foretold

BOOKS BY CARRIE RYAN

The Forest of Hands and Teeth
The Dead-Tossed Waves
The Dark and Hollow Places

foretold

14 Stories of Prophecy and Prediction

EDITED BY

CARRIE RYAN

This is a work of fiction. Names, characters, places, and incidents either are the product of the author's imagination or are used fictitiously. Any resemblance to actual persons, living or dead, events, or locales is entirely coincidental.

 Published in the United States by Ember, an imprint of Random House Children's Books, a division of Random House, Inc., New York. Originally published in hardcover in the United States by Delacorte Press, an imprint of Random House Children's Books, New York, in 2012.

Visit us on the Web! randomhouse.com/teens
Educators and librarians, for a variety of teaching tools, visit us at RHTeachersLibrarians.com

The Library of Congress has cataloged the hardcover edition of this work as follows:
Foretold : 14 stories of prophecy and prediction / edited by Carrie Ryan.
— 1st ed. v. cm.
Contents: Gentlemen send phantoms / by Laini Taylor — Burned bright / by Diana Peterfreund — The angriest man / by Lisa McMann — Out of the blue / by Meg Cabot — One true love / by Malinda Lo — This is a mortal wound / by Michael Grant — Misery / by Heather Brewer — The mind is a powerful thing / by Matt de la Peña — The chosen one / by Saundra Mitchell — Improbable futures / by Kami Garcia — Death for the deathless / by Margaret Stohl — Fate / by Simone Elkeles — The killing garden / by Carrie Ryan — Homecoming / by Richelle Mead.
ISBN 978-0-385-74129-3 (hc) — ISBN 978-0-375-98996-4 (glb) —
ISBN 978-0-375-98442-6 (ebk) 1. Fate and fatalism—Juvenile fiction. 2. Short stories, American. [1. Fate and fatalism—Fiction. 2. Short stories.] I. Ryan, Carrie.
PZ5.F757 2012 [Fic]—dc23 2012007067

ISBN 978-0-385-74130-9 (trade pbk.)

RL: 7.0

Printed in the United States of America
10 9 8 7 6 5 4 3 2 1
First Ember Edition 2013

For my father, who taught me
to always dream and believe
in limitless possibilities

CONTENTS

foretold

INTRODUCTION

One of the stories I remember most from school is the myth of Oedipus. In it, the oracle of Apollo at Delphi prophesied that any son born to King Laius would grow up to kill his father. Because of this prediction, Laius decreed that his infant son Oedipus should be put to death.

Of course, as is often the case in Greek myths, nothing went according to plan. The servant tasked with abandoning the baby on a mountainside instead chose to rescue him, leaving him in the care of a shepherd. Oedipus was raised far away in Corinth with no knowledge of his pedigree or his connection to the king of Thebes. When he was grown, Oedipus fled Corinth for home. During the journey, he was harassed by a group of travelers at a crossroads and was forced to kill the group in self-defense. Unbeknownst to Oedipus, one of the men he murdered was his father, thus the oracle's prediction.

Ironically, by struggling so hard to circumvent the prophecy of his death at the hand of his son, Laius became instrumental in its coming to pass.

What fascinates me about this story is the conflict between Laius's pervasive impulse to thwart the predicted tragedy at any cost and his concurrent belief in its inevitability. It made me wonder: Would it have been better for Laius to accept the prophecy? If he had, could he have escaped it? And what does that mean to those of us whose lives don't play out like an ancient myth?

It's easy for most of us to discount the role prophecies can play in the modern world. After all, few of us seek out the oracle of Apollo at Delphi and plan our lives accordingly. But the more I've thought about prophecies and predictions while editing this anthology, the more I've realized just how relevant they still are.

No, I'm not talking about how every few years there's another forecast about the end of the world. (12.21.12, anyone?) I'm talking about the more nuanced predictions: the parents who determine their child will grow up to be famous, the teen who declares she'll be a doctor one day, or the student who tells himself he'll never be anyone special. These become our own prophecies—and they can end up laying out the paths of our lives.

It's easy to cling to predictions because they give us a sense of direction. There's comfort in feeling as though a decision has been preordained and is therefore out of our hands. But that doesn't mean that giving our lives over to someone else's prophecy won't somehow blind us to the possibility of self-determination. Which then brings us back to Oedipus and his father, and the main underlying question of the myth: are we better served by embracing our prophecies, even the negative ones?

These thoughts prompted me to ask other authors for their own views on the topic—I was curious how each would approach the concept. I wanted to find out what might constitute a true prophecy to them, and I wondered how they would handle the question of whether it is better to accept a foretold future or fight against it. I purposely left the specifics vague, wanting to give each writer the freedom to explore his or her own interpretation of the theme.

I couldn't be more thrilled with the results! The fourteen short stories in *Foretold* showcase a variety of interpretations on the idea of prophecy: fantastical quests, otherworldly encounters, the power of someone else's perception to influence your life. In these stories there are worlds that end and others that begin, loves found and lost—and sometimes found again. Each story, in its own way, demonstrates how prophecies affect our lives by exploring characters who struggle to fulfill them, who endeavor to prevent them, or who attempt to ignore them altogether.

What I've discovered through these stories is that prophecies can bring us comfort or cause us fear; we can choose to embrace them as destiny and cling to them as dreams or avoid them as the worst kind of curse. Ultimately, when we face our own prognostications—whether self-generated or thrust upon us—it's up to us to choose whether we will determine our own lives or allow someone else to do it for us.

Gentlemen Send Phantoms

LAINI TAYLOR

1. A Dreamcake

Once, when the moon was younger than it is tonight and not as plump, three girls gathered by a hearth to bake a dreamcake. It was St. Faith's Day, the sixth of October, and everybody knows that on St. Faith's Day a girl can lure forth the phantom of the man she'll marry, see his face and know some of what life holds in its basket for her. That's what their mothers and nans taught them, and they'd all seen their men on St. Faith's Day and married them in the spring.

As it happens, all three girls were hoping to glimpse the same phantom, the one belonging to Matthew Blackgrace, whom they called Matty in that singsong way that girls have. He had fierce red hair and a grin like the devil, but his hands were good hands; he could braid his baby sister's hair and gentle a horse. And couldn't he sing like an angel?

The girls were fast friends—they lived in the cottages scattered through the apple orchards above Mosey Landing, and had grown up together—but that didn't mean there weren't some sharp thoughts between them that evening, with each nursing the same hopes, and in the same small room.

Ava was oldest; near eighteen already, and, as she claimed, "ripe to be plucked." She had yellow hair with a hint of strawberries, and such a bosom on her that the boys scarcely knew what her face looked like anymore, so fixed were their eyes elsewhere. It was a nice face, in any case, if just the littlest bit blank. Truth be told, Ava's thoughts were like those tethered ponies at the fair: slow and placid, ever going in circles, and with children never far off.

Ava was more than ready for babies, and more than ready for the making of them. Her eyes watched the orchard tots run and tumble, and she hummed and dreamed, and at night sometimes she held her pillow between her knees and blushed in the dark, imagining love.

She wanted Matty Blackgrace for his house as much as anything. He was already building his own—a tiny pretty thing up on Century Hill, overlooking the wide green Mosey. It didn't have a roof yet, but he'd already painted the shutters blue for luck, and planted bare-root roses that would bloom come summer. Ava wanted to get a babe on her hip as soon as may be, and start baking pies to set on those sweet blue sills. And Matty himself, well, he fit just fine in the corner of her daydream, thank you very much.

Elsie was next, and she was the colors of a fawn—golden, russet, and brown—and freckled as though the baker sneezed over his cinnamon and she got the brunt of it. "Sweet" was what she called herself, and she was—in nature and in tooth. She planted honeysuckle every year for her nan, who'd turned hummingbird on her deathbed four years past and came around all summer long for sips of nectar. And there wasn't a market day that went by but Elsie was sneaking down to Mosey Landing to fetch herself a treat, a striped lick-stick or a cone of sugar-ice or maybe a maple toad rolled in spice.

Lucky thing, she could eat all the treats she wanted and stay slim, because she was the tallest girl around—tall enough to pick apples without a ladder—but Matty Blackgrace was taller, and so Elsie thought she ought to get him for that reason if no other.

Catherine was the last, and some would say the least. They called her Pippin for being small as an apple seed. Hazard Root the Younger, whose phantom she was desperate *not* to see, had threatened once to put her in his pocket like a newt, and she said if he tried it she'd sting him like a scorpion, which was no idle threat. Pippin was small, but she was no newt, and she had troubled herself to learn witching from Nasty Mary before the old lady turned owl and swooped off in the night. Or at least, Pippin *said* she had, and she said it in this glittering-eyed way that made even the big boys wary of her.

But not Matty, oh never. Witch she was or witch she wasn't, he knew he'd nothing to fear from Pippin.

She didn't have bosoms like hummocks, and she couldn't pick apples without a ladder, but her face was the shape of a little heart and her shoulders were set and straight, and her laugh could make its way from one side of the orchard to the other, shivering leaves and spinning blossoms as it went.

Not that her life was spilling with laughter, sad to say. Her mother had died birthing her—so sudden she hadn't even had time to turn creature, and this was a bruise on Pippin's heart. She could almost have stood it, she'd think, tending her garden all alone, if that kestrel on the branch could have been her mam watching over her. She'd try and pretend it, just for the feel of company, but it was no good. Nasty Mary had told her in no uncertain terms that the blood had been like a river, and Pippin like a little otter slipping out on it, and just like that, her mam was gone and really truly-and-forever gone.

Her da never married again, so theirs was a quiet home, but the Blackgrace house was near, and she could always go there for a fill-up of elbows and clamor. Sometimes she even got to be part of a sticky kid-pile and fall asleep with all the others, cocoa on her breath and the fiddle floating in at her ears, her and Matty both in the tangle someplace—maybe that was his hand and maybe it wasn't, but it was enough that it *might* be.

That was done with now, of course. He and she were nearly grown and no longer kids to be tangling together like kittens! And sure she knew that wasn't the kind of arm-and-leg tangle that she was supposed to wish for now she was nearly a woman, but she missed it just the same. Woman or girl or in between, Pippin was lonesome, and when she dreamed of the end of being lonesome it was Matty's face she saw, and that was all there was to it.

2. Wishing and Firelight

"Remember," cautioned Elsie, "after this, no talking." The rules of a dreamcake were clear. It was to be baked in silence, with just firelight and wishing, wishing and firelight, and not a peep from any girl until morning—not even when their phantom came, no matter what.

"One last thing first," said Ava, her voice breathy with excitement. "Whoever we see, we've got to tell each other first thing in the morning. Promise!" She spoke with the easy eagerness of a girl used to attention. *She's that sure she'll see*

Matty tonight, thought Pippin, jealous of such confidence. Herself, she wasn't sure on anyone's behalf—not Ava's or Elsie's or her own. She didn't know *who* Matty fancied. He was so nice to everyone there was no way *to* know.

"I promise," said Elsie.

"I promise," said Pippin.

"And if you see *nobody,* it means you're to be an old maid. So don't be slamming the door on any phantom!" Ava looked sternly at Pippin. "Even if it *is* Hazard. Would you *really* rather be a spinster than a Mrs. Root?"

"Yes by a thousand," declared Pippin. "I'd rather be the Roots' old *mule,* by the green god's mercy, than marry Hazard." She was thinking to herself that if she couldn't have Matty she'd vanish in the woods and live like a fairy. Once, he'd told her she looked like one, and he might have meant it because she'd had briars in her hair, wild from tumbling through a thicket, but she'd always thought he meant something sweeter.

"Ready now?" asked Elsie. "It's time."

They were at Ava's house to bake their cake. It was a queer recipe and nothing you'd want to eat; it wasn't for eating. The flour was just plain flour, but the water stank from a bundle of cloud roses going to rot in it for more than a week. The salt had been buried in the garden and dug back up, and the goose egg was laid under a full moon and shadow-spelled for three nights running, first with an owl feather, then a rowan branch, and last of all a lock of hair from a pregnant woman—Mayfair Tanzy, who said that she'd go bald if one more girl came to her begging locks.

Pippin had earlier wrinkled her nose and declared the batter to be "all druidy-smelling," and it only got worse as it baked. The girls were quiet and wishful as they knitted by the fire, each dreaming of Matty's good hands unpinning her hair on their wedding night. Many a stitch was dropped and a count forgotten, and three crookeder socks you never saw than came of that night's work.

After the cake was done, Ava took it from the oven, let it cool some, then cut it in three. Each girl took her portion and scratched her initials in its surface. At sunup, if all went right, there should be another set of initials scratched beside their own.

They hugged each other, shared nervous grins in silence, and parted ways.

Ava went right up the ladder to her loft bed. She pulled her braid over her shoulder and unwove it, wondering: would the phantom just be a glimpse, or would it linger with her awhile?

Suppose it *talked* to her. Could phantoms talk? Not that she could answer if it did!

Could they *kiss*? Or maybe there was nothing *to* kiss, just air and dreams.

Ava shivered, hugged her arms around the deliciousness, and then—after a hot-cheeked hesitation—unlaced her dress, yanked it off, and dove under the quilt in her best slip to wait.

As for Elsie, she lived right across the way, so she had only to dart out Ava's door and into her own. Like Ava's, her house was empty—no family crowd to put fright to skittish phantoms. There was a fair down at Mosey Landing tonight to keep folks happy, and casks of drink and a cakewalk, and for a special treat some music-makers from across the Bigwater. All strange they were, handsome and dark-eyed and clad in patterns, with scythe-billed birds perched on their heads that made their own shivery songs in tune to the drums and chimes.

Elsie's hand shook lighting her candle, and unlacing her bodice she fumbled about as bad as if she'd got frozen fingers from making a snow troll. Finally, though, she was in her sheets, coverlet to her chin and long feet poking out the bottom. She waited, trembling and fidgeting as the flame teased shadows up and down the walls, and every single minute she thought a phantom was come, and almost died of nerves.

Now, Pippin, she was out alone in the night. She lived all the way on the far side of the orchard, no small walk, and she set off quick with her wedge of dreamcake cradled to her chest, her heart tight and sore from all her big wishing, not just tonight but all her life. Little life, big wishing. That doesn't go easy on a heart, and she thought maybe she'd stretched hers all out, how a sweater neck gets when you've shown the poor judgment of dressing the goat—though *that,* she consoled herself, was long ago, and had been all Matty's idea in any case.

She hurried. If Matty was at the Blackgrace house, his phantom wouldn't have far to go to get to hers, and she'd better not miss it if it did! But if he was in his own unfinished house, where he liked to go and work or just sit sometimes to dream, he'd have to send his phantom down Century Hill and that would give her a little time. She could get back home and fix her hair at least. . . .

But Matty *liked* her hair all fairy-tangled, didn't he?

Pippin hesitated for only a second. She crouched and set down her dreamcake on a tree root, then unpinned her hair. It tumbled to her waist, as shadow-colored as her eyes were sky, and the wind zoomed in at once to get it. This breeze tugged a strand here, this one there, and it was a snatch-grab dance of wind and hair fit for a queen of fairies.

Pippin closed her eyes. She loved the feeling—the stir of it, and the ache as her tame hair came wild-alive. Hairs got used to lying one way, so that it hurt the scalp to muss them up, but it was a good hurt—like the ache from too much laughing, or the tightness low in your belly when your eyes sparked together with someone special and lightning zinged all through you.

And then, before Pippin could pick up her cake to rush home, she heard voices and froze stock-still.

3. Gentlemen Send Phantoms

Now, magic was a true thing; a certainty. No one who had seen their nan turn creature could doubt it. They'd be wrinkled old biddies one minute, just about to gasp their last, and—blink!—they were gone, and owls or hawks were shaking off their nightgowns. Once in a while a cat or a fox, but it was flying they mostly wanted, and so they went with birds. It was a one-time, one-way change, and only women could make it, to the bitterness of the boys and men, who got up to the end of their lives just to die.

There were other bits and bobs of magic too: cures and curses; fairies and treelings dashing stealthy at the edges of sight; sweet moon milk and shadow castings and such like that. Nothing like what the Ancestors had brought here with them on their carved ships, but some things still remained.

As for phantoms on St. Faith's Day, a lot of folks thought they weren't real foretellings at all, but just the dreams girls had when they nodded off waiting and saw who they wished. And sure there was reason for doubt. Often enough it happened that two girls claimed the same phantom and argued over it till the red-faced boy in question had to speak his wishes plain, and maybe it was neither girl at all!

Pippin didn't know what to believe. She *hoped,* was all, but when those voices came clearer and she heard what they were saying, she got a sad insight into the nature of boys, and more than a spark of a doubt as to phantoms.

"I'll have Ava Gentry, all three of her," said one with a lecherous laugh.

"No, you won't, little brother. If anyone will be seeing Ava Gentry with her corset undone it will be me. You can have the giantess for yours."

It was the Breed brothers—those two thick quarry boys, Thane and Colin, and they were out in the orchard dark laying naughty plans. Quiet as quiet, Pippin moved closer to see, and she spied them rubbing flour into their hair and faces.

They grumbled more over Ava, but in the end it was settled, and trailing flour-dust, they went off, making ghostly noises and taking glugs of whiskey, to play at being phantoms.

Pippin bit her lip. She would have to follow them, of course. Her friends' fathers weren't at home, their doors weren't locked, and the Breed brothers were stupid, strong, and drunk—a woeful combination if ever there was one. But . . . if she didn't get home now, she stood to miss Matty's phantom if it called. *Well,* she thought, *I'll just be a minute, and any phantom too impatient to wait for me would make a poor enough husband!*

Leaving her cake where it was, she tiptoed after the Breeds.

The boys parted in the darkness between the two cottages, and Colin went to Elsie's door and Thane to Ava's. As Thane reached out for the doorknob, Pippin took a deep breath and prepared herself to call out, feeling a thrum of fear to be interrupting the two big boys at their mischief.

I'll be breaking the spell if I speak, she realized, and she faltered, but she had only to think of her friends in their beds with their hopeful toes curled, and these two falling at them drooling. "If you two are phantoms then I'm a hat" is what she declared, stepping into sight.

They both froze and swung to see her. Then, as one, they burst into gut laughter.

"Pippin girl, out phantom hunting?" asked Colin.

"Sure the only way you'll see one is if you catch it on its way someplace else!" added Thane, all grinning spite, and that pierced Pippin not a little, because she already feared it was true. "Maybe you should wait a year or three and see if you don't grow a chest on you."

"I hear there's a tonic for that," said Colin. "You got to rub it on every night."

"I guess Ava's been using it a while, then," added Thane, and the boys got off laughing again.

"I'll tell," Pippin said, keeping herself strong. "You go in there and I'll fetch their fathers."

"Run and fetch, then. By the time you get back we'll be done and gone, won't we, like the phantoms we are. *Oo-oooooo!*"

"Then I'll have to ring the fire bell, I guess."

Maybe that sobered them a little, and maybe it didn't. They were still laughing, but Colin glanced to where it was—the tall post with its bell and rope, part of the signal system used throughout the orchards for warnings. Two short pulls meant come quick. They all knew how to do it from the time they could toddle.

"Pip . . ." Thane sauntered toward her. "You want a kiss, is that it? Just ask, darlin'."

"I guess we can spare a minute or two for you," Colin contributed, following his brother. "The night is young and the bottle's empty."

Pippin took one quick step away and that was all there was time for. Behind her, from back the way she'd come, spoke a voice.

"Leave her be," it said, oh the beautiful, beautiful sound of it!

"Blackgrace?" asked Thane, squinting past Pippin.

For Matty it was. He came to her side and never was there a sweeter sight—though just now he didn't look sweet so much as furious.

"What are *you* doing here? Are you supposed to be a phantom?" asked Thane.

Pippin's heart lurched. Not Matty too. Was it a game all the boys played, to chase girls to their beds? No. Never Matty.

"If you are, you're a poor one, Blackgrace," said Colin. "Here, have some flour." And he chucked the sack at Matty, hard, but Matty sidestepped it so it hit the bell post and burst in a white cloud.

Thane added, "Anyway you're too late. We got here first."

"Why aren't you at the Landing?" Colin asked. "It's no secret Scylla Grey has a candle out for *you* tonight. Lucky dog."

Scylla Grey? If it had lurched before, now Pippin's heart clenched tight as a fist. Scylla Grey was a ship captain's daughter down at Mosey Landing. She was the prettiest girl Pippin had ever seen, with the whitest skin and the nicest frocks. Her father brought her fantastical things from all over the seas, like fans made of dragon fins, and a lace mantle knit of sea foam. She carried herself like a princess, and led a blinking Manx cat with her everywhere on a pink velvet leash. She wasn't even horrible, which was the worst thing about her. Scylla always had a nice word ready, and sometimes bought cakes for the tots—the good kind, even, with icing.

Did *she* want Matty too? Pippin felt her hopes slipping away. What chance could an apple seed have next to Scylla

Grey? Or next to Ava, for that matter, or even Elsie. They didn't look like tots playing dress-up, and none of them needed chest tonic, that was sure.

Matty was glowering. "What are you waiting for?" Colin asked him. "Go get your own girl and leave us be."

Matty said, "That's not the way it works. You don't barge into a girl's house with your sweaty hands. Anyone who tried that on my sisters would get a gun barrel tucked in his ear."

"Well, Ava Gentry's not your sister, so arse off," said Thane. "Take Pippin. We didn't really want her anyway."

Matty glanced at Pippin, and she couldn't read his face, but sure he wasn't jumping at the chance. "No one's *having* me," she cut in quick, before he had time to say no thanks. "Or Ava or Elsie either." And she marched over to the bell and gripped the rope. "You better go on, all of you, or I'll pull."

When she said *all of you,* Matty looked that surprised, and wounded too.

Like how it feels? she thought with a pinch of satisfaction. "Good night, lads," she said, all low and final, with that glimmer Nasty Mary had taught her that made her eyes go silver as a night cat's. The Breeds got spooked but tried not to show it. They cursed plenty, going off, but Matty lingered.

"Do I have to go too, Cathy?" he asked. He was the only one who called her that.

"That depends. What are you doing here?"

"I could ask you the same." He came closer, studying her breeze-spun hair, and she got a pang, worrying suddenly that it made her look not like a fairy but only a girl too young for marrying. Why hadn't she thought of that before?

He asked, "Shouldn't you be at home waiting for your phantom?"

Should I? she wondered, still stung by the Breeds' words,

the only way she'd see a phantom was if she caught it on its way someplace else. Well, she didn't want any stupid boy who didn't want her, not even Matty. Sidestepping his question, she said, "I saw the Breeds and I didn't know what they were going to do."

"Louts," said Matty with a frown. "Sure they're not the only ones. I wouldn't be surprised to hear a fair few of our mams met not phantoms on St. Faith's Day but our fathers out for a prowl."

"Do you think it isn't true, then? About phantoms?"

His eyes were deep in shadow, so Pippin couldn't see the green she knew was there, nor even the usual sparkle. "Oh, I know it's true," he said.

"You do?"

"Sure, for haven't I sent my own phantom down to the house I want it to go to?"

Pippin's heart missed a beat. "You . . . you have?"

"I have. Not that I wouldn't rather go myself like those two, and see my girl with my own eyes, but that isn't how it works. Gentlemen send phantoms."

Down, he'd said. Down to the Landing. To Scylla. Pippin stared off into the dark, imagining Scylla lovely in the candlelight—and sure her hair would be smooth as a waterfall, not wild as a bird's nest!—while Matty's phantom floated in the window. She thought her heart might fall into two pieces like split kindling. She didn't say a word, too afraid of bursting into sobs.

"Of course," Matty said, and he chewed his cheek and gave a stone a little kick, "maybe she won't want to see it. Maybe she'll send it away."

Was he joking, or was he really worried? He had to know that any girl would be glad of his phantom! He might not be the handsomest of all the boys, but he was better than handsome. He was *electric*—clever and able and full of life. He was the one everyone wanted to sit beside, and who they counted on to fix whatever troubles, and whose singing could spread a sudden hush and make folks close their eyes and smile. Tots and animals followed him around, and girls too, no more subtle than the big-pawed pups. And of course there was the little house he was building—all the girls were mad for it, already decorating it in their dreams.

Pippin thought she might as well yank down those gingham curtains she'd strung up in her own foolish fancies. She was never marrying Matty Blackgrace. "Sure she'll be glad to see you, Matty," she told him, choking on the words.

"You really think so?" He sounded so relieved, and Pippin nodded, mute. Matty was looking at her funny, so she dredged up a smile, and it felt like a dead thing from the bottom of the river, but it must have fooled him well enough, because he smiled back, sweet as anything.

"Shouldn't you be getting home, Cathy? Can I walk you?"

"But didn't you just come from back there?"

"Doesn't matter. I'm only wandering."

Wandering, thought Pippin, glum. Keeping his mind off his worries over Scylla is what. She thought of her dreamcake lying where she'd left it, her initials sad and lonely in its golden crust, and she thought of her house, sad and lonely too, and none of it mattered anyway because she'd broken the spell by talking. She wasn't seeing any phantoms tonight, least of all the one she wanted.

She took a big breath and tried to sound breezy. "I'm not going home. I've got other plans."

4. One True Person

"What plans?" Matty asked.

What seized her then? Pippin had no plans, of course,

only this wrenching realization that there was no end of lonesomeness coming for her, not soon and maybe not ever. Right now Matty's phantom might be with Scylla, but . . . *he* was here—the *real* him. For the moment, anyway.

She put out her chin and, feeling as wild as her unpinned hair, said, "Come with me and I guess you'll see."

"Okay," agreed Matty, easy as that, and when Pippin started walking—she didn't even know where to—he fell into step beside her.

The orchard was quiet, and they could hear the music from down at the landing, faint and foreign, those twanging weird instruments from over the Bigwater.

If it had been daytime, they'd have been able to see the Bigwater from here: a faint blue edge to the south where the sky climbed down. Sometimes it was just all one hazy blue and you couldn't make sky from sea, but other days the water was dark as ink. "Think you'll ever cross the sea?" Pippin asked.

"The *sea*?" Matty seemed surprised. "No. I never even thought of it before."

"I will." Pippin heard her voice say it, though it came as news to her own self.

"You will?" Matty sounded skeptical. "*How* will you?"

"I'll fly."

"Oh. You mean after you turn? You better pick a strong bird, then. It's a long way for a small creature."

"Small! I'm not going to be small anymore. I'm going to be a *dragon,* with wings like lacquer fans and jets of fire breath for roasting up goose suppers midair!" Pippin spread out her arms, imagining them wings. *Why not?* she asked herself. At least she had flying to look forward to, whatever else happened—or didn't.

Didn't. Didn't. Didn't. What an awful word, and an awful

fate: a whole long life of nothing ever happening! How would she bear it?

"There are no more dragons," Matty pointed out.

"Well, there will be. There will be *one,* and it will be me."

"That sounds lonesome, to be the only one of something."

"I'm the only Pippin, aren't I? I'll just be lonesome in the sky instead of lonesome on the ground."

"Maybe you don't have to be lonesome at all, Cathy," he said gently.

"Like you know about it," she said. She tried to laugh, but it came out sounding bitter.

"As it happens, I do."

"You? How could *you* know?"

"What do you mean, *me*? Don't you think everybody's lonesome until they're with their one true person, settled and sure, for life?"

Yes, thought Pippin, wanting to shout it and cry it. Imagining Scylla falling asleep with a glad smile, she said, "Well then, after tomorrow, no more worries for you."

"I'm starting to wonder," he said.

Pippin hissed a sigh. "Oh hush, Matthew Blackgrace. You're in no danger of lonesomeness. Everybody loves *you.*"

"Don't you think people love you too, Cath?"

He was very earnest. She thought he must be feeling sorry for her. She didn't want his pity. Her wildness was growing. It felt like a trapped cat trying to scrabble out. "What do dragons care for love?" she asked, then put back her head and ran ahead leaping, pretending to fly.

Matty came after, running too. Pippin twirled and whirled, wilding up her hair even worse. What did it matter now? When she finally stopped and faced him, her chest was heaving with exertion. He was standing very still, his hands shoved in his pockets, watching her. "Do you remember playing fairy ring?" he asked.

Did he think she could have forgotten? It was a game they'd played as children, when they'd pretend to have strayed into a fairy ring where they had to dance until they fell down dead, and the last one still dancing was the winner.

"Of course," she said. "I always won."

"I always *let* you."

"You never!"

"I did. But just so I could watch you dance."

Pippin blushed. What did he mean, teasing her? She turned away.

"Why don't you want to get married?" he blurted. The question was out of nowhere, and it was like a little punch in the heart. Pippin stiffened, her back still to him. "I mean," he added, "you not going home and all."

"Well, it's hardly fair, is it? Girls just have to wait and see who comes, while boys get to pick?"

"That's not how it is. Asking's just the hard part. It's the girl who decides."

Pippin looked back. "And what if the girl wants to do the asking for a change?"

"*Do* you?" He stood full in the moonlight now, and she still couldn't make out the green of his eyes. He looked different tonight, she thought. *New* in some way she couldn't name. Was it because he was a man now, come to his St. Faith's Day?

And herself, then—was she a woman? Had they left boy and girl behind, to be facing each other as man and woman? Did it happen just like that?

"Do I what?" she asked, flustered to all of a sudden be thinking grown-up thoughts like she'd opened a door to them. And . . . wasn't he looking at her like he was too? She imagined tangling up with him, but not like kittens, and she remembered his broad pale chest, when she'd come around the side of the Blackgrace house in the summer and caught sight of him without his shirt, sluicing a bucket of well water over his head. Smooth it still was, but no boy's chest, to be sure, and those were no boy's lips either.

She tipped up her face like she was under some spell, looking at his lips, and then at his eyes, which were fixed on hers, unblinking, and then his lips again. A new wanting bloomed in her. He was so near, but he was so *tall.* Like she was pulled by a puppet string, Pippin rose to tiptoe, but she was such a minuscule specimen it didn't bring her nearly close enough. If she was going to get a kiss—just one kiss to go on—Matty would have to bend closer . . . but . . . he didn't.

He *didn't.* When she rose on her toes, he straightened up taller, taking his lips even farther out of reach. It was as good as a slap.

Pippin dropped back flat on her soles, and when a big wind came and tossed her hair all about, she was that glad to hide her mortification inside the tangle of it. Somewhere nearby an owl loosed a mournful note, and it could have come straight from her own heart.

"Is there someone you want to ask to marry you, Cathy?" asked Matty, the cruelty of him!

Her heart turned hard. She said, "I told you. I'm going to be a dragon. I'm going to cast my sharp shadow over the whole world, just fly and fly and eat spice and scare kings."

"I never knew you wanted to see the world," he said.

I don't! "I suppose I should let you read my diary so you'll know every single thing about me?"

"Okay, fool girl." He was shaking his head, kind of smiling but kind of dark around the eyes too. "Let's say you *can* turn dragon, and I don't doubt your witching. You've still got your whole life to live first, before you change. What about that?"

Whole life. Whole long empty life.

"What about it? Nothing says I can't change right now, if I'm through with being human."

"Through with—?" Matty looked shocked. "Cathy, what are you talking about?"

She didn't mean it.

Did she?

No, of course not. She would never surrender her life and body and humanity just because a boy didn't love her! Fool girl? Fool girl indeed. Someday she would fly, yes, dragon or bird, and as for all the life up till then, she would endure it, even if she didn't get to have her one true person and an end to lonesomeness.

She wouldn't have him pitying her, though, rubbing in the empty years that lay ahead for her while his own phantom was off settling his future. "Oh, why not?" She flung the words. "What do you care? Enjoy your life, Matthew Blackgrace!"

Tears started in her eyes and she wheeled around and ran away and left him there, and the owl's cry floated after her, just as sad as sad.

5. Not At All Spying

Down in the orchard cottages, Ava had fallen asleep. Restless, she stirred awake again and again, and on one of those wakings she found she wasn't alone. It was John Ginger's phantom sitting there, just quiet with his legs dangling off the side of the loft. He was a boatwright from Gale, the nearest village on the far bank of the Mosey, and she hadn't even considered him, but now, blinking awake, she couldn't think whyever not. He was too shy to dance, was one thing she knew about him, and another was that he was a widower. He was young still, five and twenty at the outside, and he had a baby girl his sister was bringing up for him.

Not anymore, she's not, thought Ava, and she gave John Ginger's phantom a big, shy smile.

Across the way, Elsie did *not* fall asleep, not even for a second. She lay in her bed all stiff and antsy, watching the shadows cavort like imps on the wall, and it wasn't until her candle sputtered that, in the flash before darkness, she saw a face on one. *Hmm,* she thought, unsure, for it was Loren Dean, the apothecary's apprentice, who stood only as tall as her chin. He wore little round glasses that the sun glanced off, and he read thick books and marked his place with sprigs of herbs. All the nans liked him, both before and after they turned, so he always had birds flitting round him—and one fox that was probably Edith Moonworthy, who'd been afraid of heights—and leading him off to find hidden wildflowers for his potions, which, as it happened, were exceptionally fine.

Hmm, thought Elsie, and *hmm,* and she lay awake all night remembering every good thing she ever knew of Loren Dean—there were a lot!—and by morning she was convinced she'd wanted him all along.

As for Scylla Grey, it was a lie the Breeds told that she'd lit a candle for phantoms. Sure she had an eye on Matty, but being a town girl, she didn't believe in that phantom malarkey at all. She was down in the square, dancing to the strangers' music, spinning and twirling, and one of their scythe-billed birds took a fancy to her and came to perch on her head. Her Manx cat got jealous and tried to eat it, and in the commotion the stranger had to drop his lute to rescue his bird, and that was that. He was handsome as a pirate, and he didn't pick up his lute again all night, just danced with Scylla instead, and he danced her right to the church door at sunup, his bird riding on the Manx now, bird and cat giving each other smug looks like they'd arranged it all between them.

Up in the orchard, a squirrel came upon Pippin's wedge of abandoned cake. It had some kind of markings etched into its surface, the squirrel saw, but he couldn't read, and nor could he count to tell if there was one set of initials or two. He just ate it up, happy as only a squirrel can be who's found a wedge of cake abandoned on a tree root, even if it *did* savor of flower-rot water.

As for Pippin, when she ran off and left Matty behind, she didn't have a thought to where she'd go. Tears were streaking down her cheeks and she kept raising angry fists to swipe them away. Every time she thought of him straightening up clear of her kiss, her face went hot with shame. By the green god's mercy, what madness had come over her, trying to kiss him when she knew it wasn't her he wanted?

She stumbled and went down on her knees, biting her tongue in the process, and it was all just so pathetic. *Some fairy I make,* she thought, *tripping over branches!* Anyway, fairies didn't weep. They didn't even have tear ducts, which was why, Nasty Mary had taught her, if you ever saw fairy tears in the ingredients to a spell, you knew it was a fake. Pippin got to her feet and kept running, and soon enough she came to a path—a path made by many feet over the years, including her own. It led to just one place, and she found herself going there.

Since she happened to know Matty was elsewhere, it was sure to be empty. She came around a curve and there it was, tucked under the giant oak: Matty's house. It looked almost a toy under the great tree, and Pippin came to a halt when she saw it was lit up.

Orange light played out the windows, and since there was no roof yet, it glowed up and lit the underside of the oak too. Wind was tossing the branches and shaking loose leaves, and they swirled all around and fell right inside. "Careless," Pippin whispered, surprised that Matty had gone off and left a lantern lit. That wasn't like him at all.

She hugged a tree at the edge of a clearing and watched the house. She felt shy being here, and then mad at Matty about it. This had been a place for all the tots and kids once, the pair of them especially. They'd built a nest high up in the branches of that oak and kept watch over the whole earth, or so it had seemed to them then. They'd called it their crow's nest. She wondered if he remembered that.

But now he'd gone and built his house here and made it his own place, and worse: it would be his wife's soon enough, though Pippin could scarcely see fine Scylla living up here so far from town, and having to set her slippers to that muddy footpath all the wet winter long. *I hope your toes mildew,* Pippin thought pettishly, little imagining the other girl was at that moment clasped in the tattooed arms of a pirate lutanist from over the Bigwater, and more than halfway to falling in love.

She released her hug on the tree and went to the next, and then the next. Tree to tree she went around the little clearing, saying goodbye to each one in her way, until she came to the oak. And once she was touching it, there was no help for it, it had to be climbed. She knew the best route and was up it quick as a skink, her shoes left behind on the ground, and she told herself all the while that she was just climbing her favorite tree. She was not in any way planning to peer down into Matty's roofless house.

Because that would be spying.

And when her bare feet found themselves on the long

horizontal bough that was as broad as a bridge, she still was not going to spy, and when she skimbled down where it thinned and wrapped her knees around it so she could scooch out farther, she was innocent in her heart. Even as she found a likely branch to cling to so she could lean out and look down, it was not at all spying, and then it was spread out beneath her: Matty's house, built with his own good hands. It had three rooms; the two little ones Pippin supposed would be bedrooms. One was beneath her, empty except for a swept leaf pile and a leaning twig broom. And next door there was the big room where the lamp was lit—

—and the room was not empty!

Pippin gasped.

Matty was there. Matty was sitting there in his chair with the lamplight gleaming on his red hair and he was bent over, carving something on a plaque of wood. The hoarse leaf chorus drowned the sound of his chisel, and it must have carried off her gasp too, because he didn't look up. Pippin sat frozen. How had he gotten here ahead of her? He couldn't have! She'd run all the way!

How?

As mystifying as it was, him being here, it wasn't her foremost care as she swayed above his head like some kind of nosing tree creature. And after all her foolish talk and trying to kiss him and running off! Oh, what would he think if he caught her *spying*?

She inched backward, the bark rough between her knees, and if she'd gotten away unseen, she would have just crept off. That was the way things were unfurling. She'd have forgotten her shoes on the ground, and Matty would have found them and always wondered, and that would have been an end to the night: a sad little ending made out of pride and heartbreak.

Thank the green god then for biddies who didn't cease meddling just because they happen not to be human anymore!

Before Pippin got more than two furtive scoots back along the branch, a shape came hurtling at her with an ungodly screech. It was an owl, wings widespread and feet flexed, claws coming right at her like she was a mouse it wanted for its feast. *And why not, since you're acting like a mouse?* Nasty Mary would have said if she still had words, and Pippin gave a little cry, throwing out her hands to protect herself.

Matty looked up just as she lost her balance and fell into his house.

6. Crow's Nest

She landed in the leaf pile and wasn't hurt, only so mortified she half considered turning bird right then to escape seeing the look on Matty's face. She didn't, of course, and when he dashed in not two seconds later, what was on his face was nothing scornful—only surprise and concern. And if that was a bright dash of happiness too, Pippin missed it entirely, being as she was so busy with her own humiliation.

"Cathy! What . . . ?" Matty looked up, then at her, then up again, as perplexed as if she'd ridden in on a cloud.

She picked herself up with as much dignity as she could scrape together. "You see what comes of having a roofless house, Matthew Blackgrace?"

He blinked. "Fairies fall in?" He reached out and plucked a leaf from her hair.

"I never fell. I'll have you know an owl pushed me off."

"I see. Good thing I didn't sweep out the leaf pile." He grinned his devilish grin and Pippin bristled to see it. "Shall I leave it, do you think? Will you be needing a landing pad in the future?"

"I don't imagine I will," she said with a glare. She was

knee-deep in leaves, and kicked them aside. "I'll just be going now."

His grin vanished. "Going? But—"

Pippin stalked from the room, barefoot and with her chin in the air. Matty followed. The big room wasn't as empty as the other, with his rocking chair, a table, the lamp, and some tools lying about. There was his bit of wood carving, and there were his shoes kicked off. He was in socks with a couple of toes peeking out. Matty toes.

All this Pippin saw on her way to the door, before he came around her to block her way. "Wait. Can't I fix you some tea?" he asked.

In the stone fireplace hung a copper kettle she knew for his mother's old one. "There's no fire," she pointed out.

"I'll make one. I even have a tin of biscuits."

"Biscuits?" She stared at him. Was he really talking about *biscuits*?

"And . . ." He got shy. Matty was never shy. "I could show you the house if you wanted."

She'd wanted to see it bad enough to shimmy up a tree, but now she couldn't say why. It was like eating ash, imagining him living here with someone else. "I've seen it," she said shortly. "And I can't stay. I have dragon business, remember?"

His brow furrowed. "Dragon . . . ? Cath, are you . . . *mad* about something?"

"What would I be mad about?" she asked, in a voice that said *I most certainly am.*

He was still in front of the door. She made to go around him and he touched her shoulder. She jerked away, and he pulled back quick like she was some unpredictable cat. "What's the matter?" he asked her. "Did something happen?"

"Oh no, nothing at all," she said, flat, looking anywhere but at his out-of-reach lips.

"Didn't you . . . *see* something tonight?" Matty glanced out the window.

Only the future is what Pippin thought. "Nothing worth mentioning" is what she said.

Matty looked smacked. His face went red, his eyes mad, then meek, then mad again. "I see," he said, tight. Then, "So why are you here, Cathy?"

She took it for a recrimination. "I'm sorry, all right? If I'd known you were here I'd never have come."

"Well, why did you?"

As if she knew! "Maybe I just wanted to climb the tree one last time before—" She stopped herself and swallowed.

"Before what?"

Before there were wife things flapping on a laundry line, baby toys on the porch, and happiness-clutter that wasn't her own. She couldn't say any of that. Breaking for the door, she only said, "I don't know how you got back here so fast anyway."

His expression changed then. From dismay it squinched to lost confusion, then snapped to attention, sharp and glittering. "*Back* here?" he said, and this time when he reached for her shoulder, he didn't let her tug it away, but held her firm and gentle. "From where?"

She gave him a look. "From down the hill, where do you think?"

His response was not what she expected. His grin came back as bold as she'd ever seen it, and he looked *relieved,* and just as pleased as pleased.

More mocking, was it? "And what's that grin for, Mr. Smiles?" Pippin demanded.

He said, like he was telling her a good secret, "Cathy, I've been here since sundown. I haven't left the house." Still grinning, and his teeth so white. Before she could protest that it was a lie, he said, "I swear it. I've been sitting right here, making that for the front door."

The plaque. She saw it was words he was carving. They caught her eye. *Crow's Nest.* It was a little shock—him naming his house after their place in the oak—and it hid the big shock behind it so Pippin was slow to understand. But there it was. If Matty'd been here all evening, then . . .

Oh!

Her heart, her heart. All of a sudden it felt like the fire bell and someone was ringing it fit to summon the whole valley. Did he mean . . . ?

Matty's hand slipped from her shoulder down to grasp her own hand. "Cath, goose, I sent my phantom out for you hours ago."

"For *me*?" squeaked Pippin, scarcely daring to believe him. Had that been . . . ? Not even *him* but . . . ? It *had* come from the direction of her house, she realized now. It was looking for *her*, wanting *her*. "But . . . what about Scylla Grey?"

"Scylla Grey? When have I ever given a fig for Scylla Grey?"

When indeed? Never was when. So why had she thought he did? She couldn't even trace it back, she'd just gotten so sure and miserable.

"When I saw you here," said Matty, "I hoped you were coming to tell me . . ." There he went shy again, and blushing looked sweeter on him than it had ever looked on a human being in all of history.

Pippin was blushing too and ready to burst. She'd seen Matty's phantom! She'd walked with it and danced for it, told it foolish things and even tried to . . . *Oh.*

"What? Cath, what is it?" Matty was watching her that close, he saw her flinch at the memory.

"If it came for me," she asked, getting mad all over again,

"then why, might I ask, did it pull away when I tried to kiss it?"

He lit up like a light. "You tried to kiss it?"

Her cheeks got hot. Now, why had she gone and admitted that?

"Fool girl," Matty teased. "You can't kiss a phantom. There's nothing there to kiss."

Of course there wasn't, she thought, and hadn't she known he looked different? The green gone from his eyes—oh, but it was back now, bright and tart as apples—and he hadn't once touched her, not her elbow or her wild hair or anything, and he'd even dodged that bag of flour instead of catching it.

"But if you're brave enough to try again," he said, daring her, "I promise you I'm real now."

Brave enough? Matty had sent his phantom out for her! She was brave enough for anything. "I would but you're too tall," she told him. "You'll have to lean."

"I can do better than that," he said, and he took her around her waist and lifted her to him, and there were his lips, and he'd told true: he was real. And he was warm, and electric, and good. He was Matty.

And he was her one true person, settled and sure, for life.

Burned Bright

DIANA PETERFREUND

BRIGHT

Tonight, the lodge will be shaken off its foundation by the power of our prayers. Tonight, it will glow with our devotion and burn with the strength of our love. Tonight, the souls of the faithful will rise from our bodies and enter the kingdom of heaven. We will be free from illness, from death, from the suffering that will befall the billions of unbelievers on this sad, sorry earth when they're left behind. Tonight, everything I've been waiting for my entire life will come to pass.

The air in the lodge wavers before my eyes, thrumming in time to the rhythm of the hymns. Around me, the righteous sit with their families, hands clasped together, faces turned toward the rafters. Others stand, swaying to the beat of the music that's been playing ceaselessly since sunset. At least two of my sisters lie prostrate on the ground, overcome by the spirit. Earlier, they spoke with the voice of angels, but now they're spent. I'm sorry for them, sorry they'll be asleep and miss feeling the moment when we're all swept away into the firmament, to glow forever among the ranks of the blessed.

"Any hour, any minute, any moment," my father croaks into the megaphone. "Judgment will come." His voice is beginning to fail him at last. In sixteen years, I've never known my father to lose his voice, and he's preached for longer than this many times. I wonder if it's a sign. Perhaps his voice will go first, and then his soul. "And then . . . we will be vin . . . dicated."

He pauses, trying to summon enough moisture in his mouth to continue. He's been fasting all day—the whole family has, since hunger brings clarity to our righteous purpose. It burns within me now, shining like a spotlight to illuminate my father and the faithful, dimming at the edges of my vision so as not to distract me from my focus.

I look around the room, shining this supernatural focus on the faces of each of the faithful, one by one. I know them all so well. I love them all and am grateful they're joining us in the kingdom of heaven. There is Bethany, who cared for me in the nursery. There's Sam, who always smiles at me in prayer circles, and little Erin, who never regained her sight after the illness that swept through the compound when she was a baby. I look at them all in turn, old and young, sick and well, happy, sad, anxious, joyful. Their faces shimmer with sweat, their hair hangs in wet snakes on their brows or frizzes up around them like the halos they'll soon wear. Tonight, they'll all be saved, and I'm so ecstatic with it I could burst. Spirit rises within me and I feel the need to cry out. I hold up my arms and my father gestures to me from across the stage.

Of all his children, he knows I am the most holy, the most committed to his cause.

"Come here, Bright." His voice, ragged as it is, envelops me like a hug, carries me aloft to his side. "You have something to say?"

The words pour from my mouth into the microphone, but they're not coming from me. They're coming through me, filling my lungs and rushing forth by the mercy of a might not my own. My tongue is not equipped to shape the language of the angels and it comes out gibberish, but the meaning is clear in my mind:

"It's coming. Can you feel it? Can you feel it coming? Judgment, coming, sweeping over this earth. We few, we here, we present now, we're the only ones who have seen the light. Come to us now, and you will be saved. Join us, and you will be spared. This is the last day of Last Days, this is the night that will never give way to a day. The hour is near. The time is now. Declare your faith and live forever among the blessed!"

Hands are there to catch me as I fall, and the spotlight narrows, blackness closing in. Is it time? Is it now? Were those the last words I'll ever speak? My limbs are shaking as the spirit gushes through me. I try to fight it, but it's like fighting the current of a river.

No! I wanted to be awake. I wanted to be awake to witness the end.

The spotlight vanishes and I'm plunged into black. . . .

My skull feels like it's been cracked with a hammer. I reach my hand to my head and try to sit, but the pounding increases as I change position. A wan, uncertain light comes from gaps in the wooden walls, and the slits beneath the eaves. I'm still on the floor of the lodge.

I'm still here. On earth. Alive.

The hammer moves down from my head, slams into my stomach with enough force to shatter my spine. I retch, hunched over, but there's nothing to bring up, not even bile.

I'm still here. *I'm still here.* This can't be happening.

I lift my head again and look around. There are a few other unconscious people scattered about the floor of the lodge, but the building is otherwise empty. The others must have gone to heaven, body and soul. And left me behind.

With effort, I push to my feet and stagger toward the door of the lodge, hands pressed to my head to reduce the pain of each jarring step. Outside, everything is white with mist. It must be dawn, if there's still a dawn. I shuffle through the dust toward the creek—or where the creek used to be. Who knows anymore? My throat is desert dry. If the water hasn't turned to blood, I'll drink. I'll drink, then figure out what to do next.

I wasn't supposed to be here, to watch the world end. I was supposed to be saved. My father promised we'd all go to heaven together.

What did I do wrong?

SAM

The fog seems to part for her feet as she walks toward the creek, one hand pressed to her temple, the other held out as if for balance. She's beautiful, even with her tangled hair and dirty face and chapped lips. Beautiful, beautiful Bright. I never let myself think about it before. After all, we'd be gone from this earth long before it would have a chance to matter.

It would be easy to be angry. Erin's furious. But I'm not. Everyone makes mistakes. I walk toward Bright through the fog and she looks up at the sound of my shoes on the gravel.

"Sam!" she cries, and takes a few halting steps in my direction. "You're still here, too." She clutches at my elbows, putting more weight on them than I expected. I stand firm to give her support. "I'm so sorry, Sam. This wasn't supposed to happen. We were all supposed to go to heaven together." Her beautiful eyes are welling with tears, and they leave trails of color on her dusty cheeks as they spill down onto her chapped lips. She's dehydrated—she must be after her fast, and yet she still weeps tears she can't afford. For us.

"Don't cry, Bright," I say, hardly believing the words coming from my mouth. How can I offer comfort to Bright Child? She's the daughter of the prophet. Her very purpose on this earth is to provide us with the comfort of his prophecies.

Even if they're no help to us now.

"You're right." She sniffles and then forces a smile. "Is there anyone left other than you and me and the people sleeping in the lodge?"

"Where?"

"Anywhere." She shrugs. "We have to round them up, protect them. Things are going to get pretty bad out there, before the end."

"They're already bad," I reply. There's violence like I've never before seen in the compound—stuff that Jeremy Bright would never have allowed before. Everyone is blaming everyone else, everyone looking for the root sin that kept us earthbound.

"Are they?" She makes a little choking sound in her throat. "Oh, Sam, I'm so sorry. I'm so sorry you're here with me, that you didn't go to heaven with the others!"

I step back from her, which is when she reaches out and captures both my hands with her own. Her skin is dry as parchment but warm—warmer than any hands I've ever held. Her touch seems to burn right through my flesh. She's held my hand before—in prayer circles, during the greeting at worship, but this is different.

"I don't know why we're still here," she says, and there are tears choking her voice. "But there must be a reason. My faith is strong. Is yours?"

"I—" I don't know what to think anymore, not with Bright Child hanging on to me like I might dissolve and her eyes dancing with those strange lights and the hitch in her voice that makes it sound like she's pleading—with *me*.

"Maybe we're here to minister to those who are left," she says. "Are there very many? Anyone from your family? Maybe we remain to help guide them through the coming tribulation and onto the path to redemption before the very end of days." She perks up a little. "That must be it. There's still a place for us in heaven. We'll be reunited with our families again. We just have to make it through the end of the world."

I blink and do my best to keep my mouth shut as I realize what she's saying. What she believes.

"And I know we can do it." Her voice has taken on that tone, that special Child tone that only the prophet and his family know how to use. The one that makes my heart pound and my breath catch. But none of the others affect me as much as Bright, and never before as much as when she interlaces our fingers and adds, "Together."

"Yes," I whisper.

She straightens, and she hasn't had a drop of water, but she looks alive again. She has a purpose. That's Bright. "We should gather up the survivors. There are some in the lodge. Do you know where the others are?"

I do, but in the split second before the words cross my lips, I reel them back and recast them. "Yes. But I was running away from them when I found you."

"Why?"

I don't know if I can lie to her, no matter how much I want to. "They've changed, Bright. They're angry . . . dangerous."

She takes it all in, and her lip trembles until she clamps her mouth together to stop it. I caused that. I hurt her.

But they would hurt her more.

"My father's prophecy warned of the changes that would come at the end of days. I never thought it would start so soon."

My head bobs in agreement. I've heard Jeremy Child's promises for years. War: not just the standard fight of country against country that's been going on since the beginning of time, but war within nations, within families. People's hearts would grow hard and hating, and they'd become savages and turn upon their own. Bright has a point. What I saw this morning definitely looked like the end of the world.

Bright closes her eyes and goes still, so still the fog starts curling in to reclaim her, but then she opens them again and stares at me. Her gaze is as gray as the mist. "Okay, then," she says. "We have to do our best to prevent anything worse. Come with me."

She tugs on my hand, and seconds later, we're splashing across the creek and toward the woods. I look behind us at the water and beyond that, the compound. The mist is beginning to clear and I can just barely make out the outline of the buildings. They're still and silent, for now.

There's no turning back.

BRIGHT

My father's prophecies were quite clear: before the end of days, we chosen few would be lifted into heaven and spared the pain and suffering the rest of humanity would experience as the world was consumed. He wasn't the only one who thought that, of course, but his was the only path that was right. He was the only one who knew the hour of our salvation, his followers the only ones who'd be included.

The apocalypse would never touch us. We spent a lot of time talking about what we'd be missing so we'd better be able to communicate to our recruits the dangers they'd face if they didn't join us. The dangers that face us now—me and Sam, and anyone else left earthbound. Wars, plagues, famines, and other terrors beyond our reckoning. Demons with human faces. Hell on earth.

I used to pity the nonbelievers. They were foolish, and ignorant, and they deserved whatever they'd get when the end times came. But now, as I walk with Sam through a silent forest on the face of our doomed world, I wonder at my own sense of superiority. After all, as hard as my father tried for all those years, there were people his message couldn't reach. Perhaps, if they'd heard him, they would have joined us. And there are babies and children, too. They don't all deserve to suffer—and neither do Sam and I. But we will suffer, here on this earth, and I can mope about it, or I can mobilize and prove that I am equal to the task set before me—that of shepherding the innocent and the righteous who've been left here with me. People like Sam.

I lead Sam through the forest in silence. The only sound is our feet shuffling through the carpet of yellow and orange leaves. I'm lost in thoughts and plans for the dreadful future, and he's staring at me. They used to be shy and furtive, these looks of his, but now they're more open. Yet the reason is the same—he's waiting for me to lead him, to guide him. Father always said I was a model to all the children in the compound. I can't let him down now that I'm all that's left.

Mist still clings to the tops of the trees and pools in the hollows along the path. Tree trunks the same pale shade of gray stand like ghosts in golden gowns and watch us as we walk. I used to love the trees, and though I know they have no souls, I'm sorry they will be lost when the world goes dark. I'm sorry for the animals, too. I wonder if there are forests in heaven.

"Where are we going?" he whispers at last, and in the stillness of the forest, it sounds like a shout.

Father's stockpile is stored in the side of a hill three miles into the woods. He made all his children memorize the location in case the police ever came and we needed to protect ourselves. In case they ever took him away. I bet he never thought we'd have to use it like this. Or maybe he did—a gift for those of us left to fight. A final miracle for the righteous to carry us through the end of days. After all, he was granted the prophecy. He must have known there would be some of us left behind after it was fulfilled.

Maybe he even knew it would be me.

There's food and water there, medicine and fuel and blankets—enough for the entire congregation to last six months, and I'm sure longer when it comes to supplying only the people who are left.

Sam's eyes are wide as spotlights when I unlock the door and he sees the shelves and the cans and the storm lanterns arrayed along the wall. They go even wider when he sees the guns.

"What are those for?"

I shrug. People used to say horrible things about Father and the rest of us. They called us a cult. They accused him of lying to us, and made all these dire and false predictions about how he planned to make us all commit suicide with poison pills or lethal Kool-Aid. It was ridiculous. Why would we commit suicide and risk the eternal life we were promised?

Sometimes they even made threats. I remember times

when Father had to lock the gates outside the compound against people who wanted to break in and kidnap their family members or friends who had heard the truth and decided to come live with us. They wanted to hurt our followers, to kill Father. We needed to protect ourselves, protect what we'd created out here.

Of course, it never came to that. And the government left us alone, no matter what the critics said. Father always supposed it was because at least some of the people in the government knew his prophecies were true.

And though the occasional doubter did manage to turn a follower away from our righteous path, it never led to violence. In fact, the worst violence I ever heard of was from one of the followers who had been kidnapped by his family. They'd locked him in a room for weeks, interrogating him, starving him, trying to break him. He finally recanted all his beliefs in Father and in us so they'd let him free. As soon as he was able, he came home and told us what had happened to him.

People on the outside can be so evil. No wonder this wretched earth needs to be washed clean.

Obviously we can't carry too much with us, but at the same time, we need to bring enough to fulfill any immediate needs, as well as to convince the remaining people on the compound that I have their best interests at heart, and that I'm fully prepared to provide for them. Sam watches me gather supplies for a little while, then places his hand over mine.

"You know, Bright . . . maybe we shouldn't go back right away."

"Why not?" I ask. "What's to gain from letting people suffer?"

He looks at me. "You don't think you can stop their suffering, do you?"

He has a point. The end times will be terrible, no matter what I do.

"And," he continues, snatching his hand back and looking about the storeroom wildly, "everyone is so angry right now. I think maybe it's not safe. . . ."

Safe? Sam must have seen something awful to run away. How fitting that the violence everyone assumed we were capable of arrives only after our truth has come to pass. My father was right to teach me how to use the guns.

"Like if we wait a few days, maybe people will be calmer, more willing to listen to what—to whatever you plan to tell them." He meets my eyes. "Do you know what you plan to tell them?"

I bite my lip. "No. But you're right. A plan would be good."

SAM

A plan *would* be good. Unfortunately, I don't have one either. It's been two days since Bright Child led me into the woods. Two days of camping out in Jeremy's stupid storeroom, watching Bright pray and plan and eat, and two nights of lying beside her while she sleeps, listening to her breathe and feeling the heat pour off her skin and smelling her hair when I pretend I'm just rolling over.

She wants to go back to the compound. I don't know what I'm going to do. I wasn't thinking ahead—I don't even think I know *how*. Before, there was no point. Bright's father, Jeremy Child, already told us what was going to happen. Don't bother studying—the world will end before we ever go to college. Don't bother brushing your teeth—you won't have to worry about cavities in heaven. Don't look at that girl—you'll die long before you ever get your first kiss.

Lies. All lies.

Being here with Bright has pushed it out of my mind, but in the night, when all is still and the earth is turning and I can hear the sound of helicopter blades whirring high above the treetops, the truth comes blaring back to me. Everything is a lie. I've been lied to by everyone—my parents, my teachers, my friends. And they've been deceived, too, by Jeremy Child. We were *supposed* to be in heaven. We were *promised* heaven.

But instead, I'm in hell. Hell is Bright Child, two inches away from me, softly sighing, with her shirt riding up as she tosses and turns on the hard ground. I can see the strap of her bra and the curve of her back.

I should be mourning the destruction of everything I've ever known, and instead all I want to do is touch her.

It's night number three and I give up. I sneak out of the storeroom once I know she's asleep. Today has been the hardest yet. All she wanted to do was rehearse speeches to give to the congregation about our new mission, but the longer we're away from the others, the more sure I am that I can't ever lead her back. Even now, still dressed in her jubilation clothes, with matted hair and smudged skin and the sickly sweet smell of old sweat, she's more like an angel than a girl.

Her father named her well. There's a flame inside her. Her faith is almost blinding in its intensity.

The trip through the woods is treacherous in the dark, but I can't risk turning on a flashlight and leading them back to our hideaway. As it is, I don't know how long we have before the others come for the contents of the storehouse. All things I haven't considered—all very important pieces of information that go right out of my head whenever I'm near Bright.

Because when you listen to her talk, her steadfast belief, her dire and glorious convictions, it's easy to agree.

I cross the creek and see the lights glinting off glass panes in the buildings on the compound.

Easy, but not true.

No one is outside at this time of night, and no one sees me creep up to the windows of the prayer house and peek inside. The elders are all in their little folding chairs, their faces dead and hollow. Shadows lie heavy on their cheekbones and they sit slumped, defeated, and watch Jeremy Child with eyes devoid of the righteous flame I've seen in Bright.

This is why I've taken her away. I can't bear to watch the fire extinguished in her.

Jeremy is at his lectern, and he's in full pounding mode. But this time, his words are not about the End of Days.

They're about Bright.

"And is it any wonder that she, the most dutiful and righteous of all of us, should have gone ahead? My dear little girl, our darling angel, is even now making a place for us in heaven."

Is he like Bright, steadfastly clinging to his belief despite his disappointment? A lot of the elders are missing from the congregation—including my mother. Where are they? Where does my mother think I am? I wonder if anyone even cares.

I keep listening for a few more minutes, hoping to hear a word about the other people missing—maybe even about myself—but it's all about Bright. Our angel, Bright. Our savior, Bright. He argues his prophecy was correct—at least in part. Bright will guide us, Bright will lead the way.

When Jeremy finally releases them, I duck into the bushes.

Before, the elders would burst out of their prayer meetings, on fire to share with all of us Jeremy's newest revelations. Tonight, they're more subdued, talking among themselves in low voices.

"They don't believe me." The voice is very close and I flatten myself against the wall of the building. Jeremy Child is standing at the window, watching the elders walk away.

"Yes, they do." Bright's mother, her voice the usual soft whisper at her husband's side. She's nothing like her daughter—Bright takes after Jeremy. "They're just disappointed. We all are."

"If they don't believe me, they'll keep leaving. So many have already gone."

Is my mother one of them? I wonder. Did she leave the compound without me? Did she leave looking for me?

Or did she leave because while her son vanished along with his daughter, Jeremy could only allow that *Bright* was holy enough to make it into his imagined rapture.

Above me, Jeremy's voice grows firmer. "But I suppose it is their loss if they wish to brave the world without my guidance. Their loss if they wish to give up their place in heaven."

His wife is silent for a long moment, and when she does speak, her words sound more like a shout carried over a great distance. "And . . . Bright?"

"Bright is in heaven," Jeremy says firmly.

No, she's not. I want to pop out of my hiding place and say it out loud. I want to tell Mrs. Child the truth.

"Jeremy—"

"She's in heaven," he repeats, and the window slams shut.

This is his new deception, his new lie. Rage flares within me, but it's tamped down as I realize that I'm no different. He's lying to the elders, to all of them, telling them that

Bright is in heaven while we're all stuck here on earth. I'm lying to Bright and telling her the exact opposite.

It has to stop.

BRIGHT

When I wake, Sam is gone, and for a second I'm scared he's been swept up to heaven with the rest. It's hard enough imagining doing this with his help—I don't know how I'll ever be strong enough to do it alone.

Why have I been chosen for this task? They've always told me I'm as strong as my father, but I don't know how anyone could be strong enough for this. It was hard enough to get people to see the light before. Now, when the world is falling apart, how can I get the survivors to keep their faith alive?

Out here in the woods, safe with my father's stores and security measures, I've been filling my head with visions of what is going on out in the world. Each idea is more terrifying than the last—those who remain of my father's followers, dying of disease or starvation, tearing each other apart as the world falls to pieces around them. How will it end? Will the sun bake the earth? Will the seas rise up to drown us? Will we succumb to a plague and wither where we stand?

Or is it worse than that? With most of the righteous gone away, evil now walks free on this earth, poisoning the hearts and minds of men. The end times will be brutal, filled with demons and monsters. Maybe they've already infiltrated the compound. Will the end come through some new horror the likes of which even my father didn't foresee? The thought sends me back to my knees, praying for guidance, for strength to stand firm against whatever trial lies before me.

One thing is clear. I can no longer afford to sit in the woods and leave my father's followers to fend for themselves against whatever the end times have to offer. I must return to them, bearing supplies and a message of hope. It's what my father would expect me to do.

I'm packed when Sam returns. He stops on the threshold of the storehouse, staring at me with my bag filled with food, medicine, and yes—protection. "It's time to go back," I announce to him in the voice I learned from my father.

"Y-yes." His eyes are wide. "I came to bring you back. I was wrong, Bright. Wrong to bring you here. They need to see you—"

I nod.

"And—and you need to see them. It's not what you think, Bright. I—I didn't know how to tell you. I didn't want to—"

"Don't worry, Sam." I put out my hand toward him. "I understand."

He looks ready to cry. "No, no, you don't. It's just . . . your faith is so strong, Bright. I can see it now, shining all over you. You think you can save everyone."

"I can." I wave to the storehouse. "Look at all of this. It will be easier for us to keep the faith if I can ease some of the physical suffering."

"No, Bright." Sam's head is down, his voice cracking against the words. "The world's not ending. We were all wrong."

I bite my lip. Poor Sam. "I understand that's what you want to believe, Sam. I truly do. I would give anything not to have to face the trials before us. But we've been set a sacred task. We have to keep the faith of my father's followers. We have to help them."

He tries to speak again, but he erupts into sobs and he splutters, covering his face with his hands. "No, Bright. No.

You don't understand. I—I lied to you. Everything. Everything is a lie."

He's so distraught, he can hardly breathe. He stands half crumpled, collapsing under the weight of his despair. Living through these times will not be easy. I step forward, dip my head to meet his, and press my mouth against his lips. "It's okay, Sam," I whisper, and kiss him again.

We stand like that for a long time, our mouths pressed together. I don't think he's even breathing, and when I pull away, he says nothing at all, just stares at me with eyes like Armageddon.

I shoulder my backpack and lead the way back to the compound.

The sun is just beginning to break up the mist as we cross the creek. The buildings of the compound hunch in the dust. The first person to see me is Bethany, and she drops to her knees. "Bright. You're back."

"Yes," I reply, and reach out my hands to her. "Everything will be all right, Bethany. I've come to make sure you know that."

She starts to cry as I touch her. Similar responses greet us with every person we pass on our way up the path.

"Bright. You're here! My prayers have been answered."

"Bright, have you come back to help us?"

"Bright, I knew you wouldn't leave us!"

To each of them, I say the same thing: "Gather everyone you can and meet me at the prayer house. I want to talk to you all."

They shudder with excitement, ecstatic and relieved that someone has come to take charge at last. I look at Sam. "We should have come back days ago. They're desperate."

Sam appears pretty desperate himself.

"Never fear," I say, and my hand finds his across the path. "We'll do this. *Together.*"

And then Sam shudders, too.

My father's poor followers. They've been so lost without a member of the Child family to lead them. For so long, they've listened to my father. Well, I was always his favorite, and I won't let him down now. I will help them in his absence. I will be someone they can look to in these terrible end times.

Before us, even the door to the prayer house gapes in wonderment at our arrival. Behind me, people are gathering, traipsing after me, the murmurs of their relief and admiration floating in the misty air.

Ahead of us, a figure appears in the doorway of the prayer house, his face puffed almost beyond recognition. No—his face is the same, it's only the eyes that have changed. The eyes that were once so clear, that shone with a light some called divine. The eyes that were kind and strong and knowing and true.

His eyes are dead.

"Bright." His mouth moves, and the whisper is in the voice of my father. But his eyes—those eyes!

I stop on the path so quickly that Sam bumps into my back. What is he doing here? My father is in heaven. He's *supposed* to be in heaven.

Though I recoil from his touch, he grabs my shoulders and pulls me in tight. "You've been in heaven for the last few days," he whispers into my ear.

"No," I say. "I've been out in the woods. I thought you—"

"Just go with it," he hisses quickly and spins me around to face the crowd. I am surer than ever that something is wrong. My father has never asked me to lie. He's never had to—why would he, when the truth of the prophecy burned brighter than the sun?

And now, as the last of the mist clears from the ground and I can see clearly the entire compound, and all of the followers gathered before, me, waiting, I know what has happened. It's the end times, just like my father warned us. And it's more horrible than I could ever have imagined.

I look at Sam and he's staring back, as usual, his mouth drawn tight, his eyes aching with pain. He gives a slight nod. This was what he feared to tell me. This was what he's been scared of, all these days.

I drop the bag from my shoulders as my father's voice rings out, and reach in to find what I need.

"Bright has returned to us!" he cries. "She has come to bring us good news. She has come to lead the way." He turns in my direction.

The second his dead eyes meet mine, I shoot.

"Demon." I spit at the thing that looks like my father. It falls against the steps, choking. The gun is hot in my hands, and righteousness is the inferno in my veins. "Did you think you could trick us? My father is in heaven."

I think I hear screaming. I can't be sure.

There are many horrors to face, here at the end of the world.

The Angriest Man

LISA McMANN

On the day the angriest man died, his bones cursed the bed they lay in. Inside the box, the bones seethed and growled. And underground they exploded into dust and lay there, dormant, one hundred years.

From the dust rose a flower. To the flower came a bee. From the bee, a stinger grew, and it dripped with the venom of the bones of the angriest man.

The bee buzzed around, its yellow jacket glistening, until it came upon an open window. Inside the window was a woman, ripe with child. From the woman came a baby, a boy, who was still and blue, until he was stung by the bee that dripped with the venom of the bones of the angriest man.

Then the baby roared to life and growled, six long years, until the mother went mad and sent the boy away.

• • •

This is the story my mother told me in the final days. "That baby is you," she'd cry, "and this is what you have become!"

"I'm sorry," I'd growl, but to me it was a whisper.

"You are an evil, bad child. Bad to the *bone.*" Her macramé hair hung in her face. A mole throbbed at her temple.

"Yes," I said. I pressed my fingers into my evil kneecaps and cursed them.

Today is the anniversary of the death of the bee, and I am free from all ties. No one will miss me, and I am done with this. I am eighteen and wasted, not from any substance, but from life. I don't care about this foster home, these people who feed me. I don't call them anything. They put me in the basement because of the growls. They lock the door for fear I am a werewolf.

I sit up in my bed for the last time. My bag is packed and I will go once they unlock the door. There are no choices; there is only one ending to the story of a boy so bad as me.

I make my bed and brush my teeth. Tie my shoes. The shoestrings are dirty and frayed, having lost their aglets long ago. I am bad. I haven't taken care of my shoes properly. I hear my mother's screams above the growls and grip my elbows, prodding their evil points. I picture them exploding into dust, which calms me down.

At school the teachers will welcome my absence, for I am disruptive. "Not a *bad* student," one emphasized on my report card, "he just makes bad choices." If only the teacher knew the truth. I try to tell him that I *am* bad, that it's okay to say it, but he, like all the others, takes a nervous step back when I approach. Invariably his eyes dart to the door, his fingers crawl over his desk to grab a pen, a protractor, a book. Anything to use as a weapon, or as protection, against the growls.

I'm angry, they say, echoing my mother. Angry to the core. Or perhaps I have a throat disease, or a nervous disorder, but no one knows what it is. All I know is that they hear things I do not say, see things I do not do, relay stories about me that didn't happen. But I can only shrug, for I am cursed with venom, formed from ancient angry bone dust.

It didn't take me long to begin to do the things they accused me of. Why not? The consequences are exactly the same. Being bad is my destiny, and mine alone.

"David?" quavers the voice at the top of the stairs.

I jump, and the motorcycle growl in my throat revs. I didn't hear the click of the lock on this, my last day. I'm not sure what that means, but it can't be good. "I'm here," I say.

Of course you are, whispers the lock in the door.

"Do you want to come up and say goodbye?" the woman asks.

"No."

She answers with footsteps moving away.

I stare at my frayed shoelaces, waiting for the usual morning rush above my head to subside. Waiting for the growl in my breath to subside too, but it never does. It's my punishment for being born dead, which she wanted, then coming to life, which she didn't. I feel like it's the bee's fault. Like I did the right thing in the beginning.

When they are gone I sling my bag over my shoulder and climb the stairs. I don't look back—who wishes for a final look at nothing? I eat something, but in twenty seconds I'll be unable to recall what it was. Then I set my house key on the sill and open the door, turning the lock carefully and pulling the door closed behind me. At the end of the driveway I stop and close my eyes, waiting for the growl to lead me.

• • •

In my dreams there's a girl who growls too, but I know she can't exist, because the bee died immediately. My mother saw it dead on the floor as the welt swelled on my cheek. She told me, "It took one look at what it stang, and died."

In third grade, my teacher said that female honeybees die naturally after they sting, which gave me hope. I repeated the angriest man's story in my head, pausing at *"To the flower came a bee." A bee. A bee.* I willed it to be "a *female honey*bee," but the words wouldn't stick there, no matter how hard I tried to make them.

I pretended many things:

That my growl was the bee inside of me.

That my mother killed the bee trying to save me.

That it really was a female honeybee.

But my daydreams made my growl louder, and after school some jerks stuck me in the janitor's closet. The mop stared at me, wearing my mother's hair. *Bad to the bone,* it whispered. *That's what you are.* I took the mop and smashed all the cans and bottles and bags off the janitor's shelves and onto the floor, until it smelled like cat litter and butterscotch. The janitor let me out.

The next day I told the story of the angriest man to my teacher. She said she'd never heard of it.

Here in the driveway the growl points me west. I start walking through yards, across Lane Avenue, to the yellow field. Kids used to play freely in the field, but a few years ago somebody put up a fence. I know how to get in, though.

I walk through the tall grass to the trodden path. Milkweed plants beckon with whiter-than-white gluey tips. I stop and pluck a pod from a plant, open it up. Its fine silky hat sways in the wind like hair under water. The seeds inside aren't ready yet. I pull them out anyway and throw them to the sky, sending them off unannounced like Charlotte's daughters in the breeze, away from their mother, their sisters, without a goodbye. I drop the pod on the ground and try to wipe the sticky mess off my fingers. One feathery seed is stuck to me, absorbing evil from my bones. I pull it off and throw it into the air, but it drops straight to the ground, infected.

It growls at me and I growl back. I move on toward the big oak, the center of the universe, if the universe was this field.

The big oak is a maple tree, but what did we know? What did anybody know? Back then kids could overlook strange throat noises for the sake of playing house. I stop at the base of the enormous tree and look up. What remains of my only good summer is a trembling sheet of green-gray clapboard and dangling two-by-fours, working their way loose with the pressure from raindrops. I think about being eight in the tree fort with a strange girl whose name I don't remember. We played house and I was her good growly dog, protecting our fort from the sixth graders who probably built it.

They were scared of me.

Stop! My mother would scream whenever I got loud in public. *You're scaring everyone! You're driving me crazy!*

That tree fort girl—I thought she growled inside too. I told her so.

"No, I don't," she said, growling.

"You do," I said in my kindest growl, not quite a purr.

"I can't hear it." She folded her arms over her chest. "Nobody else can see me, you know."

I was sorry about that for her, but not for me. "I can see you and hear you. That's better than not."

Then she went away. I guarded the fort for a while. A few days. But she never came back, and I quit going to the tree fort to wait for my master because it was just too hard, sitting there alone.

Bad dog, whispers the clapboard.

Ever since that summer, I've wanted so much for her to be bad like me. She is the one in my dream.

I wiggle the bottom step with my foot—a rotting two-by-four. It has three rusty nail heads, like eyes and a nose, silent without a mouth. But other steps with more nails hiss against my growl, denying the girl's existence to my face.

I hang my head, knowing they are right.

A wave of longing ripples through my stomach, down to my private parts, and I stand frozen. Pain wrenches past my evil shield and seeps into my bloodstream, making everything hurt. All I can do is reach out and grip the tree, scraping the hell out of my arms, but at least that feels like something I can control. I close my eyes and press my body into the trunk, my cheek on its wrinkled bark, my chest and groin aching against it.

The old tree groans and ticks in the wind. I growl and groan and tick with it until my face is not my face—it is the tree, and the tree is the girl, and the girl is the antidote for the venom of the stinger on the bee that touched the flower, which grew from the dust of the bones of the angriest man.

But it's all in my rotten head.

I leave the tree behind and slog through the other half of the knee-high grass to where the field ends, at the railroad tracks, a place where pennies die and no one comes back for them. They glare at me with contempt, abandoned.

I roar. It's not my fault. I pick dead coins up and throw

them into the ditch that runs parallel to the tracks, but I can still feel those copper eyes on me. I cannot cross overtop of them, so I must go around to the road. I walk on the track toward Sixteenth Street, kicking every sad, angry penny into the ditch as hard as I can, because of my destiny.

When I cross at the road, I ignore the jeers from the ditch and the pneumatic exhale from the door of the school bus, which stops at the tracks for a moment to despise me.

The growl leads me on a long walk out of this town and into the next, past businesses and houses, schools and trees. On a different day I would be lost. But because this is my final destination, I am not lost at all.

My shoulder blades ache.

Finally, when my growl grows louder, I wind my way down a shady road and I am close, almost where I need to be. I leave the busy street behind and enter the quiet place of stone and grass and funeral flowers.

The cemetery is lush and green from the nutrient-rich soil. Rotting flesh liquefies and seeps through cracked caskets under the ground. Souls tunnel away under rows of boxes and roads, reaching out, tangling up with all the others; an enormous spirit ant farm beneath my feet. All the while bones lie in the coffins where the flesh has left them. Some of them are angry bones, but none so angry as the bones of the angriest man. Now I must find him. Bad begets bad; anger, anger. It's time.

I picture the underground cemetery world as I walk along under the cover of stretching maples. I listen deeply and my growl guides me over the paths.

There is a grove of small trees where I guess Jesus must be buried, in a grave under his own statue. Eleven disciples' stones surround him, along with some bushes. My feet stop me, so I stand and stare into the statue's eyes and think about my mother, how she always made me apologize to Jesus for being so bad. I growl, but the statue remains silent.

I stand so still that a bird flits into view and perches on stone Jesus's head. I close my eyes but hear nothing—just the sound of my own growl. I look up again and push onward, making a church with my fingers and pressing out, cracking my bad, angry bones as I walk.

The growl becomes a roar.

I am nearly there.

The hair on my arms sizzles and my skull and spine ache. The road slopes steeply down into a hell-like hollow, where little kids on bikes fall and are swallowed up. I travel the road, roaring, to the very bottom of hell's pit, to the moldy, cracked gravestone overcome with roots and weeds. A single flower chokes its way up from the crack in the stone, and the etched name of the angriest man is covered with swarming ants, unable to be read. But I know it is him. His bones have magnetized mine. I stumble to it and fall down on the grave, my skeleton searing inside me, my skin turning red. I lie on my back, six feet above the place where he was, where he is, his dust claiming mine. I scream to the sky, cursing my mother, cursing the bee, cursing the bones of the angriest man, but I am still bad. Bad to the bone. Words said can't be unsaid, and now I have to pay. The noise in my throat is my badness welling up from deep inside my marrow. I never had a chance to be good.

As I lie here, heating up, ants find their way over my body but they are nothing to me. They are not bees.

I stare at the angriest man's flower hanging above my face. An uninvited ghost emerges from its center, and I'm afraid. It stretches out, screams and roars, coming down to meet me.

It is the girl.

On her shoulder is a raw red sting, and from her throat comes a growl. Clutched in her hand, her own dead bee. She looks at me, and when we come together, my welt returns. She touches my cheek and kisses my melting lips, my first kiss. My last. My skin wrinkles like paper and ignites.

I am triumphant in my last breath.

The ghost girl, the one like me, disappears into my chest, absorbed inside of me, soaking up my liquefying flesh, my blood that boils out. The fire leaps and burns, licking a body I no longer feel. Then, slowly, the flames die.

When nothing more remains than wind sliding through evil bones, the ghost girl slips away, back into the flower, and my scorching skeleton becomes ash and explodes. The tiniest bits shoot high into the air in all directions, and then fall like evil snow in the trees, like angry pollen on the grass, like growly dust on the statue and the stones of eleven plus one. The powdery remains of the baddest boy's bones take hold where they land and curse the world . . . if this cemetery were the world.

When night falls, the last of the graveyard's creatures and bones turn bad, and all nature growls in unison. I melt away to find the girl who was sucked into the flower that sprang from the grave that held the dust of the bones of the angriest man. I go at last to the place where no bones, where no bees, can find me.

Out of the Blue

MEG CABOT

Interview of Dr. John R. Hall
RESTRICTED ACCESS: EYES ONLY

Well, I can't say I wasn't expecting you. I've been watching it on the news all morning.

I assumed someone from the base would be stopping by, so I got out their files. Patient-doctor privilege doesn't exactly apply in a case like this, I take it? No, I guessed as much.

Let me see. My first examination of Kyle and Kaleigh Claire Conrad was . . . what is it now? Just after their birth, sixteen years ago. They were delivered by emergency cesarean section. Seven and a half pounds each . . . that's fairly normal size for a single baby, you see, but huge for twins. No idea how their poor mother carried them to full term, but she managed. Her husband, the colonel, ordered her to do it, I suppose.

The last time I saw them—besides today on TV, of course—was the day after their sixth birthday.

Not coincidentally, that's the day I quit practicing medicine.

"I'm sure it's nothing." That's what their father, Colonel Conrad, said to me that day.

If I had a nickel for every time a parent has said *I'm sure it's nothing* when I've walked into an exam room, I'd have retired to Palm Springs instead of here in Peachtree County.

Tell you the truth, with kids, it usually *is* nothing.

Of course, with the Conrads, it turned out not to be nothing, didn't it?

"Let me take a look," I said. "Right arm, is it?"

"Yes," Mrs. Conrad said. She seemed about to cry. Her husband was upset, too, but not for the same reasons as his wife. "And it's *not* nothing. It's the exact same spot, on each of them. I thought at first maybe they'd been playing with Magic Markers, but then the spots wouldn't come off, even with nail polish remover. And they've been talking all morning about this spaceship—"

"There *wasn't* any damned spaceship," Colonel Conrad said, exasperated. "These kids will say anything to stay out of trouble. Yesterday Kaleigh said the one hundred and one dalmatians stole her sweater, when she actually left it at school. Now it's a spaceship, for crying out loud."

Alarm bells should have gone off then. But they didn't. Because I was sure I knew what I was dealing with. Ninety-nine out of a hundred other doctors would have been, too.

But no one's ever dealt with anything like the Conrads, have they?

Anyway, I examined both kids closely, then had them roll down their sleeves.

"Well," I said. "I can tell you exactly what those marks

are, Colonel and Mrs. Conrad, and neither Magic Markers nor spaceships are responsible. They're moles."

Mrs. Conrad looked shocked. "But," she cried, "they're *blue*!"

"They are indeed," I said. "They're called a blue nevus." Interesting thing about the blue nevus, I explained to her. It's a fairly rare but harmless cutaneous condition, occurring in only about one to two percent of the general population.

Of course Mrs. Conrad wanted to be reassured they weren't cancer, especially since she was quite sure she'd never noticed them before that morning.

I told her blue nevi can appear at any time during a child's first ten to fifteen years. True fact. And unless they show signs of malignancy—and nevi generally don't—I always advise leaving them alone. Removing them tends to leave a nasty scar.

For both the Conrad children to have a blue nevus, I said, and in the exact same spot—especially considering that they're fraternal, not identical, twins—is extremely unusual, but not unheard of.

That's when Kyle Conrad piped up. "That must be what he meant, Kaleigh," he said to his sister. "About our being destined for greatness."

Of course I asked, "What who meant, Kyle?"

Colonel Conrad answered before the little boy could say another word. "Kyle and Kaleigh claim that a *spaceship* landed in the field next door to our house last night, while they were camping in the backyard in the tent they got for their birthday."

"They say a man came out of the ship," Mrs. Conrad added, looking much more worried than her husband. "And that *he's* the one who gave them the marks—"

"Which we now know isn't true," Colonel Conrad said.

"Right, kids? And what happens when we don't tell the truth?"

Kaleigh and Kyle exchanged glances. "We get a time-out," they sang in unison.

"I just don't understand," Mrs. Conrad said, looking perplexed, "why they would make up something like *that*?"

"Because they didn't follow instructions," the colonel said. "And they knew they were going to get in trouble. I told them to wake me up if the weather got bad and they wanted to come inside. This morning when I woke up, I found the two of them snoring away in their beds, and the tent that I paid over two hundred dollars for blown halfway down the street, along with the sleeping bags, which were another sixty dollars each. Which is why," he added, narrowing his eyes at the kids, "they're not getting their camping equipment back until they've shown they're mature enough to handle the responsibility."

I'll tell you the truth: I've always thought Colonel Conrad was a little hard on those kids. They'd only just turned six, after all.

But I understood his frustration. I've heard a lot of whoppers come out of kids' mouths over the years.

And a spaceship landing in the backyard sounded exactly like something my sons would have come up with in order to get out of having to put away their camping equipment.

Still, I had to ask.

"Your father's right, children," I said to the twins. "It's never good to lie. We all know that spaceships are imaginary. So, when you were camping in the backyard last night, did you *really* see a man?"

They looked at one another in that way that twins do sometimes—like they're communicating telepathically—and seemed to come to some kind of silent agreement. Finally, Kaleigh spoke.

"Yes," she said solemnly. "We saw a man. He said what Kyle said."

Her mother and I exchanged glances. "That you were destined for greatness?"

"Yes," Kaleigh said. "He said that's why we'd been selected."

"Selected for what?" I asked.

Kyle answered brightly, "To do great things, of course. That's why he gave us these!" He held up his arm with a big grin, showing off the nevus on his bicep. "Pretty cool, right?"

Colonel Conrad rolled his eyes and muttered, "I can't believe I just wasted the whole morning on this. You take them home, Alecia. I need to get back to the base. We're testing those C-5s today."

It was Mrs. Conrad who, after her husband was gone, demanded that I remove her children's nevi, even though I explained to her that they weren't a cosmetic problem and there was little chance they'd ever become malignant.

But she insisted. Mrs. Conrad is every bit as stubborn as the colonel, in her own way.

I've never been fully able to explain what happened after that. All I can say is that Kyle and Kaleigh Conrad were the last patients I ever saw. I closed up my practice the second they walked out the door, and have spent the past ten years sitting in this house, afraid that my mind was slipping away . . . until this morning when my wife called me downstairs to show me what's been playing over and over again on every single news channel on TV.

Now I know I didn't imagine what happened in my office

that day. So I hope you'll excuse me, but I don't have time for talking. I've got ten years of living to make up for.

Interview of KC Conrad
RESTRICTED ACCESS: EYES ONLY

Look, I may only be sixteen years old, but I'm not stupid, okay? I have the highest grade point average in my class. So I'm just going to say it one more time: I invoke my right to counsel.

And even though my brother probably didn't say it out loud, he invokes his right to counsel, too.

So . . . you guys are just going to ignore that?

Fine, whatever. You want to waste my time, I'll waste yours. I'm not going to tell you anything except what you already know. My name is KC Conrad. And no, I'm not going to tell you what the initials stand for. Like you don't already know.

Just like I'm sure you already know that I'm a former member of the Pritchard High School girls' softball team, right? And current editor of the school paper? And vice president of the Volunteer Literacy Program? And secretary to the Science Olympiads?

I bet you even know I'm founder of the Pritchard High School Recycling Awareness Program? Impressive, right?

Well, not around here.

I used to think that was completely unfair, you know? People like us—I'm including you, because let's face it, in those suits, you might as well be on the Science Olympiads with me—we work our butts off trying to leave the world a better place than we found it, and does anyone even notice?

No, because the only thing anyone cares about around here is sports. Seriously, all my brother Kyle has to do is walk into a room, and everyone's like, "Oh my God! It's Kyle Conrad, the first person in the history of Peachtree County to be named to the national high school all-American baseball team (as a junior, no less), star first baseman of the Pritchard Wolves!"

And the sad thing is, I totally could have had all that.

But I have a little something called ethics. Which is why I had to quit the girls' softball team when that cow Amber Johnson got elected captain. That's why I was home last night blogging—yeah, I know, pathetic, right? Blogging, on the eve of my sixteenth birthday? Not that anyone even reads my blog except my best friend Radha—while everyone *else* in our class was out celebrating my birthday at the lake. Okay, Kyle's birthday. Whatever. Everyone except Radha because she works at the Regal Cinema over at the mall on Friday nights, and, of course, me, because I've been a social pariah ever since I quit the team.

I just kept thinking about how different things were when we were little—you know, in kindergarten? I'm sure you guys don't think about stuff like that because you're too busy watching *Top Shot*.

But for our sixth birthday, we all hung out *together*, me and Kyle and Radha and Duncan—Duncan Mulroney, he's Kyle's best friend. At least, he used to be until Kyle and Amber started going out. Kyle's basically been attached at the hip to Amber all semester, don't ask me what he sees in her. Amber Johnson is a mental case and it would be a public service if you guys could lock her up instead of me.

But whatever, everyone thinks I quit the team to spend more time with the Science Olympiads. Which I did, basically. Because the Olympiads treat their opponents with dignity and respect.

I don't know, it's probably lame. But I was just so sad for

the way things used to be when we were all younger and things were less . . . complicated. When we didn't have to lie all the time. I guess that's it. I was sick of all the lies.

So, okay, I'll admit it. I ended up doing the stupidest thing I've ever done in my life—well, maybe the second stupidest thing. And that was blog the truth about what happened to Kyle and me the night of our sixth birthday.

How was I supposed to know what was going to happen? I didn't expect anyone to read it, because no one reads my blog but Radha, not even my mom. I certainly didn't expect *you* guys to show up, much less *him*.

Well, maybe I expected *him*.

So there, I explained. You know all this, since you read it, obviously. That's why you're here. Good timing, by the way. You guys really helped. Did you note the sarcasm in my voice just then?

So, can I go now? Because I invoked my right to counsel and I don't care what agency you're with, the Sixth Amendment—

What do you mean, the Sixth Amendment doesn't apply to matters extraterrestrial in nature?

Excerpt from KC Conrad's LiveJournal

BIRTHDAY BLUES

. . . it was right after our sixth birthday party, the one with the explorer theme (remember, Radha? I got the sleeping bags and the inflatable mattresses to go with them? Kyle got the binoculars and that gigantic tent).

After you and everybody else went home from the party, Kyle wanted to try out all the camping equipment. He bugged Mom and Dad so much, they finally relented and helped us set it up in the backyard so they could keep an eye on us from their bedroom window.

Only I think Mom and Dad had a little too much wine with the rest of the parents. They conked out, and were nowhere to be found when the trouble started.

Which it totally did a few hours later when the wind began to pick up . . . so hard that a corner of the tent came undone. Kyle, Dad's Little Intrepid Explorer, was running around, yelling at me to try to help him peg the tent corner back down, only the wind was blowing so much, I could hardly see anything except flying leaves and bits of mulch from Mom's vegetable garden.

But I didn't want Kyle to lose his precious tent, so I was trying to help.

That's when I heard the roaring sound—like a freight train—and looked across the yard to the empty lot next door. . . .

Except of course the lot isn't empty now. It's where Duncan Mulroney lives. On whom, I would just like to state for the record, I do *not* have a crush, despite what everyone seems to think. Why would I have a crush on someone who doesn't even know I'm alive?

And Kyle uses those binoculars he got ten years ago to check out Duncan's mom whenever she sits around their backyard pool in her bikini. I'm sorry to say it, but it's true.

Anyway, that's when I saw it.

I can't really explain what it looked like. Imagine the most beautiful fireworks display you've ever seen.

Then imagine that fireworks display right above your head, attached to the underside of a gigantic helicopter, hovering just above you.

That's what it was like. The grass, the trees, Mom's cherry

tomato plants, everything around us was being flattened by the air coming out of its exhaust jets. That's where the wind was coming from.

For some reason I'll never be able to explain, I wasn't scared. I was *excited.* I guess I was too young to know better. When you're six, you think tornadoes take you to Oz.

And I guess you think that's where ships from outer space are going to take you, too.

Of course I threw down the tent peg I was holding and rushed toward it. I didn't think twice about it. I wanted to get on it. I wanted to go *inside* it. It looked like the world's most amazing carousel ride to me.

But Kyle felt differently. He wanted to get the heck out of there.

"Let's go, KC," he cried. Tears were streaming down his face. "Let's go get Dad. He said to, remember? He said to go wake him up if anything went wrong. And this is *wrong.*"

But I didn't want to go wake up Dad. I wanted to stay. I was dazzled by all the lights. Maybe I was just dazzled.

And though I'll always kind of hate myself for this, I turned to Kyle and said, "*You* go wake up Dad if you want to, Kyle. I'm going to stay. I want to *see.*"

That's when Kyle did something amazing for someone so young. Something that—no matter how much he annoys me with all the Amber Johnson drama today—I will never forget, and that I'll always love him for.

Because Kyle *could* have gotten away. He could have run, but he didn't. Instead, he came right up to me and took my hand.

He stood there and waited with me as the door to that ship opened. He was scared as could be—I could feel his fingers trembling in mine—but he stayed as a man stepped out of that ship (blue-eyed, dark-haired, and handsome as any nonthreatening teen heartthrob could be) and said with a great big smile, "Hello, children. Won't you come in?"

Of course, they tell you never to go anywhere with strangers, especially strangers who offer you rides in cars.

But no one ever mentions anything about strangers who offer you rides in their *spaceship*. Obviously I said yes. It was a *spaceship* that had all these shiny control panels with thousands of blinking lights and buttons and gear shifts and stuff.

We didn't really get a chance to look at them too much, though, because the man started explaining right away about how brave and smart and cool we were—way braver and smarter and cooler than anyone else he'd met on earth so far, because we were the only kids who'd chosen to talk to him instead of running away, screaming.

Which was why he was selecting *us* for the biggest honor his kind could bestow. See, his planet was in a lot of trouble: it had run out of many of the natural resources that we had in abundance on earth, such as clean water, air, and other things like that.

He just needed to analyze how we managed ours, and send that information back to his home planet. If Kyle and I would be willing to help him do that, that would be *really* amazing. And if we didn't tell anyone (because of course our helping him had to be a secret, since everyone else on earth besides us was such a big scaredy-cat), there'd be an enormous reward:

We'd become the most famous people on earth.

They were always telling us in church that we were supposed to help those who were in need. And this definitely seemed to apply to the poor spaceman whose planet was literally being *choked* from pollution. How could we not help? Not helping seemed like it would be wrong. Even Kyle, who hadn't wanted to get involved in the first place, had to agree.

All we had to do to help was let the spaceman stick a blue dot into each of our arms. It wouldn't hurt, he said. We'd just get a little sleepy. But, the spaceman explained as our eyelids drooped, that was normal during the "implementation and activation" process. When we woke up, he said, we'd feel good as new.

And he was right, we did. Until Mom noticed the blue dots the next morning, and we forgot we weren't supposed to talk about any of it, and we ended up at Dr. Hall's office, with him numbing my arm, then digging around for my blue dot with a needle.

I remember Dr. Hall muttering things like "Can't say I've ever seen one buried quite this deep. Sorry, hon, didn't mean for that to hurt," and "Appears to be some kind of foreign substance," and my mom wailing, "But you said it was harmless," and "Is it *cancer*?" and Dr. Hall saying, "If I can just get a grip on it . . ."

Meanwhile, I was sitting there with tears running down my face. Dr. Hall had promised it wouldn't hurt, because of the local anesthesia he used.

But it really, *really* hurt. I can't even describe how much it hurt. I thought I was going to pass out.

I knew Dr. Hall was going to start digging into Kyle's arm next. Poor Kyle who would never have been in this situation if it hadn't been for me. The promises we'd made the night before—the thrill of saving someone else's planet—were wearing off as quickly as the local. Who cared if some spaceman whose face we could barely remember had said we were destined for greatness someday? Right now, our destiny seemed *awful*.

Then something terrible happened—worse even than the pain I was experiencing. Dr. Hall suddenly froze up, then let out a scream, like . . . well, like someone had stabbed *him* with one of those needles, and with*out* anesthetic. I've never heard a grown man scream like that before, and I hope never to hear it again.

Then Dr. Hall dropped the tool he'd been using to remove what he'd called my blue nevus, and ran out of the exam room like his hair was on fire.

He didn't come back for a long time. Mom was pretty mad because he'd left in the middle of removing my blue nevus, with me just sitting there on the exam table, bleeding. She had to go out and get one of the nurses to tape gauze to my arm.

When he did finally come back, Dr. Hall looked completely unlike his normal professional self. His hair was kind of standing up on end, his tie askew, and his fingers shaking.

But he told Mom not to worry. He'd checked some of the tissue he'd managed to dig from my arm, and said it wasn't malignant.

"But it's what you called it, right?" Mom asked. "A blue . . . whatever?"

"It's blue, all right," Dr. Hall said. And though Kyle swears he didn't hear it, I know *I* heard Dr. Hall mutter this under his breath: "*Whatever* it is."

He told Mom to continue a pattern of "attentiveness" and contact medical authorities if there were any changes. Then he said, "I'm not going to charge you for today, Mrs. Conrad. And I'm sure we don't have to mention any of this to the colonel." Then he gave me about five billion root beer lollipops in a sort of distracted way and walked out again.

That was our last visit to Dr. Hall's office, because he closed his practice right after that and moved to a house so far out into the countryside, it was practically in another county.

But it was okay, because our blue dots never did get bigger or anything. They stayed exactly the same, just this weird blue discoloration on the same place on each of our right arms.

And over time, I started to believe they were what Dr. Hall said they were . . . just moles that appeared overnight. I started to forget what the spaceman looked like, or even that any of it had ever happened, except when I'd see the camping equipment all boxed up in the garage—Dad never did let us use it again, and we certainly never asked—or when Mom would jokingly tell other people that we'd once insisted we were "destined for greatness." Wasn't that adorable?

Still, there's one thing I've never forgotten, and that's bothered me ever since I got old enough to realize it:

How could *Kyle and I* help an alien civilization? *We were six.* What could *we* have told that spaceman's people (especially about water and air purity on our planet, if that's what he *really* wanted to know, which sometimes I sort of doubt) that he couldn't have learned from the Internet, which surely, considering how advanced his civilization must be, he'd have known how to access?

I've wondered about this ever since. It's all so unlikely: Aliens visited our planet, and they chose to visit *me*—well, me and Kyle, whatever. Was the whole thing just a freak mutual twin hallucination? Maybe there was peyote growing in Mom's vegetable garden, and some of it blew up our noses, and Kyle and I didn't know it.

But on the other hand, there *is* this thing in my arm. Is it *really* a blue nevus? What else *could* it be?

I'd like to find out . . . but I'm also afraid to. After what happened to Dr. Hall, there's a part of me that doesn't really want to know.

And who would even believe me if I tried to tell them? I'm sure you're reading this now, Radha, going, "Right. A *space*ship." And *you're* my best friend.

Oh, who even cares. It's midnight.

Happy sixteenth birthday to me.

Interview of Kyle Conrad
RESTRICTED ACCESS: EYES ONLY

Look, I know you guys need to talk to me about what happened last night. But can we postpone this till a little later? I got a girl waiting for me, and she's upset. You know how that is. So, if you could undo these handcuffs, that'd be great.

Wait, what did KC say? No, no, that's not how it went down at all. Look, I don't want anyone to get the wrong idea about my sister. I mean, she's crazy, but, she's crazy in a *good* way, you know?

Take this mole thing. Whenever anyone asks me about mine, I just say it's part of a gang tattoo that never got completed because another gang interrupted while I was getting it done and everyone in both gangs got shot to death in a rain of chaotic gunfire . . . everyone but me, because I ducked in time. I'm the lone gang survivor. Sweet, right? Girls totally believe it.

But then my sister goes and ruins it by posting the truth about it on her blog. She never even considers what would happen if anyone (besides her best friend) ever read the stupid thing.

Which is exactly what happened to me last night, driving home from the lake. I get this text from my girlfriend, Amber: "You like boobs? Fine. Go look at Duncan's mom's. You're never looking at mine again."

I didn't even know what she was talking about until I started looking at my other texts. *Everyone* had read KC's blog, it turns out. Because Amber has a Google Alert on her name and the minute KC posted, Amber read her entry and went nuts. Amber wouldn't listen when I called and tried to tell her that I only looked at Duncan's mom's boobs that *one time.*

KC posting that thing on her blog is classic KC. She's book smart—she gets great grades, and she's read every book in our school library, even the ones that aren't by James Patterson—but she's not what you'd call *street* smart, like me. There's a difference. KC doesn't always think ahead. She saw that spaceship, and she wanted to go inside it. She didn't think about what that spaceman might do to us. She blogged about me and the binoculars, but she didn't think about how mad that might make Duncan.

But Duncan's grabbing that baseball bat and showing up on our lawn to kill me as I pulled in the driveway on the way back from the lake? See now, that was overkill, in my opinion. Duncan's the single reason we won the championship last year, and why we're headed for another one this year, too. He's in my same grade, but because his birthday is in August and his mom held him back from starting kindergarten a year because she was worried he'd be the smallest kid in class, he's huge. I mean, he went from being the smallest kid in school to being the hugest guy in the county, practically.

So having a guy that big standing in your yard, holding a baseball bat—even if he's your best friend—in the middle of the night, that's pretty intimidating.

Which is why I texted KC to get downstairs and distract him somehow, and I didn't get out of the car (that I know technically I'm not allowed to drive without an adult accompanying me in the vehicle but it was like one in the morning. So, am I going to get busted for driving without a license, too? No? Cool, thanks).

Anyway, I was like, "Duncan, it was only *one time.*"

Except of course it doesn't matter how many times you check out a guy's mom in her bikini with binoculars. Once is all it takes to get a guy really, really mad.

So it was a good thing I'm so street smart and didn't get out of the car. Because Duncan wasn't ready to listen, you know? He wouldn't even let me talk. He just raised up that bat and was like, "Get ready to die, Conrad," and started to swing.

I was sure the next thing I was going to feel was shards of Mom's windshield and the Duncan's Louisville Exogrip embedded in my head. Though mainly I was worried about Mom's windshield, because then she'd totally know I'd taken her car out for some unsupervised driving.

Instead, I heard KC going, "Put the bat down, Duncan. Violence never solves anything."

Honestly, I didn't think things could *get* any scarier than Duncan Mulroney swinging at me.

But then I saw KC standing in the front yard wearing this teeny-tiny nightgown, and Duncan staring at her with his mouth hanging open, and I realized they *could* get scarier than that.

Because when I'd told her to distract Duncan, I'd meant with Mom's homemade chocolate chip cookies or something, not her *body,* which frankly I never even knew KC had, because all she ever wears are cargo pants and flannel shirts from Old Navy.

I was all, "KC, what's the *matter* with you? Go back inside and put on a robe."

And she was all, "You can't tell me what to do. Get back in the car, you idiot."

Which is when I realized I'd gotten out of the car, just like—well, what she said. An idiot.

And that I was standing there, totally defenseless, in front of Duncan, who still had his bat, and was totally mad at me for creeping on his mom (just that one time, though).

Only it was okay, because it was like I didn't even exist to Duncan anymore.

"Hey, Kaleigh," Duncan was saying, in this super concerned voice I'd only ever heard him use before with dogs and his grandma. "Kyle's right. You should put on a robe. It's kind of cold out."

KC looked at him like he was a crazy person and was all, "Gee, thanks, *Dad*. Why don't *you* go put on a robe?"

I totally understood where she was coming from, because first of all, he'd called her Kaleigh. No one calls KC Kaleigh and gets away with it.

And second of all, Duncan wasn't wearing a shirt.

He did something *completely* insane then, even for him. He actually put down the bat, walked over to the porch where KC was standing, and *sat down next to her on the steps.*

Between you and me, I've always kind of suspected there was a little something going on between Duncan and my sister. Why else does Duncan always go, "Sorry," whenever KC comes storming in when Duncan and I are downstairs in the den playing Halo, and tells us to be quiet when she's trying to study? Who says "Sorry" when a girl does that, instead of just fart and wave the fumes in her direction, like a normal person? Clearly, Duncan is in love with my sister.

And how come ever since I started going out with Amber, KC's always ragging on me about not spending more time with Duncan? Clearly, she is in love with him.

I don't know how I could have missed the signs.

Next thing I know, Duncan is asking Kaleigh, "It was you, wasn't it? You're the one who slipped the note under the Dulles County women's softball team's locker room doors just before their game against the Pritchard Wolves, warning them not to drink from their cooler."

I had no idea what he was talking about. But KC evidently did, since she sat down onto the porch right next to him and asked, her eyes huge, "How did you know?"

"My cousin's friend is friends with a girl on the Dulles County team," Duncan said. "She told him all about it. How they opened their cooler and smelled it, and it was filled with—"

"I know," KC said, wincing. "It was Amber. I didn't find out until it was too late to stop her. She'd already done it. All I could do was warn them."

Duncan nodded. "I figured as much. Right after that game, you quit the team. I just put two and two together. You did the right thing, Kaleigh. It's always best to tell the truth."

I still didn't understand a thing they were talking about. I was like, "Hello. Remember me? Could someone tell *me* the truth? *What* did my girlfriend put in her opposing team's Gatorade?"

But KC was too busy giving Duncan this big kiss—and Duncan kissing her back—to answer me.

So I just sat down on the lawn and concentrated on looking at the moon coming up over the Garrisons' house across the street, instead of how much I wanted to puke.

Until I heard the noise of tires crunching on the driveway. It was like two o'clock in the morning by then, and at first I was kind of worried it might be Amber (this one time, she thought I was sexting with her best friend, Taylor Hotchkiss, so she came over and lit our mailbox on fire).

But it turned out to be Radha, KC's best friend.

"Oh, my God!" Radha whisper-shouted as she ran across our driveway. I guess she didn't want to wake up the neighbors, or our parents. Radha should've known by now that our parents could sleep through anything, including a spaceship landing. "KC, are you all right? I just read your blog. I came right over. I—"

"They're busy," I told her.

"When did that happen?" Radha asked, meaning my sister and Duncan.

"Don't ask me," I said with a shrug. "I just live here."

She took off her cineplex uniform visor and ran her fingers through her hair, which was long and shiny. With the moon coming up, I could see that Radha's eyes were a real pretty brown, which I'd never noticed before because she and KC were always running off into KC's room and slamming the door.

"This is all very upsetting," she said. Then she started going on about how many hits KC's LiveJournal had gotten in just an hour. She thought it was because Amber had posted the link to her Facebook page.

"And you know your girlfriend's got a zillion friends," she said. "They must've posted it to *their* pages, and, well, now it's pretty much gone viral."

"Amber's not my girlfriend anymore. She broke up with me," I said. I don't know why I thought it was so important to share this news. I think it was the fact that Radha smelled a lot like popcorn. I didn't even realize until right then that popcorn is my favorite food.

So it was *excellent* that a second later, Radha threw her arms around me.

"Oh, Kyle!" She started snuggling her head and other parts of her body against me in a way that I really appreciated. "I'm so sorry about what happened to you that night when you were six! It explains so much about you, though.

How could Amber not be more understanding of what you've been going through all these years? I'm *so sorry* you and KC have had to carry this terrifying burden alone for so long."

I was like, "Uh, yeah. It *has* been pretty terrifying." To tell the truth, I mostly can't remember much about it anymore. Except that thing in old Doc Hall's office, when he was stabbing KC, and then got electrocuted himself, or whatever. That was messed up. For him, mainly.

"You should know that you don't have to be alone anymore," Radha said. "I'm here for you now."

Then our mouths kind of bumped into each other's, and I started kissing her.

I'm not saying I took advantage of the situation, or anything. I just realized I might have been going about this alien thing the wrong way, keeping it a secret and everything. Duncan was right: It's always best to tell the truth. I should have encouraged KC to tell everyone the truth a long time ago. It's an *excellent* way to get girls—nice girls like Radha who smell like popcorn—instead of girls like Amber, who I have to admit can be kind of scary sometimes.

That's what I was thinking as the moon finally rose over the top of the Garrisons' house, and flooded our front yard . . .

. . . and Taylor Hotchkiss's dad's Audi suddenly pulled up in front of our house, the brakes screeching, with Amber leaning out the front passenger window, screaming.

Interview of Radha Singh

RESTRICTED ACCESS: EYES ONLY

Honestly, I only went to the Conrads' house to see if there was anything I could do to help. I wasn't quite sure I believed what KC had written. I certainly believed *she* believed something strange had happened to her the night of her sixth birthday.

But it's difficult in this day and age to think that aliens have visited our planet and not been tracked by our own government's very advanced radar technology. No offense to you nice people, of course.

Then Amber Johnson showed up and began screaming abuse out of Taylor's car window at poor Kyle. I can't even tell you all the things she said, because it wouldn't be polite.

"Kyle Conrad," she was yelling, really very loudly. "I hate you! You can have your team jersey back. I don't want it anymore! Here are our tickets to prom . . . I don't want to go with you anymore. And here's the present you gave me for my birthday . . ."

The next thing I knew, Amber was throwing many things across the Conrads' lawn, including a bottle of Justin Bieber cologne Kyle said he'd given her (because she'd *asked* for it, he later explained. Kyle says he's not a fan of Justin Bieber) and a card he'd made for her for Valentine's Day, which happened to be highly personal in nature, I noticed as it flew by.

As if the fact that she was causing a very emotional scene in front of me and KC and Duncan wasn't enough, the wind had suddenly begun to blow quite hard, and was scattering everything Amber had thrown out of the car across the neighborhood. Kyle's team jersey flew across the street. The valentine ended up in a tree. It was really all very upsetting and quite tasteless.

"Would you please chill out?" I heard Kyle say to Amber. "This is not cool."

"You know what's not cool?" Amber screamed back. "You saying you loved me when you were in love with *your best friend's mom* the whole time!"

Then things *really* got out of control. Both KC and Duncan jumped to their feet and began marching down the lawn toward Taylor's car, looking perturbed. I didn't know what to do, so I started running after the things that were blowing away, like the valentine. I was thinking that in the wrong hands, it could be quite embarrassing for Kyle.

"And who's *that*?" Amber shouted, pointing at me. "How many sluts do you have, anyway, Kyle?"

I must say I've never in my life been called a slut. It was a tiny bit thrilling, but also quite embarrassing. I could feel myself turning bright red, and saw that Kyle had an outraged expression on his face. I will admit that this was also a bit thrilling.

Excuse me, I forgot to ask, you won't be making this video available for public viewing, will you? Oh, good, thank you.

Well, before Kyle could say anything, I saw KC grab Duncan's baseball bat and stalk up to Taylor's car.

"Hey," KC said. "You ladies want to live?"

I must say, mine wasn't the only jaw that dropped. Amber's did, too.

"Are you *threatening* us, KC?" Amber asked. "You better cut it out, or you aren't going to know what hit you."

"No," KC said, angrier than I've ever seen her. She was still holding the baseball bat in the air. But she wasn't looking at Amber. She was looking up. "In about ten seconds, if you don't get out of that car, *you* aren't going to know what's hit you."

I looked up, following KC's gaze.

And I realized the light I'd been seeing that I'd been mistaking for the moon wasn't the moon at all.

It was a large spacecraft . . . its engines were what had been causing all the wind.

And a second later, it landed directly on top of Taylor's car.

Interview of KC Conrad
RESTRICTED ACCESS: *EYES ONLY*

It was a pretty dramatic entrance, landing on Taylor's dad's car like that. I don't mind admitting, I was scared. Someone could have been seriously hurt.

But of course thanks to my warning, no one was. Taylor and Amber escaped just fine . . . not that you'd have known it from the way they carried on. Neither of them was the least bit grateful to me, either. It was like they thought he'd done it on purpose. Which I'm sure he didn't. He wouldn't want to draw that much attention to himself.

Things had changed a lot since the last time he'd been there. Now ours wasn't the only house in the middle of a bunch of empty lots. So he couldn't just swoop in and out undetected, the way he had ten years ago. Dozens of other houses had sprung up all around ours.

Which meant everyone in the whole neighborhood came out onto their front porch to see what the racket was when Taylor's dad's car got squashed . . . including my parents, Duncan's mom and dad, the Garrisons, everyone in town, practically, who wasn't already up and on their way over to my house because they'd read my blog entry, like you guys.

And those of our neighbors who didn't grab a cell phone and start filming what they were seeing used their phone to call the local news and tell them to get over there right away. It was an instant media frenzy.

Which I'm sure is what made him switch on the force field. That's what the big blue light was that came out from his ship and circled it . . . and us, Kyle, Radha, Duncan, and me. It totally freaked out my parents. Like they weren't freaked out enough that there was a spaceship on the front lawn.

"Don't worry, kids! I called the base!" Dad yelled. He'd rushed down to the side of the ship. "General Henry and the rest of the boys are going to be here any minute. They're bringing everything we've got. Whatever this thing is"—he banged against the force field—"it doesn't stand a chance against those new Phantoms we just got in. We'll have you out in no time!"

This was so like my dad. Someone was messing with his kids? He'd call the Air Force base where he worked and get them to drop a missile on them. Never mind that he might be starting an intergalactic war.

Meanwhile, next to him, Mom was calling to us reassuringly, "It's all right, kids. It's going to be fine. You're destined for greatness!"

That almost made me laugh. Because Mom didn't remember where she'd heard that the first time. *We'd* told her that. The guy who'd crash-landed his spaceship on Taylor's dad's car had said it.

But I didn't feel like laughing a few seconds later when the door to the ship started to open.

Because even though Duncan was right—it's always best to tell the truth—I'd never intended for *this* to happen. It wasn't the same thing at *all* as outing your brother's girlfriend for unsportsmanlike behavior.

Now because of me, the poor spaceman who'd only wanted help saving his planet was probably going to get nuked.

Kyle must have realized how terrible I felt, since—just like that night on our birthday a decade earlier—he reached out to grasp my hand.

"Mom's right, you know," he said, when I glanced over at

him. He was smiling. "He selected us for a reason. It's going to be all right."

But I had trouble smiling back. Sure, we'd been selected . . . probably because I'd been the only person on earth—or at least in Peachtree County—who hadn't had the sense to run away.

So why, because of my stupid mistake, did poor Duncan and Radha have to be dragged into it? They were innocent bystanders.

Not that they were looking that upset about the situation—in Duncan's case, anyway. Radha had reached out to grasp Kyle's other hand a bit worriedly, to be totally truthful.

But Amber had apparently gotten over her near-death experience, and was now jealous that she wasn't the focus of the Channel 4 news crew that had pulled up and was filming us through the force field. Taking a cue from my dad, Amber started banging on the side of the force field, only she was demanding to be let inside, not that we be let out.

The spaceman completely ignored her—and everyone outside the impenetrable barrier he'd erected around us—as he leaned out of the door of his ship and smiled at us.

"Children," he said, "I'm so sorry about the mess."

Just like ten years ago, I found myself hypnotized by the blue of his eyes . . .

. . . until I saw him glance—for the briefest moment—in the direction of my dad.

"Hurry up!" Dad was yelling into his cell phone, his expression stricken. "He's got my *children*!"

"Don't worry," the spaceman said in a soothing voice, glancing back at us. "You'll be completely safe with me. Come in."

But if we'd be completely safe with him, this tiny part of my brain asked, what did he need the protective force field for?

That's the only reason I brought the baseball bat into the ship with us. So I guess you can call it premeditated if you want to. Something told me I'd need it.

And it turned out I was right.

Interview of Duncan Mulroney
RESTRICTED ACCESS: EYES ONLY

I'm only going to say this once, because I don't like how you guys have been running this little show. So listen close.

That space dude may have been all smiles and blue eyes for the cameras outside that ship. But inside, where no one was taping, it was another story.

All Kaleigh was trying to do was ask him why, if he wasn't planning on doing anything wrong, he needed the force field. Fair enough, right? She'd known this guy since she was a kid. She was concerned. She was trying to protect him. And us, too. She was trying to explain how that kind of thing might not look good, especially to a guy like her dad, who's in charge of a squadron of fighter jets.

But did the dude listen to her? No way. He was completely ignoring her, messing around with a bunch of switches on his control board.

That's when we noticed the mucus. It was soaking through his human suit. Because that's what he was wearing: A human suit to cover up the fact that he was actually a six-foot slug.

We found that out when Kyle stepped up and pulled off the dude's mask. Underneath, he was . . . well, I'm all for diversity, but where those blue eyes had been were tentacles. Instead of a mouth, he just had a gash . . . a gash filled with razor-sharp teeth.

Once the mask came off, things got ugly. Pun intended. The dude picked up what looked a lot like a gun and pointed it at all of us.

"I only bothered disguising myself to look as disgusting as you to make you trust me," he hissed. "There's no need for that now." He pressed a button, and this blue laser appeared at the tip of the gun he was holding. "I warned you never to reveal my presence to anyone, and you didn't listen. So I will take the implants now. There must be no evidence I was ever here."

"Uh," Kaleigh said. I have to hand it to her. She looked scared, but she stood her ground. "It's a little late for that. There was a news crew out there, not to mention two dozen people with cell phones. Video of what's happened here is probably all over the Internet by now."

"*Outside* this ship," the alien said. And I swear, he smiled with that slug mouth as he turned the gun toward us. "But no one will ever know what's happened *inside.* Because no trace of any of you will ever be seen again."

So, let's say some alien civilization from way out there in the Andromeda Nebula discovered our planet. What do you think they'd do? Share with us all their advanced technology, so that we too could roam the universe in search of new worlds, like James T. Kirk and the rest of the crew of the starship *Enterprise*?

No freaking way.

First, they'd send out scouts to gather as much intel about us as they possibly could . . . their own Christopher Columbuses. Especially intel about our military and defense systems.

Only they couldn't just go strolling into government offices and military bases, could they? Not when the mucus of their *real* skin soaks right through their human costumes in about five minutes. Sure, it might fool a kindergartner hopped up on birthday cake. But no one else.

So they'd need another way to gather all the information required for the mass invasion they've been planning. Because ultimately their goal would be to colonize us, after first enslaving us, then kill us off when they didn't need us anymore.

That's exactly how we've always done it when we've discovered new worlds. Why should they do anything differently?

This guy's solution was to find little kids—especially ones whose parents work for the government, the military, or even local hospitals in some capacity—to stick these little data recorders in, and gather as much info from them as he could.

Up until now, no one's ever been the wiser, because everyone's just thought they were these little blue moles. Any kid who's ever said, "An alien put it in me," has gotten laughed at.

But what that slimeball failed to count on was Kaleigh blogging about what had happened, in a post that would get forwarded so many times by her brother's crazy girlfriend, a quarter of a million people would read it in one night, including you guys, causing our little alien friend's mission to be completely compromised.

So he panicked. He knew he was going to have to get rid of the evidence so there'd be no way anyone could verify what she'd written, and his people would have the benefit of a sneak attack when they did get here.

But he was a little late. And his landing was a little off.

So you tell me. What exactly would you have done? I get that he was an alien life form, unique to our galaxy, and all of that.

But would you really have just stood there and let him butcher your best friends, then escape to send vital information about our planet back to his galaxy that they could use to annihilate us?

I don't think so. You'd have done what I did, and taken him out.

Interview of KC Conrad
RESTRICTED ACCESS: EYES ONLY

Duncan said he did it?

What? No, I'm not crying. I have something in my eye.

He's just lying to protect me. *I'm* the one who was holding the baseball bat. It's on all the videos, remember? I was holding it when I went in.

He was a walking slug who was going to kill us. Not just me, but Kyle and Duncan and Radha. I had no choice. You'd have slammed a baseball bat into his head, too. Or the area where his head appeared to be.

Let Duncan and Radha go. They had nothing to do with it. My brother, too. It was all my fault. Where's that lawyer I requested?

Interview of Kyle Conrad
RESTRICTED ACCESS: EYES ONLY

What? She said that? *Duncan* said that? That's just . . . that is whack. Because *I* did it.

He wasn't exactly ET, was he? I mean, you guys saw the body. He wasn't here for Reese's Pieces.

Speaking of which, have you got any? I'm starving.

What? A guy's gotta eat.

Interview of Radha Singh
RESTRICTED ACCESS: EYES ONLY

I'm sorry, while I'm very saddened by what ultimately ended up happening to that . . . *creature,* I simply cannot agree with your assertion that had you been able to take him alive, the outcome would have been at all different. You did not meet him while he was alive. I did.

And he did not strike me as someone who'd have been agreeable to negotiating peace between our two galaxies. Far from it, actually.

Though it does appear, from what we were able to gather after his demise, when we looked at the data on his shipboard computer—before we disabled the force field and all of you lovely people burst in with your guns and bulletproof vests—as if the invasion won't be happening anytime soon. While their ships do have the ability to achieve super–light speed, their planet is still over two and a half million light-years away from ours.

By my calculations, it will take at least fifty years for their battle fleet to arrive, by which time our planet's population is going to be approximately ten billion, give or take a billion. So we should have plenty of time—and people—to form an intergalactic militia and overtake *them* before they ever get a chance to invade us . . . especially if Kaleigh and Kyle are put in charge. Everything they've done has been in the best interests of Earth. You should be treating them like heroes, not criminals. Now you have the ship, from which you'll learn a great deal. You even have that *thing's* body on which to perform a nice alien autopsy.

I highly suggest you move on and accept the facts: It's a whole new world now. Contact with extraterrestrial life has been established. And those extraterrestrials are very, very hostile.

All right? I can go now? Oh, thank you. I didn't want to have to remind you that, in addition to being president of the Science Olympiads, I'm also president of Pritchard High School's Junior Law Institute, and you had a legal obligation to release us, as . . .

Interview of KC Conrad
RESTRICTED ACCESS: EYES ONLY

. . . none of us has *actually* been arrested, nor have our rights been read to us, and in fact, it's illegal for you under the Sixth Amendment to continue questioning me after I invoked my right to counsel. Did I forget to mention I'm vice president of Pritchard High School's Junior Law Institute?

Oh. I can go now? We can *all* go?

Okay. Well, thanks. Nice meeting you.

Interview of Amber Johnson
RESTRICTED ACCESS: EYES ONLY

Is that on? Is it taping? How does my hair look? Does my hair look okay? It does? Okay, good.

Well, the first thing you should know is that my father is the biggest personal injury lawyer in Peachtree County, and I'm going to make sure that he sues Kyle Conrad, his sister Kaleigh, and the entire Conrad family for the emotional and physical duress they've put me through. Because by KC's own admission in her blog, they've clearly known for years that dirty, filthy space aliens exist.

But did they ever share that knowledge with the rest of

the community? No, not until it was too late. That's straight-up negligence.

Also, my friend Taylor's dad's Audi A4 was completely *destroyed* when that ship landed on it. If we hadn't gotten out in time, we would have been crushed to death.

I will probably have post-traumatic stress for the rest of my life, and I'm not just talking about the car, or KC coming at us like a crazy person with that baseball bat. I mean, KC's always been a weirdo, but that was simply uncalled for.

I mean the fact that Kyle Conrad used to tell all the girls he went out with that that thing on his arm was a gang tattoo, when we all know now what it really is, don't we? Some kind of camera for those nasty aliens to *spy* on us.

And the fact that the whole time he was dating me—the *whole* time!—everything I did was being recorded . . . that is also completely actionable. Who knows what Kyle intends to do with those recordings, if they ever figure out a way to get that thing out of his arm? Where is my percentage on what he's going to make from those recordings if he decides to go to a network with them? Or feature film? That's what my agent wants to know.

So Kyle and Kaleigh Conrad have to be held accountable, since they endangered not just me and the future of my professional career, but the entire population of Peachtree County, if not the world. I don't care how often they appear on the cover of *Time* magazine, or that Kyle is going out with that Radha girl now, or that Kaleigh is with Duncan Mulroney, and that they were all named sergeants in the new World Army Against the Extraterrestrial Threat. I refuse to be treated like this.

And all of you guys, with your black sunglasses and helicopters and night-vision goggles? You didn't exactly help matters, did you? Kyle and Kaleigh didn't even get punished. You just *let them go.* And now they're celebrities because some intergalactic war is coming, and get free airline tickets to Washington, DC, to see the president, and got to go to the Teen Choice Awards? No. That is not right.

So, even though you may be big-time secret agents and all, I'm going to make sure each and every one of you gets sued, too.

That's pretty much all I have to say. Oh, wait. Is this going to be on CNN? Because if so, I just want to say hi to my friend Taylor and also Justin Bieber, if you're watching this, oh my God, Justin, I love you! I'm on Facebook, friend me.

Wait . . . *what?* That is not true! How dare anyone accuse me. . . . No one actually *saw* me pee in the Dulles County team's cooler.

What are you people going to do with this tape? If this ever gets made public, I will make sure my father sues you for every penny you've got. I don't care if you're the government, I'll . . .

Fine. I said *fine,* I'll drop my lawsuits, if you won't tell anyone about that thing with the cooler.

God, I hate this planet.

One True Love

MALINDA LO

It is never lucky for a child to kill her mother in the course of her own birth. Perhaps for this reason, the soothsayer who attended the naming ceremony for Princess Essylt was not a celebrated one. Haidis had barely finished his own apprenticeship when the summons came. He knew that delivering the prophecy for this princess was a thankless job, because no soothsayer in his right mind would attempt to foretell the life of a girl-child born out of death.

His mentor and former teacher told him to sugarcoat the prophecy as much as possible. "She's unimportant, in the grand scheme of things," said Gerlach. "King Radek needs a son; he'll find a new bride soon enough and the princess will simply be married off when she's older." He gave Haidis a sharp glance. "Make sure your prophecy sounds true enough, but remember that the king doesn't need the truth; he only needs a benediction."

So Haidis went to the naming ceremony prepared to omit any problematic details from the prophecy he would deliver. He planned to stop by the soothsayers' temple afterward, to make an offering to the God of Prophecy to counteract whatever bad luck he might acquire from being in such close proximity to the princess.

It was a small ceremony, as Haidis expected, and the king himself seemed a little bored, his mind likely focused on his next journey to the war front rather than the baby held in the arms of the nursemaid nearby. The child wouldn't stop crying, her voice a thin, angry wail that echoed in the cold, stony throne room. When Haidis approached her with the Water of Prophecy and the Sceptre of Truth, she screamed even louder, her mouth stretched open in a tiny O of frustration, her eyes screwed shut. She had wisps of reddish hair on her scalp, and her cheeks were ruddy. He wondered if she would ever grow into a beauty; her mother, the late Queen Lida, had been known for her inheritance, not her looks.

King Radek barked, "Get on with it before the girl makes us all deaf."

"Apologies, Your Majesty," Haidis said. He lifted the pewter bowl containing the Water of Prophecy and dipped his fingers in it, dampening the girl's forehead and cheeks with the liquid. Her squalls stopped as if she was shocked by his touch, and she opened her eyes. They were a vibrant green, as vivid as springtime in the woods outside the castle, and Haidis was as startled by her as she seemed to be by him. She might not become a beauty, he thought, but those eyes were certainly a marvel.

He picked up the Sceptre of Truth and held it over the princess as he began the incantation that would bring him into the trancelike state required to foretell her future. He didn't expect to fall deeply into the trance; he was too aware of the king glaring at him, not to mention the princess's luminous green eyes. He kept his own eyes half open, so he saw the moment when the girl reached up with her baby fingers and wrapped them around the Sceptre itself.

This was unusual, and Haidis knew it. He knew it because the Sceptre changed into a living thing at the princess's touch, and he had to hang on to it with all his might to prevent it from flying out of his hand. His eyes widened, but he did not see the nurse's astonished expression, or the way the king sat up in surprise. He saw, instead, the princess's future, and this vision would remain with him for the rest of his life, for it was the first time he had seen true, and he could not resist speaking it wholly, without any of his mentor's suggested sugarcoating.

"The princess shall grow into a young woman strong and pure," Haidis intoned. "But when she finds her one true love"—the nursemaids standing in the throne room giggled—"she shall be the downfall of the king."

The attendants and guests erupted into shocked whispers. Haidis's vision cleared with a snap, and he saw the baby Princess Essylt gazing up at him with what appeared to be a smile on her face. Terror filled him as he realized what he had said. He pulled the Sceptre of Truth away from the princess, and as it left her hands it became ordinary again.

Behind him the king roared, "Take this abomination away! She shall never be the downfall of me! Take her away or I will have her killed, *and she will join her mother in the grave.*"

The nursemaid clutched the Princess Essylt to her breast and fled. Haidis swayed on his feet as he wondered if he had sentenced the baby girl to her death with his careless speaking of the truth.

• • •

It was the king's most trusted advisor who devised a solution to the problem of Princess Essylt's prophecy. "We shall simply never allow the princess to find her true love," he told the king, "and so your safety will be assured." Of course, the advisor had ulterior motives—he believed the princess might one day be useful, politically—but he kept that to himself, and the king consented to his plan.

From that day forward, Princess Essylt was restricted to the castle's West Tower under the supervision of her nursemaid, Auda, and was not allowed to see any man except for her father. He visited her rarely, for he had little desire to see the cause of his prophesied doom. The few times he did visit, he glared down at the princess and demanded, "Are you being an obedient little girl?"

She shrank away from him at first, running back to Auda, who would turn her around forcefully and whisper in her ear, "This is your father, the king of Anvarra, and you are his daughter, a princess, and you must behave as such."

As the years passed, Essylt learned to bow to her father, and she came to see him as a sort of duty: one that she had inherited by birth, but not one that she enjoyed. She knew that he did not particularly like her, but she did not know why, for Auda kept the prophecy that had relegated her to the West Tower a secret.

Auda was a skilled and loving nursemaid, and she took her job seriously. She knew that the only way Essylt would be content in the tower was if she thought her life was entirely normal. For several years, Auda was quite successful, for she made the West Tower into everything a little girl could wish for. When Essylt wanted new dolls, Auda ordered them; when she asked for playmates, Auda invited the princess's young female cousins to visit; when she yearned for a pony, Auda convinced the king to deliver one to the gardens adjacent to the West Tower. She even arranged for a female riding instructor to teach Essylt how to ride. Whenever Essylt voiced questions about why she couldn't go through the heavily carved oak door in the hall, Auda said, "We must keep you safe, for you are the princess of Anvarra, and you must be protected."

The only times Essylt left the West Tower were on the occasions of her father's weddings, for it was deemed too unseemly for the princess to remain locked away on such an important day. For those events, Essylt was dressed in veils from head to toe so that no one could see her face. The veils also had the unfortunate—or perhaps intentional—side effect of rendering her mostly blind, so she had to hold Auda's hand the entire time. That meant that Essylt's experience of the greater castle was confined to careful study of the floor, glimpsed in flashes through the gap at the bottom of the veils.

During Essylt's childhood, King Radek married several times, for his wives had a troubling tendency to die. Essylt's mother, of course, had died in childbed, as did the king's second wife. His third wife bore two stillborn children—sons, the king noted in despair—before succumbing to a fever. After that, several years passed before the king decided to marry again. Some believed he worried that he was cursed, but others noted that he was merely distracted by a new war that had broken out between Anvarra and its eastern neighbor, the kingdom of Drasik. This war went on season after season, and Essylt passed her thirteenth and fourteenth and fifteenth birthdays with her father away at battle, and no new bride on the castle threshold to draw her out of the West Tower.

As Essylt grew older, she became increasingly curious about the court and her father and why he did not return except once or twice a year, and Auda reluctantly began to answer her questions. In this way, Essylt learned that King Radek had sought an alliance with the island nation of Nawharla'al, which had once been invaded by Drasik but had successfully driven them out through an ingenious use of poison-tipped arrows that spread plague through the Drasik soldiers. In Essylt's seventeenth year, Anvarra and Nawharla'al fought and won a decisive battle against Drasik. In celebration of victory, the king of Nawharla'al gave his seventeen-year-old daughter Sadiya to King Radek in marriage to further cement their alliance.

Sadiya, like all Nawharla'ali people, had brown skin and black hair, with eyes the color of rich, dark soil. The first time King Radek saw her—in a tent on the side of the road after the last battle—he felt lust stir within him, for he had never seen a girl as beautiful and exotic as she. The king saw the way his attendants looked at her, too, and black jealousy rose within him, even thicker than his lust. He ordered that Sadiya be taken immediately to the West Tower and locked inside until their wedding, which would take place in exactly one fortnight.

Sadiya did not understand what he said, for she had not yet learned the Anvarran language. She only knew that the king's voice was covetous and greedy, and when he lifted her chin with his hand, she could almost smell the desire on his breath. It took all her years of royal training to not spit in his face, and she prayed to her gods that something would come to deliver her from this marriage.

On the day of Sadiya's arrival, Essylt was poring over history books in the West Tower's small library when she heard the heavy oaken doors in the entry hall flung open. Startled, she ran out onto the balcony overlooking the hall and saw a stream of women in strange, colorful clothes entering the tower, bearing a series of curious objects: wooden trunks carved with unfamiliar animals; a golden cage containing a bird with brilliant purple and green feathers; cushions the color of sunsets. Amid all this movement, Essylt saw one girl standing stock-still in the corner, her arms crossed around herself protectively. She was wrapped from head to foot in azure scarves, with only her eyes peering out.

Auda came running into the hall, demanding to know what was going on, and a woman in a plain blue dress detached herself from the entourage of attendants to speak to Auda in low, intense tones.

Essylt came down the stairs. She was drawn to the silent girl in the corner, who looked up at that moment and saw her. A shiver ran down Essylt's spine: quicksilver, insistent. *Go to her.*

As Essylt approached, the girl unwound the veils from her face to reveal brown skin, full lips, and dark eyes: a beauty unlike that of any Anvarran woman. This girl took a step away from her corner and extended her hands, palms up, toward Essylt. In the center of her palms a design was painted: swirls and loops that connected to form a pattern that was like a flower, but no flower that Essylt knew. Instinctively, Essylt reached out and covered the girl's hands with her own, paler ones, and when their skin touched, a tremor went through Essylt's body. For the first time, she became wholly aware of the way her fingers and toes were connected to the pulsing of her heart, to the breath that fluttered from her lungs to her lips, to the heat that spread over her cheeks.

Behind her, Auda said in a strained tone of voice, "Your Highness, this is the Princess Sadiya of Nawharla'al." There was another round of feverish whispers between Auda and

Sadiya's chief attendant, who spoke Anvarran with an accent that Auda had never heard before and thus found difficult to understand.

"Sa-*dee*-ah?" Essylt said uncertainly.

"*Sah*-dee-ya," the girl corrected, and her name sounded like music on her lips.

Sadiya's chief attendant said something to her in Nawharla'ali, and Essylt heard her own name amidst the stream of foreign words. "Ess-*elt*," Sadiya said tentatively, her gaze never leaving Essylt's.

Essylt's heartbeat quickened, and she realized that Sadiya had wrapped her fingers around her own, and it was as if a faint dusting of magic had settled over them, fixing them in place so that they might look at one another for just a bit longer.

It was Auda who broke the spell. "Your Highness," she said, "Princess Sadiya will be staying here in the West Tower until your father returns in ten days. Then they will be married. The princess will be your new stepmother."

"My new stepmother?" Essylt said, and saw Sadiya's attendant whisper something urgently in her ear.

Sadiya pulled her hands away. She knew that her attendants were shocked by how Essylt had touched her and how she had accepted it. The proper greeting would have been for Essylt to hover her hands over Sadiya's and then to incline her head ever so delicately, but of course Essylt did not know Nawharla'ali customs. Her mistake could be excused, but what had caused Sadiya to hold Essylt's hands, as if she were a lover rather than a stranger who would someday become her stepdaughter? Sadiya's face flamed as she realized what a scene she was making.

Essylt did not understand how she had erred, but she saw that Sadiya was uncomfortable, and she regretted it, for already she wanted to ensure that Sadiya was happy. "Welcome," she said, but then her mouth went dry. She could think of nothing more to say except *You are so beautiful,* but even Essylt, unpracticed in courtly manners, sensed that others would find that odd, so she bit her lip and remained silent.

But that was enough, and Sadiya smiled, and her face was so exquisitely shining that Essylt was certain that another sun had burned into being right there in the entry hall to the West Tower.

From that moment on, Essylt and Sadiya were inseparable. Essylt taught Sadiya the words for the flowers and plants that grew in the West Tower's garden, and Sadiya taught Essylt the Nawharla'ali equivalents. Their progress was remarkably fast, for they spent every waking minute together, exclaiming over the sounds of words and the way sentences formed when they spoke them to each other. Essylt learned that Nawharla'al was a kingdom of many islands, and each island was named after a different tropical flower, and each flower was worn by the prince of that island on state occasions. Sadiya learned that summer was short and hot in Anvarra, and she had arrived at its beginning, when the days are long and lush and sometimes so humid that sitting in the shade brought sweat to the skin. Essylt learned that the women of Nawharla'al wore long, loose skirts dyed in shades to match their islands' flowers, and they preferred to leave their arms bare, binding only their breasts in scarves that matched their skirts. Sadiya learned that the women of Anvarra wore layers of undergarments beneath heavy skirts and bodices that gripped their torsos with whalebone, and she wrinkled her nose at these gowns and said, "I will not wear those," and Essylt laughed at the expression on Sadiya's face.

The days they spent together seemed to stretch out

luxuriously in the peaceful isolation of the West Tower, but as the fortnight drew to a close, neither girl could avoid the increasing sensation of impending doom, for soon Sadiya would marry Essylt's father. The night before the wedding, they walked the garden together in silence, as if not speaking would stave off the future. When they parted to sleep in their separate chambers, Essylt held her hands out, palms upward, in the way Sadiya had upon her arrival. Sadiya was surprised, but she hovered her hands over Essylt's unmarked ones, a bittersweet sadness sweeping through her.

Then, as if she were a knight in a storybook, Essylt raised Sadiya's hands to her mouth and kissed the knuckles, her lips brushing soft and quick over Sadiya's skin. A flush spread across Sadiya's face, and she saw an answering emotion in Essylt's green eyes.

"Sleep well," Essylt whispered, and she wished she could sleep beside Sadiya and guard her against any nightmares that might slip into her mind that night.

"A blessing upon you," Sadiya said in Nawharla'ali, and then backed away before the tears could slip from her eyes. Essylt watched her go, her scarves fluttering in the dim evening light.

The wedding was held in the castle's Great Hall, which was hung with golden ropes in honor of the God of Matrimony and wreaths of snowbell flowers for the Goddess of Fertility. The morning before the ceremony, which was to take place at noon, Sadiya's attendants bathed and scented and dressed her in the Nawharla'ali bridal finery they had brought with them. They wrapped her body in fine white linen, and then draped her with scarves the color of the sea in every shade from deepest blue to azure and aquamarine. They hung jewels from her ears and twisted them around her bare arms and throat, and when she stepped into the sunlight she glittered with reflected light. Her lustrous black hair was brushed out and woven with the little white flowers plucked from the gardens around the West Tower, and though they were not the tropical blossoms of Nawharla'al, they served well enough. Essylt especially liked to see the flowers she loved in Sadiya's hair.

Auda had taken care while dressing Essylt that morning, as well, though Essylt's gown was much plainer so that she would not outshine the bride—and so that she would draw no man's eye. Essylt did not like the way the tight stays cut off her breath; she found the layers of skirts confining; and she thought the dove gray of the gown itself was ugly in comparison to the brilliant colors of Sadiya's clothes. But the thing she hated most was the gray linen veil she was forced to wear, obscuring her hair and face and swathing the whole world in dimness. As they left the West Tower, Essylt followed in Sadiya's perfumed wake with Auda's guiding hand on her arm. She felt suffocated and suppressed, each layer of clothing like a hand over her mouth.

In every Anvarran wedding ceremony, a series of customs is dutifully followed in order to ensure that the union is a fertile one. As with every naming ceremony, a prophecy is given, and to be chosen to deliver the prophecy at a royal wedding is a high honor. Haidis, the hapless soothsayer who had presided over Essylt's naming ceremony, was present at King Radek's marriage to Princess Sadiya of Nawharla'al, but Haidis had not been chosen to officiate. He came as a guest of his mentor Gerlach, who was prepared to deliver a prophetic benediction on the king's marriage to the exotic foreign princess if he had to lie to do it.

The wedding prophecy, however, would not take place until after the initial prayers to the God of Matrimony and

Goddess of Fertility, led by a high-ranking priest, who intoned the traditional phrases in a voice devoid of emotion. Sadiya was expected to kneel on a cushion at the feet of King Radek during the prayers, and though she did as requested, she refused to lower her gaze, for she did not believe in these gods. To her right, seated in the first row of ornate wooden benches, she could just make out the corner of Essylt's veil, shroudlike in comparison to the bright colors worn by Sadiya and her attendants.

Essylt did not need to bow her head, for no one could tell if she participated in the prayers at all. Instead, she clenched her hands into fists and hid them beneath the voluminous folds of her hot, scratchy gown. A deep ache began to spread in her, from belly to chest to throat, until she felt as if she might choke from it. She heard the priest ending his series of prayers, and she knew that after this would come the ceremony itself, when Sadiya's hands would be bound with golden rope to the King's left wrist, and from that moment on, Sadiya would be her stepmother.

Essylt watched through her veil as the priest picked up the rope and approached Sadiya, still chanting the blessings for matrimony. The rope dangled over Sadiya's head like a snake uncoiling to strike. The ache that gripped Essylt hardened. A desperate anger galvanized her. She lurched to her feet and felt Auda's hand reaching for hers, but she shook it away. She ripped off her veil and cried, "*No! Please, no.* Sadiya, you must not marry him."

Essylt lunged for the rope and tore it out of the priest's hands, throwing it behind him onto the stone floor.

Sadiya stood, astonished and terrified and hopeful.

At first everyone in the Great Hall was simply too startled to move, for none could remember a time when a royal wedding had been disrupted in such a manner. In that moment of stunned immobility, Essylt took Sadiya's hands in hers and pulled her away from the king. Sadiya said to her in Nawḥarla'ali, "You are mad, my love," and Essylt responded in the same tongue, "I am mad with love."

Haidis had watched in shock from his seat as Essylt leapt to her feet, jerking away the marriage rope. As she clutched the hands of the foreign bride, Haidis realized that the prophecy he had delivered on Essylt's naming day was coming to pass. He stood up—he was the first among the audience to do so—and said under his breath, *"The princess shall grow into a young woman strong and pure, but when she finds her one true love—"*

Gerlach's hand gripped his arm. "Do not speak any more!" he hissed, and Haidis's mouth shut tight in fear as the Great Hall exploded into shouts.

King Radek's thick, strong hand clamped down on his bride's shoulder, and as Sadiya winced in pain, he dragged her from his daughter. "What perversity have you wrought on my bride?" he demanded of Essylt, who tried to reach for Sadiya again but was wrenched back by the hands of the king's soldiers, who had leapt forward at his command. "What damnation are you bringing upon my kingdom? You have been cursed since you killed your own mother, and it was only my mercy that kept you alive." The king would not take his hands off Sadiya, whom he held near him like a plaything. He growled to his soldiers, "Take Essylt away to the farthest reaches of the darkest forests of the north, and abandon her to the wolves. She is no longer my daughter. May she die alone."

Essylt heard the words as if from a distance, for all she could focus on was the look of terror on Sadiya's face. As the soldiers dragged Essylt from the Great Hall, she tried to struggle but her skirts were too heavy and her bodice too tight, and then someone struck her across the face. Pain burst in her cheek and nose. She screamed and lunged away from the soldiers, but they grabbed her and hit her again and again. The last thing she saw before she fainted from the pain was the glimmer of blue in the jewels around Sadiya's neck, liquid as the faraway sea.

Essylt awoke in a cage on a moving wagon. She winced as the wagon jolted over a bump and caused her hip to bang against the wooden floor. Outside the bars she saw green fields rolling past beneath a clear late afternoon sky.

She was outside the castle.

This fact alone overwhelmed her. She had never been outside the castle, and her heart began to race as she sat up, hands gripping the bars. She drank in the unfamiliar landscape: stone walls rising and falling over the fields; solitary trees standing watch in the distance; an occasional farmhouse or barn, with horses grazing nearby. It was almost dark before she realized that a man was riding behind the cage, watching her.

A soldier.

She shrank away from the bars, and everything that had happened rushed back to her: Sadiya and her father's wedding, the marriage rope hanging like a noose above Sadiya's head, her father's words. *May she die alone.*

As the sun set she wondered whether it was still the day of the wedding. Was this the wedding night? Her stomach twisted. When she had first begun her monthly bleeding, Auda had told her what it meant, and Essylt knew very well what her father desired from his wives: sons. There was a chance that her father had not gone through with the wedding, but the way he had treated Sadiya made Essylt doubt that he would give her up. No, he would take Sadiya as his bride regardless of how perverse he thought his daughter was.

Essylt wanted to throw up, but she hadn't eaten all day, and she could only cough up bile, bitter and acidic.

The soldier behind the cage rode closer and banged his sword on the bars. "Don't choke to death, Princess, we've a long way to go yet."

The journey to the wild forests of the north took a week. There were two soldiers: one who drove the wagon, and one who rode behind. They gave her a bowl of water every night that she had to lap up like a dog, and once or twice the driver slipped her a piece of dried beef out of pity, but she was given no other food. Neither of the soldiers ever let her out, so Essylt was forced to relieve herself in one corner, humiliated by the stench that began to rise from her body.

She watched the countryside when she was awake, but as the days passed and she grew weaker, she slid into a half-sleeping doze in which she saw Sadiya's face hovering over her, radiant and beautiful. She clung to those visions as tightly as she could, the memory of the last words that Sadiya had said echoing in her mind: *You are mad, my love. Mad, my love. Mad.*

Finally, they reached the pine-forested border of Anvarra. The driver drew the wagon to a halt in a small clearing in the woods and climbed down from his seat. The soldier riding behind dismounted, pulling a black iron key from the chain attached to his swordbelt. Inside the cage, Essylt sat stiffly with her arms around her knees, her bright green eyes wide in her pale face. The soldier unlocked the cage door, which groaned open on its hinges.

"Welcome to your new home," he said, and laughed. "Time to get out."

Essylt didn't move until the soldier reached inside and clamped one hand on her ankle. Frightened, she kicked him in the face. He cursed as blood spurted from his nose, then grabbed both of her ankles, his nails digging into her skin, and dragged her out until she landed with a bruising thump on the ground.

"Never seen a man except your father, eh?" he said, and the tone in his voice made her skin crawl. He began to unbuckle his belt.

Essylt tried to scramble away, but she only banged into the wagon wheel behind her.

"There's a reason you turned out wrong," the soldier was saying, a horrible grin on his face. "You need to learn what's right—"

"Shut up," said the driver. He smashed a wooden staff into the side of the soldier's head, knocking him to ground, unconscious. The driver shook his head and looked down at the princess. He had a sister her age, and he would never forgive himself if he let the soldier have his way with her. Even if she *was* perverse. He jerked his head toward the woods. "You'd better run for it, Princess. You're on your own now."

Essylt didn't hesitate. She jumped up, her legs tingling as she stood for the first time in seven days, and she fled.

She ran over unbroken forest ground, her thin-soled court shoes doing little to cushion her feet from fallen twigs and upturned stones. She ran as the daylight faded and turned the forest into a land of murky shadows, and she slowed down only enough to prevent herself from tripping on the uneven ground. She found a riverbed where the trees parted to reveal a sliver of black night sky strewn with stars, and she knelt down and drank the water from her cupped and dirty hands, and then she kept going.

At some point she removed her whalebone corset so that

she could breathe more freely. She stripped off her encumbering underskirts and wrapped her torn shoes in the cloth to cushion her feet. When she was too tired to walk any farther, she made a nest for herself in a bed of fallen pine needles and slept with her head resting on her arms. When she awoke, she continued. She saw no one.

She was hungry, but she did not know what she could eat in the forest, and her book learning had taught her to be wary of unfamiliar plants. A few times she thought she glimpsed the shadowy movement of wolves nearby, and she prayed to the God of Safe Passage to watch over her. She did not know where she was going, but she knew she had a destination. With every step she took, even though her body felt weaker and weaker, she was more and more certain that she had something to live for. Sadiya. *Sadiya.* Someday, she vowed, she would go back for her. She would return to Anvarra City and save her, and King Radek would pay for what he had done.

One morning, after Essylt had walked in a stubborn, starving daze for hours through the dark night, she stumbled through the last of the pine trees into a clearing where she saw a little cottage built of logs. Smoke curled out of the chimney, and the windows were hung with cheerful plaid curtains. She dragged herself the last few steps into the clearing before she collapsed, her body giving up at last.

The cottage belonged to a retired knight named Bowen, who lived there with his wife, Nell. It was Nell who discovered Essylt later that morning, lying in a crumpled heap at the edge of their garden, and it was Bowen who lifted the princess in his burly arms and carried her inside, laying her down on their bed.

Essylt did not wake until evening, and the first thing she

saw was an older woman rocking in a chair nearby, knitting. Essylt was not frightened, for the woman had a kind face and reminded her of Auda, but she was disoriented, and she pushed herself up and asked, "Where am I?"

Nell put down her knitting and studied the girl, whose eyes were a remarkable shade of green. Her reddish-gold hair was disheveled and knotted up, and her face was dirty. In fact, all of her was so dirty that she smelled rather unpleasant, but neither Nell nor Bowen would turn away a girl who so obviously needed their help simply because she also needed a bath.

"You're in the village of Pine Rest," Nell told her, speaking with an unfamiliar accent. "I found you in our garden this morning. I am Nell, and my husband's name is Bowen. He is outside. What is your name?"

Essylt stared at the woman, whose gray hair was wound up in braids coiled at the nape of her neck. She seemed kind, and Essylt wanted to trust her, but a knot of fear still held tight within her, and she did not wish to reveal her true identity. "My name is Auda," Essylt said, and flushed slightly at the lie.

Nell nodded. "You must be hungry."

Essylt's stomach awoke at those words and growled so loudly that it embarrassed her. But Nell only smiled and got up from her chair. She left the little room and came back a few minutes later with a bowl of soup. "Something gentle for you," she said, "while you regain your strength."

Essylt took the bowl from Nell's outstretched hands and inhaled the fragrant scent of broth and herbs. She drank every last delicious drop, and then lay down again in Nell and Bowen's bed and fell asleep instantly, feeling safe at last.

In the morning she met Bowen, who was large and gentle and had lost all his hair except for the bushy white eyebrows that seemed to speak long sentences on their own. She learned that the village of Pine Rest was just over the border from Anvarra in the neighboring kingdom of Ferronia. Essylt remembered from Auda's geography lessons that Ferronia was rarely concerned with Anvarran politics because the Black Forest that separated the two countries was mostly impassable—and this Essylt could now attest to personally, having crossed it herself on foot. Bowen had been a knight serving the king of Ferronia, but after many years of service he had retired to the village where he had been born. Bowen and Nell's son, Petra, was a swordsmith whose forge was in Pine Rest, and Petra drew much of his business from Bowen's old knightly acquaintances.

As the days passed, Essylt regained her strength while Bowen and Nell fussed over her as if she were their long-lost daughter. They set up a pallet for her in the loft over the main room of the cottage, and Essylt began to help out with the chores. She grew strong from tending the garden with Nell and learning how to chop wood with Bowen's hatchet. And though she came to know the other villagers and to love Bowen and Nell, she kept her secret. Pine Rest might be far from Anvarra City, but the news of Princess Essylt's depravity had reached Ferronia via traveling minstrels who sang of her tragic lust for the queen. Essylt worried that Bowen and Nell would turn their backs on her in disgust if they knew who she was, so she grew accustomed to being called Auda, and swallowed her own feelings of shame and sorrow. Every day, she thought of Sadiya and her vow to return for her. Every night before she slept, she whispered Sadiya's name to herself so that she might never forget how to pronounce it.

She spoke with Petra, who had traveled to Anvarra because of his skill as a swordsmith, and began to plot her own return journey. She laid aside a store of food, stealing as little as she could. From the old trunks in the loft where she slept, she discovered a cloak that was moth-eaten but could still keep her warm at night. She felt guilty for taking these things from Nell and Bowen, but she promised herself she would return one day and pay them back if she could. She did not let herself think of where she and Sadiya might go. Was there a place in this world that would have them? She did not know, and it was easier to accept the emptiness of not knowing than to face the fact that she might rescue Sadiya and still fail in giving her a happy life.

One morning she awoke and her body felt ready. She was strong and healthy again, and she had finally stocked enough provisions to last for the several weeks' journey to Anvarra. But when she went outside to pump water as usual, snow was falling from the sky. She stood on the doorstep in shock as white flakes tumbled down, thick and fast, from iron-gray clouds. How had the summer passed so quickly? She hoped that the snowfall was an early anomaly and that it would only delay her journey by a day or two.

But the snow continued to fall, and it stuck to the ground, and the air became colder and colder until, weeks later, Essylt had to admit that winter had come early and hard, and she would not be able to journey to Anvarra until spring.

It was Nell who found her, weeping silently at the woodpile, her tears turning to ice crystals on her cheeks. "My dear," Nell said, "whatever is the matter? Come inside and be warm."

That night, exhausted from the subterfuge, Essylt told her the truth. "I am Essylt," she said, and speaking her own name out loud broke a dam inside her and she sobbed. Nell gathered her into her arms and stroked her hair and rocked her back and forth as if she were a baby. "I am Essylt," she said again and again. When at last her tears were spent, she told them of growing up in the West Tower, and the unexpected joy she had felt when she met Sadiya, and the anguish of being forced apart. She told them of her plan to rescue Sadiya, and finally, her voice diminished to a tentative whisper, she said, "I will leave if you will not have me here any longer. You have been so kind to me, and I have only defiled your home."

Bowen had sat silently in the corner as Essylt confessed her truth, but as Nell's hands stilled on Essylt's hair, he said, "It is never a crime to love someone."

Essylt looked at him in surprise.

Anger darkened Bowen's face. "The king of Anvarra is a bastard. In the spring you shall ride to Anvarra City and save your true love, and we will help you."

"But—but why?" Essylt asked.

Nell had drawn back a little, and Essylt saw that tears streaked down Nell's face as well. She shook her head. "My dear, we love you like a daughter. That is why."

As Essylt looked from Nell to Bowen, she felt as if her heart might overflow with gratitude and love for them. "I have never felt like anyone's daughter," she said, "but I will do my best to make you proud."

All winter, Essylt trained with Bowen. "You will need to learn to fight," he said to her, "for the king will not give up his wife without a battle."

Bowen took down the old tools of his trade from the attic: his broadsword, which was so big that Essylt had to carry it with two hands, and his armor, which was now darkened with rust. During the days, he forced her to run through snowdrifts with the sword strapped to her back until sweat streamed down her face. At night, she helped him polish the armor until it gleamed. It was too large for her, but Bowen said that Petra could adjust it to her size. And so she began to visit Petra at the forge, where he fitted various pieces of steel to her, muttering under his breath about fashioning a special breastplate.

Essylt could not understand why Petra was willing to do this for her. She knew that he knew who she was now, for he called her Essylt instead of Auda. She thought perhaps he was simply his father's son, and would not speak out against anyone his father loved. It wasn't until well past midwinter when she noticed the way Petra spoke to the blacksmith who shared the forge with him: Markus, a broad-shouldered, black-bearded man who sometimes came to supper at Nell and Bowen's home. There was a certain angle to Petra's body as he approached Markus, and then Essylt saw him reach out and smooth his hand gently over the man's shoulder: a caress. Essylt realized with a jolt that Petra did not merely share the forge with the smith; he shared a life with him. She felt a great sense of wonder steal over her, and she had to turn away as tears came to her eyes.

From that day on, she felt as if she had found her family. She would hate to leave them in the spring, but she could come back. She could come back with Sadiya, and they could be happy here.

Petra finished the full suit of armor in late winter. It was light and well balanced, but when Essylt put it on she felt the strength of the steel close against her muscles, and she knew that it would protect her. To her surprise, Petra also presented her with a sword, forged specially for her height and weight, and the first time she swung it in an arc, it sang in the cold winter air.

She spent the last month of winter parrying with Bowen, and sometimes with Markus, who had been a knight's squire in his boyhood. She learned how to ride a horse in full armor, her red-gold hair braided and coiled beneath her helm. She learned how to force back a man twice her size with her sleek, elegant sword, her gauntleted hands gripping the beautiful hilt that Petra had designed. And she thought of Sadiya, as she always did, keeping her face alive in her memory, as fresh as the first day she had seen her, standing behind the oak door to the West Tower, swathed in azure scarves.

The news came before she was entirely ready to go, but as soon as she heard it from the mouth of the traveling minstrel at the tavern in Pine Rest, Essylt left to pack her supplies. The Anvarran king had discovered that his island-born wife had been drinking a concoction she had brought from Nawharla'al to prevent herself from conceiving a child. This, King Radek said, was treason. He sentenced Sadiya to die by beheading on the first day of summer, which gave his people time to travel from their villages to witness her public execution.

When this news reached Pine Rest, the last of the winter snow had barely melted, even though the first day of summer was less than one month away. Essylt decided to ride directly through the Black Forest to Anvarra instead of following the highway south. It was dangerous, but it would cut two weeks from her journey.

"There are wolves," objected Nell, worried.

"They didn't kill me before," Essylt said. "They won't kill me now."

Bowen and Petra wanted to go with her, but she refused to allow them to come.

"It is my task, and my choice," she told them. They relented, for they saw the determination in her eyes.

She departed at dawn, riding Markus's white mare—a horse he insisted she take—with her saddlebags full of food that Nell had prepared. The forest was quiet as she rode south, with only the sound of her horse's passage to accompany her. Petra's armor sat lightly on her shoulders, and already she was so familiar with her sword that when she slept, she rested her hands upon it. She did not feel threatened by the wolves she glimpsed sometimes at night, their eyes reflecting the light from her campfire. They saw her weapons, and they left her alone.

She emerged from the Black Forest two weeks later, and struck out on the hard-packed dirt road that led southeast toward Anvarra City. At first she was alone on the highway, but as she drew closer to Anvarra City, other travelers joined her, all on their way to the execution. At night, she camped as far from the other travelers as she could. She kept her armor covered with her long brown cloak, and she did not remove her helm in the daylight. She could not reveal who she was, for the Princess Essylt was supposed to be dead.

She arrived on the eve of the execution, and though she could have ridden into the city and bought herself a room at an inn, she could not bring herself to pass through the gates. In the distance she saw the West Tower—her old home—and now she recognized it as a prison. She wondered what had happened to Auda, and her gut wrenched, for though Auda had always maintained a certain formal distance from her, she was the one who had raised her.

All night, Essylt lay awake beneath a spreading oak tree on the side of the highway, watching the silhouette of the castle on the hill. When dawn broke, Essylt was already mounted on her horse and waiting outside the city gates. Hundreds of other people surged around her, eager to view the death of the traitorous foreign queen. Their jubilation made Essylt sick with rage, and her fingers trembled as she curled them into fists on her thighs.

A stage had been erected at the northern edge of the central square, and on that stage the executioner's block was waiting. Essylt rode into the square, surrounded by the crowd and unnoticed by the soldiers who stood guard along the perimeter. She found a place near the stage, beside a fountain that shot cool water up into the warm summer morning. The scent of snowbell blossoms hung thick in the air, sweet and cloying. The people in the square chattered about the coming event, but Essylt paid no attention to them. Her entire body was tense and alert, her heart beating a war drum in her chest. She could sense Sadiya approaching—as if they were connected, flesh and bone drawn together—and when the murmur of the crowd crescendoed, she looked to the north and saw the king riding into the square on a black stallion.

He was flanked by soldiers and followed by a wagon with a cage strapped onto it—the same kind of cage that Essylt herself had been locked into. Within the cage, Sadiya was seated with her hands bound behind her back.

The crowd exclaimed at its first glimpse of her: hair loose and tangled, a rough sackcloth dress draped over her body, her face bruised but defiant.

Essylt felt as if an arrow had torn into her belly. She had to suck in the muggy air to calm herself down, for her mare sensed her nerves and began to prance in place. Essylt wanted to rush forward at that very moment and seize Sadiya from the soldiers, but she remembered what Bowen had taught her, and she forced herself to wait.

She waited as the executioner mounted the stage, his black cowl hiding his face from the crowd, the sun glinting on the blade of his axe. She waited as the king, resplendent in purple robes, joined the executioner. She waited as the cage door was unlocked and Sadiya was pulled out, barefoot, onto the cobblestones of the square. She waited as Sadiya was hauled onto the stage by two soldiers who bent her arms back at an angle that made Essylt wince to see it.

She waited until the king said: "For betraying me, and by extension, your people; for dishonoring me, and by extension, your people; for murdering before birth my very own children and heirs; for all this, you are sentenced to death."

Then—and only then—Essylt threw off her cloak. Her armor shone silver-bright in the sun, and her white horse leapt through the crowd that parted before her, their mouths agape in excitement. Everyone on the stage turned to see a knight riding toward them, sword raised in the air. From the margins of the square, the king's soldiers raised their bows and shot, their arrows flying toward the rider.

Essylt felt an arrow slam against her back, but Petra's armor held. Then she was at the edge of the stage and the archers had to stop shooting, because the soldiers were in their line of sight. She pulled herself onto the stage and met the first soldier with her sword raised. She shoved him back with all her strength, her steel blade screaming against his. The soldier stumbled, startled by her assault, but he had a second to back him up, and then Essylt had to fight two of them.

But the soldiers wore standard-issue armor, not nearly as well crafted as hers. She could slice their breastplates off with ease, and beneath that, they weren't even wearing chain mail. No one had expected an attack at the queen's execution. Essylt disarmed one and slashed open his side. He yelped and fell off the stage into the crowd. The other came at her with his broadsword, but she used his momentum against him and flipped him onto his back, knocking his weapon out of his hands and tipping the point of her sword against his throat. His eyes bulged up at her and for an instant she hesitated—was she going to kill a man?—but out of the corner of her eye she saw him pull a dagger from his boot and ready it to throw at her. Before his weapon left his hand, she cut his throat.

She looked up and across the stage, her heart pounding, and called, "Sadiya!"

Sadiya had watched the knight beat back the king's soldiers with a rising sense of hope, and when she heard the voice behind the helm, she knew who it was, and hope exploded into joy. She tried to run to her, but the king grabbed her arm, yanking her back. He shouted, "Who would dare to act against me?"

Essylt took off her helm. The long braid of her red-gold hair fell out over her shoulder, and she said, "Father, I dare."

The king's face was a mask of fury as he beheld his daughter standing before him—his daughter who should be dead, and yet she was alive and breathing, her green eyes glinting like emeralds as she raised a sword against him, and he unarmed.

"Give me a weapon!" the king cried. The executioner stepped forward and handed the king his axe.

The king swung it in an arc, and Essylt met the axe handle with her sword. The thunk of metal meeting wood rang through the square. She jerked the sword back and leapt away as the king advanced, his eyes wild with anger. She parried him again, and this time the handle of the axe broke as the sword cleaved through it. The axe head clattered onto the stage.

"A weapon!" the king shouted again. A soldier in the crowd tried to shove his way through to give the king his sword, but the crowd—riveted by the spectacle before them—would not let him pass.

"I will not kill you unarmed," Essylt called. "Let us go and you will never see us again."

"Never," the king snarled. "You will die. Both of you will die here today."

Suddenly Sadiya stepped over the body of the dead soldier and said, "She may not kill you unarmed, but I will." She lunged toward the king and shoved the soldier's dagger into the king's chest, thrusting it straight through the rich purple velvet, and the king fell, howling, to the wooden boards of the stage.

Sadiya stood above him, gasping, her hands bloody, and spit on his face.

The crowd roared.

Essylt saw the hatred in her father's eyes swept away by fear and bewilderment as his hands scrabbled furiously at the dagger. Sadiya turned to Essylt, wiping her bloodied hands on the ruins of her dress. Essylt reached for her and crushed her into her arms, and Sadiya's body shook against Essylt's armor. All around them the crowd murmured. Those who had been close to the stage had heard Essylt declare who she was, and now they passed that knowledge back across the square, until all who had gathered for Sadiya's execution understood that Princess Essylt was not dead—she was alive—and the words of her naming-day prophecy were repeated until it became a slow and steady hum.

The princess shall grow into a young woman strong and pure, but when she finds her one true love, she shall be the downfall of the king.

Prophecies, the people said, were not always straightforward, but if they were real, they were true. None who saw the way that Essylt and Sadiya held each other that day could deny the strength of their love. But for many years to come, they debated whether it was Essylt or Sadiya who had been the downfall of the king.

• • •

No one stopped Essylt and Sadiya as they left the city. No soldier lifted a weapon to harm them; no man or woman shouted a curse. They rode as far as they could before stopping to rest their horse. They found a sweet little spring bubbling out of a rocky cleft in a hill near the road, and dismounted to allow the mare to drink.

Then Essylt took off her armor, and Sadiya peeled off her soiled dress, and they waded into the water and scrubbed the dried blood and sweat and dirt from their skin. When they emerged from the spring, naked and wet in the warm evening air, they saw each other as if for the first time: one woman dark and slender; one woman fair and muscular. Essylt took Sadiya's hands in her own and pulled her close, their breasts and hips sliding together, slick and soft, and her breath caught in her throat as Sadiya whispered, "You are my one true love."

Essylt wrapped her arms around Sadiya's waist. Her fingers found the hollow of Sadiya's lower back, her spine like a string of jewels, and she leaned in, pausing to remember this moment always, and kissed her.

This Is a Mortal Wound

MICHAEL GRANT

Here is what I said to Ms. Gill: "All you care about is being in charge and pushing us around. I thought school was supposed to be about learning stuff."

Here is what Ms. Gill had said to make me react that way: "You were told exactly what to read, Tomaso. And, Tomaso, you were told exactly *how* to write the report. I did not give you an F because what you wrote was wrong, Tomaso. I gave you an F, Tomaso, because you didn't do what I told you to do."

Notice the way she kept saying "Tomaso"? Like she relished the sound of it. It came spitting out of her lipsticked mouth like it had hard edges and could hurt me. Like she was spitting Tomaso darts at me.

Clearly she started it. Right? Maybe I escalated it. But where did she get off with that "my way or screw you" stuff?

So next—after I'd said the thing about her just wanting

to push me around—she got very pale. I would say that the blood drained out of her face, but that would make it sound more gross than it was. She did not gush blood. She just got very pale. The only color her lips had came from the makeup counter at CVS, and those mean pomegranate (or possibly currant) lips drew back a little, like she wanted to show me her teeth. If the next sound out of her had been "Grrr!" I wouldn't have been surprised.

"You. Rotten. *Brat.*" Each word sounded like she had just discovered it in her vocabulary list and really, really enjoyed it. Then she did a variation. "You. Rotten. *Arrogant.* Privileged. Narcissistic. *Brat.*"

That last word was like, *bRRRR-at!*

And her hands, which were at her sides, clenched and made little half fists. Twitchy, hesitating fists. Fists that wanted to, wanted to oh so badly, but couldn't.

At this point I escalated things again. Why? Because I'm a passionate lover of fairness, that's why. Because I believe in justice, that's why.

Can you already kind of picture me waving a "Don't Tread on Me" flag? Like one of those guys in the Revolutionary War? Standing up for liberty? No?

Okay, actually, if you want to picture me, just Google Tomaso Hockmeier. Believe me, with that name you're not going to get a million hits. There are only two. One is a seventy-two-year-old retired plumber from upstate New York, with a white fringe beard. The other is a thirteen-year-old kid with dark, longish hair, sort-of-green eyes, and the amazing body of a star athlete. If by "amazing body" you mean average-sized and completely undistinguished.

Look at my profile pics, check me out for yourself. And ignore the baby pics my parents put up thirteen years ago. Especially the one with the gigantic fat cheeks and the tiny wiener. (Yeah, thanks, Mom and Dad, that was just so excellent of you to do that.)

Anyway, I said to Ms. Gill, "Look, you can't just call me names unless you're going to stand there while I call you a burned-out old witch who hates kids and isn't smart enough to get a job salting the fries at Wendy's."

Later accounts would vary on this detail: some kids claimed I said "McDonald's," others said I mentioned In-N-Out. But it was Wendy's. Because I prefer the fries at Wendy's.

And of course some kids claimed the word I used wasn't exactly, precisely *witch*.

I think I'll just leave that ambiguous. Consider it a mystery.

Anyway, later that day I was invited to leave the school immediately and never come back. Which turned out to be okay because my mom had just taken a new job in San Francisco and my dad was going to look for something there as well.

And San Francisco, according to everything we had read, was much more advanced when it came to schooling. They were part of the new OutSchooling thing.

In fact, I said as much to Ms. Gill as she watched ever-so-happily while the security dude and the vice principal escorted me to the front door to be picked up by my poor father.

I said, "Your day is over, you old witch. This school is over. The days of mean, ignorant old frauds like you pushing kids around is over! No more teachers! No more schools! Wake up and smell the 2017!"

Excellent parting shot, I thought.

But then Ms. Gill said something that froze me. Knocked a step out of my swagger.

"You think you're free of teachers, Tomaso? You'll never

be free of teachers. You'll never be free of me, Tomaso! Do you hear me, you little brat? You'll never be free!"

My dad explained that what she probably meant was that some memory of her, some influence from her, would be with me always. That she wasn't making some kind of prediction or laying some eternal curse on me. Or threatening me.

But I was inclined to be more literal. And more worried. I was just a wee bit scared, to tell the truth.

Until I finally moved.

So, let us leap forward in time. Shall we? It's a two-year leap. Earlier I was thirteen. Now I'm fifteen. The year is no longer 2017 but . . . okay, I'll let you do the math.

Now we live in the Marina District in San Francisco. My mom ended up hating her job and got a different one. My dad loves his job, which is . . . Well, I'm not totally clear on it, something to do with design. (Maybe later I'll look him up and see.) So we're here in San Fran and probably for good. And whoa, school? The whole OutSchooling thing?

Well, let me walk you through it.

My school day starts whenever I'm ready.

I'm usually ready about ten-thirty. In the morning, not at night—I'm not a vampire. I just seem to naturally wake up around nine or nine-thirty, depending. Then I take a shower and drink a Red Bull and eat something tasty instead of whatever grotesquely nutritious thing my mom left for me.

Yes, I know that caffeine and a s'mores tart are not the best way to start the morning. I've dipped some nutrition, so I get the whole "food pyramid, diversified diet, blah, blah, blah" thing. But just because you have knowledge doesn't mean you have to apply it in real life.

Anyway, I like to get math out of the way first thing, because it's my most suckalicious subject and once I get it done I feel free, freeee!

I do math at home, before I head out. Because if you're basically a moron at something, it's better to be a private moron than a public one.

So I dip some math and it's a lecture from Neal Stephenson on codes and encryption, and it's actually kind of cool because he's got some high-end video and then does a thing where he plays some music and you can see the math kind of concealed within the music. And it's really a great lesson and all, and I kind of sort of understand it. The PT ('Puter Tutor, for those not familiar with current Bay Area slang) says I have a 72 percent comprehension, which my friend Crystal pops up on my screen to say is too optimistic.

"Yeah, right, like you understood any of that," she says from the three-inch square on the corner of my screen. She's still at home, obviously, since her hair is all up in a towel and her bare shoulders are still beaded with shower water.

She does this just to mess with me. You realize that, right?

"I understood it," I argue. "And I will continue to understand it for at least the next ten minutes or so. Now. Are you going to tilt that camera down or not?"

"Oh, you want me to tilt it down?" she teases. "Like . . . like this?"

At which point she tilts the camera down to reveal that she's wearing a tube top and jeans. She takes the towel from her perfectly dry hair and laughs at me. "You are so easy."

"You're a very bad person, Crystal."

"Well, duh. See you at Sweek?"

"On my way. But I still hate you."

Of course I don't so much hate Crystal as kind of, you know, the other thing.

Anyhoo, all of that takes us to eleven-fifteen-ish, at which point I head to Sweek. Sweek is a so-called edu-pub. Which means it's mostly a coffee shop, but on school days half the place is given over to kids. I guess it's a new thing, because my folks both bitch about how great things are for kids "nowadays." And how back in their day . . .

Off-topic: what is *the exact time frame of "nowadays"? And when exactly was "their day"? Why is "nowadays" plural and "their day" singular?*

Back on topic: I get to Sweek and Crystal's already there and I can tell from the three grins pointed my way that she's told everyone about the fake shower thing. So I give everyone a good-natured middle finger, grab a beverage, and flop onto the couch beside my best friend, Allison.

"You are such a loser," she says by way of hello.

Next to Allison is her girlfriend, Jen, who's okay but is kind of jealous that Allison and I share a love of Magnum bars, which we talk about far too much.

But seriously: they are the best. Especially the white chocolate. (No. Do not argue with me about this. Best ice cream bar ever.)

And in the big Morris chair—which I will grab the first chance I get—is Turbo. Turbo . . . Well, let's just say Turbo has not been entirely successful with his bipolar meds. The boy is in one of his down phases.

"Did you hear about the kidnapping?" he calls out instead of saying "Hi."

"And a fine good day to you, too, Turbo," I say. I pull my Link out of my pocket and say, "Full screen," and the unit unfolds itself to forty-four-centimeter size, stands itself up—avoiding Allison's raspberry scone—and pulls up what it guesses will be my first course. It guesses right: epistemology. The menu gives me an array of lectures, text, video, TV/movie references, whole books, animations, comedy bits, and so on. I often like to start with a comic take on a new topic, so the Link already has a Penn and Teller magic bit on epistemology at the top of the queue.

"It's serious, man," Turbo says. "Third kid in like two weeks. No bodies. No clues. And they're all about our age."

"Yeah, well, the cops'll get them," I mutter, wanting to get to work, not deal with Turbo's paranoia.

"You know how many crimes go unsolved in San Francisco?" Turbo says.

With a conspiratorial glance, Allison, Crystal, and even Jen say, "Query: How many crimes go unsolved in San Francisco?" so that all our Links answer in unison with a whole array of statistics.

"Very funny," Turbo says, pouting.

We all think it's pretty funny.

A brief digression:

The other day I was cleaning out my files and came across the report that got me in trouble with Ms. Gill. It was about Alexander Hamilton.

Who was Alexander Hamilton? Well, if you believe the nine-pound book I used to haul around at my old school, he was one of the most boring people ever to live. I read that book—just as Ms. Gill had told me—but then I Googled him. You know, just on a whim, just in the desperate hope that maybe there was something interesting . . . Turned out, um, yeah, there was.

Alexander's parents weren't married. His dad took off and his mom died when Al was either twelve or thirteen. Then his worthless father claimed Al's mother was a whore and ended up taking everything she had left to Al and his brother.

Nice, huh?

That wasn't in the book.

He didn't get much school, but he educated himself. He

even became a lawyer after studying for like three months. But before he did all that, he joined up with Washington and became a pretty good soldier. Later he was secretary of the treasury.

That was in the book. But this next part? Not:

Once he was secretary of the treasury, Al was set up by his political enemies with what used to be called a "honey trap" back in the day. This dude James Reynolds got Al to hook up with his wife, Maria. Yes, you got that right, some guy pimped his own wife out to Alexander Hamilton.

Then he blackmailed Al: *Give me money or I will rat you out for sleeping with my wife.*

Now, okay, Al was in the wrong here because he was married himself. So, definitely uncool. But still you have to give the top uncool points to Maria and her amazingly sleazy husband.

The whole thing was investigated and it turned out that Al was definitely a hound, and yes, he had paid blackmail money to pimpster James Reynolds. But he'd used his own money, not the money from the treasury, which would have been a crime.

Then—and here's the reason I ended up liking old Al—he totally overreacts and writes a ninety-seven-page pamphlet laying it all out. Including a whole lot of details about his thing with the lovely Maria.

As my mom would say while attempting to sound young and cool: Can you say Too Much Information? And she'd be right. It's TMI colonial-style. And the whole colonial country was like, "Seriously? He said *that*?"

Also, the book did mention that Al died in a duel with Aaron Burr, who was vice president. Yes: the vice president shot the secretary of the treasury in the guts for dissing him.

But the book didn't have the details. The way they all

had to sneak around. The way they had to row across the river from New York to Jersey. The way no one knows who shot first, or whether Al even meant to shoot. And it left out the fact that Al, with a pistol bullet through his stomach and lodged in his spine, diagnosed his own case before the doctor could even check his insurance card.

"This is a mortal wound, Doctor."

The story starts out with a smart loser of a kid, a dead mom, and a less-than-admirable father, but the kid says forget all that, nothing is going to stop me! And he becomes a soldier and one of George freaking Washington's posse, figures out how to be a lawyer, gets to be secretary of the treasury, gets trapped with a married babe, writes a scarily detailed pamphlet, and ends up bleeding out from a gut shot on a misty August morning in New Jersey.

See, to me that was a better story. So I didn't really care about sticking to what Ms. Gill told me to stick to. In the book he was some guy in a wig who did some good but kind of boring stuff.

I didn't care about that boring stuff until after I realized that I kind of liked the dude.

So, day over, heading back home from Sweek, walking along right at the corner of Avila and Beach and a van pulls up and stops, double-parking like maybe they're making a delivery or whatever.

I pay no attention to the van because I'm more thinking that the woman walking toward me down Avila looks kind of familiar.

About fifty feet away my brain makes the connection. And my mouth says, "No way."

And Ms. Gill says, "Wrong again, Tomaso."

I gulp and my heart skips a couple of beats, because seriously, what is she doing here? This is a long way from Utah.

But what can I do? I can't turn away like I'm scared. I'm not scared. I'm creeped out, not scared.

"Ms. Gill. It's . . . good to see you?"

"Get into the van."

"Actually, I have to get home. But, you know . . ."

At which point a beefy, hunched-over dude in a cheap short-sleeve shirt appears, coming around the van. Holding a gun.

Have you ever had a gun pointed at you? Well, time stops. Just stops.

And your visual field suddenly shrinks down so that you don't see the sky or the street around you. You don't see the person holding the gun. You just see the gun.

It looks very large.

For once in my fifteen years of life, I have nothing clever to say.

The only reason I don't wet my pants is that I'd prudently taken a leak before leaving Sweek.

But still, I'm not going to get into that van. I might be paralyzed with shock, but I'm not stupid. You never get in the van. Never. Everyone knows that. Much better to let whatever is going to happen play out in a public place.

I say, "No, I'm not—"

And then I wake up in the van. Hog-tied. This means that my ankles are tied by rough rope, that my wrists are also tied, that I'm facedown, and that my ankles are tied to my wrists in such a way that I form a sort of squashed letter U.

It's very uncomfortable. The van's suspension's pretty bad and every time we hit a bump it's like a kick to my stomach.

I haven't been shot. But I have an amazingly painful headache and a swelling on my neck where someone must have hit me with something hard.

Ms. Gill's in the passenger seat. The guy with the lame shirt is driving.

And then I notice that there's an Asian kid my age lying trussed up beside me. We're both gagged or I might say hello, how are you, and why the hell are we in this situation?

Instead I just grunt, and he stares back at me with wide, scared eyes.

We drive up and down the hills for a while, and I try to keep track of where we are. Mostly I'm listening for sounds indicating that we're crossing one of the bridges. But I don't get that. Nor do I get freeway-type noise. So I figure we're probably still somewhere in the city, and then, at last, the van lurches to a stop.

Ms. Gill turns around, arm over her seat, and says, "Vice Principal Edgar's stun gun can knock you out. Or it can merely . . . *discipline* you. So don't do anything stupid."

Ah, so it was a stun gun, not a gun gun. I can see that now.

They let us out. I guess right away that we're somewhere on the Presidio. That's a former army post in, like, the world's most beautiful location in a park overlooking the Golden Gate Bridge.

The army moved out a long time ago, and some of the old officers' quarters are rented out, and some of the other buildings, the headquarters and all. Now they're offices for various things.

It's kind of an empty place for the most part, not like the rest of the city. A weird place to do a kidnapping, I think.

The van's parked on gravel in front of a low, tan stucco building that's—inconveniently, I think—out of view of anything else. No view of the Golden Gate for us, we're nestled in pine trees.

There's a new brass plaque on the wall beside the only door on the building. It reads "Academy of Troubled Youth."

I share a look with the Asian kid and I can tell by his expression he's thinking the same thing I am. Shouts, cries, and loud prayers coming from a place with that kind of name would go unheard. Deliberately unheard. No one wants anything to do with "troubled youth."

We march through the front door and down a narrow, gloomy hallway to a side door. Ms. Gill opens it with what I can only describe as an expression of smug satisfaction. By which I mean that she opens the door with her hand, while having on her face a look of smug satisfaction.

"Class," she says in her brittle teacher voice, "we have two new students." And with that, the guy pulls off our gags and we're pushed into a room.

With a chalkboard at the front.

I . . . I can't breathe. There's a teacher's desk in the corner.

My God, and bookshelves! Shelves double-stacked with every kind of horror, across all age groups: from Magic Tree House books to *A Tale of Two Cities* to biographies of people no one cares about.

And then, I see . . . desks! Student desks. In four rows.

And in half of those desks are . . . kids!

"Sweet Lord," my co-kidnappee breathes. "It's a classroom!"

It is indeed a classroom. It has the classroom look, the classroom clutter, the classroom smell of boredom and despair.

And no computer. Not even a Smart Board.

I can't breathe. But I fight the panic. Freaking out will accomplish nothing. But my throat's tight and my heart's pounding and for a minute I think I might pass out from the sheer horror.

We're shackled by our legs to desks and Ms. Gill says, "Introduce yourselves, children."

There are five other kids in the room besides the two

of us. All shackled. All hunched over actual books. Books inked up with other people's notes and drawings.

The same books are in front of me. And on the board, written in chalk, are words that strike terror into me.

Reading: Chapters 9–12 on U.S. House of Representatives and its committees.

I jerk against the chain at my ankle.

Ms. Gill doesn't even bother to look up.

"I'm Peter," a sullen kid says.

"I'm Annette."

My God, they're actually doing it! They're introducing themselves! Like this is an actual classroom and not some nightmare of Ms. Gill's creation.

"Tomaso and Nguyen, since you haven't had time to read the assignment, just try to keep up with the class discussion."

Am I dreaming? Is that it?

"You'll find college-ruled spiral notebooks and number two pencils in your desk. I'd advise you both to take careful notes. What we're covering will be on the test."

She looks right at me when she says that.

On the test.

On. The. Test.

No. Maybe Peter and Annette and Nguyen and that other girl, and that dude with the lazy eye, and Jennifer—who under other circumstances I might ask out—will sit quietly and read their paper books, and stare at the chalkboard and take notes with a pencil. On paper!

Not me.

I pick up the spiral notebook and throw it on the floor.

And do you know what I learn from that? I learn that stun guns really hurt. (It's actually better when they're set to knock you out.)

Here's what you want to imagine. Ever see one of those

old-fashioned marionettes? (If not, just do an image search.) They're basically puppets with too many joints, dangling from strings.

So, the Taser hits, and for about twenty seconds I am one of those marionettes and an ADHD three-year-old is yanking me around by the strings. Legs, arms, head, all twitching away like a crazy person.

"That was the lowest setting, Tomaso," Ms. Gill says. "Next time I'll ask Vice Principal Edgar to raise the voltage a little." She comes toward my desk, doing the teacher strut, leans down, and says, "Not so smart now, are you? Now pick up the book. And the notebook. And . . ." She pauses for extra relish. ". . . the number two pencil."

We spend the night shivering in narrow bunk beds. Our ankles are chained to the metal frames.

I don't sleep well. For one thing, Nguyen has an impressive snoring thing going on.

For another, I'm seething with a range of unfamiliar emotions: white-hot fury alternating with cold, dark despair.

My normal emotions range from cool beige amusement to somewhat warm taupe irritation.

See what I did there with the color and emotion thing?

The point is, I'm not happy in a way that I've never been not happy before. I've been abused. Parts of my brain are probably permanently damaged from reading about the permanent committees of the U.S. House of Representatives—a political body included in the Constitution with an eye toward causing future kids to weep with boredom.

"They'll never find us, will they?" Nguyen whispers. I should have known he was awake: the snoring had stopped.

"Of course they'll find us," I say. "The whole city is looking. You can't just 'disappear' seven kids without people noticing. Not even in San Francisco."

"We're hidden in plain sight," Nguyen moans. "They'll figure we were taken to the East Bay or something. Over the bridge."

"Over the bridge," I muse. "Listen to me, Noo—you don't mind if I call you that, right? Were you carrying a Link when they grabbed you?"

"Well, duh," he says. "But they broke it."

"Yeah, mine too, I imagine. But there will be a GPS record of where we both were when we were picked up. Suddenly, bam, we go off-grid, right? So if we're the cops, what do we do? We check those areas for witnesses. And better yet, we check for any kind of security camera."

"It's probably a stolen van. They won't be able to trace it."

"They don't have to trace it by the license plate, Noo, they can check bridge cams—they'll see that it never left the city. They'll know we're still here."

"But we're in the Presidio. This is the one part of the city where no one ever goes!"

He's right, and I have no clever answer for that. Why hadn't they taken us to the Castro—an old woman with a bunch of kids would have been spotted in a heartbeat.

Ms. Gill had obviously set this up carefully. She would have had to rent the building, set up her bogus "Troubled Youth" organization, bring in desks and so on.

And who would ever suspect a teacher of being a kidnapper?

"They'll find us," I say bravely.

But as I say it I know it isn't what I want. I don't want to be found chained to a desk and learning from books, cut off like some kind of primitive throwback, reduced to a caveman existence. I don't want to be humiliated that way.

I don't want to be a victim of forced hierarchical learning.

There has to be a way out.

If only I could have two minutes online . . .

If only . . .

But it's not going to happen. I'm de-Linked. I fall asleep eventually, thinking of Crystal. And Magnum bars.

A day passes.

And another.

On the third day I get a B-minus on a test.

On the fourth day I lose it. Four days without any sort of Link-age. I go a little crazy, thrashing against the chain that holds me to my desk, throwing things, cursing.

The so-called vice principal—who I think may just be a hobo—is about to Tase me, but Ms. Gill holds up a hand and stops him. I see the look on her face. A look of triumph. Victory!

On the fifth day I have a paper due. I stay up late and study. With a book. It's full of dated references. It stinks of mildew. It's utterly linear. And whoever owned it before me has highlighted, like, every word, in yellow.

There's no way to turn off the highlighting.

No way to stop the cursed yellow that permeates the unchanging, static page.

I stare at the page and cry.

Noo hears me. He has the top bunk. He leans over the side and says, "Dude, it's not that hard. It's just biology. I could help you—"

"Damn your help!" I shout. "What good is your help? All you have is the same stupid book I have. What if it's wrong, Noo? What if the science has changed since they wrote this in—" I pause to check the front of the book and I'm shocked. "No! It's older than I am! It's as old as my mom!"

Noo checks his. "Not mine," he says. "Mine is only ten years old."

"Only?" I shrill sarcastically. "Only ten . . ." And then I

freeze. Okay, then I unfreeze, leap as far as my chain will allow me, and snatch the book from Noo's hand.

Oh, it's *Life: Elements of Biology,* all right. But it's the tenth edition. And my *Life: Elements of Biology* is the eighth edition.

The next day is Day Five.

I'm going to study for it like I've never studied before.

"Tomaso, why don't you tell us what you learned about mitochondrial DNA," Ms. Gill demands.

"I'm afraid I can't, Ms. Gill."

She stares pretty hard. I smirk hard back at her.

She's seen this smirk before. She knows I'm up to something. But her natural teacherly arrogance won't let her back down.

I'm counting on that.

"Did you do the assigned reading?"

"Yes indeed, Ms. Gill."

"Then you know the answer, Tomaso."

"On the contrary, Ms. Gill. I am unable to find *the* answer. Not . . . *the* . . . answer."

She gets up from her desk.

She walks toward me. Heels click click click.

I can hear the vice principal–slash–hobo unholstering his stun gun.

"Open your book to the appropriate page." She sucks in a breath and spits out, "Tomaso."

I open my book.

She stabs at the paragraph with her finger. Is that finger trembling just a bit? Oh, yes, it is.

"There," she says triumphantly. "There is where it says that except in very rare cases each individual has only one type of mitochondrial DNA. There! If you had read the assignment!"

I stand up, too. Toe to toe. Nose to nose. Marshall's blouse to Target T-shirt.

"Oh, I read it, Ms. Gill. Then I read it again." I grab Noo's book and hold it up so she can get a good look at it. "I read it again, in the tenth edition. And guess what, Ms. Gill?"

She takes a small step back, faced with the rage of my knowledge.

"It seems they originally believed heteroplasmic mitochondrial DNA to be quite rare, but we now know—as of this, the tenth edition, Ms. Gill—we now know that heteroplasmic DNA is present to some degree *in almost all tissues*!"

She swallows hard.

"In . . . almost . . . *all* . . . tissues!" I repeat.

I lean in for the kill. "The facts, Ms. Gill, cannot be ascertained from the reading assignment you gave me. And who knows what further details have emerged about mitochondrial DNA in the decade since the tenth edition, let alone the thirty-seven years since the eighth edition?"

"No," she gasps.

Then, almost pleading, "No."

"Well, Ms. Gill." And I totally spit out the words *Ms. Gill* with the same sharp-edged tones she uses to say my name. They are some cutting syllables. "Who knows? Who *knows*? I'll tell you who *knows,* Ms. Gill: the Internet knows, Ms. Gill."

I let the book drop from my hand.

She flinches at the sound of it hitting the floor.

"The. Internet. Knows," I say with grim finality.

Well. I wish I could say that her head explodes. Because that would be cool.

But instead what happens is that the FBI and the SFPD burst into the room. They grab Vice Principal Edgar after a brief struggle.

And they handcuff Ms. Gill.

She doesn't struggle.

She doesn't say a word.

She just stares at me with a look of terrible loss. I've crushed her world. And compared to the defeat I've inflicted on Ms. Gill, her arrest, trial, and subsequent plea-bargained sentence of twenty years in the minimum-security women's prison in Chino will be nothing.

The FBI and the SFPD may have rescued me.

But I have already defeated Ms. Gill.

It's been fifteen years. Wow. Time flies.

I got married. Not to Crystal. This is real life, not a romance novel. Anyway, Crystal wasn't right for me. A fact I came to realize shortly after she dumped me.

If by "shortly after" you mean "following three weeks spent sobbing into my pillow."

Anyway, forget Crystal. My wife's name is Gala. She's nice. I mean, more than nice, obviously; I love her.

I got a job designing multisense orbital advertising. If you've seen, heard, and smelled the orbital logo for GebEx, you've seen, heard, and smelled my work.

I wouldn't say I'm rich, but I have a hoverhouse in Marin, and yes, a flying car. (I know: finally, am I right?)

And we have two kids, Jake and Julia.

We had a big decision to make a few years ago when Chipster first came out. I mean, obviously I'm the last guy to get hung up on traditions, but it seems weird to me that kids today don't have to even speak a search term, let alone actually type on a keyboard.

It seems incredible and maybe a little wrong that a five-year-old should be able to think about the U.S. House of Representatives or Alexander Hamilton and then, boom, there it all is inside their brain, thanks to an implant the size of a grain of rice.

The last I heard, Ms. Gill had been let out of prison after doing three years, and had gotten a job at the Museum of the School, in Fresno.

I flew over there one day. Did I expect to run into Ms. Gill? I don't know. Maybe.

Maybe I wanted to say, "See, I turned out okay."

And maybe I wanted her to say, "You know, I was wrong about you, Tomaso. You turned out to be a fine young man."

That would have been nice. Because the one thing a Link never really does is look you up and down and say, "You turned out to be a fine young man."

Yeah, that would have been nice.

Really nice.

Instead, I did run into Ms. Gill, and when I smiled at her and said, "Hey, it's me, Tomaso!" she Tased me and tried to shackle me to one of the desks in the life-sized holographic diorama of the Ancient Schoolroom.

Don't worry about Ms. Gill, though—she didn't get sent back to prison. Only the worst cases get sent to prison. In Ms. Gill's case, for this second kidnapping they just performed minor surgery.

Yep. She has a nice fresh Chipster in her head now. It warns her when she's having crazy thoughts. And if she *does* something crazy, it messages the police.

And as a bonus, with just a thought she can instantly access whatever there is to know about mitochondrial DNA.

Misery

HEATHER BREWER

Misery was a strange name for a town, and Alek wasn't at all certain that it was fitting. He had, in the three years that he'd called Misery home, experienced nothing worse than a strange sense of loss. An odd, unexplainable grief wafted through its windows and doors at every hour, as if the town's inhabitants had been glazed in a thin film of sorrow and, perhaps, regret. But even with that strange, ever-present gloom, the town's name had never made much sense to Alek. No one who lived here was miserable, exactly. They simply *were.* Nothing more. Nothing less.

And just as Misery simply was, so too were its citizens. Alek could not recall, no matter how terribly he strained to do so, his life before Misery. Nor could he remember having moved here. Not exactly. One day, he wasn't here. He was somewhere else—somewhere with many colors. And the next, he was.

He supposed he should be grateful for remembering the

colors of his past. The only colors in Misery were black, white, and a palette of grays. Apart, of course, from the eyes of everyone who lived here. Alek's eyes were a vibrant green. His best friend, Sara's, were bright blue. He loved looking at his neighbors' eyes. They were a brief reminder of something before Misery. Something that Alek could not recall, and could not identify with any measure of certainty.

Not that he minded being here. Not really. After all, it wasn't exactly a miserable kind of place.

"Morning, Alek." Mr. Whirly passed by on the street, tipping his bowler hat in Alek's direction. He didn't have a smile on his face, but no one ever seemed to smile in Misery. It was, Alek thought, strange that he recalled what smiling was at all.

Mr. Whirly was dressed in a three-piece suit of varying grays, his silver cuff links gleaming in the morning sun. He always looked so dapper, and made a point of greeting everyone he passed. Except, of course, for Sara, whom he still hadn't forgiven for running over his freshly sprouted daisies with a lawn mower last spring. Alek smiled and nodded his hello. "Morning, Mr. Whirly."

It was never a *good* morning in Misery. Just morning. Then afternoon. Then evening. Nothing was good. Or bad, really. So Alek felt rather guilty about questioning the absolute blandness of it all. Like the colors, the actions they all took here seemed so repetitive. It worried him sometimes, though he'd never had the guts to voice his concerns to anyone but Sara—who was currently waiting for him near the town center.

The town's center was marked by a massive, ornate fountain. At its peak stood a large crow. Its shiny glass eyes peered down at passersby. Alek didn't much care for it, for reasons he couldn't quite explain. The statue unsettled him, tying tight knots in his stomach whenever he looked at it. But he couldn't stand to not look at it, either.

"You're late." Sara cocked her head to the side in a way that reminded Alek of someone's mother, rather than their best friend. But then, Sara had been like that since the day they'd met—judgmental and protective of him in only the best manner.

Alek half shrugged. "I was busy."

"You were delaying the inevitable." She cast him a concerned glance, one that said that she hadn't forgotten about their conversation the night before. "Still nervous?"

Alek swallowed hard. Nervous? He was actually pretty terrified. So much so that he hadn't slept a wink last night, and every moment this morning had been consumed by his absolute fear of what was to come today. Not that he should be worried or anything. He didn't know of one person in the town of Misery who'd received a Gift they hadn't liked. Of course, his subconscious continued to insist on reminding him, there was always the first time. What if that first time belonged to him? "Yeah. Kinda."

"You are the only person I know who gets nervous over receiving their Gift." Sara frowned. It wasn't that she was upset or anything. She was merely concerned for him. Still . . . Alek could have done with a reassuring smile from her this morning. "It's not like you didn't receive a Gift last year, y'know. Or the year before. And have any of them been bad? No. So what are you worried about, exactly?"

Sara's irritation merely framed the obvious in gilded, extravagant swirls. Alek's nervousness over something so simple, something so very ordinary, made her nervous too. And that was precisely why Alek hadn't told anyone else in town about the way his stomach clenched every time he thought about receiving his upcoming Gift. It was better, in a place like Misery, to just go with the flow, and not upset anyone with his strange reluctance. He couldn't explain why, exactly. It was just . . . *better* this way.

Alek shrugged, trying like hell to keep his attention off the stone crow perched atop the elaborate fountain, despite the fact that its glass eyes were sparkling brightly in the sun, begging to be examined closer. "Two years ago, my Gift was you. Last year, my Gift was my own room at the boarding-house. What if this year doesn't compare?"

She examined his face carefully, narrowing her eyes just a bit in suspicion. When she spoke, her voice had fallen into mere whispers. "That's not really it, is it, Alek? You're afraid of something. I know you. I can tell. What are you afraid of?"

It amazed him at times how well Sara knew him, and how she could predict so easily when things weren't sitting so great inside his mind.

When it came to predictions, to knowing things that were unknowable, the citizens of Misery turned to a woman by the name of Jordan. Jordan was psychic, or sensitive, or just incredibly talented when it came to understanding the annual blessings that were bestowed upon the people here. No one knew where the Gifts came from or who sent them. Like anything else in Misery, people simply accepted the Gifts as the norm, refusing to make waves by questioning the Gifts' origins.

Two years ago, Jordan had told him that a new friend was coming to Misery, and that she and Alek would become very close in a relatively short period of time. Maybe it had been Alek's loneliness talking, but he'd doubted at the time that his Gift of friendship would ever come true. The very next day, Sara had found him at the town center, not so far from the spot they were standing at now. He'd vowed that day that he'd never doubt Jordan or her abilities ever again. And yet here he was, his stomach all tied in knots, his palms slick with anxious sweat.

"Fine. Don't tell me." Sara folded her arms in front of her and turned, leading Alek down the sidewalk in the direction of Jordan's house. As they came to a stop at the corner across from Vinnie's Sales and Sundries, she continued her thought. "But I'll bet you just about anything that you're wrong. It's your *Gift,* Alek. How can that be anything to worry about?"

"Morning, you two. Causing trouble early today, are you?" Virginia called to them from where she was kneeling in her flower beds. Beside her was a pile of weeds, as gray and dull as the flowers themselves, but somehow more lifeless. She wore a big floppy hat to block out the sun's rays, and had to hold up the brim just to meet Alek's and Sara's eyes.

Sara put on a pleasant demeanor. "No, ma'am. Just walking over so Alek can receive his Gift."

"Oh, has it been so long already? I swear, after so much time here, every year seems to blend into the next." Virginia stood and brushed dirt from her knees before approaching the white picket fence between her and the sidewalk they were standing on. "Are you looking forward to your Gift, Alek?"

Alek gulped as silently as he could manage, swallowing his hesitancy at receiving something he knew on the surface would be satisfactory. Then he nodded at her. "Every year. When do you receive your next Gift, Virginia?"

She wiped a bead of sweat from her forehead with the back of her hand as she considered his question, leaving behind a smudge of soil. "Well, let's see. If you get your Gift today, my next Gift must be in about two months. But, you know, after last year, I don't really need another Gift."

Alek shrugged. "Maybe you'll get some new flowers to put in your garden."

Virginia sighed. "You know what I'd really like? Some color. Maybe some color for my roses. Oh yes, I'd like that very much."

The three of them exchanged looks. Looks that spoke volumes.

Then Virginia stammered, as if she were afraid that someone might overhear them. "Of course, I'm not complaining. I like Misery just the way it is. It's just that you have such beautiful green eyes, Alek. I wish I could see that in my garden too. Anyway, you two should scoot. Don't want to be late to receive your Gift."

"Yeah." Alek's heart felt hollow and heavy. His voice dropped off, into an almost whisper. "I wouldn't want that."

Alek moved down the sidewalk, his steps hesitant. Beside him, in direct contrast, Sara's stride was confident and sure. Lining the street were large oak trees. A strong wind gusted high above the two friends, blowing several leaves in varying shades of gray from the branches. The leaves danced and fluttered on the wind before settling gently on the grass and in the street. High in the sky, tucked halfway behind a gray cloud, was a hot white sun. The scene should have been serene, should have settled any upset in Alek's nerves and calmed the churning of his stomach. But it didn't. The quiet simply added to his stress, though he couldn't exactly point to what was stressing him out or why.

At the end of the street stood a large Victorian house, with three floors and a high-peaked round tower that loomed above the surrounding homes. The house was painted a charcoal gray. The front porch was wide and inviting, and in front of the stark white door sat a mat that read "Welcome All." Under each window was a charming flower box, and planted inside were small blooms that seemed cheerful, despite their lack of color. The shutters were carved with amazing detail—

storybook images on each piece—and painted stark black. Alek's favorite image was carved on the shutters surrounding the window nearest the front door. One side featured a house made of candy, with two children skipping merrily up to the door. The other showed a woman peering out of the home's window, grinning menacingly. The image had always appealed to Alek, but today it felt sinister. He tore his gaze away from it and rapped on the front door, ready to receive his Gift. Maybe Sara was right. Maybe he was just being stupid about the whole thing.

Besides, the last two Gifts he'd received had turned out even better than expected. So what was he so worried about?

A singsongy voice called from within, "Be right there!"

Alek's heart skipped a beat, but he willed it to steady its rhythm, and cast Sara a reassuring glance—not that she was the one who needed any reassuring. He hoped it reassured her, at least. But he was pretty sure she knew he was full of crap. He was scared, and they both knew it. They just didn't know why.

The door opened in, and Jordan poked her head out. Her brown eyes were bright and dazzling amidst all the gray. She wore a floral apron around her waist, over her tasteful dress. Her curly hair was held neatly back from her face with a floral scarf. On any normal day, Alek really liked coming to visit Jordan. There was a motherly quality to everything she said, everything she did. It was comforting. It was nice. But today, it wasn't helping. "Come on in, Alek. Sara, you can wait on the porch swing. I left you some lemonade and cookies to munch on, but this shouldn't take long."

Sara gave Alek's shoulder a comforting squeeze and turned on her heel toward the porch swing. He watched the bounce in her step for a moment before turning back to Jordan. She held the door open for him and he stepped inside. The table just inside the front door held its usual platter of fresh-baked cookies. As he grabbed a gooey snickerdoodle, Jordan closed the front door behind them and said, "Are you excited about your Gift, Alek?"

He really wished people would stop asking him that. He bit into the cookie, which wasn't as sweet as he'd wanted it to be. The cookie he'd had last year had definitely been sweeter. But then, last year he hadn't been nervous at all. He chewed and swallowed, and the bite went down hard. Suddenly, he wished he had some lemonade to wash it down with. "To be honest . . . not really. I've felt a bit . . . off all day. Is that weird?"

"Hmmm." That's all she said. Just a thoughtful noise. Not even a word, really. It did little to settle Alek's nerves. She tilted her head, looking him over for a moment, before gesturing to the parlor door behind him.

Alek nodded and sat his unfinished cookie on the table before turning to the parlor. The door to the parlor wasn't really a door at all, but an archway. Grand black velvet drapes held back by large silver tassels separated the space from the foyer. As he moved inside, a medley of herby smells wafted over his senses. He couldn't identify which herbs had blended together to create the aroma, but he rather liked the way the spicy-sweet scent tickled his nose.

At the center of the parlor was a small round table, also draped in velvet, and sitting to either side of it were two small stools that reminded Alek of mushrooms. On the rounded walls hung several picture frames containing photos of people that Alek didn't recognize. He'd never dared ask who the subjects were. It wasn't really his business, anyway.

Jordan plopped down on a mushroom stool and gestured for Alek to do the same. Once he had, she held out her hand

and said, "Well, let's see what we have here. Close your eyes and hold out your dominant hand."

He lowered himself onto the stool and slowly held out his right hand. His fingers were trembling slightly, and just as Jordan took his hand in hers, he noticed a small grouping of cookie crumbs on his palm. He thought about mentioning it, but before he could, her fingers had already brushed them away. She squeezed his hand, closed her eyes, and released a cleansing breath.

That was what she called it. A cleansing breath. As if every problem in the world could be lessened by simply taking a deep breath and letting it out slowly.

Alek took a breath and blew it out. If nothing else, it didn't hurt to try.

The room suddenly seemed very quiet, although it was no more silent than it had been just a moment before. After a few seconds, she frowned, as if he'd done something wrong. "Relax, Alek. You have to relax or I can't sense what your Gift will be. You're so tense, I'm not getting it right now. Just breathe, okay?"

He took a deep breath, and as he released it, he focused on his muscles, relaxing each and every one as well as he was able. Maybe his concerns were baseless. Maybe he was just being stupid, worrying about his Gift. But he'd never know if he didn't chill out and relax.

"Ahh. Hmmm." She opened her eyes then, but averted her gaze from meeting his. She patted him on the hand in a way that was designed to comfort him, an act that sent his heart into a more concerned rhythm. Was something wrong? What was his Gift? Last year, she'd reacted brightly right away. The year before, she'd hugged him. But this year, her eyes were wide with concern and darting all around the room. Maybe his gut had been right after all. Maybe his Gift wasn't going to be much of a gift after all. Or maybe he wasn't receiving a Gift at all. It would be a first in Misery, unheard of, but Alek's imagination was running wild.

He gathered up what courage he could and asked, "What . . . what is it?"

She shook her head, and shrugged, a strange cloud settling over her usually cheerful exterior. "It's . . . nothing."

Alek blew out a breath, instantly relaxing. Nothing! It was nothing. He couldn't have felt more relieved. He settled back on the mushroom stool, every bit of tension leaving his body. "Oh, man. That's great. You have no idea what that means to me, Jordan. I was so worried all morning that it would be something bad."

Then Jordan met his eyes at last. She gripped his hand once again, but this time as if to keep him from running away. When she spoke, her voice was tinged with panic. "No, Alek. You're not understanding me. Your Gift. It's nothing."

"You mean . . ." His heart beat twice, hard and hollow inside his chest. A sick feeling filled his pores, seeping deep inside of him. "You mean I don't get a Gift this year?"

It was ridiculous and horrible and not anything at all that could possibly happen in Misery. So why was it happening to him?

"That's not what I'm saying." She cupped one hand over the top of his and gave it a squeeze, as if trying desperately to comfort him in a situation where no comfort could be found. "Listen. When I tap into a person, I generally receive a vision of what their Gift will be. And this year, yours was . . . nothing. I saw nothing. It was a cloudy haze. It was . . . nothing. For your Gift, you are receiving nothingness. Nonexistence."

The last word she spoke sat in his chest like a hot stone. "Nonexistence? You mean . . . I'm going to die?"

Everything in the room suddenly seemed smaller. The

table, the mushroom stools, the picture frames, the walls. As well as every molecule of air that was available to breathe.

"No," she said, after a too-long pause. "You won't die. You're just not going to *be* anymore. By the end of this day, you're no longer going to exist."

Alek's heart was pounding in his ears. His breaths came sharp and quick as the panic took hold of him, and it felt very much like something had gripped his lungs and was squeezing them as tightly as it could manage. He shook his head, giving himself over to denial, and met Jordan's eyes. He wanted to see even a hint of a smile in them, like this was all just some sick, cruel joke. But all he found was the truth. He was going to blink out of existence by the day's end.

Tears welled up in Alek's eyes against his will. This couldn't be it, couldn't be the end of him. He was just a kid, just a teenager. He hadn't even kissed a girl yet. When he spoke, his voice shook slightly. "Please, Jordan. You have to help me."

She grew very quiet, brushing a few tears from the tip of her nose and her cheeks. He'd fully expected her to shake her head, to tell him that there was absolutely nothing that they could do to preserve his future. But she didn't. After a moment, she released his hand and sat back in her chair, wrapping her arms around her waist, darting her eyes about the room, as if a thought had popped into her head. One that had deeply disturbed her.

Alek sat forward, his eyes locked on her grief-stricken face. "What is it, Jordan? What can I do? There has to be something! And if you know and you don't tell me—"

"There is something." She met his eyes, and then blinked, as if she were shaking off a bad dream. "Maybe. But I can't help you with it. And it might not even work. It probably won't work at all."

"But it might." He wasn't feeling a burst of optimism, but he did know that if they, if he, did nothing to prevent himself from dying, blinking out of existence, whatever you wanted to call it, then that was exactly what was going to happen. "Please?"

She stood, arms still wrapped around her waist, and began pacing the small room slowly. "Have you ever heard of a man by the name of Cameron Boswell, Alek? Probably not. He was here a bit before your time."

But Alek did remember him. Not from memory, but from whispers around town. People said he was a troublemaker. People said that Misery was better off without him here. But people said little else about him.

She didn't wait for an answer. She merely paused for a moment and became lost in thought again, leaving her parlor, Alek, and the entire town of Misery behind for the time being. In her eyes, Alek could tell that she was someplace else. Someplace better. Then worse. A brief almost-smile touched her lips before crumbling away like ashes in the wind. Whatever she had been thinking about had made her happy—incredibly happy—but whatever that was was gone now, and all that was left were shadows. "He was a kind man. Outgoing. Generous. But not well liked around town. Maybe it was because he was different from everyone else. Not in any way that you could see just by looking at him. But Cameron . . . Cameron was different."

Her almost-smile returned long enough to lightly brush the edges of her lips before fluttering away again. After all, there were no smiles in Misery. "On his fifth anniversary in town, Cameron came to me to receive his Gift. It was the same as yours, Alek. His Gift was nothing."

Alek sucked in his breath. He wasn't the first to receive the Gift of nothing, and what scared him most about that was that Cameron was nowhere to be found. Blinked out of existence, maybe. He swallowed the lump in his throat and said, “What happened to him?”

She moved to the archway and stared out into the foyer at nothing in particular. Slowly, she raised her right hand and gripped the drapes gently, as if they might help to steady her should she fall. “He came to me with this crazy theory. He thought that if he could manage to leave Misery, he might not cease to exist. If he could somehow get past its borders and head for the next town, then maybe he’d be all right.”

Alek’s forehead creased as he strained to recall where exactly the border to Misery was located. Had he ever been to the edge of town? *Was* there an edge to town? He wasn’t certain. He only knew that ideas were only crazy sounding to those who had other options. If Cameron had actually left Misery and was living out his days somewhere else, if he had proven that it could be done, then Alek was totally on board the crazy train, without hesitation. “Where is it? The way out of town, I mean.”

“I’m not sure anyone really knows. Cameron thought that you could leave Misery by heading north and climbing that really big hill there. He said the other side of it was the border. I don’t know if he was right or not.”

But Cameron had known. And Alek very much wanted to know that too. That there was a way out. That he didn’t have to blink out of existence just because Misery had deemed it so. He stood at last and brushed past her into the foyer, determination driving him forward. “I’m going. I have to try.”

But before his fingertips could make contact with the doorknob, she gripped the back of his shirt. “Wait! You can go. You should! But don’t tell anyone else. The people who live here . . . in a way, they are Misery. If they know you’re trying to leave . . . I don't know. It's not safe, Alek. They'll stop you."

Alek paused, letting his hand fall back to his side, before turning back to Jordan. If he didn't ask her now, he might not ever know. "How do you know all of this, Jordan? I mean, I get that the Gift giving is some kind of psychic deal. That's not exactly a secret. But how do you know all about Cameron?"

Her eyes glistened with tears, and when she spoke, her voice cracked slightly. "Cameron and I were engaged."

Engaged. And then Cameron went away forever. It had to be an impossible thing to face—losing your fiancé in one way or another. Either by him disappearing completely or leaving town forever. "I'm sorry."

"The day I gave him his Gift, he told Mr. Whirly and me about his plans to leave. Mr. Whirly used to be a joyous man, full of a bubbly, infectious spirit. But he changed after hearing Cameron's plans. He just seemed . . . darker." She lifted the corner of her apron and dabbed at her eyes. "Cameron didn't really have a chance after that. He made it to the bottom of the big hill before he disappeared. I was there. I saw the whole thing happen. He simply . . . ceased to be. It was horrible. I don't want it to happen to anyone else."

Alek watched her for a moment, wishing he could take her pain away. Then he reached out and gave her hand a squeeze. She squeezed his back, and they exchanged nods before putting on false pleasantries. By the time Alek opened the door, all seemed well with the two of them, though it was anything but.

Sara crammed the remainder of a half-eaten cookie in her mouth and chewed fast before swallowing. As she skipped across the porch to Alek, who was closing the door behind him, she said, "So? What's your Gift?"

Alek remembered what Jordan had said about Mr. Whirly. "I can't tell you just yet. But I know where to go to get it."

"That's weird. Where do you have to go?" She followed him down the steps, a doubtful crease in her forehead.

Alek paused as they reached the next block. He had to get rid of Sara, couldn't risk her changing like Mr. Whirly had with Cameron. What if Jordan was right? What if the townspeople really were the town? He couldn't fully trust anyone. Maybe not even Jordan—something that sent a nervous chill down his spine. Shrugging casually, he couldn't help but notice Virginia toiling in her flower beds again. "The north side of town. I can go get it and bring it back."

"Don't be stupid. I'll come with you." The words had no sooner left her mouth than Virginia looked up at them, a burning curiosity in her gaze. On any other day, Alek might not have noticed such blatant curiosity. But today was different. Today was his last day in Misery, one way or the other.

He lowered his voice, trying to keep any sense of nervousness out of his tone. "I'd kinda like to get it on my own, okay?"

Sara threw her arms up in exasperation. "Why are you acting so weird?"

Virginia had stood up then and approached her picket fence. Mr. Hoffman had stopped on the sidewalk where he was walking his poodle. Both stared at Alek with an intensity that solidified his belief in Jordan's words.

Alek tugged Sara's sleeve and headed north. He had no choice but to take her with him. "I'm not. Come on, then."

Sara moved up the sidewalk with him, but slowly, almost reluctantly. They'd moved two blocks before Alek felt eyes on him, almost burning their gaze into his back. Glancing as casually as he could manage over his right shoulder, he noticed Mr. Hoffman following from about a block away.

He was pulling back on his poodle's leash as it barked and showed its teeth in a way that Alek had never seen it do before. Behind Mr. Hoffman by a matter of steps was Virginia, who had seemed so kind and caring just a few minutes before he'd set foot in Jordan's house. But there was no kindness in her face now. Misery had changed with the mention of a single word: *nothing*.

"Alek, slow down!"

Sara was jogging beside him now. Alek hadn't even realized that he'd instinctively picked up his pace. But he couldn't slow down, couldn't face whatever it was that Virginia and Mr. Hoffman had planned for him.

As he reached the final street block at the foot of the hill, Sara panting behind him, he dared a glance over his shoulder again. Several more townspeople were hurrying to his current location, none of them looking happy at all. Mr. Whirly was bringing up the rear. Alek couldn't be sure, but he thought he saw a large gray crow circling overhead. But the hill was right there! He was so close to freedom, so close to being safe. He turned back to the hill with a determined breath. And a familiar hand fell on his left shoulder.

Alek turned to face Sara. She was still his best friend, still the girl he told everything to, and why should this be any different? Yet as he opened his mouth to explain, his eyes met with hers. Only her eyes were different now. They sparkled like glass in the sun. Her eyes were that of the crow's from the fountain. Because she was a part of Misery as much as it was. Her mouth contorted into a maniacal grin. "You can't leave us, Alek. You can't ever leave us."

A familiar voice—Jordan's voice, though he couldn't see her from where he was standing—shouted, "Run, Alek! Run for your life!"

Alek screamed and bolted up the hill. Behind him, he

could hear the townspeople scrambling after him, but he couldn't look back. He didn't want to see what was coming, couldn't bear to see what had happened to his friends, his neighbors. He ran, digging his sneakers into the soft earth, and at last he reached the crest of the enormous hill. He hurried over its peak to the other side.

He was there! He was free!

But as he leaned forward on his knees to catch his breath, a moment of utter terror hit him.

His hands. His hands, which should have been on his knees, were gone. Invisible. Disappeared. They were nothing, and that nothingness was quickly moving up his arms. He was fading, and fast. Tears poured down his cheeks and he shouted into the sky, "Nooooo!!! I made it! I made it!"

Alek fell to his knees, which he could no longer see, and waited for something to happen—for Misery to consume him, or for his nothingness to be completed. His heart pounded in terror. In the distance, on the side of the hill facing away from town, he saw a flash of something. It was probably the crow's eye, he mused.

Only . . . it was something purple. Bright purple. A color, unlike anything at all in the town of Misery. Then there was another flash. This time orange. Then pink. Then red.

And then Alek stopped caring that he was disappearing, because a memory slipped back into his mind. A memory of colors and warmth and joy. It was a memory of home, his home before Misery. He recalled his family, his neighbors, and the way that life had been. Life—that's what it had been. Not the place between lives, the way that Misery was. After all, he recalled, that was what Misery was—a place where people went between their actual lives.

And now, he was going home.

The Mind Is a Powerful Thing

MATT DE LA PEÑA

Joanna's sixteenth birthday celebration kicked off at a small apartment in West L.A. where her and her girls always went to pre-party. It was Joanna, Tessa, Kelly, Laura and Tessa's Auntie Helen, who owned the apartment. After devouring some cheap Chinese in the tiny kitchen, they gathered in the living room on metal folding chairs where they sipped out of plastic cups filled with red wine from a box. Power 106 played on the radio in the background. Everyone was talking excitedly about heading to Campos later to celebrate Joanna's sweet sixteen—everyone except Joanna, that is. Joanna was staring at the ominous fortune she'd just pulled out of her cookie:

"The Hour Has Finally Arrived."

Fear slowly spread through her veins, because she knew exactly what it meant.

Someone would be hurt tonight—most likely Joanna herself.

Her brain had always worked this way, immediately jumping to the darkest of possibilities. She was obsessed with news shows about forced entries, kidnappings, brutal killings and serial rapes. Every night she'd rig her bedroom window with old CD cases so they'd come crashing down if someone tried to break in. She lined up empty bottles in front of her bedroom door. First thing she'd done when she got her last cell was program 911 into every speed-dial setting. Her dreams were all nightmares filled with dark basements and slowly creaking doors and hulking men in ski masks—and coming home to her ground-floor apartment in Mar Vista one night only to find her mom and little sister massacred on the living room rug.

A message carved into their naked corpses:

We'll be back for you, Joanna!

Joanna tried to shake herself from these thoughts. She'd step outside for a quick smoke to calm her nerves, but she was trying to quit. She took a big sip of wine instead, slipped the folded fortune into her pocket and rejoined the conversation. Her girls were now talking about what they always talked about before they went out together: how wack the dudes at school were.

"I can promise you this," Kelly said. "Things were different back when we were freshmen."

Everyone agreed.

"The seniors were way more mature. You remember Miguel Davies, right?"

Joanna did. She'd never met the guy personally, but she could still picture him cruising outside the quad with his boys.

"He looked good and he was funny," Kelly said, "but he also knew how to be around girls. Remember how he'd never let you walk on the traffic side of the sidewalk?"

"What happened to Miguel anyways?" Tessa said.

Kelly shrugged.

Joanna swallowed another sip of wine, said: "Didn't he go into the army? Maybe he got deployed or whatever."

"It's depressing," Kelly sighed. "They're all a bunch of wannabe gangsters now. You know dumbass Ricky got himself a gun last week, right?"

A gun? Joanna's eyes widened as she thought of her fortune.

Technically, Ricky was still Kelly's boyfriend. But for the past two months he'd been "dumbass Ricky" and she'd been going on and on to Joanna about how she was over him. Ricky didn't take his future seriously enough. He was too jealous. He never did anything sweet anymore, like show up at her door with flowers. Instead of breaking up with him, though, like Joanna suggested, Kelly had started seeing some new kid on the side. A skater type they all referred to as "Marcus from Venice."

And now Ricky had a gun? This could be really, really bad. She fingered the pack of cigarettes in her bag.

"What's Ricky need a heater for?" Helen asked.

"He claims it's for 'protection,'" Kelly said, doing air quotes.

"Either they're packing heat like Ricky," Laura said, "or they're geeky mama's boys. There's no in between no more."

More nodding from the girls.

Joanna pushed Ricky out of her head and pictured her best friend, Ronny. He wasn't a wannabe gangster, that was for sure. Never tried to act hard. Didn't even have a single tattoo. In fact, the only time Joanna felt halfway safe in her own bed was when she was talking to Ronny on the phone—back when hers was still working. She'd huddle under the covers, make him stay on the line until she fell asleep. She woke up most mornings with her cell still pinned against her ear.

"Just talk," she remembered telling him during their first marathon conversation, almost a year ago.

"About what?" he'd said.

"Anything. Your day at school. Stupid World of Warcraft. Whatever you want."

It went quiet on the phone for a few long seconds, Ronny probably second-guessing why he'd wanna be friends with a schizo like Joanna in the first place. Finally he said: "I don't get it, Jo. Why watch all those crime shows if they're just gonna freak you out?"

"So I can be prepared, okay? Girls gotta learn all the things that could happen so we understand the warning signs."

A few more seconds of dead air.

"Yo, Ronny," she said into the phone. "You hang up I'm just gonna call your ass right back."

"You shouldn't fixate on that stuff," Ronny told her. "Some people believe the kind of energy you put out into the universe is the same kind you'll get back. You ever heard of a book called *The Secret*?"

Joanna laughed right into the receiver. "Look at Mr. Hot Yoga all of a sudden."

"I'm serious, though. It's like a self-fulfilling prophecy."

"I didn't realize I was on the line with Deepak Chopra."

She could hear Ronny start chuckling, too. That's when she knew they were gonna be tight.

After a few seconds Ronny cleared his throat, said: "You at least know you're crazy, though, right, Jo?"

"Rather be crazy and alive," she told him, "than some stable bitch who gets sliced up by a serial killer."

Somebody's cell went off.

Joanna knew it wasn't hers, because the piece of crap in her bag had died a week ago. She'd been saving up babysitting money to get a new one, but she probably had another month to go, two or three if she wanted one of those iPhones. But could she really wait *three months* to get back to her and Ronny's nighttime conversations?

Joanna watched Kelly check the screen of her phone, roll her eyes and hit mute.

Auntie Helen started talking about back in her own high school days, but Joanna was still stuck on Ronny. A couple weeks back he'd asked if they could have a talk. Turned out he wanted to be more than friends. They already hung out all the time, he explained as he walked her home from school. Both in person and on the phone. And it's not like they were seeing other people. And what if he told her he was developing feelings? The next-level kind?

Joanna ducked out of the conversation by saying she needed time to think.

Since then she was always making mental lists of pros and cons.

Ronny definitely wasn't the gun-carrying type, Joanna told herself, sipping more wine. *Thank God!* But it's not like he was a mama's boy either. In fact, his real mom passed three years ago from complications with her diabetes. Ronny stayed with a family friend now, some landscaper guy named Jessie and his wheelchair wife—both were super nice whenever she called their landline. Ronny could also be funny sometimes. Knew all Chris Rock's standup bits by heart.

The only thing with Ronny, Joanna decided, was he

had a little geek in him. Didn't play sports. Never been in a fight. Spent entire days locked inside his tiny bedroom playing World of Warcraft, barking nonsense into his ridiculous headset like: "Nuñez, make sure you buff everyone with horn of winter," and "All right, guys, just remember. No DPS until five sunders are up. Got it?"

Whatever *that* shit meant.

But Ronny was cute. And he had good hair. And maybe for Joanna to actually feel safe around a guy, he needed to be a little geeky.

Auntie Helen was now showing pictures on her phone. Retro shots of her in a prom dress and her leaning against a school wall with her hair all gelled up like a chola. Everyone was cracking up.

"Oh, my God," Laura said. "They're totally in black-and-white, too."

"For artistic purposes. I'm not *that* old."

"Wait," Tessa said, standing up in her excitement. "Tell them what we figured out last Saturday. When we were walking around the Apple store at the Promenade."

Helen rolled her eyes, said: "Tess likes to get hung up on little details."

"Check it out," Tessa said to everybody else. "There was no such thing as email when my auntie was in high school. Can you even believe that shit? No email!"

"Like, it wasn't invented yet?" Kelly said.

Laura nearly fell out of her chair she was laughing so hard.

Helen was in her early thirties and had recently left her husband. Joanna suspected domestic abuse. For the past few weeks Helen had been letting the girls come over to her new apartment to pre-party. "I know you guys are gonna drink anyway," she said whenever she held open her screen door for them. "Might as well be here where I can chaperone."

In private, Tessa claimed her auntie was just lonely.

"Watch," Helen said, walking over to the box of wine for a refill. "Once you graduate high school, time flies by. One day you guys'll wake up and be in your thirties, too."

"Yeah," Tessa said, "and you'll be a wrinkled-ass geriatric."

They all cracked up, including Helen, who said: "Touché." She poured herself another cup of wine and sat back down. "Seriously, though, tonight isn't about Yahoo dot com. It's about Joanna turning sixteen."

Everybody nodded and turned to Joanna.

Laura raised her wine, said: "To the birthday girl."

They all tapped cups and drank.

Joanna knew the wine was already hitting her hard, because she couldn't stop picturing Ricky with his gun. And she kept connecting the gun to the words from her fortune cookie: "The Hour Has Finally Arrived." She made herself smile to her girls, even laugh a little, but secretly her heart was beating out of control.

Kelly's cell went off again on the car ride to Campos Tacos.

Joanna watched her check the screen and turn it off, slip it back in her bag. "That Ricky who keeps calling?" she asked from the backseat.

Kelly shrugged.

Joanna peered into the wine cup in her lap. Because Ricky was out of town, Marcus from Venice was supposedly stopping by Campos Tacos tonight to meet all the girls for the first time. But why'd Ricky keep calling? Joanna had a bad feeling about it. She looked up, told Kelly: "Just watch yourself, girl."

"Ricky's all the way in Oxnard," Kelly said. "With his family. You need to stop stressing so much, Jo."

"Right?" Tessa said. "All Joanna thinks about is aggravated assault and shit."

"Excuse me for worrying about the guy who carries a concealed weapon."

"Real life isn't one of your crime shows, Jo."

"You all need to wake up," Joanna said, snapping her fingers. "According to this crime site I found, last year almost two thousand women were murdered by their man. You know that's like three per day, right?"

Laura nearly spit out her wine in the backseat. "Did she just throw down a bibliography?"

"You like that?" Joanna said. "How about this one: Every two minutes someone in the U.S. is sexually assaulted. Every *two minutes*!"

"Come on, Jo," Tessa said. "It's your birthday celebration. Why you trying to bring everybody down?"

"You think about one thing as much as you do," Laura said, "it's more likely to come true."

Joanna shook her head. Now *everyone* was sounding like Ronny.

"Why you think I concentrate so much about getting skinny?" Tessa said.

"The mind is a powerful thing," Helen added from behind the wheel.

But Joanna wasn't done. "And sixty-six percent of those assaults—guess who they're committed by, Kel. Someone who *knows* the victim."

Kelly tapped Tessa on the shoulder. "Can somebody please explain to me why she's bringing up sexual assault?"

Tessa shrugged. "Maybe 'cause she's *Looney Tunes*?"

They were all staring at Joanna as Helen pulled the Camry

into the mostly empty Campos parking lot. Joanna knew she was taking it too far, that everyone just wanted to have fun on their Friday night, her birthday. But they didn't understand it like she did. The data clearly showed that they, too, would be affected by a violent crime at some point in their lives. Either as a victim or a witness. Helen had already dealt with spousal abuse. Joanna would bet money on it. Why else was she being so quiet in the driver's seat? But at least she'd lived through it. Would Joanna, Tessa, Laura and Kelly be so lucky?

As everybody climbed out of the car and slammed their doors closed, Joanna thought about her fortune again. What if the hour really *had* arrived? What if this was it?

She already regretted leaving her bag with her smokes in the car.

"You know what we *wanna* hear about, right?" Laura said, after Willy, the owner of Campos Tacos, seated them at their usual table inside the main dining area, the one against the window overlooking the entire parking lot.

"I believe I do," Kelly said.

"So? Does Marcus have any cute Venice friends?"

Kelly got a big smile on her face and nodded. "Single, too."

"Single like *you're* single?" Joanna said picking up her menu.

"Here we go," Tessa said, rolling her eyes.

"You know what, Joanna?" Kelly's smile had disappeared. "If I want your judgment, I'll ask for it. Okay?"

"Who's judging?" Joanna said, laying her menu back down. "I'm just saying, Ricky's really jealous, right? And now you tell us he's carrying a gun? Say he finds out—"

"What's he gonna find out?" Kelly interrupted. "He's not even in L.A."

"Everything's not just about you!" Joanna said, pounding a fist on the table. "You're putting us all in danger!"

Kelly stared at Joanna in total shock. Then a sarcastic grin slowly spread across her face. "You wanna worry about someone," she said, "maybe you should start worrying about your little puppy dog boyfriend."

Joanna gave Kelly a blank look. "Who, Ronny? Me and him aren't even together."

"You think it's healthy how he follows you all around, Jo? Every single place you go?"

"Okay," Laura said. "That's enough, you guys. Everybody just chill the hell out."

But Joanna was too pissed to chill out. "You should leave Ronny out of this," she said, pointing at Kelly. "He's the nicest friend I've ever had!"

Kelly chuckled a little, picking up her menu. "Obsessed people do strange things," she muttered. "Even the supposedly nice ones."

Laura leaned forward and got in both of their faces. "I'm serious! That's enough out of you two! Jeez!"

They all went quiet for a minute, watching the busboy set down their waters. Joanna couldn't believe Kelly, though, bringing up Ronny like that. Saying they were together when she knew it wasn't true. Joanna was fuming. Why had she left her stupid cigarettes in the stupid car?

Soon as the busboy left, Tessa said sarcastically, "Wow, you guys. I'm really in the mood to party now."

"Right?" Laura said.

Helen pushed back her chair and stood up. "Look," she said. "Jo may be a little bit of a *Dateline* freak. But she's our girl, right? And tonight's her sweet sixteen. Now who's gonna sing 'Happy Birthday' with me?"

Joanna followed Helen's eyes to the restaurant owner,

Willy, who was coming out of the kitchen with a chocolate cake. It took her a couple seconds to realize the cake was for her, and then her mood instantly changed.

"There's the birthday girl!" Willy said. "Your friends, they stop by this afternoon. Help bake this specially for you." He set the cake on the table. The white icing spelled *Happy Birthday Joanna!* He flicked a match, lit the first candle, then used that candle to light the rest.

"Oh, my God," Joanna said, feeling her anger disappear. She turned to her girls. "You guys made it homemade?"

They all smiled and reached across the table to hug Joanna, one at a time. Even Kelly, who whispered in her ear: "You frustrate the shit out of me sometimes, Jo. But you know I love you, right?"

"I love you, too," Joanna whispered back. And she genuinely meant it. She loved all her girls. Maybe it was partly the alcohol, but she found herself fighting back tears.

As everyone sang for her, Joanna stared at the sixteen little flames and thought about Ronny. Maybe he really was obsessed. He didn't have many other friends—unless you counted people from his video game, who were probably twelve. And he *did* send Joanna like fifty texts a day. And what about the big talk he kept wanting to finish?

Wait a second, Joanna thought, swaying a little from the wine. Was Ronny actually dangerous? Why had she never thought of this before?

After polishing off the cake, the girls sipped "virgin" daiquiris (which they'd spiked under the table with miniature bottles of rum) and talked and watched the parking lot start filling up outside. Joanna was beyond buzzed now. But it was her birthday. Her sweet sixteen. You were supposed to be buzzed the night you turned sixteen. And it felt like a celebration again, because everybody was back to being friends. She'd even managed to quit stressing about Ricky's gun and Ronny's possible obsession.

After the busboy cleared their plates, Willy shocked everybody by bringing out tequila shots "on the house." He put a finger to his lips before passing them out and told everyone: "This happened never, you understand?"

Joanna clinked glasses with all her girls and downed the shot in one go, and they all sucked on lime wedges and looked around at each other, cringing and grinning.

That was when things started to blur for Joanna.

Thoughts spinning just beyond her grasp.

Marcus from Venice and a couple of his boys suddenly appeared inside the restaurant. They were pulling up chairs and sitting with the girls. Kelly wasn't lying, they all looked good in that Vans-wearing, skaterish way—especially Marcus. Hooded sweatshirts and baggy jeans, chains connecting wallets to belt loops. But at the same time, they looked sort of rough, too. Marcus had the Venice Beach zip code tattooed on the side of his neck. One of his boys had a jagged pink scar under his right eye, like he'd recently been knifed. Joanna wondered how well Kelly even knew these guys. Before she realized what was happening, she had started chanting her fortune to herself, over and over: *The hour has finally arrived the hour has finally arrived the hour has finally arrived the hour has finally . . .*

She only stopped when Kelly got up and sat next to her.

"I'm sorry about earlier," Kelly was saying in a low voice. "I actually like Ronny. I just wished you supported my decisions, Jo. Even when they're not exactly perfect."

"You honestly think he might be obsessed, though?" Joanna asked.

"Who, Ronny?" Kelly smiled and shook her head. "Nah,

I think he just really, really likes you. Probably every girl secretly wishes her man liked her that much."

But Kelly's eyes told a different story.

They shouted: *You're the only one who doesn't see it, Joanna! Ronny's extremely dangerous! He's on his way to a life of violent crime! If you don't get away now, you'll be his first victim!*

Joanna was about to ask Kelly how she knew, but Kelly was pulled into a conversation with Marcus. So Joanna just sat there swaying, eyes all bugged, jonesing for a smoke to calm her nerves. She suddenly remembered an old *20/20* special about a guy who worked in a bank. He seemed normal enough to all his coworkers. Dressed like a regular guy, always said hi in the halls. Nobody had any idea about his secret obsession with a blond coworker. One night he followed the woman home after their shift together, snuck into her parking garage and grabbed her by the hair near the stairwell. After a brief struggle, he stabbed her forty-seven times. The whole thing was caught on a surveillance camera. According to reports, when the cops arrived on the scene, the man was just sitting by the woman's body, rocking back and forth. He admitted to everything. When they asked why he did it, tears began streaming down his face. He loved her, he said. With all his heart. Nobody would ever love her the way he did.

In the middle of remembering the mug shot of the man that flashed across her TV screen, Joanna glanced out the restaurant window. What she saw made her drop her daiquiri glass and scream.

It was Ronny.

Staring in at her.

"Jesus, Jo," Tessa said, looking down at the shattered glass. "Are you completely wasted?"

Joanna pointed out the window where Ronny was

standing alone, holding a paper-bagged bottle and a bouquet of flowers. He grinned and gave a little wave.

Joanna knew in that moment that her life was in jeopardy.

"It's just Ronny," Tessa said.

Joanna turned to look at her. "He was supposed to wait till I called." She was paralyzed with fear. She couldn't focus her eyes.

"Yo, is she okay?" one of the Venice guys said to Kelly.

"You should go talk to him, Jo," Laura said.

Joanna's heart pounded as she pushed back from the table and got up. She stumbled past the hostess stand and approached the front door thinking of the Chinese fortune folded in her pocket. The hour really *had* arrived. Finally. 'Cause maybe this had always been her destiny. To become a *Dateline* special, a case that girls all over the country would watch in terror. She imagined the reenacted parts as she pushed through the door. The actress had to be strong, though. That seemed important. Which meant Joanna would have to be strong from this moment on.

Ronny was on one knee in front of the restaurant, holding out the flowers. "For the beautiful birthday girl," he said with his sociopath smile. How had she never noticed this before?

Joanna snatched the flowers out of his hand, said: "What are you doing here?"

"I got you a gift, too, Jo. It's in my ride."

"What ride?"

"Jessie let me borrow the Durango. Him and his wife say happy birthday, too, by the way."

Joanna was spinning from the booze. She had to lean against the wall to stay upright. But she wouldn't let Ronny think she was scared. "I was supposed to call you," she barked. "After I hung out with my friends—"

"I know, I know," Ronny said. "But I had to at least drop off the flowers."

She looked at them for the first time. Pink and white roses. Didn't this color combo symbolize murder?

"But you don't get the gift until later," he said. "That's the surprise part."

"Oh, that's what you're calling it now?" Joanna said. "My *surprise*?"

Ronny looked confused. "What are you talking about, Jo?"

She pointed at the paper-bagged bottle by his feet. "And what's going on there? You don't even drink."

Ronny reached down, slid the bottle out of the bag. Grape soda. "Look," he said. "I'm not trying to cut in on girl time. Go have fun and text me when you're ready to head home. I'll just take a walk or something."

Joanna could see right through Ronny's little act. How had she not noticed any of this before? The shifty eyes. The way he nervously played with the small hole in his Raiders sweatshirt. God, she'd almost agreed to be his girlfriend. She glanced out toward the parking lot, saw the Durango. She definitely wasn't getting in no car with Ronny.

He gave her a little salute and turned to take off. He only made it a couple steps, though, before he spun back around, said: "Try not to drink too much, Jo. I was thinking we could finish our talk on the way home. About me and you."

Joanna stood there, swaying, heart racing.

And if he didn't get the answer he wanted? Was that when he'd pull the knife from the glove box? Drive it into one of her vital organs?

As she watched Ronny walk out of the parking lot, she could already hear the voice-over for her *Dateline* episode saying: *And then the victim made what proved to be a fatal mistake.*

She followed young Ronny Muñoz back to the borrowed Durango to retrieve a promised birthday gift. Less than twenty-four hours later, Joanna Garcia of Mar Vista, California, would be buried alive in a remote northeast corner of Runyon Canyon Park.

Joanna stumbled back into the restaurant just as everyone else was filing out. "Come on," Laura said, "we're all getting fresh air."

Joanna swayed as she watched everybody move past her, toward the parking lot. Laura, Marcus from Venice and his boys, Kelly. Tessa stopped to ask if everything was okay. Joanna wanted so badly to tell her about Ronny. How she was scared of him for the first time in her life. How she was considering whether or not to call the cops now, before he had a chance to do anything. But she was afraid if she let out even one word, she'd start sobbing. And that wasn't how she wanted people to remember her.

"Girl, go get yourself some water," Tessa said. "You're not looking super stable. Helen will help, she's still in there talking to Willy."

Joanna only made it a few steps inside the restaurant before she heard arguing coming from the kitchen. Sounded like Helen and Willy. To be sure, she checked their table by the window. Nobody. Then she heard a loud crashing sound in the kitchen.

Joanna stood there stunned.

Maybe this was the crime she sensed was coming. Maybe Willy was in there hurting Helen. Joanna had read on the Internet how common it was for women to go from one abusive relationship to another. She had to save Helen.

Joanna marched toward the kitchen, pushed through the saloon doors. It was Helen and Willy, all right, but they weren't fighting. They were making out on one of the kitchen counters, surrounded by scattered slices of lime.

When Helen looked up, Joanna took off.

She was so confused. And so drunk. She stumbled back to their table by the window and sat down to think. She was more convinced than ever something awful was going to happen. She just didn't know what. And she didn't know where to look or who to keep an eye on. Maybe she was wrong about Ronny. Like she was wrong about Helen and Willy. She pulled out her fortune and read it again. "The hour has finally arrived." The words seemed to swim around on the slip of paper, like they were alive.

She shoved the fortune into her mouth.

Maybe if she swallowed it whole she'd get rid of its power. But that was too crazy, so she pulled it from her mouth and held it over the candle flame, watched it slowly catch fire and then twist and shrink into blackness.

The embers reminded Joanna of her cigarettes, and she reached into Helen's bag for the car keys. Even though her stomach was off, and the room was spinning, she had to have something to calm her down. If she was still alive tomorrow, she'd throw away the pack.

Just as she stood up with Helen's keys, though, she heard screeching tires in the parking lot. Through the window she saw Ricky's tricked-out Civic.

Her heart climbed into her throat.

She had it right from the beginning. Ricky and his gun. Marcus from Venice and his thugged-out friends. Suddenly things grew clear for Joanna. She had to save Kelly's life.

She raced out into the parking lot as Ricky revved his engine and inched toward Kelly and Marcus. His tinted windows were all down. Hip-hop thumped on his system.

"No!" Joanna shouted, but her words were drowned out by the rattling bass.

"Yo, Kelly," Joanna heard Ricky shout out his car window. "Who's this guy supposed to be? You think I'm stupid?"

Soon as Joanna saw the look in Ricky's eyes, she understood.

Her entire life had been moving toward this very moment. She didn't faint like she always thought she might. In fact, she grew stronger. And things slowed way down, like she was seeing everything before it happened.

She knew Laura would rush over to tell Kelly, and she knew Tessa would duck behind a black SUV. She knew Marcus would let go of Kelly's hand and shout back at Ricky. She knew Willy would come flying out of the restaurant holding his cell phone, screaming for everyone to leave before he called the cops. But most of all, Joanna knew she'd sprint over to Kelly, grab her by the arm and start pulling her toward Helen's car.

She hurriedly unlocked the passenger door, shoved Kelly into the bucket seat, then raced around to the driver's side and dove in and started the engine.

All she knew was she had to get Kelly away from danger.

Fast as she could.

Before Ricky could pull his gun and fire on her out of jealousy.

Kelly was sobbing and shouting at Joanna to slow down, but now was not the time for conversation. Joanna flipped the car into reverse and jerked it out of the tight parking space, then gunned it for the lot's only exit. Just as she was pulling into the road, though, she had to slam on the brakes. But the car didn't stop fast enough and she plowed right into a pedestrian.

The last thing Joanna saw before cracking her forehead against the steering wheel column was Ronny's terrified face.

• • •

When Joanna came to, she was on a stretcher, surrounded by cops and paramedics. Her friends were all holding each other and they looked like they'd been crying. Kelly was there. She was okay. Over Kelly's head, Joanna saw the slow spinning lights of multiple cop cars.

Then she saw Ronny.

There was a huge gash on the side of his face and his head was taped down to the stretcher so he couldn't move. His right pant leg was covered in blood. Joanna's heart broke. She'd run over the one person who made her feel safe. How could she have ever thought he had bad intentions? Two paramedics were wheeling him toward the open doors of an ambulance.

"Wait," Ronny said as they passed Joanna.

The paramedics slowed to a stop.

Joanna's head was still in a fog from the booze, and from the accident, but she clearly saw Ronny trying to reach for the bulge in his right pocket. He couldn't get his hand down far enough, though, because of the way he was secured in the stretcher, so one of the paramedics had to help. The man reached into Ronny's pocket and pulled out a wrapped package. He asked what he should do with it, and Ronny motioned toward Joanna.

The man placed the package on Joanna's stretcher, then they loaded Ronny onto the ambulance and drove off.

People were leaning over Joanna, asking questions. Cops with their notebooks and paramedics. Her friends. Auntie Helen. But Joanna couldn't focus. Her forehead was throbbing where it had slammed against the steering wheel. And the world was still spinning. She managed to pick up the package and pull apart the poor wrapping job. And when she saw what it was, she immediately started sobbing.

They wheeled her toward a second ambulance. Two paramedics lifted her stretcher and slid her toward the back, and one of them hopped in with her. The last thing Joanna saw before they closed the doors was the paramedic handing the iPhone box Ronny had given her to Tessa, who looked at it and then looked at Joanna, tears running down her cheeks.

Joanna was still crying, too, as the doors shut out all the outside sound. She felt the engine start, and she stared at the blurry ambulance ceiling, imagining the fortune that would be imprinted in her mind forever: "The hour has finally arrived."

It had taken running Ronny over in a car to understand what those words actually meant. Not that she would be hurt, but that it was time for her to stop pretending. She'd wanted to be Ronny's girl all along. And tonight she was supposed to tell him. On her birthday.

She shouted his name. "Ronny!"

Again and again she called for him.

But nobody could hear her.

And nobody could take back what she had done.

The Chosen One

SAUNDRA MITCHELL

I suppose there's nothing to distinguish Vernal, except that it's my home, and it has a prophecy. It starts like this:

> *There will come a day when Evil will pierce the Heart of the Green City. Questing through wilds and dark and peril, the Light-Forged Champion alone shall claim the Fabled Cup and restore the kingdom's Heart, and with it, all our joy. Praise Vara.*

There are also bits about three flaming witches, the Breathless Reaches, and an Earthenwork Defiler. It doesn't sound like much, does it? Though admittedly, it only rhymes in the original tongue.

Nevertheless.

Like Vernal, there's little to distinguish me, except that I am myself and no one else can claim that.

My father is the king, my half-sister, the crown princess:

respectively, the head of the kingdom and its burgeoning heart. I am nothing. I rolled out of the wrong side of His Majesty's sheets. Consequently, I can't be acknowledged, but neither can I be entirely ignored.

I'm close to the court, but not in it; cared for but never coddled. The king is a wise man and knows enough to walk a balance with me. I have nothing to resent, and I never feel entitled to anything more than the pleasant position I have: my sister's bed mistress. I dress her hair and hear her secrets, and I love her completely.

Everything about her is exquisite, from her coiled black hair to her curved ankles. Likewise her voice of spices and honey, which she uses to beckon me.

"Corvina—"

I glance over my shoulder, still busy polishing her bronze mirror. It takes a fine touch—too much sand and the face will go hazy. Too much acid and it will go dark. "Yes, Lucia?"

With a smile, and a net made of her dark lashes, she casts for me. "Come sit awhile. Come talk."

"Oh no, I can't. I'm slaving for you," I say, with my own smile.

"I'll rub your feet."

I put the mirror aside and turn, scrubbing my hands clean on a cloth. Though I pretend reluctance, I have my sandals half-off before I reach her side.

"If you insist," I say, and sprawl in her linens.

And she does, the crown princess of Vernal, rub my feet. She's quite good at it, and cheerful, too. Hints of lavender and orrisroot waft around me, perfume from the herbs folded into the mattress. I taste bliss, and sigh with it.

"Yes, sweet?" she prompts.

I curl a hand over my head and beam at her. "Perfect."

Lighting with that, Lucia doubles her effort and resists

the temptation to tickle. Over my toes, she peeks at me and whispers, "I've figured out my Betrothal Quest."

"Then tell me."

"It will be a Decade of Conversations," she says. She digs her thumbs into the arch of my foot, on purpose, I think, just to make me collapse. She's pleased with herself, all but humming now.

Melting in dozy pleasure, I smile at the canopy and tell her, "Somehow, I don't think Father's going to let ten years pass before you pick a consort."

"I knew I should have used another word," she mutters. "What I mean is, I'll choose my suitors, and they'll each have to have ten conversations with me."

Teasing, I say, "Last one standing takes your hand?"

"Hush." She flicks me, just hard enough that her fingers snap against my heel. "They're supposed to take clues away from our talks. After all ten, they'll go questing for the thing that will win my hand."

I lift my head again. "And what thing is that?"

"Whatever I like. A perfect quince from Queen Vatia's garden. A Lycean bone spoon. I don't know. It doesn't matter." She shrugs. "Because I'll tell nine of them, 'Good luck unraveling my clues. Go forth and seek my prize!'"

Warming all over, I push onto my elbows. I see precisely where she's gone with this, and it couldn't amuse me more. "Then your favorite you'll tell to fetch a Lycean bone spoon, and be quick about it."

"Exactly. It seems like it rewards cleverness, and you know how Father admires that."

I tug the ribbons on her sleeves. "So you know, I admire *you.*"

"Flattery gets you nothing," she says, but then her hands still. The weight between us shifts, heavier as something troubles her. With a halfhearted squeeze, she asks, "Will you come with me?"

The weight lifts, at least from me. If she weren't so entirely serious, I'd joke with her—bother her with demands and impish conditions. But this matters; it's written in the depths of her eyes and the set of her lips.

Quickly, I say, "Yes, of course."

"In my court," she promises, "you'll be allowed to do what you please."

What she means it that she'd let me get married. All the stars in Lucia's eyes are for romance, though I suppose she'd let me become a sea captain or an oratrix or actress, if I really wished it.

Still, for her, it comes back to love, always love. It doesn't matter that the accident left me with no eyelashes to bat, no eyebrows to darken with kohl. She couldn't care less that I'm bald and mostly earless and mottled. I look like a brown egg, oblong and unnatural. Yet, in her mind, I am her lovely little sister; any suitor would be lucky to have me. Her stars leave her blind.

No one else shares that sentiment; no one knows that better than I. I'm seventeen, the king's bastard daughter. My mouth is unscarred, and my lips full—but no one's ever tried to kiss me, not even for machination's sake. The rest is too disturbing to try.

Most days, I wind scarlet silk around my head, to give the impression that I might have hair. That way I merely startle people coming and not going. I can't help that. I'm melted and molten; I don't like it, but that's my face.

Nothing will change it.

But because Lucia believes the only thing keeping me from romance is our father's strategies, I loop my arms around her and press my forehead to her temple. She's been eating candied quince again. I smell it when she sighs and shifts her weight into me.

"It's a kind thought," I say. "But hush now."

"I mean that," she insists. "You can do anything you like."

Petting her, I swear, "I already do."

My sister has been poisoned.

Or cursed, or taken ill—none of the royal physicians agree. I stand at her bed, bathing her fevered brow with ginger water, and try not to resent each expert for being stupider than the last.

"It's all wolves," Lucia says. She turns her face toward my hand. A thick, raised rash spreads over her body—she looks like a coal crusted with fire and ash.

"There are no wolves," I answer.

Lips parting, Lucia begs soundlessly. A dark halo of sweat outlines her body, her trembling hands clawing at the covers. Mindlessly, she pushes them off, then keens for them once they're gone. I feed her water from my fingertips, and shudder at the sensation of her leather tongue rasping for more.

My beloved sister has fallen, and the physicians argue amongst themselves. None comfort her but me, so I start over again with the cloth: bathing her face, her chest, her searing arms and hands.

Our father arrives, and Cilo barely bows before saying, "It's quite possibly hysterics, my lord. To fall ill on the eve of naming her quest, surely it's nerves."

Praise Vara, our father dismisses that with a waved hand. "Ridiculous. Laenus? Gemella?"

The eldest of the three, Laenus relies on that seniority to add gravity to his diagnosis. He tugs his white beard and pronounces, "Poison. Yesterday, she was fit and well; today, struck down and out of her head. It's too sudden to be anything but malfeasance."

"All due honor to my mentor," Gemella says, cutting a look at Laenus that says she'd prefer not to honor him at all, "she's burning with fever and beset with the scale. We've had word that villages in the outer provinces have seen the same of late. Either there's a spree of poisonings—"

Wrapping himself in a decided chill, Laenus shakes his head. "Augusta Lucia hardly spends her days scrabbling with wild animals and dung fields. You cannot compare unlike cases."

"She *is* mortal, you dolt."

I say that.

No one expects it. Until then, I am invisible. A servant, actually busy at my task and minded by no one. Now Laenus minds me quite a bit, though Father seems unperturbed by my outburst.

Seeing her chance to win the diagnosis, Gemella tightens a wrap around her shoulders. "Certainly, Laenus should offer a bezoar against poison. But Her Majesty *is* mortal. What harm can come of treating this as illness, as well?"

Father nods. "I agree. Make all due haste."

The doctors file out, muttering among themselves. And to my surprise, Father reaches for the bowl in my hands. Once his gaze falls to Lucia's face, it doesn't raise again. He dips the cloth and squeezes it, wiping new sweat from her brow.

"She's never been ill," he says. He settles, bound by shadows, at her side. "*You* were always the uncertain one. You caught every little pox, it seemed, and then the fire . . ."

Suddenly, my feet ache from standing; my head hurts from too much upset. Folding my hands, I say, "I'm sorry."

"Don't apologize, Corvina. Children get sick. Accidents happen."

He dips the cloth again, and the light catches on the silver streaks in his black curls. For a moment, I'm confused by them. My father has always been the king; kings are strong and young.

But I newly realize that his youth is just an impression. In truth, he is growing older, and his voice is vulnerable when he says, "But they must not die before their father does. Promise me you won't."

I'm much too surprised to say anything more than, "I won't."

"We'll make sure Lucia promises when she's well again."

The ground beneath me shifts ever so slightly. The tenderness in his hands I find remarkable. They have done this work before; he doesn't shift uneasily. He's not guessing how to tend Lucia, he *knows*. And he's just said that she's never been the sickly sort—not like her mother, Vara bless our death-kept queen.

I don't know that my father has ever *said* he loved me, but it seems he's been doing just that all along.

This weighs on me, but I cannot consider it too deeply. There are dragon's galls to be forced down Lucia's throat, and willow bark tea to be poured after them. I make a hundred compresses if I make ten. Well after dark each night, I harvest ice from the straw pit in the atrium and pack it into her bed.

She cries, and I cry, and none of it makes any difference. The physicians still argue: it's magic, it's disease, it's a sanguine fever—no, a consumptive one—no matter, the cures are all the same now. Bloodletting and cinnamon tonics. Cinnamon poultices and more bloodletting. Her chambers stink of both and I'll never eat a sweet bun again.

The seizures come; the rumors start. The physicians retreat, for the crown princess is dying, and no one wants to bear the responsibility for that. No one dares approach my father, who has made camp at Lucia's side. He's consumed with grief in anticipation.

This is why it wounds me to wound him, when I slip from the castle and steal Gavrus, one of his finest horses. Love aside, I'm still the nothing daughter—the stable master knows I'm not entitled to a steed. The cook knows I have no right to a bag of provisions.

And I'm certainly no Light-Forged Champion—but Lucia is my heart, the kingdom's heart, and if it takes a Fabled Cup to restore her, I'll find it.

"I just need a place to water my horse and sleep for the night," I beg.

I rub my fingers on my tunic, as if I can wipe off the bone-deep sting of having them caught in a closing door. It doesn't work, but if I can do nothing, I prefer to move while I do it.

"We've got nothing for you!" This farmer's wife is perfectly suited to her job. She is broad-shouldered and strong, and doesn't hesitate to protect her home from threats perceived and real.

I shouldn't have knocked after dark; I should have found a place in the wood to camp for the night. Truthfully, I found a place. The clearing was cool, sweetened by a spring and wild-growing sage.

But the darkness overcame me—I was unprepared for true night, one without torches and strong walls to shape it. Beasts of every sort, perhaps bigger for my ignorance, crept all round me. I clung to my satchel and my horse as long as I could bear it.

When something screamed (and Vara willing, it was a bird, please let it have been a bird), I fled. The sound echoed, chilling my spine, filling my ears—it bound me with a fear that went on and on.

My life in the palace was more comfortable than I realized, but realize it now I do. Laying my cheek on the rough wood door, I knock again helplessly. "Some straw in your barn? Anything, please."

"I'll have no abomination on my land," the farmer's wife cries.

Something on her side of the door makes a terrible sound. A wooden latch closes, a plucked wire whines. With a sharp breath, I straighten and that saves me.

An arrow shears through the slats. I taste its hiss; the shaft burns my cheek. The latching sound comes again, and my blood and bones, far wiser than my thoughts, move instantly. The narrow keen of another bolt zings past me, and I leap onto Gavrus' back

The direction doesn't matter. I'm animal instinct, my only thought is *Run, run, run!*

We streak through hills, as dark trees claw at the stars. Great, flying leaps carry us over acacia thorns and thin streams more mud than water. Edging the woods again, I start to laugh. All of my innards remain inside; I'm gloriously unpunctured. My head swims, sparkling with the giddy intoxication of escape.

Wind on my skin and night on my back, I have scarcely imagined the pleasures of adventure.

And scarcely imagined they are, when I find myself lost. Vernal is a good kingdom, better than most. But even the best kingdoms have brigands. Even the finest adventures have dangers.

Gavrus slows. Already exhausted, he's now burned to a

stub. To push him further would be to ruin him. Just as it's true I've done little camping, I have done even less hiking—and it would be cruel to break such a steady companion besides. My drunkenness fades; I must face the situation on cunning instead of instinct.

Sliding to my own feet, I shiver when the ground sinks beneath me. *It's alive,* I can't help but think; *it wants to swallow me.* But that's madness, unsettled thoughts fed by fear and unfamiliarity. I'm tired, and new-broken from riding, that's all.

Just then, the sharpness of an evergreen distracts me. No, not evergreen—bay laurel. My stomach rumbles in confirmation. The scent isn't as rich as when it rolls out of the kitchens, because these trees gleam with life.

Laurel trees are full of spirits—they're the wooden bodies of maidens forever safe from ravishment. It's a sin to cut their wood-made flesh. Leaving Gavrus close to the stream, I slip inside a fragrant cloud of leaves. They shiver and whisper, hanging thick on spindling branches.

I can barely see out; certainly no one will see in. In the morning, I'll head east and hope that the three flaming witches exist. This is my last thought before I sleep.

"My lady," a man says.

No, a boy—no, I'm not certain, only that he's strange and broad and beautiful. He crouches, holding the laurel's branches open to peer at me in the morning light. His hair gleams around his head, dark at his scalp, the curls bleached copper by the sun.

I manage only to blink at him in confusion.

"My lady," he repeats, offering his hand. "I'm sorry to wake you, but you very nearly lost your horse."

Joints crackling, I have no choice but to crawl out of my

bower. Down is always easier than up, and I take his proffered hand. Hot and rough, it swallows mine. There is easy strength in it; he could pluck me off my feet if he wished to, I'm certain.

And I'm dwarfed beside him. At my full height, I can't even see his collarbone. My nose brushes the rough weave of his shirt, and I breathe him, I'll claim on accident, and discover he's not perfumed but seasoned. Ginger and black pepper, a sting of cardamom—he's an exotic giant in homespun.

He raises our still-joined hands and tips my chin up. "Can you speak?"

I want to say, *Do you know your eyes are green as olives?* But I don't, as he must know, and it's ridiculous besides. Blessedly, my voice comes out steady and regular when I do say, "Yes, thank you. What of my horse?"

He knits his brow and smiles crookedly. Letting my hand slip from his, he turns to gesture to Gavrus and another beast so massive, I hesitate to call it a horse. It's a thick, wild thing, with tufts at its hooves and eyes as big as pomegranates.

"Carnifex and I found him a ways upstream." Admiration creeps into his voice. "Never seen a finer mount, I must admit."

My senses return bit by bit. Chest tightening, I stare at the animals and fend off a chill. He could have taken him—it's not as though I would have known it. Then I'd be lost, on foot, and too far from home to save myself, let alone Lucia.

Now that I'm awake and aware of myself again, I reach for my satchel. "I'm in your debt. Can I reward you?"

His laughter rings through the grove, low and rich. "If I weren't a gentleman . . ."

Because of my scars, no blush stings my cheeks. But it *does* burn my throat, an unpleasant prickling. I'm no innocent—my life has always been perched at the edges of court, and all its perversions and pleasures.

I don't speak in innuendo, and no one's ever mistaken me for it, either. I'm not a desirable thing, no matter the romantic notions that roll in my sister's head. But I *am* a thing that desires. I want to touch this giant's mouth and pull his curls straight; I wonder at the shape of him beneath his tunic.

This is stupid, and useless—and distracting me from my quest.

"I meant bread," I correct. "That's all I have to offer."

"Company," he counters. "Let me ride with you awhile."

"Why?"

His crooked smile returns. "So I can moon over your horse."

Some tiny spark inside me darkens. Shaking my head, I loop a hand in Gavrus' bridle. "You can't, I'm sorry. But I'll make sure your kindness is repaid. What's your name?"

"Valerian," he says. He whistles sharply, and Carnifex stirs, wandering to him like a pup to its master.

From boxes at circuses, I've seen great cats coaxed through rings of fire, and pushed into pools to prove they can swim. Bears dance if encouraged with whips; elephants will too. But never have I seen a creature—much less a terrifying wall of creature such as Carnifex—greet a man so willingly, with so much affection. He butts his head against Valerian's, and huffs when he's rewarded with a fond stroke.

Ignoring the possibility that it's madness to trust a horse to judge a man's character, I relent. Climbing astride Gavrus, I remind myself that the prophecy is already ruined. If I'm no champion, there's no reason to seek my prize alone. Turning eastward, toward the sun, I bow my head ever so slightly. "Have you a sword?"

Valerian reaches for the scabbard at his hip in reply.

"Are you accomplished with it?" I ask.

"Extremely."

"Then please join me," I say, and ride ahead of him, to let the wind wash the blush away from my throat.

Stopped at a crossroads, Valerian studies the signs with great interest.

If we keep to the east, we'll ride into Alisca, a town bordered by farms and renowned for its spirits. To the north, we'll find Castra Curia, a village that exists mainly to support the Anchorites of Vara, who live in the temple complex there. To the south are cliffs and sea, open to whatever world can be found on the back of a ship.

"It would help," Valerian says casually, "if I knew where we were going."

I twist Gavrus' reins around my hand. There's little point in lying. Nevertheless, I hesitate. It's been a long morning ride to this crossroads. Valerian's raced me down hills, and plucked blossoms from trees to weave in Carnifex's mane.

He shared his wine bladder with me, and covered the place where my lips had touched it with his. This mad, happy creature talks to me easily. He looks me in the eyes. He looks at *me*.

And none of this is my purpose. Shame fills me. In her cool chamber, Lucia burns with fever, and what am I doing? Fantasizing and laughing and fooling myself. I pinch myself as a reminder. This is no game, no adventure for pleasure. I tell him the truth.

"My sister's dying, and I seek the Fabled Cup."

To his credit, Valerian doesn't boggle. He merely looks thoughtful. "Which tasks have you finished?"

Nudging Gavrus with my knees, I look toward Alisca. The horizon darkens with smoke from cook fires, balanced by the white puff of sheep wandering the hills outside town. "I've only just set out."

Amused, Valerian turns Carnifex, to come up beside me. "How far?"

"I'm still looking for the three flaming witches, if you must know." I sound sharper than I mean to, but it's embarrassing. I have no plan. My path is uncertain. And all I've got to guide me is wishful thinking.

"With that, I can help," Valerian says. He turns Carnifex once more, urging the beast to leave the road. When I don't immediately follow, he calls back. "If you don't hurry, we'll miss it."

"Miss what?" I ask, but take off after him.

The fields give way to us, high grasses whispering against our boots as we ride through. Cottages dot the horizon, more sheep and cattle wandering in lazy waves. Everything smells sweet here, of fresh greens instead of the road's dust. Soon, we crest a hill and Valerian points at the rise of the next one. Something has cut into the earth, exposing long gouges of white chalk.

"I grew up here," he says. "And do you know what we call those chalk cuts?"

Slowly, I shake my head.

"The White Witches."

I turn back to the hill and say, "But I need three *flaming* witches."

"They will." His face brightens, and he looks toward the horizon. "Hop down. These good beasts could stand a rest."

Dismounting, we let Gavrus and Carnifex wander. They find a shallow stream and stand there shoulder to shoulder. Those horses could be no more content in a fine stable; it's plain from the way they flick their tails and drink their fill.

I follow Valerian to a small clearing in the meadow. Before I can sit down, Valerian bends his knee and offers one hand. At first, I don't understand what he intends. Then he tips his head, his eyes glancing at his own shoulder.

"You'll want a good view," he explains.

My mouth drops open, and I close it with a snap. I'm not sure what possesses me, as I've never been especially graceful or brave. But I step onto his knee and let him heft me to his shoulder.

My heart races as I perch there like a falcon, curling my hand around his shoulder for balance. Banding my ankles with *his* hand, he doesn't seem to notice that his touch makes me shiver.

The view *is* better here. From this vantage, I understand how the horses so easily found the stream. The grasses are darker along its edges, and it winds into the distance in a serpentine wave. Subtle shapes cast shadows from this height. I make out an old path, and a new stile, and even the nests of meadow birds.

"Here it comes," Valerian says.

The valley fills with the sunset. It's mostly orange, the fields drenched in bronze. But the longer light stretches to crimson. It strikes the chalk and the hill goes up in flames. A sound slips from me, one of surprise and wonder.

The witches flicker, playing with the sunset and strange shadows. Glimmering, dancing, they seem to bow and twist toward the sky. They're *alive.* Until this moment, I've never seen a dragon or a spellcasting—I can't say that I believed in either. But this is magic. True magic.

Just before the horizon swallows the sun, the chalk witches throw one last illusion. It burns like a brand against the hill, a cartographer's symbol. It's unmistakable, and for a moment, it seems like it will burn away the grasses to leave a permanent mark.

Then, at once, it's gone. There's nothing left but a crumbling rise and the coming of night.

"South by southwest," I say on my first new breath. Thoughtlessly, I card my fingers through Valerian's curls, and lean over so I can see him when I speak to him. "We should get going."

Clasping my hip, Valerian bends so I can slip from his shoulder. When I hit the ground, my scarf comes loose. It snakes down my back, coiling at my feet. Valerian manages to pluck it up before I can, and he offers it to me.

He's surprised—of course he's surprised. Lucia's the only one I've never caught staring at my scars. I'm a horror, and without his asking, I answer.

"When I was very small, my mother dropped me in the solstice bonfire. Gossip says my father planned to send her away, as he did all his mistresses, and to keep me." I wind my scarf around my head once more, feeling strangely hollow. "Father swears it was an accident."

"Was it?"

"Who's to say what the truth is?" I shrug. "I don't remember, and the result is the same. She died and took the answer with her."

Instead of offering this time, Valerian simply takes my hand and nods toward the horses. We walk toward them, and I'm unsettled. It's not dark yet, but it's coming, and the air between us is much heavier than before. His grip is tight when he finally speaks. "What's it like?"

I could answer so many ways. I decide on facts, which is probably what he means anyway. "Well. I'm sensitive to heat, and my eyes get dry. The physicians used to split the scars on my birthday, to let me grow. But not on the last one. They think I'm as big as I'll ever be now."

Towering above me, Valerian hums, and his expression

is a mystery. I wish he would come down to my height; he's so tall, this giant. And I don't mind explaining. It's a bit of a novelty to talk about it, actually.

Most people, the polite ones anyway, stare hard and try to pretend they're not curious. (The rude ones call me an abomination and run me off their land with a crossbow.) To prove I'm not wounded by his silence, I add, "Sometimes I can't tell my nose is running until I can taste it."

There is silence. Then he starts to laugh.

"I'll ask my mother if she has an extra handkerchief," he says. He releases me, to give Carnifex a good petting before he climbs back into the saddle. "She'll feed us tonight. I hope you like stew."

"We mustn't stay long. My sister fevers; she doesn't have time to wait."

"On my honor, we won't even stay long enough to lick the bowls."

Nodding, I put my foot in the stirrup and throw myself astride Gavrus. Valerian follows suit, and soon I'm following him toward a cottage just outside Alisca.

I cannot let myself wonder why he would present me to his mother, or honestly, why he's still with me. If I did, I would suspect him of something. Court intrigue has taught me to examine every kindness twice over. I am *not* a desirable thing.

But there's a sliver of my heart that doubts that when Valerian looks my way.

The stew is perfect. Its savory scent taunts me, daring me to wolf it down with no manners at all.

But Iulla, Valerian's mother, watches me. Her eyes are gray as a petrel's, and just as keen. She has wrested her thick silver hair into a crown of braids, and presides over her cottage as a queen keeps her court. I don't dare eat like a beast before her.

"She says, 'I'm a scholar, making a history of these lands,'" Valerian lies, smiling at his mother over the rim of his bowl. "So I said, 'You'll need a guide. I know these hills better than any.'"

Iulla smiles, but it doesn't reach her eyes. "You come and go with the seasons; you just needed an excuse."

When Valerian stands, he has to bow his head so it doesn't scrape the ceiling. His shoulders fill the room, and he steps over benches to get to the basin by the door. "It's true. But this is my best excuse yet, don't you think?"

"Be a pet and fetch your poor mother some water."

Moving to stand, I say, "It's the least I can do for the meal, please let me."

"No, no," Iulla says. She catches my wrist. Though her hands are birdlike, they clasp tight. There's an edge of force to it, but she still smiles. "Let Valerian. It keeps him humble."

Unaware of the strange tension that passes between us, Valerian smiles. He bows humbly, then sweeps out the door with a bucket in each hand. When he fades into the night, I look to Iulla and offer a smile of my own. "He's a good soul. You must be very proud."

Iulla ignores that. She lets go of my hand and catches my chin instead. It startles me; most people don't touch me at all. No one but Lucia touches my face. Valerian's mother tips my head sharply and before I can pull away, she retreats.

"Well, Augusta Corvina, Your Highness," she says, cold creeping over her like a mantle, "isn't it a pleasure to serve you?"

Her voice is brittle. It snaps and cracks, and honestly, it surprises me. She has been uneasy since she saw me, but most people are. That's an impersonal sort of distance. This is frighteningly intimate.

Squaring the bowl in front of me, I shake my head. "If you know my name, you know I'm bastard-born. I have no title. I'm a citizen and subject, just as you are."

"And what would a citizen and subject want with my only son?"

I blink. That question is just as sharp and cold as the last one, but now I recognize her look. Her meaning. She isn't angry; she's *afraid*.

"I don't want anything." Earnestly, I press a hand to my heart and swear, "He doesn't even know who I am."

"Neither do you," she says. Her words are clipped and direct. "Augusta Lucia is dying, and the king's remaining heir is missing, believed kidnapped. There's a reward for her safe return."

"And you wish that reward?" I ask. The words stick in my throat.

A ripple of disgust crosses her face. "I have all I need, Your Highness. I have my home, and my hearth, and my *son*."

Baffled, I say, "Then what—"

She cuts me off with a black finality. "If you're safely returned, your father will forgive *any* method used to accomplish it."

Now I feel her cold, from within instead of without. My father is a successful king by every measure of kingship. He sends young men to war and calls them into service. He can sentence the guilty and pardon them alike. Without hesitation, he does both. His power rests easily on his brow, but he's not known as The Good or The Gentle.

He's known as The Immovable.

How many people lie awake tonight imagining how they would spend that reward? How many would cut Valerian to pieces to get to it, knowing all their sins and crimes are already forgiven?

Quickly, I stand. I fumble for my satchel, pulling it over my shoulder. My belly turns to stone, and a tight band stifles my breath in my chest. I want to rail at the gods, at the sky, at my father. No one at the palace is supposed to miss me! There should be no prize for my return.

"Tell Valerian . . . ," I start, my gaze trailing toward the open door. He's out there somewhere, bemused and carrying water. And safe—safer still, the more distance I put between us.

I never should have let him accompany me in the first place. I never should have held his hand, or—no. These are useless thoughts. I shove them down and open the back door. My voice cracks when I finally finish my thought. "Tell him thank you for me."

As I creep away in silence, I doubt very much that she will.

After two days' riding, I come to the end of the world. Or more accurately, to the end of the island.

The Straits of Lixus separate me from the plains of Ticinum. Those are Queen Vatia's lands, and she's our ally. Should I succeed in my task, it's likely her second son will come for Lucia's Betrothal Quest.

Sliding from Gavrus' back, I walk to the cliff's edge. This precipice is exactly south by southwest—I can go no farther unless I find a ship and someone to captain her. I measure my steps and follow a narrow path down to the shore. Though I've heard that some beaches are smooth with powdery sand, this one is entirely stone.

The water seems to smile and beckon. Moonlight plays on the waves, twinkling like stars. Down here, I taste salt with each breath and turn my face into the cool wind.

The prophecy says that the three flaming witches will point the way, and the Light-Forged Champion will survive the Breathless Reaches. Valerian found the witches; it's up to me to figure out the rest.

Suddenly, a wave rolls onto the shore. It soaks my sandals and recedes between the rocks, white fingers pulled back into the sea. Another follows it, swelling as if taking great breaths, and then collapsing on itself. It lures me closer. Perhaps I can catch the stars on the waves. Perhaps I can step onto them and walk the waters as if they were land.

I hold my arms out as the next wave comes in.

It wants to push me over. It tries to pull me in. It's a grasping, living thing and now I'm openly thwarting it. I don't know why, except the hard spray stings my skin, and the cold clarifies my thoughts. If I just let it, I think the waters will scrub me clean. I'll be selfless again, worthy of the Cup.

I'm stronger than the sea. I'm greater than my foolish, infatuated heart. I don't wait for the next wave; I step into the water to greet it. The crash and the call roar in my ears, a long gasp that blocks all but the sound of my own heart beating. Water strikes. This time, I sway with it. It clutches me. It drags.

Overhead, the moon swells bright, full and round as the goddess herself.

Cold swallows me, my bones aching. A sheer black wall rises before me. In its shadow, already weighted with waves, I stare at it in wonder. How beautiful a thing, this lithe column made of the sea. I can see garlands of watergrass hanging in it, the bright white sparks of shells as they're carried along.

Reaching to touch it, I gasp when a spark lights in me—

a memory. Stories of sailors enchanted by the waves, dazzled by the full moon reflected in the sea. Once I had wondered how water, simple water, could call so many to drown.

Now I know.

I try to scramble back, but the wave collapses on me. It sweeps my feet from underneath me. Now that I'm unfooted, my satchel is an anchor. It drags me deeper; I'm stripped by the descent. My headscarf peels away, hanging like a drop of blood above me.

Everything is quiet in the below, all but the hum of my last breath escaping in a stream of silver bubbles. At first, the peace drowns my panic.

Then my lungs start to burn. I don't remember the solstice fire. And I don't remember the months afterwards, either, thank Vara. But my *flesh* remembers it. Fire sleeps within me, roused when I stand too close to the hearth, or even when Lucia's hand lingers too long on my cheek.

And now. A thousand pinpoints of fire—of pain—strike my chest. Water should douse fire, but it doesn't. It rises into my throat; my lips swell and even my eyes burn and bulge.

Thrashing, I twist and find my arms. I take a few strokes, but where's the surface? I can't tell. I'm fighting my own flesh. My chest screams for a breath; my mind refuses to take it. Once I'm full of water, I'll belong to the sea forever. I know that, with all certainty I know that, and I give up on thinking. I just swim.

I hear the dull thud inside my head before I feel the rocks cutting my scalp. Heat pours from me, cold clasps me. Digging my fingers into stone, I try to follow its shape. Strange silver domes cling to this rock wall, caught on ledges. They waver like jellyfish, little, impossible moons beneath the waves.

When I drag my fingers through one, it turns to bubbles. I almost laugh, hysterical and delighted. I'm saved, I'm saved! Pressing my face into one of the domes, I draw the air from it, a tiny sip. I have to clamp a hand over my mouth. Instinct begs me to draw deeper, but I can't. I mustn't.

Half-floating, half-dragging, I pull myself along the wall. I inhale every bubble I can find. It's not enough, but my head stops spinning. My panic softens; I can think. Peeling my satchel off, I let it drift away. I'm lighter now. Bit by bit, I rise.

Catching a sharp edge, I duck beneath it because a huge streak of silver gleams there. When I lift my face to it, I don't just find a pocket of air. I find the surface. The sound of the splash echoes all around me. Air cools my face; a stone ceiling arches high above my head.

A cave. I've found a cave. I can pull myself from the water here, and I do. No matter that the rocks cut my bare flesh. If there are sightless beasts, they're welcome to crawl and bite. I'm too weak to fight them off, so let them come. Shivering, I open my eyes wide to take in light, the same way my mouth gapes open for more breath.

Logic tells me that I should be swathed in perfect darkness. The ceiling is solid, the walls too. I lie beneath sea and stone, completely entombed. There are no torches but the obsidian flecks in the wall glitter all the same. Unsteady, I pull myself to my feet.

Now that I'm not drowning, my body complains about the other abuses it's suffered of late. My hips feel wide and breakable from riding; a headache blooms from the gouge in my forehead. It's like my flesh is mapping the past few days, recording the journey.

But I can't get ahead of myself. It's not over yet. I have to survive the Breathless Reaches and pass the Earthenwork

Defiler. If Iulla's news is accurate, I have little time remaining. I turn, following the leap and spark of obsidian, until I make out a thin white ribbon of light.

It leads me into a tunnel. At first, the walls are sharp and irregular. But the light grows brighter, and they grow smoother. In some places, they're so polished that I catch rippled glimpses of myself as I walk past. Then black glass gives way to colorful tesserae.

These tiny tiles swim along the tunnel walls in intricate patterns. Spirals and twists stretch out, bordering what appear to be more complicated mosaics between them. In spite of the dim light, the images come to life. They're remarkable, as fine as any of the mosaics in my father's palace. Each scene inhabits its own frame, but I can see they're connected.

In the first, a white-shrouded figure looks down at a city. In the next, the figure kneels before three crones blazing inside a hearth. My heart suddenly quivers as I take in the third. Now clad in blue, the figure kisses a silver mirror—or draws a breath from a trapped bubble.

I can't read the runes, but I don't have to.

This is the prophecy; perhaps the first recording of it. I'm on the right path. I'm almost to the end!

Hurrying to the fourth panel, I'm disappointed. It should explain what the Earthenwork Defiler is, give me some hint how to reach past it. Instead, the figure wields a sword, thrusting it into *nothing.* The border of the mosaic cuts off the tip of the blade. I move down a few paces, hoping the next panel reveals all.

It doesn't. It's victory, finality: a pair of hands hold the Fabled Cup aloft. Light streams from it, and these tesserae are flecked with gold. I can't help but notice that the hands are made with alabaster tile. They're pale and unmarred. My own hands are dark—bruised and scored, and even if they weren't, I have no sword for them to bear.

Exhausted, I walk back to the fourth panel, but it remains a mystery. The sword still cuts into the border, nothing beyond it to be seen. There's nothing. Nothing! I stand there, all too aware of the things I don't know. That I have come this far by chance and luck and no wit at all.

My entire life, I've been *in* the court, but not *of* it. For my father to name me his heir, he must have known he needed one. All my petty litany of complaints, that I'm tired and cold and hungry, fades away. My sister is dying. She may well now be dead.

Lucia is good. She's kind, and she's clever; she would be the queen that Vernal *deserves*. My insides turn to liquid, a hot wine that bubbles and boils. It feeds my hands and makes them clench; it fills my belly and sears me from the inside out.

The shadowy weight of grief has no chance to settle on me. How stupid I've been, to waste her last days chasing a fable. How fantastically absurd I was to think that I could be the one to fulfill a prophecy that has, all along, excluded me.

I pound my brown fist against the white hands in the mosaic. I'm no champion. I'm forged of nothing but damaged flesh. Again, I beat the wall. My teeth feel sharp with pleasure, and I grind grim satisfaction between them when the tesserae come loose. They sound like glass breaking as they fall at my feet.

Uselessly, I beat against the wall. More tesserae fall. I dig them out; I break the soft mortar and let it fall like ash. I'm mad with ending this prophecy, and I'm viciously relieved when my fist finally strikes wet earth. It's done; it's obliterated.

A few tiles cling yet, but I've torn away the Cup, the hands, even the border. As I heave great breaths, I stare and let the last of my anger drain away. And then I tip my head in surprise. Light pours from the mud, a single pinpoint almost blinding in its clarity. I sweep my hand in front of it. It's not warm, it doesn't burn—but it doesn't waver, either.

With careful fingers, I widen the hole. More light pours through, and soon I'm bathed in it. It spills from a hidden chamber, appointed in marble and gold. My vision blurs, and I'm assaulted by the rich scent of burning marjoram and dittany.

A hand reaches out to take my elbow, startling me, drawing me forth. Everything glows so brightly that it's like standing in a lantern. The touch, now strangely soothing, slips from my skin, and a woman says, "I always find it interesting to see who comes for the Cup."

Perhaps I've drowned after all. Perhaps this is a dream I'm having, fevering alongside Lucia.

In the temples, Vara gazes down from her sculptures with a slightly maternal air. Her hips are wide and round, her breasts full. Her hair coils around her head in braids, and she is always, always rendered in bronze.

Now I see why. I don't mean to stare, but what is the proper response to seeing a god made flesh? I hope it's trembling and confusion, because that's all I can manage.

"Sit," Vara says. She fills a basin and brings it to me. "Here. Let me get you a cloth."

The water in the basin is warm. Steam rolls up, and it feels like a kiss on my scoured skin. For a moment, I consider drinking it. It would be just like tea, I think.

"You'll have tea in a minute," Vara says. "That's for washing."

Chastened, I take the cloth she offers, and do just that. I'm filthy from digging in the walls and crusted with salt. If I could climb into the basin, I would; the temptation to empty it over my head is great.

It's a remarkable bit of work, the basin. It seems to be simple pottery, but the water inside it never fouls. When I scrub mud from beneath my fingernails, or wipe clean the blood from the soles of my feet, each time I dip the cloth, it comes back clean.

"Better?" Vara asks.

"Much," I say.

She exchanges the basin for a cup, and nods at me expectantly. I drink deep. The bright, astringent herbs make me shiver, then warmth sweeps all through my bones. It leaves a pleasant burning in my chest, an ember to drive away any chill.

Before I have half finished my tea, Vara produces a chalice and sits before me. Only when she pulls her chair a bit closer do I realize that all of these things she's given me have been drawn from the air. There were no chairs until we sat upon them. There was no basin until she gave it to me. I want to tremble again, but her dark eyes are too kind. Her strong hands too gentle. She should frighten me, but she doesn't.

"This is the prize," she says, offering the chalice to me.

I wrap my hands tighter round my teacup, soaking up heat through the pottery. "But I'm not . . . I failed, didn't I? I'm not light-forged. I never found the Earthenwork Defiler. I survived the Breathless Reaches by accident . . . someone else showed me the witches."

Vara smiles crookedly. "*You're* the Earthenwork Defiler. Look what you did to my mosaics. You survived the Reaches, and that's all that matters. I don't care how you found the witches, you found them."

My warmth turns to a flush. "I don't . . ."

"The quest was never meant to be difficult, if you were meant to be on it."

She offers the Cup in all its fineness and I take it this time. It weighs nothing, though it should. It's beaten silver, inlaid with carnelian and lapis, bedecked with sapphire and ruby. It feels so insubstantial in my hand that I raise it to my lips, just out of habit.

"Don't. You'll waste its magic," Vara says. "Each Champion may use the Cup but once. We both know it's not for you."

Clutching the chalice to my chest, I say, "My sister is sick. She's dying."

"Then let her drink deep." Vara waves a hand, and smoke twines around it like a bangle. "Go, Champion."

As I stand, I dare to ask, "How many are there? How many Champions?"

"Not many. Most people assume a prophecy isn't meant for them. Or that the time isn't right. Or their need is not so great. Others think they're entitled to my gifts. None of these would-be champions are light-forged."

She opens a door that wasn't there before, and we look into the sea. Something holds the water back, and I marvel. Colorful streaks of fish stream by. A creamy shark cuts sharp curves in the distance, following the shadow of a ship on the surface. From here, I can see the moon—it's full and low, and looks like a pearl.

"It's not enough to want the Cup," Vara says. She plucks my satchel from nowhere and drapes it over my shoulder. "You must *need* it, and seek it selflessly. And you'd better hurry. Your sister waits."

Before I can thank her, Vara commends me to the ocean.

Cold shocks my skin; the salt burns my eyes. I twist

around, yet I see nothing but a sheer rock face, and silver bubbles clinging to its imperfections. The golden chamber, and the god inside it, are gone.

This time, I know my way. The tea's heat still courses through me, and I have enough air in me that no panic can unsettle my path. Unafraid, I rise toward the moonlight. When I surface, I breathe and I bask, and I start the journey home.

The guards would keep me from Lucia's chambers, at least until they realize who I am. There's an advantage to a face like mine. No matter how bedraggled I am, despite my dirty clothes, I am entirely recognizable.

Nonetheless, I dare them to raise their axes to me, and push past them without hesitation. When I burst through the doors, I'm struck nearly senseless. A fire burns in the stove, and herbed water boils away on it. The chamber swelters, and it captures the stink of sickness.

Sour sweat and acrid vomit, and something dark and awful, like flesh decayed while it still lives—that all hangs in a miasma that only barely stirs when I walk through it. The physicians are long gone.

They've left a salt circle around Lucia's bed and dotted it with stone amulets. These are their last, feeble attempts, magic instead of medicine. I can hardly blame them; it's the same remedy I sought.

My father cries out when he sees me. He's haggard, and throws himself at me, crushing me in his arms. His new beard scratches my face as he murmurs, "Thank Vara, they found you, they found you."

"No," I correct him. "I came back."

As much as I'd like to steep in the novelty of a father who loves and acknowledges me, I have more important things to attend to. All my years as his bastard, mostly ignored, generally tolerated—they remain yet in my memory. For now, I only have time for the one who has always loved me openly. Wriggling from my father's grasp, I pull the Cup from my satchel.

I perch at Lucia's bedside, my poor, dear sister who is yellow and drawn. Her skin clings to her bones now; her lips are dry and cracked, crusted with spittle and blood. It pierces my heart to see her like this. I cannot imagine how she's lasted so long.

But these are thoughts I cannot indulge. Instead I lift her head, trying not to shudder at the hair that slips free of her scalp when I do. Pressing the Cup to her mouth, I say, "Just take a sip now."

Like the basin in Vara's chamber, the Cup fills itself. At first, the water spills down Lucia's chin, but a few drops slip onto her tongue. With a sigh, she stirs, opening her mouth against the weight of the Cup.

Each swallow dilutes the deathly shade of her skin. Each taste fills the hollows of her cheeks and darkens the luster of her hair. Though Lucia's the one healing, I feel it in my bones and in my body. I am full with it, all my fear and anger tempered into joy.

Behind us, my father sobs and prays, and it sounds as if there are people gathering. They press closer to witness a miracle, to be the ones who can later tell their grandchildren that once, they saw the Fabled Cup.

I pay them little attention; I help my sister drink until her eyes open.

"Corvina," she says. She's the one that sounds like a raven, her voice rasping and broken. With a gentle hand, she traces the wide gouge that splits my forehead, so carefully that it barely hurts at all. "Oh, sweet, what happened?"

"You mad thing, don't mind me," I say. I raise the Cup for her, urging, "One more sip."

She takes it, and we're both surprised when the Cup unwinds itself. It's like watching a spool of silk thread unfurling, only this makes nothing but a spark before it's gone. One last bit of magic, as if Lucia's return weren't sorcery enough.

Disbelief turns to surprise when Lucia looks up at me. "What . . . ?"

"I'll tell you everything," I promise. "But wouldn't you like a bath first?"

All of Vernal celebrates Lucia's return from the dark. Wreaths of laurel and heather pile high at the palace gates; each night, my father sends a priestess to accept these offerings, and to burn them so the smoke sweetens the sky.

I still attend my sister's chamber; I still dress her hair. But now, when I walk through the halls, people bow their heads and call me Augusta Corvina. My station has changed entirely. The most interesting thing about that is that my father makes no announcement at all. It's his will, and somehow, it's known. He remains immovable.

Because I'm now a full princess, I sit at Lucia's side on the dais on the opening of her Betrothal Quest. Second sons, army captains, and peasants alike are admitted to the throne room. While our father still lives, Lucia will keep her own court in the country. But there is no mistake—she takes a consort, not a king-to-be.

One day, Vernal will be hers entirely to rule. First sons are for alliances, not for marriages. Peasants are welcome to apply only if they're born of this land and pledge to remain in it. This is how we'll keep our kingdom whole and individual.

So suitors of all manner arrive at the gates at dawn. Lucia sends most of them away—the ones that are too old, the ones with gimlet eyes, the ones who cannot keep from openly recoiling when they see me. I take some miserable satisfaction that this matters to Lucia, though I admit, seeing it happen again and again does sting.

Tasius, Queen Vatia's second son, makes the cut. So does Gracilus, a merchant from Nasos, a fuller named Libo, and a pair of Lycean twins who look as surprised as my father does when Lucia gives them a favor to keep between them. I think it's because they've made her laugh. They can no more share a single wife than she can enjoy two husbands.

Evening comes, and the last of the suitors trudge away. Lucia's favorites stay—they have ten conversations ahead of them, and they must remain at the crown princess's leisure. Just as the gates begin to close, a thundering of hooves approaches. A monstrous black horse fills the entire gate, and the rider flings himself from the saddle before the beast comes to a stop.

Valerian throws up a hand, and he calls out, "Wait!"

Effervescent, I knot my hands in my lap. My giant has come and the crowd skitters away from him. They form a terrified aisle, filling the space behind him once he's passed.

It's foolishness, madness—surely they can see how kind his face is. Certainly they must realize how carefully he threads his way to the dais, what is there to fear? Leaning her head toward mine, Lucia murmurs, "Vara save me, he must eat whole goats for breakfast."

I barely have time to mask my surprise before Valerian reaches us. But it's good that I've masked it, for I'm surprised again when he kneels before my sister and bows his head. His gaze never trails my way; it's as if I'm invisible.

"Augusta Lucia," he says. "I present myself as a freeman of Vernal, humble of birth, loyal to the crown, and ask for your favor."

This can't happen; I beg the gods to spare me, for a spell of fainting or a sudden opening of the ground. He doesn't recognize me, and yet, how is it that he doesn't recognize me? I bear that better than the possibility that he *does* know me and simply cares more for the power he would wield as my sister's consort.

From a distance, I hear Lucia's voice. The interview seems to go on forever, but all the words are distorted in my head. She takes my hand; the touch startles me. Her breath is so hot against my cheek when she leans in to whisper, "Can you even imagine?"

The question draws blood, though she doesn't realize it. Turning to her, I press my lips to her ear. "Give him a token."

"What?" Lucia smiles through her shock.

Loosing myself from her grip, I stand. Bits of my bone grind to ash; it thickens my blood and stills the beat of my heart to say it, but I do. I wrench myself open, and whisper in her ear. "Without him, I could not have found the Cup. You don't have to marry him, but at least give him your favor."

With that, I let the footman escort me away. I hurry him, as if there's a graceful way to flee an audience. I am, nonetheless, wholly aware of the collective gasp behind me when Lucia gives Valerian her coin. My hands are restless; they long to slap the gaping faces. I could dig my fingers into their bones, and castigate them for their small minds.

But I won't, because I think I've earned my rest. None shall argue when I close myself in my tower chamber; only one shall miss me when I choose not to descend. Lucia's Decade of Conversations will end soon enough, all the suitors but one will return to their homes.

When Lucia comes to my door, she knocks and speaks through it. "I stole a cake from the kitchen."

"I don't want cake," I reply, but the door opens anyway.

Winding around to sit at my feet, Lucia makes a table of my lap and dares me to ignore it. She tears off a sticky bite of the confection, waving it under my nose before she eats it. "Are you all right?"

I smear a drop of sugar glaze on my finger, then gloss my mouth with it. That way, I get a bit of sweetness that lingers. "No. I liked Valerian overmuch for how little I knew him. It was foolish to think he'd come for me."

"No, it wasn't!"

"You're wrong," I say. "I abandoned him after he showed me much kindness."

Pinching my ankle, Lucia makes a face. "Why would you do that?"

"Because Father put a bounty on me, and I didn't think death was a fair penalty for a good and innocent man." I steal a piece of cake right from her fingers. "So don't marry him, even though you'd like him."

Lucia leans her head back, brows arched incredulously. "Corvina, he's terrifying!"

"What's terrifying about him?" I demand. "He's handsome, and generous, and you would be lucky to have him. Just . . . don't have him!"

Perhaps sensing my rawness, Lucia waves a hand to dismiss it. "Fine, I won't."

She's beautiful again, now that she's recovered. Her curls are thicker than ever, and the dark fan of her lashes seems made to entice. Only a madman could resist her, so protecting my petty heart, I beg again. "*Swear* to me you won't. It's a little thing, and no hardship to you anyway."

"I swear it," Lucia says. She puts a hand to her heart. "On my honor, by pain of death, without hesitation."

I give her a little kick. "No need for dramatics."

"Did he kiss you?" she asks abruptly.

My face is cool as ever, but my chest grows hot. Taking the entire plate in hand, I abscond with her cake and retreat to my bed with it. "Of course not."

At once, Lucia is too thoughtful. She hauls herself up, and doesn't kiss my cheek before she leaves. She does hesitate, though, gesturing at the plate. "Don't make yourself sick." Then she's gone, swirling away in a cloud of dark curls and lavender.

I wonder if I've disappointed her somehow.

Valerian leaves after his first conversation with Lucia, and I'm relieved. Sulking in my chamber felt juvenile after a few hours, and this is my sister's Betrothal Quest. I don't want to miss it. Though she doesn't *need* my counsel, it pleases me to share it anyway.

On the morning she sets her suitors free to complete her quest, I dog her steps to the atrium.

"I think you should let the twins win," I say. Fussing with her hair, I pluck out the silver butterfly pins, and slip them in again to improve the arrangement. "Just to see the look on Father's face."

Lucia throws a smile over her shoulder. "Shhh, I'm in no rush to take the throne."

Threading the last pin into my headscarf, I put on my smoothest expression as the footmen open the atrium doors for us. This morning, only Father and the suitors await. When there's a wedding feast to be had, that's when the crowds will return. Today is only so much bookkeeping. Bureaucracy excites no one.

At least, no one but my sister and me. We have a wager. She refuses to tell me her selection, but she'll give me a prize if I guess before he returns. It's a game of reading faces. She's already told one of them to fetch something. In a few moments, she'll wish the rest luck divining her desires. My guess is that only one of them will be at ease.

Of course, this assumes that Lucia didn't tell her husband-to-be to make it difficult on purpose. I wouldn't put it past her.

We file onto the dais, Father greeting us with kisses. He catches Lucia's hand and murmurs low enough for our ears alone, "If they all fail, you should pick the one you like best."

Lucia's brows leap up, and I make a faint, strangled noise. Fortunately, Father turns to say a few words to the suitors and doesn't notice. Settling beside each other, Lucia and I lean in to speak at once.

"I think my fever addled *his* brain," she says.

I grin. "But only a little. You still have to choose from this motley assortment."

Because we're on display, we don't jostle or pinch. But we trade mischievous looks until it's time for Lucia's address. I sharpen my gaze, studying each man's face. One of them already knows—which one?

She *has* coached him, because they all share the same, faintly distressed expression. I study them so intently that I barely hear Lucia's final words, at least until she says my name. Father's not expecting it either. His spine straightens, and he leans back just enough to catch my eye. I shrug. Lucia does what she likes.

"Despite the fact that we have never left this palace un-escorted, my sister gathered provisions and struck out into the countryside on a quest to find the Fabled Cup. For me. Surely, she could have healed herself, but she raised the Cup to my lips, so I might live."

Now everyone looks to me, and I want to crawl into my headscarf. Lucia's been thinking long on this, apparently, but I'm mortified. The only time I raised the Cup to my mouth was out of wonder that it was real at all. I may not like my face, but it's my own. I share it with no other, and I never thought to change it.

Irritation builds in me, and I consider interrupting her. If her idea of a Betrothal Quest is to go fetch that Cup again for my benefit, we will have words. Strong, sharp words. To my relief, Lucia continues and it's not in that vein at all.

"So go forth, knowing that an example has already been set. I expect much, but I grant much in return. May Vara guide you."

She raises her hands in blessing, and I'm baffled when the only suitors who move with purpose are the Lycean twins. As if they know exactly what they seek. My mouth doesn't hang open; I have better manners than that. But Lucia couldn't have been clearer. She swore she would give the secret of the quest to her chosen suitor.

Holding my composure until the atrium clears, I tug Lucia's hem and pull her down to say, "You didn't."

With a sugared smile, she strokes my cheek with her knuckle. "Is that your guess?"

For a moment, I hang there suspended. But then I shake my head. As silly as she finds the Betrothal Quest in concept, it's tradition. She will be queen someday. Other regents arrange *every* marriage; there's never any choice in it. Lucia wouldn't jeopardize that bit of freedom just for the sake of amusement.

"You chose Tasius of Ticinum," I say.

It's a guess, but a good one, I think. He's personable at the dinner table, and reads for pleasure. And he's handsome, russet-skinned and black-haired, with fine hands and broad shoulders. There is little to dislike about him and much to recommend. Besides which, we *did* like him when we were children. There's value in shared history.

Lucia puts her hands on her hips and scowls at me. "You cheated."

"How could I?" I ask through my laughter. "Do you think I can read minds now?"

"Well, you're not getting your prize today," she says.

Lifting her hems, she sweeps from the dais, her head held high. No amount of cajoling changes her mind, either. I peck through dinner, and over our midnight tea. When I come to dress her hair in the morning, I start on her anew, but one of the atrium maids interrupts us.

"The twins are back!" the girl cries.

Lucia leaps up, sweeping a scarf around her shoulders and pulling me along with her to greet them. They bow before her when she meets them in the atrium, and then present her with a pair of monkeys. They're no bigger than their palms, with wide, inquisitive eyes.

"Oh my," Lucia murmurs.

The monkeys cling to her fingers; they climb her gown and make themselves happily at home on her shoulders. Something tells me that there was an agreement made here, but not one for her hand. Lucia kisses the twins' cheeks in turn, then produces a heavy purse.

"They are lovely, but they're not my heart's desire," she says. She offers the purse with a knowing look. "But they please me, and I've enjoyed our conversations. I hope this will help you start your traveling menagerie."

They thank her and go, leaving my sister with monkeys on her shoulders and a supremely smug look on her face. Turning, she plucks up one of the chirring beasts and offers him to me. "Your prize?"

"Hardly. You're the one mad for animals," I tell her, but I take the monkey anyway. He's warm, and he clings to my neck, darling and tame. He rubs his nose against my cheek and walks his curious fingers along the ridges of my scars. "Answer me this, Lucia. Do you have a purse for all of them?"

"Everyone has dreams," she says, smiling when her monkey clasps her finger like a babe. "This one looks like a Celeris, don't you think?"

The merchant Gracilus returns next, weighted with a basket of rare fruits. Their sweetness perfumes the atrium and makes my mouth water. Everything in the basket is a treat, and not coincidentally, it contains bundles of leaves that our monkeys find irresistible. In exchange, my plotting sister doesn't give him a proposal, either. His prize is another purse. Gracilus will finally be able to buy a trading ship of his own.

Lucia giggles when Libo returns with newly woven blankets, just big enough to make a bed for a pair of miniature primates. They're even embroidered with dancing monkeys—shamelessly perfect. For this, Libo leaves the court with funds to build a water mill for his fullery.

"You haven't even pretended to play fair," I say. It's obvious now: she told all of them to bring something specific, and she would give them the gold they needed to follow their dreams. Now I'm anxious to see what Tasius will bring her. Surely it's something greater than exotic pets and things to keep them.

We pass several days in the atrium, watching Celeris and Cursor charm all that come near them. They're happy, silly creatures, free to roam the palace as they like. They've taken to introducing themselves by dropping from the pillars onto people's shoulders.

This morning, they squeal and retreat to our laps when the door crashes open. Tasius strides in. Clothing wrinkled, hair mussed, he's ridden quite some way to be here, and didn't stop to pretty himself. Yet another check in his favor—for Lucia, at least. Swiftly, he approaches us, then drops on one knee to take Lucia's hand. "I have finished your sister's quest."

I fail to hold my tongue. "Excuse me?"

"He said," Lucia answers, leaning her head toward mine and pointing toward the gate, "he's finished your quest. Well . . . made it possible for *you* to do it rightly."

Valerian stands there, a hand on Carnifex's bridle. I feel at once curiously light and completely leaden. Vaguely, I'm aware when Lucia takes the monkey from my hands, but I can't seem to move my blood or my body.

With Celeris settling on her shoulder, Lucia stands and pulls me to my feet. "When I asked why he wished to marry me, he said he didn't. That he thought the only way to get to you would be through me."

"Then why didn't he see me? Why didn't you tell me?" I start to bristle, but I'm distracted when Valerian raises his fingers; he waves at me. He smiles.

Drawing me down, step by step, Lucia says, "Because I was arranging things. I told you, in *my* court you could do whatever you like. And now that's true in Father's court, too."

My gaze turns to Tasius. He looks so disgustingly pleased with himself, I almost want to pinch him. But Lucia casts him a playful smile; they glow with shared pleasure. And it's then that I understand.

To become Lucia's consort, Tasius had to complete whatever task she set before him. It's our law, our *tradition*. Like my father, it is immovable. So if Lucia's quest was to bring me a suitor, and if Tasius did so, earnestly, in all faith—Father would have no choice but to honor it.

One day, my sister will be a kind and clever queen.

"You don't have to marry him," she says, nudging me again. "But I'd try kissing him, at least."

Her words release me. I fly down the steps, my headscarf unraveling behind me. I run to him, crash into him—catching his hand and pulling him to my level. It's a long way, and deliciously worth it, because his mouth is hot and tastes of cardamom. It fits mine exactly. I desire, and I'm desired, and before I know it, he's hefted me to his shoulder.

I can see the whole court; I fly above it. Everything else that will pass between us, Valerian and me, is meant only for us. It's precious, and all you should know is that my heart beats with his, and I am happy.

But you should also know this:

One day, the minstrels will sing the story of the Princess Corvina's quest for the Cup; they'll make it seem as if I were light-forged all along. I hope that you'll remember it wasn't so. I wasn't the Chosen One.

What distinguishes me is that I chose myself.

Improbable Futures

KAMI GARCIA

When I was six years old, my mom sent me to school for a month. It was the first and last time I ever set foot in a real school. My mother said she was tired of moving around and decided it was time to settle down and "plant some roots." Even at six, I knew it wouldn't last, but I was willing to take what I could get. That's what you do when you don't get much.

On the first day, I wandered into the classroom holding my mother's hand like all the other kids. I was wearing a brand-new blue dress. I looked like a regular kid on the outside, which is the only part that counts. It's the face the world sees, the one you can change as many times as you want. After lunch, the teacher, Mrs. Hale—I'll never forget her name—called us to the rug in the front of the classroom. It was Share Time, and she asked us what we wanted to be when we grew up. I had no idea. I spent most of my time thinking about what I *didn't* want to be.

Hands flew up. The girl with the brown pigtails wanted to be a ballerina. The boy in the orange shirt, a garbageman. Hands kept raising and more jobs floated around the room, until the boy next to me called out, "I wanna be in the circus." A hush fell over the group as the idea circulated like a virus. After that, almost everyone Mrs. Hale called on decided they wanted to be in the circus too.

When it was my turn, I didn't say a word. One thought threaded its way through my mind: *Who would want to work for the circus?* There was only one place worse—a place where the big tent was replaced by dingy trailers and cheap amusement park rides. Where you paid to see fortune-tellers and a bearded lady instead of trapeze artists and lion tamers. The place my mother had worked my whole life, and the one I was sure we would be returning to eventually, because she never left for long.

Once a carny, always a carny.

I slip out of my jeans and reach for the peasant top and ankle-length skirt balled up on the floor of the trailer. It has tiny bells sewn around the hem that chime when I walk barefoot across the lot. Between the skirt, bare feet, armload of bangles, and tangle of necklaces laden with mass-produced charms from the mall, I'm supposed to look like an exotic gypsy. It's beyond cliché, but that's what the marks—I mean the customers—want. The illusion I'm a mystical fortune-teller, who can watch their futures unfold through a glass ball I bought online for $29.99.

Two years ago, on my fifteenth birthday, Mom offered to let me have her old crystal ball as if she was passing down a priceless heirloom, instead of the diversion I used to con people out of their money. I ordered my own the same day. There should be some honor among thieves. Even if the thief is your mother.

It's just after dark, and by the time I leave the trailer, the lot is already packed with skanky girls in tank tops and cutoffs, chain-smoking Marlboro Lights. They're crowded around the entrance to the Freak Show, flirting with Chris. I call him CR because he's a shameless cradle robber. He's twenty-five, but he looks closer to my age, which is the reason Big John makes him work the Show. The girls line up by the dozens, spending five bucks a pop to flirt with CR for thirty seconds before they check out the two-headed snakes and the Devil Baby—a disgusting silicone "alien" fetus floating in a glass jar full of murky liquid that passes for formaldehyde. CR said Big John bought it from a special-effects studio in Los Angeles that specializes in custom body parts for horror flicks. Between the flat snubbed nose and the curled claws, the Devil Baby is beyond horrific even if it is silicone. The Freak Show tent is really dark inside, but you'd still have to be an idiot to believe that thing in the giant pickle jar is a demon baby.

This whole place runs on stupidity.

Everyone knows the games are rigged, the rides are rusted death traps, the hot dogs aren't made of anything that ever resembled a cow or a pig, and the silicone fetus isn't the devil's spawn. That's why my mom and I, in our belled skirts and bare feet, are so important.

Fortune-tellers are the reason people ignore the rest of the cons at a carnival. We're the one thing they actually believe in. Even the nonbelievers. They climb into the trailer, part the silk curtains, and tell you how they know everything you're about to tell them is a lie. Until you tell them the *one* thing they want to hear. The thing that makes them believers.

We're the ultimate grifters.

Because after we reveal the secrets your future holds, we go back to our trailers, take off the hoop earrings, and throw those bell-covered skirts on the floor until tomorrow.

When I get to the trailer with "Fortune-Teller" written on the side in cheap pink paint, there's already a line outside it.

Good. Let them wait.

It only makes them hungrier for the crap I feed them when they get inside. I push past the couple standing at the base of the steps watching me expectantly. "Follow me."

Let the games begin.

I scoop up my skirt and climb the makeshift stairs, a splinter cutting into the bottom of my foot. I bite the inside of my cheek until I taste blood. The tiny sliver of wood is like all the other painful things inside me that I will never be able to dig out.

I close the door behind my customers and turn the knob on the glass oil lamps, bathing the room in dim reddish-yellow light. The walls are lined in colorful silk fabrics my mother artfully attached with a staple gun. More fabric is draped from the ceiling, twisting above the small table where my glass ball waits to decide their fate.

The two of them are holding hands, giggling and whispering. "What do you think she's going to say?" the girl asks.

"That I'll love you for the rest of my life," he says.

I steal a glance. They aren't much older than me, but I know right away the girl is nothing like me. She's happy.

"Please take a seat." I gesture to the chairs in front of the shimmering un-crystal ball. "What is it you desire to know this evening?"

They sit down, hands still tangled together. "Aren't you a little young to be a fortune-teller?" the guy asks.

Of course I am.

I should be in school, holding hands with a boy, picking out a dress for some stupid dance. But that was never the future my mother saw in her own crystal ball.

"I come from a long line of mystics and my gift manifested early." I pause, as if the ridiculous way I'm speaking isn't dramatic enough. "Which means I'm very powerful. I assure you that whatever your futures hold, I will see it here." I wave my hand over the ball with a flourish.

The girl leans forward in her seat expectantly. She has long, wavy black hair just like mine. "What do you see?"

I don't *see* anything, because I'm staring into a hunk of glass I bought online for thirty bucks. But I can't tell her that; I have to say something profound. Something that will change her life—at least for a few days.

I frown, the muscles in my face tightening in mock concern.

"What's wrong?" The girl's posture changes, stiffening to mirror mine.

"I cannot get an accurate read."

"You saw something." Her boyfriend is watching me carefully, aware that I'm hiding something. I can tell from his expression that he thinks it's the truth. He's half right. "Was it bad?"

I look away. "I don't want to say."

The girl inhales sharply and her boyfriend puts his arm around her shoulders, pulling her close. "You have to tell us. Please."

"Are you absolutely sure you wish to know?" The question hangs between us, sucking the air out of the room.

This is the moment.

The one that determines whether or not I've played my part well enough—jingled those bells on my skirt with enough resolve. You have to give a moment like this space to breathe and time to take hold.

The black-haired girl nods without taking her eyes off me.

I have her.

I can tell her anything now and she'll believe me. If I were my mother, I would weave a tale of a bright future, ticking off the number of children she and her boyfriend will have by counting the lines on the edge of her hand. I try to imagine it for her, but I'm not my mother.

The knot in my stomach tightens, born from fear and shame. The pressure and pain build, splintering into a thousand shards of glass that tear apart my insides. There's only one way to stop the pain.

I have to release it one tiny shard—one vicious fortune—at a time.

"Enjoy what little time you have left," I say. "You won't be together by the next waxing moon."

"I don't—" The girl shakes her head, confused.

"What the hell is that supposed to mean?" Her boyfriend sounds angry, but I can tell he's afraid. Fear is the easiest emotion to read.

I cover the ball with a scarf, as if I can't bear to look at it myself. "I'm so sorry. The eye never lies."

I don't need any help with that.

"But we're getting engaged," the girl pleads. "Right, Tony?" The tears are falling now, leaving pale streaks in the foundation that's too dark for her natural complexion. "It has to be a mistake."

I don't respond. At this point, silence is more powerful than anything I can say.

Tony stands up, knocking over the chair. He pulls the girl out of her seat, his knuckles white as he grips her hand. "This is a load of crap. You can't see the future! We're getting married. Aren't we, Heather?"

Heather nods, but I see the doubt spreading across her features. Tony doesn't take his eyes off me as they back out of the trailer. He reaches the door and pauses for a second, offering me the chance to take it all back—to see another future for the two of them. When I don't, he slams his hand against the door, sending it flying open.

I lift the scarf off the ball, polishing it so I'll be able to read the unfortunate future of the next person who steps inside.

I don't know how many people I see tonight. A woman with the cheap blond dye job and the pink lipstick smudge on her cigarette who wanted to know if her boyfriend was cheating—he was. An old man who had gambled away his life savings asked if he was ever going to win big at the races—of course he would. Two bad breakups on the horizon for the drunken girls showing too much cleavage, an unwanted visitor for the quiet brunette in the red sweater, and a few promises of impending bad news. There were more, but I forget most of them five minutes after they leave the trailer.

That's the way it is when you see twenty or thirty people every day for two weeks straight, until you pack up and head for the next town.

It's always the same. Only the fast-food joints change.

The carnival is winding down. It gets quiet, the whir of the rides and the rhythm of the screams from the midway fading into a loop of eighties heavy metal songs. My line started thinning around eleven. But if Van Halen isn't blaring from the speakers, it's midnight by now.

Enough tears for one night.

As I make my way back to the trailer I share with my mom, I see the familiar orange glow of a cigarette in the darkness. I know exactly who it belongs to. I also know he's waiting for me.

Big John steps out of the shadows and into the lights of the midway. The rides aren't running anymore, but the neon bulbs of the Scrambler are still flashing. I look down at him because he's half my height. Big John is a dwarf, but his nickname isn't a joke. This is a fence-to-fence operation, which means he owns everything here—the rides we work, the trailers we sleep in, and the food we eat. He owns us too, and he's an evil bastard. He calls himself Big John to remind everyone that he owns us and his stature doesn't affect his ability to hurt us.

I should know.

"You little bitch," he hisses between gritted teeth. "You think I don't know you were chasing my customers away again?"

He grabs my wrist, twisting it until I fall to my knees. What Big John lacks in height, he makes up for in strength. The pain shoots up my arm, but I barely feel it. All I can think about is the way my skin crawls from the feel of his skin against mine. And how many times he's touched me before.

The first time was four years ago, but it feels like it's been going on forever. Like nothing existed before that day and nothing could exist after it.

I can't exist after it.

He steps closer, his pockmarked face inches from mine. "Need me to teach you a lesson? 'Cause it would be my pleasure." He presses against me, and there's nothing but the smell of stale cigarettes and sweat. Nothing but a thousand more nights like this in my future. Unless I want him to leave my mom and me in one of these crap towns, with nothing but the clothes on our backs.

I wouldn't care, but this is the only life my mother knows.

I remember the month she spent as a checker at the grocery store when I was in kindergarten, trying to decide what I wanted to be when I grew up. She told me it was the longest month of her life. She missed the dizzying lights and outdated music of the midway, the bells on her skirt that made her feel like she was something special, and the rush of predicting futures that would never come true.

"You listening to me, Ilana?" Big John's pinched red face stares back at me, anger coming off him in waves.

I don't respond. Anything I say will make him angrier, and my own rage already threatens to eat me alive.

Finally, he releases me and I can breathe again. Big John flicks his cigarette at me as he walks away. "Remember what I said."

As if I can ever forget.

My mother believes that "what doesn't kill you makes you stronger." But she's wrong.

When evil unthinkable things happen, they don't make you stronger. They keep killing you over and over again. And you don't forget. You relive them, trapped in a continual loop that never ends. She swears you can make it stop by forgiving and moving forward. I'm moving forward, but I'll never forgive.

The light is on inside our trailer, which means my mom already cashed out for the night. When I open the door that never stops squeaking no matter how many times we grease it, she's unbraiding her hair in front of the mirror. My mom is beautiful, my polar opposite in every way. She's fragile and delicate looking, the kind of woman men automatically allow to walk through doors first. I'm not beautiful or delicate, or even ugly.

I'm nothing.

My mother turns to face me, and I know Big John has already been here. I can see the disappointment in her eyes. She gives me a moment to offer an explanation, even though I never give her one. She senses tonight is no different and plunges in. "Ilana, why do you keep doing this? Big John is going to kick us out if you keep this up."

That's what I want.

She puts her hands on my shoulders gently. "You're hurting people. You know that, don't you?"

I laugh, and it sounds as bitter and vicious as I feel. "And you're not? We lie to people for a living. You don't think that hurts them?"

"Yes, we lie. But these poor souls come to us for hope—to hear their lives will get better. You promise them they won't. We may not be able to predict the future, but we can influence it."

I've heard this before, but it never stops sounding ridiculous. "You honestly believe that?"

She picks up a miniature crystal ball sitting on the corner of her vanity. "Do you know what they used to call these?" She turns the ball between her fingers. "The witch's eye. People believed that only a powerful witch could see the future. We may not be able to alter the hands of fate, but the power of suggestion is very real. We affect people's lives. And we can choose to make their lives better, even if it's just for a few minutes."

There is no way to make her understand. I'm not capable of making anyone else's life better when I can't even change my own.

"I can't lie with a smile on my face. Maybe I'm not cut

out for this." Now I am lying and she knows it. I'm a better grifter than my mother any day of the week.

My whole life is a lie.

Tony was pissed. He'd spent the last two hours with Heather, trying to convince her that he wasn't going to change his mind about getting engaged, while she cried her eyes out. All because of some stupid fortune-teller at a cheap-ass carnival.

Tony knew it was crap. He wasn't going to change his mind. He was crazy about Heather. He'd already bought a ring, one of those fancy ones from the jewelry store at the mall. Tony had saved for six months to buy it, and now it was burning a hole in his dresser drawer. After what happened tonight, he almost told Heather about the ring.

But that wasn't the way he wanted to propose—with his girl freaked out because of some second-rate psychic.

Maybe he should've given it to her. . . .

Tony shoved his hands in his pockets, distracted. He was still thinking about it when he stepped off the curb. He never saw the car coming.

Jeanie unlocked the front door. The town house was quiet, a relief after the never-ending noise of the carnival. Loud music, even louder rides, and the voice of the fortune-teller she couldn't forget.

Soon you will have an unwanted visitor.

It sounded like something from a fortune cookie.

Jeanie knew it was ridiculous to obsess over a prediction made by a teenager at a run-down carnival. But she had always been pessimistic. It was hard to ignore bad news when someone actually handed it to you.

She just needed some sleep.

Jeanie didn't bother to turn on the lights in the kitchen as she poured a glass of water. She was still standing in front of the sink when she noticed the broken glass in front of the sliding doors a few feet away.

And when the junkie who broke it pointed the black gun at her red sweater.

I wake to the sound of an angry fist banging on hollow wood. Someone's at the trailer door.

"Antoinette? Ilana? Can you come on out here, please?"

I recognize the voice immediately. It's Leeds, the carnival's mender. His job is to pay off the local cops so they don't hassle us for rigging the games and selling dead goldfish. A few times he negotiated a quick exit out of town, like after the arm fell off the octopus ride with a carload of people in it, or the time some fifteen-year-old girl's father caught her behind the Porta-Johns with CR, both as naked as the Devil Baby.

If Leeds is knocking, it's not good.

"Antoinette! You get your ass out here!" Big John shouts, rattling the door handle.

My stomach seizes and I jump out of bed searching for a sweatshirt. I want to cover up every inch of my skin before my mom opens the door.

"Just a second." She gropes for her robe, still half asleep.

8:07.

Carnies don't get up before noon. Add Leeds and 8:07 together and it equals crap too deep to wade through.

My mother opens the door, and I know I'm right. Leeds is wearing his cheap tweed jacket that makes him look like one of those accident lawyers who advertise on TV at two in the morning. Big John is standing next to him, swollen and red faced in a white ribbed tank and suspenders. Anyone can tell he lost a fight with a bottle of Jim Beam, especially the cop hovering behind him.

"What's the problem, gentlemen?" my mom asks.

"You know anything about a woman getting robbed last night?" Big John points a chubby finger at me. "'Cause I swear if you do, you're gonna be the sorriest little—"

"I don't know what you're talking about," I snap.

"Then why the hell are the cops here?" His voice is hate and poison and the promise of something terrible.

"Let's all calm down," Leeds says. "Ilana, this officer needs to ask you a few questions." Leeds is talking like a real lawyer instead of a cash-and-carry con man.

The cop pulls a notepad out of his shirt pocket. "You remember telling a lady she was going to have"—he flips through the pad—"an unexpected visitor last night?"

"I probably saw fifty people. I can't remember what I said to half of them. What happened? Did she stay up all night waiting for her ex and now she wants her money back?"

It's one of the classics. A third of the women who walk into the tent want to know if their ex is coming back.

"Nope," the cop says without losing the grip he has on the toothpick between his teeth. "She spent the night in the hospital. Guy broke into her house. Robbed the place and beat her up pretty bad."

My mother crosses her arms and switches to the offensive. "I don't see how that involves my daughter. Are you accusing her of something, Officer? Because if you are—"

Leeds holds his hands up. "Calm down, Antoinette. No one's accusing her of anything. The officer is just doing his job."

"That's right, ma'am." The cop moves the toothpick from

one side of his mouth to the other without touching it. Maybe Big John should offer him a job.

I look the cop in the eye and hope he knows how to recognize the truth when he hears it. But it's doubtful. Most people can't or I'd be out of a job. "I'm sorry about what happened, but I don't know anything. People give me five dollars and I give them a story. That's all."

The cop gives me the standard intimidating stare. I look him right in the eye and he nods. "All right then. You let me know if you hear anything."

My mother's silk robe flutters gently in the breeze. She looks like the real thing. Someone who can predict your future as easily as making toast. "We'll be sure to do that."

My mom shoves me back inside and watches as the officer disappears into the midway. She twists her long hair on top of her head and slips on a tank top and jeans. The gypsy is gone. "I'll be back. I'm going to give Leeds a piece of my mind."

She stalks across the dusty lot, and I can't help but think of how she'd react if I told her about Big John—the things he's done to me. But I can barely stand to think about them myself. I could never tell her. If I did, that's what she would see every time she looked at me.

It's what I see when I look in the mirror. I can't face seeing it in her eyes too.

There's another knock at the door and my stomach sinks. Is it Leeds coming back to give me a tongue lashing for causing trouble? I open the curtain covering the tiny window. An old man is standing on the folding steps of the trailer, holding a cap in his hands.

I recognize him from last night.

What did I tell him? Something bad, that's for sure.

But his eyes are bright and hopeful.

I crack the door hesitantly. "Can I help you?"

The old man looks surprised. He was probably expecting me to greet him in my gypsy garb. "You've already helped me, miss. Wanted to thank you." He's a townie, a local for sure, grinning at me with cigarette-stained teeth and tired eyes.

"For what?" Lately, my fortunes haven't been worthy of thanks.

"You said I'd win big if I kept betting on the horses." He pauses and grins wider. "And last night, I finally picked me a winner. Odds were ten to one. Payout was twenty grand."

"You won twenty thousand dollars?"

He nods, excited. "Yep. Like I said, I just wanted to thank you."

I try to think of a response, but my mind is on overload. The girl in the red sweater and now this? What are those odds?

A thought crystallizes with perfect clarity the way the future is supposed to materialize in my cheap glass ball: *My predictions are coming true.*

Is it possible?

The proof already knocked on my door twice this morning.

"Miss?" He's watching me expectantly.

"You're welcome."

He puts his cap back on and disappears, leaving me standing in the doorway of the trailer. He passes Big John huffing through the dust, his beady eyes zeroing in on me. He's looking for me.

It's always me.

"You think you're funny?" Big John points across the lot, his face red and tense. "People don't come to see your hot little ass. They come to hear something good's about to happen in their sorry lives." He's only a few feet away, but I can already smell the sweat mixed with whiskey.

"They want a future!"

Anger churns in my stomach, the sick taste of hate in my throat. "You mean an improbable future?"

Big John grabs my arm, his fat fingers pressing into my skin. He shoves me against the door, crushing my body beneath his. "You've got a smart mouth. Do I need to remind you what happens to little girls with smart mouths?"

The nausea hits me in waves, and I have to swallow the bile to keep from throwing up.

You're not here. You're somewhere else. . . .

I can feel his sweat on my skin, thick and sticky.

Let go.

He pushes away from me, turning at the bottom of the stairs. "I'll see you tonight. And every townie that gives you five bucks better walk out thinking he's gonna be a millionaire. You got that?"

I nod. But I think about all the things he's taken from me. All the things he'll continue to take. I think about the smell of cigarettes and Jim Beam, the feeling of sweat on my skin. I feel it again.

The bells on my skirt drag in the dirt. If they're ringing, I can't hear them. The only thing I can hear is a Def Leppard song blaring from the cheap speakers above the Scrambler and Big John's voice in my ear. I walk over the trash and cigarette butts littering the midway. This whole place is nothing but trash.

Something moves in my peripheral vision near the broken cotton candy cart.

Big John.

He's leading a girl who looks a few years younger than me behind the abandoned cart that marks the edge of the carnival grounds, where the trampled grass and dirt turns into trees and darkness. I've never seen her before. Big John's hand is clamped around her wrist and he's smiling. She's not. The girl glances around nervously like she's trying to decide how embarrassing it will be if she calls out for no reason. Because he's not going to hurt her . . . right?

I can't move.

I'm not the only one.

I want to run or scream or do something, but every muscle in my body is frozen as I watch them disappear into the darkness.

Do something!

I will my legs to run. My voice to scream. But I'm frozen, trapped by the solid wall of fear I can't climb.

How long has he been doing this? How many girls?

"Ilana, there's a line!" Leeds shouts.

I focus on the trailer. The red paint. The folding steps. The line of people milling around outside, waiting for pink and yellow bulbs to light up. They don't care if half of them are burnt out and a seventeen-year-old who hasn't been to school since kindergarten is the one making the promises. No one cares.

I force my legs to move and I block everything out, the way I've done more times than I can count now.

I scan their faces—hopeful, doubtful, nervous, excited—and think about what I'm going to tell them tonight. Will they win love or lose it? Get rich or go broke? Live forever or die tomorrow?

I think about the girl who disappeared behind the cart with Big John. I wish I could predict her future. It would be happy and safe and far from here.

The night blurs around me. I don't know what I see in my glass ball or what I tell the steady stream of hopeful faces that sit across the table. Lies, I know that much. But these lies are different. They leave the marks smiling and happy, filled with dreams of improbable futures.

It doesn't make me feel better like my mother says it will.

But it makes me feel something, even if it's an emotion I can't name.

I stay in the trailer long after the door closes behind the last happy customer. I stare at the crumpled bills in the bowl on the table. I grab them in handfuls, ripping them up and tossing them in the trash. The lights on the Ferris wheel go black and I sit in the semidarkness.

I'm not sure how long I've been sitting here when the door creaks open and I smell the whiskey. Big John is standing in the doorway looking satisfied in a shiny sharkskin shirt that makes him look even sweatier. A bottle of Jim Beam swings from his hand.

My stomach contracts and twists into a knot. I think about the girl, the way I was too scared to help her, and shame burns though me. "What do you want?"

Big John hooks a finger under his suspenders and smiles. "Came to predict your future." He takes a swig from the bottle and points at the glass ball. "Says you're gonna bring your ass to my trailer in ten minutes."

The other girl wasn't enough. With him, it's never enough.

Something inside me snaps.

I think about the old man who won at the races and the woman in the red sweater. Last night, I predicted their futures and they came true. Maybe it was a coincidence. But if there is one thing I've learned in the halls of this dirty school without walls, it's how to play the odds.

"My turn." I stare at the cheap glass ball on the table and back at his vicious face—evil and sadistic and everything wrong with the world. "Fate will deal you a fair hand."

Big John laughs, phlegm rattling in his chest. "You're damn right it will. Cash out and I'll see you in ten—" He looks at his watch. "No—nine minutes."

The door slams behind him and I collect the shredded money in my hands. Time to cash out. I'm putting it in my pocket when I hear someone shout.

I know that voice. I rush to the door, bells jingling at my ankles.

"You've got it all wrong!" Big John shouts. He's holding his hands up to shield himself, the way I have so many times.

A man stands a few yards away, holding a hunting rifle. "You filthy son of a bitch. My daughter told me what you did!"

Carnies come out of their trailers, but no one moves. Even Leeds just stands there with his sleeves rolled up.

"It's a misunderstanding," Big John says.

The girl's father doesn't respond. He keeps the rifle pointed at Big John as if he can see the truth. "Tell 'em that in hell."

I don't see the bullet, but I hear the round explode from the gun. My body tenses for a split second and Big John falls in the dirt.

The man with the rifle spits on the ground and walks away.

Everyone rushes toward the place Big John's body lies motionless. I don't even recognize the faces as I push my way through the crowd.

"Ilana, you don't want to see this."

But I do.

I step through and I see him. The monster from my nightmares, staring up at a sky he will never see again.

It's something I've wished for a thousand times. But I never thought I would see it happen, or that I would be the one to do it. The realization spreads through me slowly like it's stretching after a long nap.

I did this, even if I wasn't the one holding the gun.

I turn and start walking. I pass the trailer I share with my mom. The bells on my skirt are ringing again. I bend down and rip them off one at a time. I keep walking until the carnival is somewhere behind me and I can see the highway in front of me. I won't stop until I can see my future.

Death for the Deathless

MARGARET STOHL

The year 1999, seventh month, from the sky will come
a great King of Terror.

—Michel de Nostradame, *Les Prophéties*

I. Adrienne, 13h52, le 17ème Octobre

It's not possible. It can't be. The end of the world should come at the end.

Not now.

The words of the *Prophéties* rise and fall, senseless, unreliable, as if I am trying to read a flame.

In some ways, I am. At least, Luc is. That's his job. To read.

It's only my job to believe him.

I look up. "So you're absolutely sure? That's it then?" I've said it a thousand times before, now a thousand and one. I smooth my fingers across the yellowed page, resisting the urge to seize it and rip it into tiny pieces. On the other side of the table, a pale-faced mage watches me, dark eyes in more darkness.

Those eyes, most often glued to his dull gunmetal machine, are the only fixed thing in my universe.

"Don't, Adi," he says. Luc knows how I feel, even though I can barely see his face well enough in this light to read his expression.

Les Immortels. We can be so stupid about so many things Mortals take for granted. Like, for example, when it's time to turn on a light.

When it's time to go.

Still, I don't move to light the old lantern in front of me. Instead, I hear the sound of a match striking. Luc shrugs, cupping it in his hands. "I don't make up the words. I just decrypt them. And they're all saying the same thing." The cigarette bobs in his mouth while he talks around it.

"Terror from the sky?"

He nods.

"How long? Weeks? Days?"

"Hours."

I force myself to look back to the words. "But 1999? He's a little late to the party, this king-of-the-sky person. It's 2012. Maybe Nostradamus got it wrong." I push the paper away, stubborn.

Luc smiles. "*Ah, oui, Michel de Nostradame.* Let's ask him again." An old joke, an inside joke. One that only a few would understand.

I wish I didn't. I don't want the words to be true, and I don't want to know what the truth means. More than that, I don't want to be the bearer of the news.

Which I am. Determining the prophecies, that's Luc's problem. Believing them, explaining them, that's mine.

Luc takes a drag off a cigarette from where he sits behind the machine—not the least of his dirty habits. That's Luc, the perpetual rebellion of a boy who is forever seventeen. He'll never do what you want him to, and he's no one's man but his own. James Dean ad infinitum, a thousand years in the making.

He grins at me, his crooked smile the only thing not model-perfect about his rugged face. "*Tant pis.* Too bad. So we're off by a decade or two? It's not a perfect science, what we do." His chin glows like a lump of coal in the shadows, and light flickers off the metal keyboard in front of him.

La Machine Enigmatique. The Enigma Machine. It looks like an old typewriter. Luc types the messages in French, and they appear on the other side—wherever that may be—encrypted. Likewise, encrypted messages appear in this realm on his machine in French. I don't know why Luc clings to the old protocols of World War II cryptology tech. I suppose old habits die hard.

The message today has said that we will die harder, and die now.

Terror from the skies.

That's all the Enigma tells us, all we are given to know.

Another problem of Immortality. We're old, older than Paris, most of us. Older than the Gauls, some of us. Lone creatures of lonely habits. We don't like change. I still pin my hair into curls. Take rosewater baths. Write with fountain pens, on linen paper.

"Put that out."

"Why? Because it will kill me?" A harsh laugh.

Luc sighs, grinding his cigarette into ash. He's only doing it to humor me, though he knows not to smoke in here. The priests might smell him—his tobacco and his coffee and his sleeplessness—and they barely tolerate our presence as it is.

We don't have time for words with them now. We are the children of the devil, by most accounts. Still, things have improved in my long lifetime. No more stakes. No inquisitions. Not for a very long time, at least.

It's what makes today possible, this small room filled with papers and smoke and bad news and a typewriter that is not a typewriter and my old friend with his dark eyes.

So Luc and I sit here, in this smallest room of this large cathedral, perhaps the most famous in all of France, certainly Paris. An anteroom to an anteroom to an anteroom, hidden away on the Ile de la Cité. Ours isn't a room you'll ever see, or one you'll ever know existed. I'm not sure it does, to be honest. Not in the Mortal world, if that's how you define existence.

How do you define existence? Does it even matter anymore?

I consult my watch. "Five minutes. We'd better go."

"And then?" Luc holds my eyes with his, but I can't bear it.

I look away, rising to my feet, smoothing the deep creases in my rumpled summer dress. The washed-out floral print seems incongruous, given the situation. I wish I'd gone home and changed. A pencil skirt, maybe. My good silk blouse, the one with the navy and white polka dots. *La Société de Notre Dame Immortelle,* the deepest secret organization from the darkest corner of the supernatural world, they're not used to seeing me like this. It's one of the countless vanities of Immortals in a Mortal world; we look good even if we don't have to. Especially because we don't have to.

Not that it matters now.

How do you dress for the end of the world?

The others are waiting. The meeting will start soon, if it hasn't already. I grab the page, holding out my hand to Luc. He slips on his battered leather jacket and takes it, cold as death, soft as butter.

It's time.

That's all I know for certain.

II. Luc, 14h02, le 17ème Octobre

I watch her move and it's all I can do not to touch her. No man is immune to the pull of *la Sirène,* but of all men I am the least. Hair. Curves. Bare neck. Bits of wrist and ankle, above and below her wrinkled dress.

I would do literally anything on heaven or earth to have her.

Heaven. I snort.

Mon Dieu, *you're pathetic. You act like a* loup-garou*—a werewolf. Like you want to eat her, not kiss her.*

And so it has been for as long as we have worked together, as long as I can remember. I close my eyes, swallowing. It sounds like a wave crashing in my ears, but I know she can't hear it any more than she can hear my heart pound.

I follow Adrienne down the narrow hallway. Gas lamps flicker dimly from the stone walls, but I can see what I want. What I need.

The light illuminates the curve of Adi's legs through the thin cotton of her dress. I can see plenty.

At a time like this, I shouldn't be thinking about her perfect *derrière,* but I do. It's how she walks. *Elle marche toute en beauté comme la nuit.* In beauty, like the night. You'd write a sonnet to that pair of curves, too.

It makes me want to punch the wall. Instead, I finger the pack of cigarettes in my jacket pocket.

Two years, that's the age difference between us. In Mortal years she's just nineteen. But those gypsy eyes, those black curls—they've been tormenting guys like me for two hundred, more.

Elle est trop belle et trop jeune pour mourir. That's all I can think now. Unlike me, she is too pretty and too young to die.

She stops at the dark wooden doors. Her hand on the iron handle, she draws a deep breath. *Courage,* I think.

"Don't." The word slips out before I can stop myself.

"What?" She doesn't turn around.

"Don't tell them, Adi," I say, catching her hand. She twists to me, a strange expression playing across her lips.

"I have to."

"Of course you don't. Yes, you're the *Voix de Prophétie.* But just because you're the voice of the future doesn't mean you have to tell the others." I think of the society, the room ahead of us teeming with immortal life. "They'll go crazy. They can't imagine facing death, let alone the end of the earth."

"Luc."

"Let's get out of here. I have my moto." I sound as desperate as I am. "You don't know what they'll do. It's not safe."

What happens now? How do you tell Immortals that they're about to die?

How can they hear it?

How can we?

She laughs. "Of course it's not safe. Nothing is. But not because of them." She looks at me, her smile fading into softness. "Not because of us, Luc. We're just the first to know."

When she says my name, I want to cry.

I don't. I know she's barely holding it together as it is. I also know she's bluffing.

And terrified.

Adrienne doesn't want to say it out loud, not this news. Still, she knows it's coming. She knows it will be bad. We both do. Adi, and me, and the few we've told at the Council.

The few we needed, to call the meeting. Everyone we've brought it to.

Any one of us who says otherwise is lying.

It's been brewing for years now. Since the sixteenth century, in fact—the first day I got the first message in a spilt puddle of black ink on yellow paper. The day we met.

Les Prophéties de Nostradame is the public record of everything we've learned over the centuries, as our oracles became seers became prophets became tea leaves became scryers became machines.

Now there's only the Enigma.

The Enigma, and me.

Et Adrienne.

Nostradamus, he's just a name, a personality we invented—the group of us—so we could disseminate information throughout the mortal world. Nostradamus's real name is the *Société de Notre Dame Immortelle.* He's us, the whole lot of us, our joke—named for the church where we hold our meetings. Adi and I carry the truth to the others, and they decide what to do with it. What to tell the Mortals.

But the source of the words, the other end of the line, the sender-recipient of the messages I type out so carefully on the Enigma, that's no joke.

That's a different thing entirely.

I've stopped knowing what to make of it. More and more, all I get are glimpses of disaster. At some point, news stops being news. What else is there to say, when every message is like this—

At forty-five degrees the sky will burn, Fire to approach the great new city: In an instant a great scattered flame will leap up.

Or this?

Earthshaking fire from the center of the earth will cause trem-

ors around the New City. Two great rocks will war for a long time, then Arethusa will redden a new river.

Who writes them? Who sends them? Who is it that cares enough to say? Who knows what is coming our way?

Another person—more philosophical, more religious, at least more curious—would obsess about the source of the message. Me, I'm more concerned with the message itself. What it means. What time I have left.

Besides, I have a god already, and she's standing here in a rumpled dress, beside me.

Adrienne takes a step closer to me. She takes my hands in hers, crumpling the piece of paper she carries between us.

She's standing so close to me I can smell her. Lavender and Earl Grey tea. Chocolates and new bread and rain on the pavement. Wind. Life. Eternity.

That's what I want her to smell like. That's how I'll remember her, for as long as I can.

"Luc. Do you know what your name means?"

I nod. "Light," I say, thinking of my mother and her warm lap.

"Do you know what mine means?" she asks.

Beautiful, I think. Perfect. The thing that defies explanation. "*Non,*" I say. "*Pas du tout.* Not at all."

She smiles, sadly, from somewhere faraway. "Darkness. According to our birth names, you're the light, and I'm the dark. See? This is what I was made to do. Funny, isn't it?"

She doesn't laugh.

Neither one of us does.

Instead, she drops my hands, sliding hers up to my shoulders. For a moment, she lets her head linger on my chest, resting.

I can feel her breathe. And I can hardly breathe myself.

Because the wooden doors are all that stand between us and the end of what has always held us together.

The *Société*—our people, the closest thing to family we've known for hundreds of years—will learn the truth.

That death comes for even the deathless.

I want to stay on this side of the brown doors forever. I want to circle my arms around these dark eyes and dark curls and turn us to stone, in the middle of this stone hallway.

I want to tell her I love her, and that I know somewhere inside that crumpled dress, above those wrists and beneath those curls, she loves me too.

All the things we have never said.

Instead, I say nothing, and she pulls away from me, turning her face like a bubble is popping between us.

III. Adrienne, 14h12, le 17ème Octobre

The door groans as I pull it open.

The faces surround me in the wide chamber of our council room. *La Société de Notre Dame Immortelle. Les Enchanteurs, les Sorciers, les Magiciens, les Vampires et les Loups-Garous*—even a few *Fantômes* with nothing better to do.

In other words, the Immortal Undead, in all our many forms.

They've come to Paris, but they're not from here. Not all of them. They're from everywhere, from cities where they live among the Mortals, from graves and caves where they remain in isolation.

The faces around me are drawn, worried; everyone is sitting too far forward in ancient hardwood chairs. We've called this meeting suddenly, without warning. They know that is never a good sign.

But then, there are few good signs now, not for us. Not anymore. All the cryptic messages have led to today. Now.

The King of Terror, the great waiting death from the skies, is upon us.

There's no point in drawing it out.

I step up to the podium in the center of the room, a carved stone half-pillar, in front of a lone row of crushed-velvet chairs.

I lean against the stone, looking out at the faces in the shadows of the cavernous space. I feel their eyes on me.

I take a breath.

Let the words come.

Give me the courage to say them.

I don't know who I'm asking, not exactly. Luc? Myself? That enigmatic presence on the other end of our clumsy encryption machine?

Does it matter?

Is anyone there?

I raise my voice. "*C'est fini. Le fin.* The end. We need to accept the truth of our predicament. It's getting worse. We don't have very long now." I look up, but I can't meet their eyes. "I'm so sorry, but in this matter, we are beyond doubt."

I smooth the paper out on the stone in front of me, focusing only on the typed words.

"There's more," I say.

I keep my eyes on the page as I speak.

It's the only way I can bring myself to do it.

I tell them, again, about the world killer. About the unthinkable mass, and the trails of fire and stars. We ourselves have predicted this for six centuries now. Our Nostradamus. The thing we hoped would not be. The event some of us even prayed—*to whom?*—would not occur. I unfold the paper, repeat the final words.

"All that has been foretold will come to pass, on the last breath of this, the last day of the last month of eternity. The King of

Terror, the great death that falls from the skies, is upon us. And even death will not spare the deathless."

It couldn't be clearer. Death will not spare us. Even our immortal lives will end today.

From what we can tell, Mortals will believe it is an asteroid. That's what Luc says.

The word itself, which means "starlike," seems a cruel joke, because this star isn't bright and won't bring hope or create life. It will utterly destroy it. Without feeling, without motive, without reason.

I tell them it's not a mistake. The Enigma Machine has typed out only this message, every day, for the last week.

Each message names this day as the last.

No predictions have ever been so detailed, so complete.

Seven lines, repeated seven times.

I tell them it won't be long after that.

Minutes, maybe seconds.

Today.

Luc stands with me. He doesn't say a word, but he doesn't have to. As usual, as always, his presence is the one fixed thing.

His presence, and his *prophéties.*

His eyes do not look away.

My voice sounds strange and steady in the darkness. I do not feel anything beyond the words I speak.

I am dark, I think.

This is how it should be.

The moment I finish speaking, my words die in the air above me. I understand the truth of the prophecy.

There is no reason to keep our powers in check, not anymore. No reason to do or not do anything at all.

I have lost control of the room.

The most powerful creatures in the world, who sit within it, have lost control of themselves. I can see it in the look of their eyes, the twitch of their impatient fingers, the crazed flush of their faces, the glow of their auras, their staffs and talismans.

We don't have to wait for the terror to come from the skies. It begins now, as soon as the words are spoken.

Shock turns to rage turns to chaos. Despair. Rage. Disbelief. They will do this now, themselves, on their own terms. I step back as the haphazard violence of power surrounds us, engulfs us.

Ancient rivalries and unnatural behaviors held too long in check explode from every corner of the room. There is no holding back now.

No point or reason. No higher power or accountability. Only the madness of powerlessness, perhaps the only thing we've never felt, not in this room.

There is nothing left to say, only to do—and they all begin to do it, in their own way.

All we can do is watch ourselves in horror.

"I told you," hisses Luc, grabbing my arm. "It's not safe here. They have nothing left to lose. They're going to riot."

Just as he speaks, an ancient *sorcier* erupts into blue flame, sending from each outstretched arm an electrical pulse wave that floods up the sides of the cathedral walls, all the way to the point of the highest spire. His power surge immolates everything it touches into ash, least and most of all the *sorcier* himself.

It's the supernatural equivalent of throwing yourself off a burning building.

A Ruina spell. Unimaginably destructive, and completely irreversible.

Like today, I think.

Burning timbers fall around us, and Luc pulls me closer to him, shielding my head with his arms. I see a patch of blue sky now, at the seam where the walls should be meeting the ceiling—where the world is falling apart.

"We have to go, Adi. Now!" I can hear Luc, but I can't move. My feet feel as much like stone as the altar in front of me.

Luc picks me up, yanking me from the path of a vampire. I cannot help but watch as the creature dives out of the way of the fires, reaching instead to instinctively pincushion the nearest flesh, rooting about for anything to sink his teeth into. Our baser instincts seem to have overtaken all of us.

An elderly *enchanteur* does not resist, closing her eyes until it is over.

"Don't look," Luc says, but I can't help it. Smoke fills the room, stinging my throat, stuffing my ears, but I cannot close my eyes.

It is not over.

A chair flies over our heads, and Luc staggers closer to the broad cathedral doors. Between us and the streets, *a loup-garou* kicks and hurls chairs against the wall. Blood spatters as he looses his jaws, free to bring his own destruction now.

Luc doesn't try to stop him, slamming instead his own back into the massive wooden doors at the front of the church.

I wait for another patch of blue sky to appear, but it isn't there.

It doesn't come.

All that I see are more faces, curious bystanders crowding up the front steps of Our Lady of Paris, struggling to see what all the ruckus is about.

The *loup-garou* doesn't wait, and as Luc pushes through the crowd in front of us, I hear the screams of the poison inside the room leaching into the streets. Luc stumbles, and I wonder if he feels the blood slick beneath his scuffed boots.

He slides me onto the back of his moto, kicking it into

gear with one arm still around me. He turns his face, just so. His mouth is against my forehead as he shouts into my matted hair.

"Hold on, Adi. No matter what, don't let go."

I nod. I won't. I promise.

Not now. Not yet.

It doesn't matter what comes after this, I think. What falls from the sky. We had less time than we knew.

My words alone were a world-killer.

IV. Luc, 14h41, le 17ème Octobre

We fly, bumping, over the seam where the cobblestones give way to smooth asphalt.

I pull into the space between Dumpsters and beneath the laundry line where I keep my bike.

I turn off the moto.

The silence is surreal; the alley behind my apartment is strangely quiet.

Nothing has happened here, not yet.

No one knows what is about to happen.

Someone next door has begun to roast a chicken. Marceline, across the hall, will be home from school any minute now. An open window above mine broadcasts a football game from inside.

Paris SG versus Marseille, I think, pulling out my keys. Out of habit, I listen for the score, even as we rush up the steps and push our way through the little gate.

Only Adrienne's eyes tell me it is real. When she looks at me, I see flame and ash and blood. I see the brokenness and the ending, the rising panic.

Wordlessly, I swing open the door and scoop her effortlessly into my arms. Her head drops against my shoulder as I carry her inside.

My room is a bed and a window and a kettle. I let my eyes follow hers, a circle around my room. The walls are bare. The shelves empty. Dirty coffee cups piled in the sink. A lone bag of leeks sits on my counter. Leeks? What was I thinking? The end of the world and a bag of leeks.

We need only the bed.

I place her on the mattress gently, as if she were a dandelion. A dream. A wish.

But she isn't.

Adrienne is stronger than that. Harder. She sits up and looks past me, out my good window, and I turn to see the fire burning across the city. Our Lady in flames. I listen for the sirens.

Then I close the window.

Enough.

"Don't you want to see?" she whispers, looking at me sadly. I smile down at her, pulling a stray curl loose from the corner of her mouth. A single tear catches on her lashes. "For the last time? How it ends?"

Adi's lips are the color of pink champagne.

"I do. I want to see everything." I lean closer to her, until I can feel her breath on my cheek. "For the first time. How it begins."

It's you, I think.

You are the beginning and the end.

You always were.

Her eyes meet mine.

She pulls my leather jacket down my arms, without looking away from me. Our gestures become frantic, and I fumble with her buttons, nearly yanking her dress in two.

I give up and let the fabric rip. A button strikes my temple and she smiles.

She pulls my shirt over my head, pulling me down to her side.

Instinctively, I slide my hands down, moving her on top of me. Her skin is slippery as pearls, as petals between my fingers.

I'm still wearing my jeans, and she's still in her dress, pooling down around her hips. Her camisole is lacy and red. A tiny tattoo of what looks like a half a heart rests just above the curve of her perfect left breast.

Then I see it isn't a heart.

It's a flame.

I stare, wonderingly.

She looks down. "That? My candle in the shadow." She touches my chin. "For you, Luc. My light."

I can't look away.

For me.

She carries me next to her heart.

Me.

Red lace and fire between her wrists and her hem. Two things I never knew.

I kiss her, hard, but I cannot kiss her hard enough. She pulls away, breathless, and I bury my face in the hollow of her neck.

Near the flame.

"I'm still here. I'll be right beside you, Adi. I'm not going anywhere." I hold out my hand and she takes it, threading her fingers between mine.

Her eyes are wet with tears that hang in the fringe of her eyelashes, refusing to fall.

"I know."

She doesn't say anything else.

"Luc."

Her voice breaks on my name.

It is only one word, but it is mine. It is enough for me.

"I'm here." I kiss the pattern of her fingers. "It's the only place I ever wanted to be." I rub her hand against my closed eyes. "Go to sleep, *ma belle*."

She smiles. "I'm not afraid. Not now. Not anymore." She pulls free, wrapping her fingers in my hair, raising her mouth to mine.

I am afraid, I think.

I'm afraid it isn't happening. I'm afraid I'm not really kissing her, that I'm asleep in my own bed, alone. That I'm going to wake up any minute now, to bad coffee and worse cigarettes.

But I don't wake up. I won't.

I'll never wake up again.

It's real.

Everything, all of it. She's real, so I'm real too. Even if only for a moment.

It is peaceful here, in her kiss.

I can rest here.

Finally.

I lay my smile against hers and we don't stop kissing as the last sparks of the known universe fly.

Our flames climb even higher than that.

V. Adrienne, 15h00, le 17ème Octobre

I stare into Luc's eyes, wrapping my fingers in his hair. I pull his mouth to mine.

We aren't kissing anymore, I don't think.

We're breathing.

I want every part of our bodies to touch, as long as they can. I want my skin to grow into his, like two webbed fingers of the same amphibious creature.

Heart to heart. Hip to hip. Toe to toe.

Cell to cell. Blood to blood. Bone to bone.

Ash to ash.

They say we all die alone, the Mortals. But I know now it's not true. Not for Immortals, anyway.

It's only now that I am dying that I am finally not alone.

We are here now, for this one moment.

Really here.

Mortals and Immortals, the planet and the people.

The dogs and the cats and the birds, Luc and me. Everyone and everything, all history and all time, *tous ensemble.*

We all go down together.

And when we do, I know what happens. I bring Luc home to the peace that belongs only to us. We take each other into the dark.

It is our first time as much as our last, our beginning, in our end. A lifetime lived in one forever hour.

Love is its own oblivion; death seems somehow smaller.

VI. Luc, 2h00 le 18ème Octobre

We sit in the darkness at the edge of *la Cathédrale de Notre Dame,* as close to the perimeter as the fire trucks and the police and the ambulances and the shocked crowd will allow.

Adi wears my clothes. I keep my hand fixed to her waist, beneath my old black sweater. We have become one thing. Even so, everything has changed. Her curls are wild, her lips are purple. Her eyes are red, like she herself has been lit on fire.

She has been. We both have.

Our Lady is gone, taking with her *la Société de Notre Dame Immortelle,* every last one. The end of the universe came, all right. *Oui. Le fin.*

But not for the Mortals.

Only for everyone and everything we knew.

Our Nostradamus, gone.

My Enigma Machine, gone.

And the prophecy?

Adi points to the distant place, the line where one darkness gives way to another. "*La Seine,* it's red with fire, see? The reflection?"

I nod. "*L'Ile de la Cité* must be burning all the way down to the water." It's true. The island where we stand, in the middle of Paris, is going up in smoke.

She looks at me, aghast.

"*The prophecy,* Luc." She can barely speak the words.

"Scattered fire from the skies," I say, remembering. I pass her a paper cup of bitter coffee. Her hands are shaking.

"The King of Terror?" She glances at me from the corner of her eye. She already knows the answer. She has, I think, since the first moment she saw her words themselves could bring on an apocalypse of their own.

I shrug. "Who knows. Does it matter?"

She shivers. "It does to me."

I see the last flickers of doubt and wonder on her face. Who was at the other end of the machine? The Great Enigma himself? Can anyone ever be certain?

She shakes her head.

She is certain. She knows.

And she knows I am certain too.

I pull off my jacket, wrapping it around her.

"C'est moi."

"It's me."

Fate

SIMONE ELKELES

—1—
CARSON

As I step off the bus with my duffel, I stare at the sign across the street welcoming me to my new home. *Seaside Campground and RV Park.* I never thought I'd be homeless at the age of eighteen. Well, I *was* homeless. Today, I'm the proud owner of a crappy RV on the smallest piece of land at Seaside RV Park.

With the hot Florida sun at my back, I enter the general office and find the property manager at the front desk. I already know the guy from the phone conversation I had with him, and it's pretty obvious he doesn't have a stellar work ethic.

The dude is sitting beside a big box of half-eaten donuts. "What do you want?" he barks in what he probably thinks is an intimidating voice. He has no way of knowing that nothing intimidates me.

"I'm Carson Miller," I tell him. "The new owner of the RV on lot twenty-six."

"All right." He takes a clipboard with a bunch of papers attached to it and hands it to me. "Fill out all the info, sign the agreement, then give it back to me with your deposit for the monthly rent on the lot."

After filling out the forms and giving him the cash, I'm officially a resident of Seaside.

I sling my duffel over my shoulder and walk down a winding dirt road lined with campers, tents, and RVs. I stop in front of an RV that looks like it's seen better days. Lot 26.

Home.

The red and orange sunset painted on the side is faded and dirt-encrusted, and a banged-up screen door is lying in the dirt next to the RV like it's the door's final resting place. A bunch of bright yellow and red flowers perfectly outlining the rectangular lot looks out of place. I walk up to the door and put the key in the slot, but realize pretty quick that the lock doesn't work. I probably should've checked it the first time I came to look at the RV, but all I was interested in was finding a cheap, permanent place to stay. I got lucky that the woman selling the RV just wanted to get rid of it, fully furnished with dishes and utensils and everything. Supposedly it was her father's place and he'd died recently, so she had no interest in keeping it.

"Are you moving in?" I hear a squeaky, excited voice from behind me.

I turn around and see a red-haired girl wearing dirty, ripped jeans and a football jersey that's seen better days.

"Yep."

"Where are your parents?" she asks.

I stand frozen for a second before answering. "Don't have any."

She gives me a look of disbelief as she walks toward me. "Of course you have parents. *Everyone* has parents. If you didn't, you wouldn't be alive."

"Thanks for the biology lesson," I mumble.

"That's okay if you don't want to talk about your parents. Half the time I don't want to talk about mine, either. By the way, I'm Willow. Willow Baxter."

I wonder how Willow hasn't gotten the not-so-subtle hint that I'm not in the mood to talk. I don't intend to make any friends while I'm living here. My goal is to work and save up so I don't have to worry about paying off the rest of the loan I got for the RV or paying rent on this small piece of earth that my RV is on. I open the door and catch a whiff of some nasty odor coming from inside.

I walk into the place, feeling a small sense of pride. This is mine, and no matter how crappy it is, nobody can take it away from me.

I drop my bag on the bed and start opening the windows to let the place air out. Who knows how long it's been since someone lived here.

"What's your name?" Willow practically yells through the ripped screen as if I'm hard of hearing.

"Carson."

"Were you named after someone? Because I was named after a tree. And before you go thinking it was any old type of tree, it wasn't. It was a tree that my parents carved their initials into when they fell in love."

"I wasn't named after anyone . . . or anything."

"Oh. That's too bad."

Is this chick for real? "Not really. Listen, I'm gonna clean up the place and start unpacking. See you later."

She knocks on the side of the RV, the sound echoing inside. "Need help?"

"Nope. I got it."

"Okay. See you later, Carson," she says, waving wildly.

I watch Willow until she turns around and disappears. Alone now, I lean on the edge of the small kitchen counter. I sigh, and it feels like I'm releasing a bunch of demons. This is a new beginning, a place to start a new life and forget my past.

—2—
WILLOW

"I met our new neighbor today," I tell my parents as we sit down for dinner. "His name is Carson."

"That's nice," Mom says.

"I think we should invite him over for dinner or something."

Dad reaches out and grabs one of the cornbread muffins that I made. "That sounds like a great idea, Willow." He takes a bite, then turns to my mother. "This is delicious. Our daughter has a talent, Betsy."

"Yes, she does," Mom says, smiling at him. "She's also got a green thumb. Have you seen what she's done next door?"

"I sure have. I hope that Carson fella appreciates all the hard work you put into his property."

After Mr. Yates died, I've made sure that his yard is taken care of. He used to pay me to do it, but it wasn't like a job, because I like to garden. I don't know if Mr. Yates appreciated the well-groomed yard, or if he just liked having me come over so he could have someone to talk to. He was lonely and his family didn't come around much. I wonder if Carson is going to be just as lonely as Mr. Yates.

• • •

Carson's lived next door for two weeks when I decide to make a housewarming cake for him. It's a special recipe I made up two years ago one day when I was bored. I call it Creamy Apple Pie Upside-Down Cake. I sold the recipe to this bakery called The Cakery Bakery in town, and it's one of their best sellers.

I find Carson outside his RV, sitting on a folding chair in front of Mr. Yates's old fire pit. He sits alone every night like this, staring into the fire as if the answers to life are gonna jump out of the flames and smack him in the face. I don't want to burst his bubble and tell him that's not gonna happen.

"Hi, Carson!" I say cheerfully as I walk toward him. "I made you a housewarming present."

He eyes the cake in my hand.

"Here," I say, handing it to him. "Take it."

"Thanks," he mumbles before putting the cake inside his RV and coming back out.

I sit on a stump a little ways from the fire. "I'm glad you moved in. It was sad having no neighbors after Mr. Yates died. He was a nice man, and had the most awesome stories about when he was a teenager, like the time he dressed as a girl to get into his girlfriend's dorm room."

Carson watches the fire without responding.

I say something to fill the void, which I figure is better than uncomfortable silence. "How old are you? You know, if you don't mind me asking."

"Eighteen."

"Oh. I'm sixteen. I have a cousin Tracy who's my age, and she's dating this guy Jake who's eighteen." I laugh nervously. "Jake's really different from you, though. He's really rude. And he's got his ears pierced with lug nuts. Tracy told me that once his ear got infected by the lug nut and all this pus started oozing out of it. She said that—"

He looks up at me and shakes his head, as if he's completely uninterested in the pus-infected lug-nut ear-piercing story.

"TMI, huh?" I say.

He nods.

Okay, so I guess Jake's oozing ear probably isn't the best conversation starter. "You don't talk much, do you?"

Carson leans forward on his elbows. "Listen, Willow, I've got to be honest with you. I probably won't be as good of a neighbor as Yates, so don't go having high expectations."

"Why not?"

"Well. Like you noticed, I don't talk much."

"I don't mind," I tell him. "I can talk for the both of us until you're ready to, you know, reciprocate."

He picks up a stick and tosses it into the fire. "I may never reciprocate."

I pick up a stick and toss it in the fire, too. "You need to talk to people, Carson. You might not know it yet, but you will."

"What I need is money. Lots of it."

"For what?"

He looks up at me again, the yellow fire flickering in his green eyes. "Did anyone ever tell you that you ask too many questions?"

"I'm curious by nature," I say proudly.

He gives a cynical laugh. "Yeah, well, I'm not."

We sit for a while. Carson stares into the fire while I study his face. I don't think he realizes how good-looking he is. I can't pinpoint his best feature. He's got a straight nose, a strong jawline, and eyes that are so piercing he could probably attract any girl he wants. I can't look at them for too long or else I get all tingly inside. I've never seen him smile, but I'd bet that if he did it would brighten up whatever room he's in.

I'm about to tell him I was chosen to be the head debater on the debate team at school when he looks up and asks, "How did your dad lose his arm?"

I don't really think about it much, although I guess it's obvious to the rest of the world that my dad only has one arm. He doesn't walk around with a prosthetic limb or anything . . . he said it's no use trying to hide or be ashamed of it. It's been three years since he came back from the Middle East. At first I couldn't stop staring at the place where his arm should be, and I was afraid to hug him. Eventually it became a nonissue, and now I don't even remember what he was like before. "The army. He was serving in Iraq and he kind of ran into an explosive."

"That sucks."

"He's alive. That's really all that matters."

"You always look at the positive side of everything?" Carson asks.

I think about it for a second before answering. "Yeah, I do. I just don't see any use looking at things in a negative way. It'll only make you sad. Why be sad if you don't have to be?"

He shrugs. "I don't know. It seems to be the theme of my life lately."

"Well, you need to change that."

He laughs. Not a small, polite laugh designed to make me feel good. It's a real laugh, the first one I've ever heard come out of his mouth. It's so genuine it makes me smile just hearing it. "I don't know if anyone can change, Willow. Especially not me."

"Everyone can change, Carson," I say. "*Even* you."

—3—
CARSON

I'm building wooden pallets from scrap wood when Willow walks past me on her way home from school. She's got her backpack slung over one shoulder and her eyes locked on the sky above. Willow isn't a classic beauty, but she's definitely got something about her that makes you look her way. It could be her long red hair and the headband that she always wears, showing off a freckled face that looks so innocent you wonder if she's for real.

"Yo, Willow. Talk to me."

It amuses me that she doesn't hesitate. She's not cautious and skeptical, like me. In fact, she's the exact opposite.

"Need help?"

"Maybe. Want to help me make these pallets?"

"Okay, but first you have to tell me what a pallet is."

With hurried steps, Willow comes over and hangs her backpack on one of the thick low-lying branches of the only tree on my lot.

The first time I met Willow, I thought she was the most annoying girl I'd ever met. I mean, seriously, the girl cannot keep her mouth shut for an entire five minutes. If she did, she might instantaneously combust. And she's got this annoying habit of being upbeat and optimistic about everything and anything.

Every instinct in my body tells me to run and hide whenever I see or hear her. Instead, I find myself being strangely amused by my red-haired neighbor. I've gotten used to her hanging around.

"This is a pallet," I say, showing her the square structure I've nailed together with wooden slats. "I sell 'em to companies for nine bucks apiece. It's not much, but I make enough to pay for this place."

"What do you want me to do?"

Truth is, I really don't need her to do anything. I can practically build these pallets blindfolded, but I figure hearing Willow and her crazy stories will stop me from thinking too much. I need to stop thinking.

"Set up the wood pieces in a square pattern and I'll come around and nail them down."

"Okay."

It doesn't take long before Willow and I get into a rhythm and we've got a pretty good assembly line going. Maybe I was wrong and I do need her to help me so I can finish faster. Forty-five minutes later, Willow announces that we're out of scrap lumber and we're done. We finished a stack of ten pallets in record time.

"I owe you dinner," I tell her.

She smiles shyly. "No, you don't. You owe me a *favor*."

"What kind of *favor*?"

She stands in front of me with furrowed eyebrows. "I don't get people to owe me favors much, so I better save this one for a rainy day. I'll let you know as soon as I figure it out."

"You're not like any other girl I've ever known."

"Is that a good thing?" she asks, but then holds her hand up. "Wait, don't answer that question."

"Why?"

"Because my mom once told me never to ask questions I don't want to know the answer to."

I nod. "I wish I'd gotten that advice from my mom."

"What's the best advice she ever gave you?" she asks.

"She didn't." I look off into the distance, because the truth still stings after all these years. "My mom left when I was nine years old. She visited every couple of years, but I haven't seen her in a while. I guess you could say my mom wasn't a permanent fixture after she moved on. She was more of an acquaintance."

"I'm sorry."

"Yeah, well, it is what it is. No need to dwell on it now."

"Do you know where she lives?"

"Nope."

"Aren't you the least bit curious?" she asks, then backs up and puts her hand over her mouth. "I'm sorry. I know I ask too many questions. Just forget I asked that last one."

She reaches up to slide her backpack off of the branch, but I put my hand over hers to stop her. "You don't have to leave." I look into her eyes and tell her the truth. Not because she's prying, but because I want to. "I don't blame her for bailing. I would have left if I was her, too."

Willow leans forward and wraps her arms around me. "Thanks," she murmurs into my chest.

"For what?"

She keeps her arms around me but looks up, her big brown eyes showing nothing but empathy. "Being real."

I hug her back. "Thank *you,* Willow."

"For what?"

"Letting me be real."

—4—
WILLOW

I have a crush. A big one.

I didn't mean to fall for Carson. Maybe it was the way he laughed when I told him to always be positive. Or maybe it was the way he hugged me two days ago, after I helped him make the pallets. I could always blame my crush on his eyes—those bright green, fire-reflecting eyes.

But deep down I know it's not his eyes.

A loud banging noise outside interrupts my thoughts. I push our curtains aside and peek out the window. Carson is standing in front of his RV, making pallets. His muscles bunch up as he manipulates the pieces of wood and nails them together.

I watch him for a while, stupidly staring as if I'm watching the most captivating home improvement show known to man. When he wipes sweat off his face with his shirt and glances in my direction, I snap out of my trance and quickly let go of the curtain.

Show over.

Just as I'm vowing not to stare out the window at Carson and admire everything about him ever again, there's a knock at the door.

Oh no.

Maybe I should ignore it and hope he goes away so I don't have to explain why I was spying on him.

I wince as I slowly open the door, ready to apologize to my neighbor for spying on him. But it's not Carson standing in the doorway. It's my friend Katie.

"Hey, Willow!" Katie says. Her curly blond hair is up in a ponytail and she's wearing shorts so short they ride up her butt. I know this because her locker is next to mine and I always catch her picking her shorts out of her crack between classes. "Umm . . . is that your new neighbor with his shirt off?"

"Yes," I say slowly.

Katie flips her hair back and says enthusiastically, "Wow. He's even hotter than what you described." She glances at Carson. "Invite him to the lake with us."

"Carson!" I yell out. "Want to come to the lake with us?"

"Maybe later," he says.

I'm ashamed to say that I wish he'd simply said no, for

the mere fact that I like spending time with Carson alone. I know it's weird, but when I'm with him I feel like we have this connection. If other people are with us, I'm afraid the connection will disappear. Or maybe I don't want him to come to the lake because I don't want to share him with anyone else.

I'm so selfish.

I head to the lake with Katie and give a short wave when we pass Carson.

"Have fun," he says.

"We will," I call out.

At the lake, our friend Dex is leaning back on his elbows, his face pointing toward the sun. Dex's best friend, Tyler, is skipping stones near the water's edge.

I sit on the bench next to Dex. We talk for a while . . . about school, life, and how sports is the center of the universe—that's according to Dex.

"Katie tells me you've got a boyfriend," Dex says.

"I do not have a boyfriend," I tell him.

"She's got a major crush," Katie chimes in while Tyler is teaching her how to skip stones. "He's not her official boyfriend . . . yet."

I can feel my face getting red-hot just thinking about the prospect of Carson being my boyfriend. It's a fantasy, not reality. "He doesn't even know I like him," I tell them. "Besides, we're just friends."

"With benefits?" Dex asks.

"No, it's not like that."

When Tyler and Katie challenge each other to jump in the lake fully clothed, Dex turns to me. "Is that *the boyfriend*?"

I look to where his attention is focused. My mouth goes dry when I see Carson walking over to us. "Shh, don't embarrass me," I tell Tyler in a hushed whisper.

Carson stops right in front of me and smiles. "Hey."

"Hey." He's wearing a tank top, showing off muscles that I'm itching to touch. I feel like my face is on fire just thinking about it. "Carson, this is Dex, Katie, and Tyler. They live at Seaside, too."

Carson shakes Dex's hand, then nods to Tyler and Katie.

Carson finds a spot next to me on the bench and nudges me with his shoulder. "So these are your friends, huh?"

"Yep. Just so you know, sometimes they act normal, but it's not often."

"We were just about to have a competition," Dex says. "You game, Carson?"

Carson shrugs. "Depends on what type of competition."

"Basically," Dex explains, "you have to skip a rock and the one who makes it skip the most times wins."

"Sounds easy enough," Carson says, now standing.

"I forgot to tell you what the losers have to do." Dex grins. "They have to jump in the lake . . . naked."

Carson looks toward me and I shrug. "I told you they weren't normal." I toss a stick at Dex. "Carson isn't playing, so go find someone else to challenge."

"Why not?" Dex says. "He chicken?"

"No," I tell him. "He just doesn't want to make the rest of us have to look at your naked body."

I stand up. "Come on," I say, grabbing Carson's hand and leading him back toward our homes. "We'll see you later."

"Don't do anything I wouldn't do!" Tyler calls out, then laughs.

I'm painfully aware that we're still holding hands as we walk through the gravel paths of Seaside. I don't want to let go anytime soon, and savor the warmth of his skin on mine. I wonder what it would be like to be Carson's girlfriend.

When we reach his place, he releases my hand and points to a pickup truck parked a few feet away. I'd noticed it earlier, but thought it was one of the neighbor's new trucks.

"New wheels?" I ask him.

"Yep. Like it?"

I saunter around the truck, taking in all the scratches and dents.

"It needs a little work," he admits.

"It has character," I tell him, then pat him on the back. "Like you."

"You sayin' I need work?" he asks.

"We all need work. You especially." I push him back playfully, then try to dodge away from him but trip on his foot and lose my balance. He reaches out and grabs my arm, keeping me from falling.

"Ow!" I say, clutching my arm and pretending his grip was too rough. "That's gonna bruise."

"I'm so sorry." He steps toward me, suddenly serious. "I didn't mean it."

He gently holds me against the truck and pulls up my sleeve.

"I'm just kidding," I say, laughing.

"Don't joke about that." His face is close to mine now, his expression grave. He brushes stray hairs out of my face, his fingertips gently touching my cheek. "I would never hurt you."

"I know."

He looks down at me, his eyes piercing mine so intently I feel like I'm getting a glimpse inside his wounded soul. Being so close to him makes my heart beat a million times a minute. I've never wanted to kiss someone so badly. My entire life has been waiting for this moment.

As if he can read my mind, he bends his head down to kiss me. I'm ready for this. More than ready.

I lift my head up so our lips are just inches apart now. I close my eyes and wait for his lips to meet mine, but they don't. A car passes us, and instead of ignoring it Carson leans back and the moment is gone.

"Sorry about that," he murmurs, then rubs the back of his neck in frustration.

"About what?"

"Forget it." He starts to walk away from me. "I gotta go."

"Wait," I call out. He stops, but doesn't look at me. I don't want him to walk away just yet. I liked the way he looked at me when he was about to kiss me. I want to hold his hand again. My words stream out of my mouth without my brain fully registering what I'm saying. "I'm calling in that favor you owe me."

He raises an eyebrow.

"Take me on a date, Carson."

—5—
CARSON

I look at myself in the small, old mirror in the bathroom as I shave after taking a long, hot shower. Tonight is the night. My date with Willow.

How did I get myself into this mess?

I didn't have anything remotely decent to wear tonight. I went to the thrift store in town this afternoon and bought a button-down shirt and jeans that don't have holes in them. I figure Willow wouldn't appreciate me showing up for a date in my usual ripped jeans and T-shirt.

At eight, I knock on her door. Her father answers it, but

doesn't invite me in. Instead, he says, "Willow, Carson is here," then motions for me to follow him as he walks outside.

"So . . . besides the occasional small talk, I haven't had a chance to really get to know you," Baxter says. "Tell me about yourself, son."

"There's not much to tell. I'm eighteen, originally from Miami, and, well, let's just say I'm trying to figure out life."

"My daughter speaks highly of you," he says. "Seems like you two have some sort of friendship."

I nod.

Baxter pats me on the back. "Just remember that she's a special girl . . . my only child. And she's sixteen."

"You have nothing to worry about. We'll be home early."

My words seem to satisfy him. "Good. I think we're on the same page. Let's keep it that way and we'll get along just fine."

The door to the Baxters' RV opens and Willow steps out. She's wearing dark jeans that hug her curves. Her shirt is cut just low enough to give a small glimpse of the curve of her breasts. Damn. I didn't know up until now that the girl had curves.

But she does.

She's even got makeup on, making her look older than sixteen. My body is reacting to her, and I wasn't expecting that.

"You look great," I tell her when she steps closer.

She smiles sheepishly. "Thanks."

My instinct tells me to scan her up and down a second time, but I stop myself. I sense that both of her parents are staring at us, analyzing our interaction. The entire situation is awkward. It's no wonder I never wanted to meet my ex-girlfriend's parents when I was in high school. I'm used to running away from parental scrutiny, and I'm itching to get out of here.

"Ready?" I ask.

"Yeah."

In the car, Willow sighs. "Thanks for taking me out. I know you don't want to."

"It's cool," I tell her. "We'll have fun."

Once I drive away from Seaside and we're on the road, Willow stares out the window. I expect her to talk my ear off, but she's silent, and it feels strange.

At a stoplight, I turn to her. "Talk."

She looks at me innocently. "About what?"

"Hell if I know. I just got used to hearing you blabber on about stupid stuff. It's what you do. I miss it."

"Sorry." She fidgets with her hair. "I guess I'm nervous about tonight."

"No need to be nervous. This isn't a *real* date, Willow. Think of it as two friends just hanging out, okay?"

She nods. "I joined the debate team, but I don't like it. I mean, they give us time limits on our speeches, as if debating is a time-sensitive sport."

"Sport?" I question. "Since when is debate a sport?"

"It is. I'll tell you why." I can tell she's getting excited by the way she shifts her body and talks with her arms waving around as if they're an extension of her words. "It's something you either win or lose, like any sport. It's something you have to practice, like any sport. And it's exhausting, like any sport. Am I right or am I right?"

I laugh.

"What? You don't agree with me?"

"I'm afraid not to agree with you, Willow. For fear I'll have to get into a debate with you."

"Would that be the worst thing in the world, actually talking and debating something? At least you'd be talking."

"I talk. Just not as much as you. And I don't debate."

"It's like fighting, but with your brain and words instead of fists."

"I don't fight."

"You're going to tell me you've never been in a fight? Ever?"

"Sure, when I got in the middle of my dad beating the crap out of my mom. I got in fights then. That was in the past, though. I've moved on."

—6—
WILLOW

After dinner, we get in Carson's car. "Are we going somewhere else?" I ask. I don't want the night to end so soon.

He looks at me sideways as he turns onto the main road leading to Seaside. "I thought you'd want to go to a movie. That's what people do on dates, right?"

"Absolutely. But since you insisted on paying for dinner, I'll pay for the movie."

He shakes his head. "No way. This is a date and I'm paying."

"You said it wasn't a real date earlier. Remember?"

"Maybe I lied."

The entire night has felt like a real date, and even though this is my first one it feels as real as they get. At the box office, Carson asks me what movie I want to see. There's an action movie called *Trigger* and a romantic comedy called *Hearts on Fire.* In the end, I choose *Trigger.* I know Carson will like it, and to be honest I like action movies just as much as romantic comedies. A bunch of kids from school are in the theater, and I'm suddenly self-conscious.

"Willow Baxter's in the house!" Tyler screams from the back row.

Dex waves us over. "Yo, lovebirds, come sit with us!"

I look up at Carson. "Please ignore them. I swear I didn't know they'd be here. If you want to see *Hearts on Fire* instead—"

"Nah," he says, taking my hand and leading me to one of the middle sections of the theater. "It's all good."

"You don't want to sit with us?" Dex asks.

Carson gives him a short, mocking salute. "Get your own date, dude. I'm not sharing mine."

Carson and I share a drink and a bag of popcorn he bought at the concession stand. I'm hyperaware that other kids from school are staring at us—especially Mandi Milner, who just walked in. Mandi is the popular senior girl who every guy wants to date. She's got long, perfect hair and a face that is so cute and feminine every other girl looks manly next to her. Especially me.

I watch as Mandi scans the theater, then eyes Carson and proceeds to lead her group of friends into our aisle. *Please don't sit next to my date,* I say silently to myself.

But I'm not that lucky. Sure enough, Mandi plops herself in the seat next to Carson.

"Hey, Willow," she says, smiling as if we're best friends. "Who's your friend?"

"Mandi, this is Carson," I mumble, wishing the previews would start so it'd be too loud to have a conversation.

Carson nods to Mandi and says, "S'up."

I know she's going to take all of his attention. To be honest, I don't even blame her.

"I'm so excited about this movie," she says, trying to start a conversation like I knew she would.

But he doesn't take the bait. Instead, he leans toward me and puts his arm across my shoulders and pulls me in close so I'm leaning into his warm, muscular chest. As the previews start, he leans in to my ear and says, "I bet she doesn't make pallets half as good as you do."

I laugh. "I bet you're right."

Carson's arm doesn't move from my shoulders for the entire movie. Afterward, he takes my hand as we leave the theater. I can see out of the corner of my eye that Mandi and her friends are watching us, and I feel invincible and desirable and pretty.

It isn't long before we're back in the car on the way back home.

"Just so you know, you're an awesome date," I tell him as he makes the turn into Seaside.

"Thanks. I had a good time, Willow." He stops the car in front of his place and turns to me. "It's been a long time since I had a good time. You're a super cool girl."

A huge grin crosses my face and that tingly sensation that only appears when I'm with him settles in my stomach. He reaches for the door handle to get out of the car, but I put my hand on his arm to stop him.

"Carson," I say, "will you kiss me good night? And not because you owe me a favor or anything like that. I've never really kissed a boy before, and I want you to be my first. I mean, I had a great time tonight and it really felt like a date even though you said it wasn't real."

Our eyes meet.

I swallow hard, then close my eyes as the truth spills from my lips. "I know we're supposed to be friends, but I have feelings for you here. . . ." I point to my heart.

He lets out a low breath and runs his hand through his hair. "You're sixteen. I just don't think—"

"Stop. I get it. Don't say anything more."

Humiliation rushes through me when I realize that he doesn't remotely feel the same way about me that I feel about him. When he put his arm around me at the theater tonight, he was being polite . . . he was acting like a good fake date in front of Mandi and her friends. It was solely for show.

"Willow, don't get upset."

Tears start to form in my eyes. "Forget I asked you to kiss me. Forget what I just said. Forget everything I said tonight."

I hurry out of the car and head for home, but he catches up to me and blocks my path. "Look at me," he says.

"I can't."

"Look at me." He tips my chin up with gentle fingers and urges me to look up. "'Cause I have something to say, and you need to hear it."

—7—
CARSON

Willow's eyes are glassy and a tear is running down her cheek. Damn.

I came to Seaside to get away from emotions and commitments and connections, and here I am, standing in front of a crying girl. I'd be lying to myself if I thought of her as just any girl. It's Willow, the girl who made me want to talk again—the girl who wouldn't take my silence and curt behavior as a hint to run far away from me.

"What?" she asks, then blinks teary lashes.

I cup her cheek in my palm. "I want to kiss you. I shouldn't, but I do."

I lean down and touch my lips to hers, reveling in the warmth of her sweet, full mouth on mine. I keep the kiss soft and it feels so good I'm tempted not to pull back for a long time.

When I finally do break the kiss, her eyes are still closed. The vision of her makes me smile.

"That was *great,*" she murmurs as she slowly opens her eyes and becomes aware of her surroundings once again. "You're perfect."

"I'm far from it." I kick my foot into the dirt. "I got a lot of baggage I'm carrying."

"Because of how your dad treated your mom?"

I nod.

"Where is he now?"

"Jail."

I expect her to back away, or ask me details on how and why my dad got locked up, but she doesn't. Instead, she wraps her arms around me and holds me tight.

"You're not your father," she tells me.

She's the first person to tell me that. Deep down I knew it, but nobody ever put it into words before. I actually think my father thought he was a good role model, and was proud to tell people I was a chip off the ol' block. I was always afraid that I'd end up a monster just like him.

"And I'm not gonna leave you like your mother did," she adds.

Willow has helped me, whether she meant to or not. I was trying to ignore my feelings for her, especially tonight, because I was afraid to admit I care about her more than just as a friend. Being in a relationship means commitment. Being in a relationship means I'm not alone. I thought alone and noncommittal was where I wanted to be.

It's not. Well, at least it's not when it comes to Willow.

I want to express how much she means to me, but words don't rush off my tongue easily.

Maybe I don't need to tell her how I feel . . . I can show her.

"Wait here," I say, then walk inside my RV and take out a switchblade I'd found in one of the kitchen drawers after

I moved in. My heart is pounding wildly, like I'm about to jump off a cliff without a bungee cord to hold me back.

I don't need to hold back, not anymore.

I find Willow waiting for me. I take her hand and lead her to the tree on my lot and start carving out my initials.

"What are you doing?" she asks, confused.

"You'll see."

When I'm done, I carve her initials below mine, then move away so she can see my handiwork.

Her eyes light up. "You carved our initials on the tree."

I nod.

"Does this mean what I think it means, Carson?"

I take her hand in mine. "It means I can't imagine my life without you. I'm falling for you, Willow."

She looks up at me with a mischievous smile on her freckled face. "It also means if we ever get married we'll have to name our first kid Crabapple."

The Killing Garden

CARRIE RYAN

They say my father wept at my birth. Not from joy, but from agony that I was born a daughter rather than a son. Until me, my father's family had run an unbroken line of male heirs, each one of them growing strong and following in the steps of those who came before as Gardener to the Emperor. It was a prestigious position that brought with it wealth and power.

My father took one look at me in my infant's crib and declared, "She'll never be strong enough for such a role." Perhaps it was true, as the Emperor's Gardener was not only in charge of the lush acres surrounding the palace but of pruning his court as well. This was accomplished through strangulation, and no one had taken to his role as Gardener more fiercely than my father.

In his first five years after assuming the title, my father strangled more than five thousand people. It was not enough for him to simply kill; he turned it into a sport as well. He raced the condemned through the gardens he maintained so meticulously, their finish line the execution platform. If the condemned won, he'd merely suffer banishment rather than execution. If he lost, my father strangled him and threw his body into the river.

Virtually no one ran faster than my father.

Except for me.

No daughter has ever worked as hard for her father's approval as I have. From the moment I could walk, I ran instead. When I learned to speak it was in full sentences, always showing respect for my elders. At night, when the monsters came in my dreams, I suffered in silence rather than wake my slumbering parents.

As my mother's only child I was showered with the best of everything; no cost was too great for tutors or clothes. Every birthday was a lavish affair, each milestone in my life marked by exuberant announcements and grand fetes. I grew into a darling of the Emperor's court.

But I wanted none of that. What I truly craved was the acknowledgment of my father, any scrap of his attention. From the moment I learned of his disappointment in my birth I determined that I would make him proud and prove I could sustain the family honor.

I vowed to take the role as Gardener, but the only way to do that was to beat him at his own game. In secret I began my training. Long-sleeved gowns became the rage at court once I began wearing them to cover the scratches on my arms from sprinting through the gardens at night. The calluses on my hands I hid with brightly colored gloves.

When, on the eve of my fifteenth birthday, I announced my intention to challenge my father, I expected some kind of gleam of pride, a moment of weakness in which I could find his adoration for me. Instead he merely lifted one brow and nodded.

I asked my father before the race if he'd ever felt remorse for any of the deaths. "Were there any for whom you questioned their guilt?"

He didn't look down at me. His eyes were trained forward toward the gardens. He knew them intimately—every intricate turn and dead-end path—which was an advantage during his races with the condemned.

But today I was his opponent and I knew the route just as well, eliminating any advantage he would have.

"Mine is not to judge," he told me. "But to run."

I found that his answer did not settle my thoughts. "It's not difficult for you? When you have your hands around their necks, you never wonder if they deserve it?"

This time he did look down at me. "Everyone dies, Tanci. Now or later, by my hand or someone else's. We are all guilty of something deserving of punishment."

That was when the marker called for the race to begin. My father's bare feet were already pounding the garden path by the time I took my first step. No one, including him, thought I could win this race.

The number of paths to the execution platform is almost infinite, but my favorite has always been through the hedge maze. Most condemned avoid this route; there are too many false turns and confusing twists unless you've grown up with these trails as your playground.

As I expected, my father turned toward his preferred course along the Crying River, but I veered away and sprinted toward the topiary garden. Every turn was indelibly mapped in my head: left at the cockatrice, right at the manticore, straight past the twin alce, double back around the wyvern.

And here was where I knew I would win: there are no rules to this race. It is simply a matter of which of the two runners arrives first, and any means of accomplishing this goal is allowed. Too few condemned ever realize this. They may try to ford the Crying River or hop over the border between whispering beds, but never do they presume to truly break the boundaries of the ordered paths.

To them the hedges are walls. To me they are shortcuts. This was what I'd trained for: toughening the skin along my arms so that I could hold them over my face as I pushed through the interlocking shrubs with thorns as long as antelope horns and sharp as snake fangs.

There were gouges along my shoulders and shins as I climbed my way up the execution platform, but that didn't matter. What mattered was this: I was the first to arrive.

My father's steps did not lag when he rounded the final turn of his course and saw me, nor did his speed flag as he raced the final bit of distance between us. I waited for him to say something, to congratulate me or smile—anything—as he climbed the steps to stand beside me, but he was silent, his face betraying nothing.

Behind me stood a score of attendants used to pin the condemned if he or she chose to fight this final act. But they were unnecessary this morning: my father voluntarily knelt before me. His fingers didn't fumble as he released the intricate knots holding the stiff leather Gardener's collar, the symbol of his position, tight around his throat. The skin underneath hadn't seen light or breathed air since he'd taken this same collar from his own father so many years ago.

No matter how hard I tried to control my body, I trembled. In all of my dreams I won this race over and over again, but I never dwelt on what would come after. For the briefest moment I wondered if perhaps my father had been correct all those years ago and I wasn't strong enough to assume the role of Gardener.

All this time as my mind swam, my father knelt before me on the execution platform. Beyond him the Emperor and his retinue sat watching from the balcony, news of our race having brought a rather large crowd.

My father reached forward and took my hand in his. Here was a man whose fingers could squeeze the life out of any soul, but with me his touch was gentle as though my fist were a fluttering fledgling.

Blood leaked from the cuts in my arms and my father ran his thumb over one of the trails, smearing red across my wrist. His next words crushed me.

"I did not want you for this," he said.

He lifted my hand to his throat.

I felt small in that moment, emotionally and physically. Even with him kneeling and me standing, his head reached the height of my chin. The tips of my fingers grazed the ridge of his spine; my thumbs pressed against the blood vessels on either side of his windpipe. His position forced me to hold my arms out straight, no way to leverage my body weight.

Either my hands alone were strong enough to strangle my father or they were not.

My father did not move his eyes from my own. Not when his breathing became labored. Not when his face burned red and the blood vessels began popping in the whites surrounding his pupils. He stared at me through every moment.

Tradition held that the new Gardener did not have to execute the former but needed only to prove his strength and fortitude. Normally, choking the predecessor to unconsciousness was enough.

But of course all mercy rests in the heart of the Emperor. After my father's tongue pushed from his mouth and his body fell forward, my hands still wrapped around his throat, I looked up toward the Emperor's box, my glance alone a request for mercy.

It didn't come.

In that moment I had a choice: kill my father and take the Gardener's collar or release my hands and admit that my father was right: I would never be strong enough.

I stared down into my father's purple face and remembered him telling me that every person is guilty of something deserving of punishment. If only I knew what *his* guilt was, then perhaps I could determine whether he was deserving of this sort of retribution.

But I knew, as clear as the sun on a bright day, that were our roles reversed and it was my father's fingers ordered to circle around my neck, he would do so without thought. As he himself said, his role was not to judge.

If I was to follow in his path, then mine wouldn't be either.

The last flutter of my father's pulse was struggling against the blockade of my thumbs when the Emperor gestured for one of his men to call mercy. I released my hands instantly, muscles so cramped my fingers were frozen in the form of claws.

A deep sense of relief welled within me, causing me to stumble back. On the execution platform my father choked and wheezed, heaving as he lurched to his feet. He bowed, short and sharp, to the Emperor in thanks for the mercy before bending to grab his discarded collar.

He said nothing as he stepped behind me, his fingers fluttering soft around my throat as he knotted the collar so tightly that breathing became a chore. My neck was shorter than that of my male ancestors, so the edges of the leather bit against my collarbones and chin, making it difficult to move my head.

Only two things would ever necessitate the removal of this symbol of office: death or defeat at the hands of a challenging executioner.

After the trumpeters heralded my success and the Emperor showered me with gifts—my own retinue of servants, my own set of rooms in the palace, a festival to mark my ascension to the new position—I found my way to my parents' residence.

My mother greeted me with tears in her eyes, a mixture of joy and sorrow. Bruises ringed the dark skin of my father's throat and he stood formally as I sent my new servants to pack my belongings.

I'd never seen him without the collar that now encircled my neck. He looked vulnerable and even a bit weak. Until that moment I hadn't considered what he would do now that he was retired from gardening. The chase and the kill were his life, his passion, and I had no idea how he'd fill the chasm of time just opening in front of him.

"Do you have any advice?" I asked him, hoping that by sharing this common bond I could tempt him into showing me validation for my choices. After all, at my birth he'd claimed me too weak for this role and I'd proven him wrong. I wanted him to tell me he was proud.

"Run fast," he said simply. "And remember that you are nothing more than a tool to the Emperor."

The servants carried my trunks from my rooms, and my mother placed her hands against my forehead, my mouth and then my heart in a gesture of goodbye. She never let her eyes settle on the collar around my neck. I would always be welcome in my parents' house, but from now on it would be only as a guest.

My father said nothing, which agitated me. I'd done everything he'd ever asked of me, exceeded every expectation

I'd understood him to have for me. For a brief blaze of a moment I almost wished the Emperor hadn't granted him mercy, and this thought brought shame to my cheeks.

"Do you have any regrets?" I asked him as I stood in the doorway to leave.

He stared me straight in the eyes. "Only that you now wear the collar."

The position of Gardener wasn't easy, but I took to it just as fiercely as my father. The difference, though, was that he had found a sort of joy in the role, while I felt only a deep need to prove my worthiness. I quickly gained a reputation for being ruthless and swift. I'd walk into a room at the court and people would fall silent. The Emperor needed to simply nod in someone's direction for them to find themselves on the line to race me to the execution platform the following morning.

I never lost. There had been times during my father's tenure when the condemned would win, thus earning banishment rather than death. I vowed to exceed his record in all ways. To be sent to race against me through the gardens was to be sent to certain death by my hands around your throat.

Sometimes they fought or begged or sobbed. Their mouths would dribble excuses even with their last gasping breaths. I never listened. As my father told me: I was a tool of the Emperor, and mine was not to judge but to run. For years that was what I did.

Until one morning when I found myself standing at the starting mark next to my best childhood friend. Her hair was unbound, flowing over her shoulders in tangles, and I realized that I hadn't even known she'd been married. Since becoming Gardener I'd lost touch with my former life.

The marker called for the race to begin before either of us could utter a word. My body was well honed, it knew nothing to do but run, and as I sped along the Crying River I tried to understand what crime could have brought my best friend to the garden. Growing up, she'd been as gentle and subservient as a butterfly in a breeze.

Of course I made it to the execution platform first; it had never occurred to me to do anything otherwise, and it would have been difficult to claim that someone like Sifri could have outpaced me. High-born women had no reason to run, and my best friend was no exception. By the time she stumbled to the clearing, she was winded, and limping from a cramp in her side.

She came to the platform willingly, and for this I was grateful; sometimes the execution attendants broke bones as they pinned the condemned. Sifri chose to lie on her back rather than kneel, and I could feel her body trembling as I straddled her torso with my knees.

Her hair spread around her like a void, and my fingers tangled in it as I placed my hands against her neck. How many times had I braided this hair as a child? How often had she run her own hands through mine?

The words whispered out of my mouth before I could stop them. "What did you do, Sifri, to end up here?"

It was a scandalous question, one that would cause the Emperor consternation if he learned I uttered it. His word was law and I was a tool of enforcement. Sifri's answer would have no bearing on that; she would die by my hands regardless of what she said next.

But she said nothing as my thumbs found the thrumming arteries along the edge of her windpipe and pressed. It was a gentler death to cut the blood to the brain before choking off the air. Her breaths came frantic, her ribs straining against my thighs where they kept her pinned.

I was proud of her grace in this moment, as her eyelids fluttered and her lips parted in an anguished and frightened gasp. I was the last person she would see, and I wondered if she thought of me as friend or executioner in that final moment before her brain pulled her to darkness.

Strangling someone takes more patience than most people realize, as such a death does not come quickly. I spent several minutes sitting atop my best friend's body with my fingers tight around her throat, staring down into a face I'd once known as well as my own.

I realized then that I craved to understand what brought people to such a fate by my hands. Not that I proposed to question my duties as Gardener or my role as a tool of the Emperor. I simply felt that I owed it to those I executed to know what guilt they were atoning for.

Thus I began a new routine as Gardener. Before my races I'd stroll through the cage dungeons and visit with those against whom I'd be running. I quickly found that my red collar caused many condemned distress and resulted in most refusing to speak with me, so I took to wearing high-necked gowns and bright scarves that concealed my true identity.

I was often assumed to be merely a courtier coming to give a final bit of comfort in the form of a willing listener to their confessions. I heard from murderers and thieves, rapists and adulterers. But there were also those whose only offense was to have whispered a rumor about the Emperor or to have amassed too much power.

The Gardener wasn't expected to just prune the obvious dead leaves, but to ensure the shape of the overall hedge, and sometimes this meant trimming branches that grew out of place, no matter how healthy they may have been.

None of my forays affected my ability to continue my duties just as I had before. I was still the fastest runner, still lethal in my ability to kill any who raced against me and lost.

And not once had I lost. Not before Sifri's execution, and not after.

There were a few condemned who came to the platform and expected leniency from me when they realized I was the one who'd sat patiently outside their cage, hearing of their guilt and fears. But I disabused them of any such thoughts the moment I wrapped my hands around their throats and squeezed.

The condemned still begged, but only the Emperor could grant them mercy.

The dungeons were never pleasant. They were situated deep enough underground that my ears popped as I descended the winding stairs, and the darkness was so oppressive that even the air felt heavy. I never relished visiting the cages strung about the echoing chambers, but I saw it as my duty to speak with the condemned and I never wavered in the face of what was expected of me.

On this particular visit I pulled a wooden stool in front of one of the cells and smoothed the silk of my skirts around my legs as I sat. "I hear you are to race in the killing garden soon," I said.

The condemned lay on his side, curled in a ball with his back to me. When he heard my voice he stretched and turned, his movements sinuous and fluid like a tiger's. His cage was too small for him to ever be able to straighten himself out fully, but it was suspended in its own corner of the dungeon, away from the worst smells and sounds, which was a benefit in and of itself.

He stared at me for a long moment, his eyes amber in his dark face. If he was surprised by my presence, he didn't show it. "I am," he said. "I hear the Gardener is fleet of foot and that I'm unlikely to win against him."

I toyed with the scarf hiding my collar. "Yes, she has yet to lose a race since taking the position."

"She?"

"Our Emperor's Gardener is a woman," I told him. "She claimed her role from her father several years ago."

The condemned thought on this as he slid his legs around beneath him and leaned against the back of the cage, facing me. "I'm sure there are many who think this must give them an advantage, assuming someone of the gentler sex would be too weak for the job," he said.

I bowed my head a moment to hide my smile. "They may think that until her hands close around their throats."

"Why are you here?" He asked the question quick and sharp, so different from the languidness of our earlier banter. Briefly I considered whether he'd been toying with me and knew my true identity, but I pushed the thought aside. If he didn't even know the Gardener was a woman, he wasn't a man of the court who would recognize me on sight.

"I'm here to ask what brought you to your execution," I told him.

He frowned. "Why?"

This was the trickier question. I stood from the stool and paced behind it. I'd already run three races that morning and my legs hummed from spent energy. "I like to understand those who are taken to the garden."

"Does it ever make a difference?" he asked.

"In what way?"

"Has anything you've ever been told spared a condemned from the race?"

"That is not for me to give—only the Emperor may grant mercy," I reminded him.

He leaned forward. Like most condemned, he wore only a cloth tied at the hips and I watched his abdomen contract as he shifted to the front of the cage. The muscles along his legs were long and lean, the mark of someone used to running. It was rare that my speed was tested, and my stomach fluttered brightly at the idea of having a real race.

"Have you ever asked the Emperor for mercy?" he asked.

The question unsettled me, and I felt my hands clench into fists behind my back. I took a deep breath. "Only once," I told the condemned. "For my father," I added.

"And did he grant it?" The man's fingers slipped around the bamboo bars of his cage.

It took me longer than it should have to answer him. For some reason I was compelled to tell the truth as I never had before. "That would depend on whether my father felt his life was worth living after that moment."

The condemned wasn't done with his questions. "Did you think his life was worth living?"

I was caught fully off guard as I realized my answer: that I lived my father's life every day. I didn't tell this to the condemned, though. Instead I gave him a tight smile and bade him good-bye.

When I was several paces away he called out after me: "You never found out why I'm here."

I turned and dipped my chin. "Perhaps another time."

He'd shifted to his knees, tilting the cage forward with his weight. "What if I'm sent to the gardens before then?"

"Only the Emperor knows when that day will come," I answered him. It was mostly the truth.

For several days my stomach tightened every time I entered the garden, and it took me a few races before I understood what this new feeling meant. I was worried that I'd step up to the mark and I'd find that condemned man with the amber eyes waiting.

I realized with a sudden sinking clarity that I wasn't ready to kill him yet, but I didn't understand why. At first I avoided the cage dungeons, hoping to purge the memory of him from my head, but this only made my thoughts more frantic and focused until I could take it no longer.

Late one evening I strode down the steps into the dungeon but didn't bother dragging a stool to the same condemned man's cage. I remembered too late that I'd forgotten to cover my collar and I hissed in irritation. I wasn't ready for him to know who I was. Before he could turn to face me I ripped the torches from the wall and threw them to the floor, casting the corner into deepest shadow.

His voice rippled from the darkness. "You seem angry."

It was impossible to see much of him, only the flash of his eyes now and again. I heard the shifting of his body, the protest of the chains keeping his cage aloft. He'd yet to take on the stench of most condemned: the combination of desperation and starvation.

"What is your name?" It wasn't what I'd intended to ask. I wanted him to tell me why he was here, that was all.

"You're pacing," he said in answer.

I realized he was right. My legs itched to move, even though I'd endured seven races that day—more than any other day since I'd taken the role of Gardener. I forced myself to still, the hem of my silk dress whispering as it settled around my feet.

I said nothing more, waiting for him to fill the silence with his name.

Instead he asked his own question. "Have you asked the Emperor for my mercy yet?"

I laughed, a sharp, barking sound that surprised me. "The

Emperor is the one who condemned you. Why would he change his mind?"

"I had hoped." There was less bravado in this statement.

"Hope is useless," I told him, not to be cruel but to be realistic. "You will race the Gardener and you will lose."

His response came softly spoken. "Will you be there to watch?"

My back bristled and I forced myself to squeeze my hands together tightly. Never had anyone had the ability to catch me so off guard as this man. "Why would you want me there? I'm no one to you."

He shifted, setting the cage swinging slightly, like a pendulum ticking away the seconds of his life. For a moment there was silence, broken only by the squeaking of the chains rubbing against one another, measuring time.

"Down here there may be days or hours, but all I ever know—all that exists for me—is you."

I didn't know what to say to that or how to feel. So I did neither. Instead I turned on my heel and walked away.

As I left he called after me: "My name is Rete." I don't know if he heard how my steps hesitated or that I opened my mouth to tell him my own name but then thought better of it.

On my way from the dungeon I paused by the keeper's pedestal. He was used to seeing me here, though I had never once spoken to him. "When is the condemned Rete scheduled to race?" I asked.

The keeper ran his finger along a scratched wooden board with a list of names written in charcoal. He didn't meet my eyes as he answered. "The Emperor has yet to set a date, Gardener."

I nodded once and left.

• • •

My nights became restless, and more often than not I started the mornings stiff, with sleep in my eyes. I became distracted, once almost losing an afternoon race to a swift political prisoner when a member of the court accidentally stepped in front of me as I ran through the garden.

To win I had to push my way through the hedge maze, something I hadn't resorted to since I'd run against my father years ago. I beat the man to the platform, but my hands were slippery with my own blood, which made it difficult to keep a firm grasp on his neck. His was not an easy death.

Nothing had changed in my life and yet suddenly everything felt duller. Appearances in the Emperor's court became more difficult to endure, and I grew less patient when, during conversations, people's focus invariably drifted to the collar at my throat.

The only time my heart ever truly raced was when I ran, but even those moments seemed bare and ordinary.

I found that what I craved was to be caught off guard. I lived my life so rigidly that even the slightest deviation from course became a thrill.

And only one person had that ability: the condemned man in the cage.

More times than I cared to admit, I found my thoughts wandering to him, and any tether I was able to keep on myself during waking hours came loose the moment I fell into dreams.

When I slept his body prowled around me like the tiger I'd first imagined him to be, muscles long and languorous. He never touched me, not once, but that didn't matter, as his eyes seemed to know everything and promise even more.

After one such torturous night I leapt from the bed at dawn and went straight into the dungeon to his cage.

"Tell me what you have done," I demanded. "What brought you here?"

His body was sharper than it had been the first time I saw him, bones tight against the skin where before there had once been muscle. He moved slower, still with grace, but that of an aged cat rather than a prowling tom.

When he saw me he seemed genuinely surprised and pleased, his mouth tilting into a predatory smile. The expression couldn't hide the gauntness of his cheeks; he was being starved and was growing weak.

My stomach clenched and I tightened my hands into fists. The Emperor was ensuring that Rete would have no chance against me in the race. He didn't trust me to win on my own.

I inhaled a sharp breath and walked away. Rete called after me: "Wait! Wait!" his cries growing more desperate with distance.

The keeper didn't even need to ask who I was talking about when I told him, "I will not race against him weakened like that. Feed him, and do it well. He comes to the marker at full strength or he doesn't come at all. Understand?"

"But the Emperor dictated—"

"How many?" This cut him off. "How many have you starved before sending them to the garden?"

The keeper's eyes glistened, his loyalties torn by fear. I leaned forward and placed my hands on the podium. "How fast can you run?"

He dropped his head. "He will be fed, Gardener. From now on, all of them will be."

The next time I saw the condemned man his skin looked less like the ash of a broken fire. "You are being fed?" I asked, though the answer was clear by the satisfied swell of his stomach.

"Is it you I have to thank for that?" he asked.

I smiled. He had a maddening way of answering my questions with his own. Never had I been treated with such disrespect, especially not since binding the red leather collar around my throat.

"The Gardener requested that you be strong when it came your turn to race," I told him.

He lifted a brow. "You said yourself I've no hope of winning against her."

"You should at least be given the chance." I realized, as the words slipped through my lips, that I'd spoken them gently, with a certain sort of yearning coating each syllable. Immediately the sheen of arrogance dropped from his expression.

He shifted to his knees, moving toward the front of the cage, where he curled his fingers around the bars. I stared at the half-moons of his nails and remembered how in my dreams I desired nothing more than for him to trail them along the deep curve in the small of my back.

"You would care if I won or lost?" he asked. His knuckles were white, his posture held rigid.

I nodded, feeling the stiff collar around my throat hindering the movement.

He still didn't relax. "Which would you want more?"

Our eyes locked. I catalogued every speckle of brown scattered through the amber. His pupils flared wide, and this caused something warm to begin unspooling inside me.

"Your fate is not mine to decide," I whispered. "That is for the Emperor."

"No." He shook his head. "It is for the Gardener."

I swallowed, the collar around my throat feeling too tight. After my father first laced it on it took months for me to learn to live with the choking feel of it. I had to figure out how to run all over again, taking shorter and shallower breaths. At night I'd wake up gasping, my lungs screaming for air. The stiff leather bit deeply into the skin along my chin and collarbone, chafing me raw until calluses formed.

The collar was more than just the symbol of the office, it was a reminder of the power we wielded. As we strangled, so were we strangled. Sometimes there were days I'd forget I was wearing it. Other times, like now, every breath was a struggle.

I stood close enough to the condemned man's cage that he could reach his fingers through and twine them around my scarf. He tugged, pulling me even nearer, until only the width of the bars separated us.

My breathing was uneven, my heart racing as it never did in the gardens.

Slowly, Rete unwound the knots of my scarf. His fingers then fluttered over the buttons of my high-necked gown until he laid bare the red leather collar around my throat.

"Which will you choose for me, Gardener?" His words caressed me as his lips could not.

I felt a welling at the base of my throat. "Neither." And then I added, foolishly, because I could think of no other way to keep him safe, "I'd keep you here."

He laughed and pulled away from me so abruptly that it sent his cage swinging. It bumped against me, knocking me off balance and causing me to stumble.

"You would keep me trapped down in the dungeons like a pet, then?" he asked sharply. He crouched to his feet, hands tucked under his arms to make his elbows like wings. "Your pretty bird. I can sing if you'd like." He began to belt out a raucous tune, off-key and loud.

I felt stupidly exposed with my scarf in a limp pile on the dirty floor and my dress unbuttoned and spread wide to show my collar and a stretch of skin beneath it. Other condemned began to join the song, their voices rising in a discordant cacophony.

My jaw clenched as I tried to control my breathing. But nothing I did could stop the stinging heat of humiliation coursing through me. He'd pulled free emotions I'd never acknowledged; he'd given them light and air so that they'd flourished and grown. Until the moment his fingers danced along my jaw, I hadn't realized just how much I'd come to care for him.

He'd been the first person to ever seek for *me* past the bit of leather lashed around my throat. And now he was mocking me. I wanted nothing more than to flee, to run faster than I ever had and leave this dungeon and this man and this world.

I'd go to my father's house and I'd put his hands around my neck and I'd beg him to finish it, as he should have all those years ago when he learned I'd been born a girl.

But I didn't. Instead I stood stiffly as I buttoned my dress methodically and rewound the scarf around my neck. I made Rete watch as I let my emotions, any compassion I'd ever felt for him, leach out of me until I was once again as I had always been: nothing more than a tool to the Emperor.

The girl who would have strangled her father to death if she'd been asked. The woman who had killed her best friend without knowing the reason.

I was the Gardener. And I would race against Rete and I would win.

For three days, every time I stepped to the mark in the garden I expected to face Rete. Never was it him. The dungeons belched up all manner of condemned—men who'd languished underground for years waiting for their chance to run. It was as though the Emperor was punishing me, sending me into race after race as he purged his cages.

Twice I vomited from the extreme exertion, my body protesting every time the marker called for the race to begin, but never did I stop running. The days were a punishment I relished, leaving me so exhausted that I fell into sleep the moment I stepped from the platform after the last execution.

I hated how the anticipation of Rete's race became a sort of torture in and of itself.

And then something happened that had never occurred before. I lost my concentration leaping over the Stream of Sorrow and my foot caught the edge of a rock, sending me crashing into the shallow water. Bits of gravel scored over my arms, drawing blood, and my teeth tore into the side of my cheek.

The worst came when I pushed back to my feet and tried to run: an excruciating pain that raged from my ankle up my leg. I'd dealt with pain before. I'd borne the scars left by forcing through the hedges in the maze, and I'd pushed myself through lung cramps and muscle tears and flus and headaches.

But this was pain like none other, something deep and grinding, like the shattered ends of two bones scraping against each other. I tried to limp, and when that didn't work I resorted to crawling, not caring about the skin being grated off my knees and palms.

For the first time in my life I was second to the execution platform. A hush buzzed through the crowd as I drew near not like the champion I'd always been but like a dog, on my hands and knees. I was handed a staff to lean against as the Emperor gave the condemned his sentence of banishment, and I stood on the platform, my one good leg trembling with exhaustion, long after the man had been led from the gates and sent forth into the vast emptiness beyond the city walls.

Eventually the Emperor's surgeons came and took me back to my suites in the palace. When they set the bones between stabilizing boards I refused any medication to deaden the agony; I needed to know the repercussions of my mistakes. Every time the dagger-sharp edges of errant bone chips sliced against muscle and flesh I thought about the moment my foot had slipped across the rock in the stream.

I'd been thinking of Rete.

The Emperor called a moratorium on the races while my bones knitted. I tried retaking my place in court, using a clever mechanism of a platform on wheels to take the pressure off my shattered ankle as I made my way through the palace chambers and gardens. But everywhere I went I was met with hushed silences, followed by tittering gossip the moment I rolled from the room.

Some were pleased to see me brought low, and I began a list of them all in my head. They might have thought me weak then, but there would come a time when I'd return to the gardens, and my tools would be sharp and searching for new plants to prune.

The one place I could not manage on my own was the dungeons, with their myriad steep and twisting stairs, and I refused to ask for help. Some days my forced absence felt like a curse and others it was a blessing. Never before had I felt even the smallest fissure of weakness, and my first thought of comfort was always Rete.

I wanted him gone from my mind, yet he was all I could think about.

For weeks I resorted to spending the days in my chambers, looking out into the gardens and watching the hedges grow ragged and the paths fill with weeds. My staff still tended to their duties as ever, but without my constant presence they had become lazy. I added all their names to the growing list of condemned in my head.

• • •

My recuperation was lengthy and my strength slow to return after the stabilizing boards were finally removed. The day the surgeons pronounced my leg healed and rehabilitated, the Emperor called for the races to resume on the next morning. His dungeon was overflowing, and his court had grown soft without the ever-present threat of the gardens.

Besides, he'd lacked entertainment throughout the dull months of summer.

I'd always thought the first place I would go after being released by the surgeons would be to Rete—after all, his was a constant presence in my thoughts—but instead I found myself standing in front of my parents' house, staring at the bright brass knocker on the door.

My mother greeted me as she always did, placing her fingers against my head, my heart and my lips, a gesture of love and blessing. She called for spiced cakes and honeyed tea and drew me toward the solarium, but my attention was not for her.

When she could not coax me to settle and focus on her wandering conversation, she sighed softly and said, "He's outside." I nodded before rising and going toward the door, wincing at my slight but lingering limp.

My father stood in the middle of his personal garden, a miniature of the emperor's. There were small hedges twisted into unnatural shapes, meandering paths and a rock waterfall that fed into a pond flashing with bright fish.

It was nothing like the grandeur of what we'd both been used to, and my father seemed to have shrunk along with his duties, as if the measure of the man were determined by the scope of his importance.

He was the first to speak. "You are to resume running

tomorrow." I couldn't discern whether it was a question or a command.

I nodded, but with his back to me he couldn't see the gesture. He knew the answer anyway; asking was only one more formality in the long line that had defined my upbringing. "The gardens have grown a bit wild in your absence," he added. We both knew it wasn't the orchards and elaborate hedges but the members of court he spoke of.

"They have," I acknowledged, my jaw tight.

With the deliberateness so familiar over the course of my life, he stepped forward and raised a thin knife, trimming back an errant sprig from a flowering dragon.

I crouched and drew my finger across the surface of the pond, watching the ripples blur the colorful fish beneath. The moment I'd seen my father standing in his garden I'd known why I'd come to him.

"You lost races. Why?"

His blade flashed in the light as if he'd been startled. A few tender green leaves drifted from where he'd accidentally sheared a twig. He bent to collect them. "Because I was not always the fastest."

I thought about Rete and the anxiety I'd felt over expecting to meet him at the starting mark. "Did you ever consider losing a race on purpose?"

He straightened, brow furrowed, and looked at me for several long moments. Between us was only the trickle of the waterfall and the buzzing of insects. He held out his blade, sharp and cold in his palm.

"We are the tool," he said. "It has no thoughts, it knows nothing about right or wrong. It simply exists. It is up to the one wielding the blade to determine what should be cut and what should be left to flourish."

I took a step forward; I couldn't help the emotions raging through me. "But that blade just sheared a branch because the person holding it made a mistake," I argued, pointing at his hand.

My father sighed and moved toward a nearby bench to sit, his shoulders slightly slumped. If possible, he appeared even older. He set the knife down carefully beside him. "If I regret one death, where then does it stop? There is not enough room in a life for fourteen thousand regrets."

His gaze, when it met mine, was pleading. It set me off balance, my thoughts spinning. I had never seen my father like this—lost and vulnerable. Even when my hands had closed around his throat after I'd won the race to succeed him as Gardener, he'd seemed so sure of life and his role in it.

"You've never come to watch me race in the garden, have you?"

He glanced at the collar around my neck and then away. "No. I never wanted to see you like that, Tanci."

A rage flashed through me, heating my cheeks and causing my fingers to tremble. The achievements I was proudest of, and my father never even recognized them. Without saying anything more, I spun on my heel, trying not to wincc as my leg protested, and strode from the garden.

In the middle of the night, after sleep had eluded me for too long, I made my way into the dungeons. If the keeper was surprised to see me, he knew better than to show it. He merely nodded when I demanded the list of those set to race against me in so few hours and said nothing as I ran my finger along the scrawled names. There was only one that mattered, and when I saw it my jaw clenched.

I did not bother to hide my collar as I stormed through the dungeons, and while most of the condemned turned away when they saw me, others called out, an echoing riot of lascivious jeers.

Their time would come soon enough, I told myself as I ignored them all.

Rete's cage still hung in its own corner, slightly separated from the rest of the cells. Only one torch still burned along the wall, and it cast a flickering shadow along his body. The first time I'd seen him his skin had been a rich darkness, but now, after so many months trapped away from the sun and fresh air, he'd taken on more of an ashen appearance that made me ache inside, though I struggled to keep my face neutral.

After all, the last time I'd been down here Rete had succeeded in humiliating me, and it wasn't a feeling I wanted to experience again. But I'd made a promise to myself to visit with each condemned in the days before their race, and I would treat him no differently.

He lay on his side, curled around himself, with his back to me. Even as I approached, he did not move. I let my eyes devour him, tracing each knob of his long spine, watching the curve of his ribs rise and fall with each soft breath. He slept with his hands tucked beneath his chin and with one foot hooked behind the other.

In the end I found myself staring at his neck, the rhythmic throbbing of his pulse fluttering just beneath the surface. My hands squeezed into fists and I turned away, intending to leave.

"Tanci." His voice was gruff from sleep.

It was the second time I'd heard my name used that day. I'd almost forgotten the sound of it; over the years I'd learned to respond to nothing except Gardener.

I faced him but said nothing.

He was kneeling now, his cage swinging slowly back and forth from the movement. "Are you okay?"

I had to press the back of my hand against my mouth to stifle the choking laughter I felt surging forward. For all the definitions of the word "okay," I could think of none that applied to me. "How did you know my name?"

"I asked," he said. "When I heard about your leg, I was worried."

There was an edge to my voice I couldn't control as I demanded, "You weren't thinking about how it would buy you more time before your trip to the gardens?"

"I was thinking about you." His words were laced with an emotion unfamiliar to me, something tender and burning all at once.

I shook my head, taking a step toward him. "Why would you be so stupid? Don't you understand that tomorrow we race? There will be no mercy—the Emperor has planned this. My entire reputation will rest on this race—my future will depend on my making it to the execution platform first. The Emperor's Gardener cannot show weakness, and that's what you are to me."

My words finally seemed to mean something to him; his breathing became more strained. Tomorrow, Rete would die by my hand.

"Please tell me you're a fast runner," I begged him softly. I reached out a finger and placed it against the ridge of his knuckles.

He twisted so that he gripped my hands in his. "You think your strength lies here," he whispered. The cage tilted as he reached through the bars to trail his thumb along the ridge of my collar. "And here."

My pulse thundered, each breath feathery light. He let his hand fall until it rested against my chest. I knew he could feel every crushing beat. "You silence your heart in order to run; you were not made to lead such a quiet life. Being the

Gardener does not make you strong, and being Tanci does not make you weak."

I jerked away from him, but I could still feel his touch even through the silk of my tunic, the warmth from the pad of each of his fingers. As I fled through the dungeon I remembered what my father had said the day I was born: *She'll never be strong enough.*

The only way to prove him wrong was by killing Rete, the only man who'd ever looked for more behind the Gardener's collar.

It was not enough for the Emperor to simply resume the races; there had to be pomp and circumstance, turning what had once been merely routine into a celebrated event. He wanted his people to know that his Gardener was well again, that any courtiers who grew out of line would be pruned with brutal efficiency.

The same people who had nattered behind my back as I fled ballrooms only a few months earlier now paraded through the gardens and stuffed themselves into the spectator boxes around the execution platform. They wore their brightest colors, each of them almost shining under the harsh sun.

The air had the feel of a carnival, of the whispered excitement before the curtain rises on a new opera or play. After the race there would be more displays of the Emperor's might with battle demonstrations in the arena and lavish parties starting early and lasting late.

It made my legs jittery, my pulse uneven and my stomach anxious. There were those who had come today to see me fail. Who would delight in witnessing the Emperor's darling Gardener being laid low so they could continue with the empty tittering.

But if that was what they were expecting, they would be

sorely disappointed. I never stepped to the mark unless I intended to win, and that was exactly my plan that morning.

By the Emperor's orders I was paraded through the gardens, flower petals strewn about me, so that his court could see up close my strength. I'd polished the leather of my collar that morning so it gleamed blood red in the sunlight, and my lips curled with delight when I saw the unease it caused those around me.

As I stood beneath the Emperor's box I caught sight of the familiar face of my father, and that, more than anything else, caused my cheeks to burn. Why he'd come to this, of all races, I didn't understand, and his expression gave no clues. I felt a fierce and familiar fire of determination blaze inside me, a desire to prove to him my worth and strength.

When I stepped to the mark Rete was already there. He was almost an afterthought to the day's proceedings, a minor token in an otherwise grand exhibition of the Emperor's strength.

I noticed how Rete shifted his weight from foot to foot in nervous anticipation, his fingers fluttering into fists and stretching straight again. As was custom, I nodded at him and he nodded back.

It looked as though there was something he wanted to say, but before he could open his mouth the marker was called and the race began. I did not hesitate and neither did Rete.

As always, I ran barefoot, but the soles of my feet had grown soft and every twig and pebble seemed to cut against the flesh. The bones of my recently healed ankle protested, but I'd been assured they were healed and could come to no more harm from the strain of sprinting.

I'd forgotten the exhilaration of movement, the wild joy of throwing myself so fast and hard that my legs could barely catch my body before I fell. I practically skipped through the Stream of Sorrow, relishing the cold water kicked up behind me.

This was racing as it had never been for me before, not some duty born from a desire to prove my worth to my father, but instead a symphony of speed. I forgot everything in those moments but the song of my heart, and I followed it through the gardens that had been more a home to me growing up than anywhere else.

I didn't know what I was expecting when I sprinted around the final curve toward the execution platform, but I knew what I hoped. I could already hear the murmuring of the crowd, and several of them gasped when I came into sight.

Everyone stared, but the only eyes I refused to meet were those of my father. I couldn't bear to witness the disappointment that would be written so clearly across his face.

Later, I knew my name would be on everyone's lips, but I'd made sure that the one thing they could never say was that I hadn't run fast or hard enough. I still struggled to catch my breath as I climbed the execution platform.

The look on Rete's face when I joined him was mostly one of confusion laced with joy and shock. He'd expected to lose and prepared himself to die by my hands. Instead the Emperor pronounced his sentence of banishment with a growl and dismissive flick of his fingers.

There would be no execution this morning, and the disappointment from the crowd was palpable. It didn't take long for the stands to clear after that, the entire mood of the day dampened. Everyone moved quickly to the arena, placing their bets against the various warriors who paraded with tigers and other jungle cats.

I was allowed to say nothing to Rete before he was led away by the execution attendants, so I remained alone on the platform, watching their small procession wend toward the city gates.

The sun burned across the sky and the garden emptied and still I stood and watched the dark speck of Rete make his way across the barren landscape of the world outside. Eventually I reached up to my neck and began to unlace the stiff leather, my fingers trembling at first but growing surer.

The collar fell away, and at the rush of freedom I felt almost light-headed. I stared at it in my hands, the leather still warm from my skin. For three years this had defined me, and I felt naked without it.

When I let it drop to the platform it landed with a satisfying thunk. Behind me I heard a rustling of movement and my heart quickened with terror that I'd be caught in my act of treason. A figure stood in the highest rows of the Emperor's box, and as my eyes adjusted to the gloaming light I recognized my father.

He said nothing, the distance between us too great to do anything but yell, and that had never been in either of our natures. For a moment he was still, and then he touched his hand to his head, his mouth, his heart and finally his bare throat. It was a gesture of good-bye and a blessing for the future.

My eyes were blurred and useless but my steps were steady as I descended the execution platform and walked not in the direction of the palace but toward the city gates. As I passed through them I picked up my pace.

I am the fastest runner I know, and I will catch up to Rete, eventually.

Homecoming

RICHELLE MEAD

I hadn't expected to be back in Russia so soon. I certainly didn't want to be.

It wasn't that I had anything against the place. It was a nice enough country, with rainbow-colored architecture and vodka that could double as rocket fuel. I was fine with those things. My problem was that the last time I'd been here, I'd nearly gotten killed (on multiple occasions) and had ended up being drugged and kidnapped by vampires. That's enough to turn you off to any place.

And yet, as my plane began circling for its landing in Moscow, I knew coming back here was definitely the right thing to do.

"Do you see that, Rose?" Dimitri tapped the window's glass, and although I couldn't see his face, the note of wonder in his voice told me plenty. "St. Basil's."

I leaned over him, just barely catching a glimpse of the

famous multicolored cathedral that looked more like something you'd find in Candy Land, not the Kremlin. To me, it was another tourist attraction, but to him, I knew it meant so much more. This was his homecoming, the return to a land he had believed he'd never see again in the sun, let alone through the eyes of the living. That building, the cities here . . . they weren't just pretty postcard shots for him. They represented more than that. They represented his second chance at life.

Smiling, I settled back in my seat. I had the middle one, but there was no way it could be more uncomfortable than his. Putting a six-foot-seven-inch man by the window in coach was just cruel. He hadn't complained this entire time, though. He never did.

"Too bad we won't have time to hang out here," I said. Moscow was just a layover for us. "We'll have to save all our sightseeing for Siberia. You know, tundra. Polar bears."

Dimitri turned from the window, and I expected to be chastised for furthering stereotypes. Instead, I could tell from his expression that he hadn't heard anything after "Siberia." Morning light illuminated the sculpted features of his face and shone off his sleek brown hair. None of it could compare to the radiance within him.

"It's been so long since I've seen Baia," he murmured, his dark eyes filled with memories. "So long since I've seen them. Do you think . . ." He glanced at me, betraying the first glimpse of nervousness I'd observed since beginning this trip. "Do you think they'll be glad to see me?"

I squeezed his hand and felt a small pang in my chest. It was so unusual to see Dimitri uncertain about anything. I could count on my hand the number of times I'd ever witnessed him truly vulnerable. From the moment we'd met, he'd always stood out as one of the most decisive, confident people I'd known. He was always in motion, never afraid to take on any threat, even if it meant risking his own life. Even now, if some bloodthirsty monster sprang out of the cockpit, Dimitri would calmly jump up and battle it while armed only with the safety card in his seat pocket. Impossible, dire fights were of no concern to him. But seeing his family after he'd spent time as an evil, undead vampire? Yeah, that scared him.

"Of course they'll be glad," I assured him, marveling at the change in our relationship. I'd started off as his student, in need of *his* reassurance. I'd graduated to become his lover and equal. "They know we're coming. Hell, you should've seen the party they threw when they thought you were dead, comrade. Imagine what they'll do when they find out you're actually alive."

He gave me one of those small, rare smiles of his, the kind that made me feel warm all over. "Let's hope so," he said, turning to gaze back out the window. "Let's hope so."

The only sights we saw in Moscow were inside its airport while we waited to catch our next flight. That one took us to Omsk, a middle-sized city in Siberia. From there, we rented a car and made the rest of our journey on land—no planes went where we were going. It was a beautiful drive, the land full of life and greenery that proved all my tundra jokes wrong. Dimitri's mood fluctuated between nostalgia and anxiety as we traveled, and I found myself restless to reach our destination. The sooner we got there, the sooner he'd see he had nothing to worry about.

Baia was a little less than a day's drive from Omsk and looked pretty much the same as it had on my last visit. It was out of the way enough that people rarely stumbled across it by accident. If you found yourself in Baia, there was a reason. And more often than not, that reason had to do with the large number of dhampirs living there. Like Dimitri and me, these dhampirs were half-human, half-vampire. Unlike Dimitri and me, most of these dhampirs had chosen to live apart from the Moroi—living, magic-wielding vampires—and instead mingled with human society. Dimitri and I were both guardians, pledged to guard the Moroi from Strigoi: the evil, undead vampires who killed to sustain their immortal existence.

Days were longer during this part of summer, and darkness had only just begun to fall when we reached Dimitri's family's house. Strigoi rarely ventured into Baia itself, but they liked to stalk the roads leading into town. The fleeting rays of sunlight ensured our safety and gave Dimitri a good view of the house. Even once he'd turned off the car, he sat for a long time, gazing out at the old, two-story structure. Red and gold light bathed it, giving it the appearance of something otherworldly. I leaned over and kissed his cheek.

"Showtime, comrade. They're waiting for you."

He sat for a few moments in silence, then gave a resolute nod and put on the kind of expression I'd seen him wear into battle. We left the car and had barely made it halfway through the yard when the front door burst open. Bright light spilled into the dusky shadows, and a young female silhouette appeared.

"Dimka!"

If a Strigoi had sprung out and attacked, Dimitri would have had to respond instantly. But seeing his youngest sister stunned his lightning-fast reflexes, and he could only stand there as Viktoria flung her arms around him and began uttering a torrent of Russian words too fast for me to follow.

It took Dimitri a few more shocked moments to come to life, but then he returned her fierce embrace, answering her back in Russian. I stood there awkwardly until Viktoria noticed me. With a cry of joy, she hurried over and gave me a hug as tight as the one she'd bestowed upon her brother. I admit, I was almost as shocked as him. When we'd last parted, Viktoria and I hadn't been on good terms. I'd made it clear I didn't approve of her relationship with a certain Moroi guy. She'd made it equally clear she didn't appreciate my input. It seemed now that was all forgotten, and although I couldn't translate the words she spoke, I got the impression she was thanking me for restoring Dimitri to her.

Viktoria's exuberant arrival was followed by the rest of the Belikov family. Dimitri's other two sisters, Karolina and Sonya, joined Viktoria in embracing both him and me. Their mother was right behind them. Russian flew fast and furious. Normally, a haphazard doorstep reunion like this would've made me roll my eyes, but I found myself tearing up instead. Dimitri had been through too much. We'd all been through too much, and honestly, I don't think any of us had ever expected to be sharing this moment.

At last, Dimitri's mother, Olena, recovered herself and laughed while wiping tears from her eyes. "Come in, come in," she said, remembering that I didn't know much Russian. "Let's sit down and talk."

Through more tears and laughter, we made our way into the house and cozy living room. It too was the same as my last visit, surrounded in warm wood paneling and shelves of leather-bound books with Cyrillic titles. There, we found more of the family. Karolina's son, Paul, regarded his uncle with fascination. Paul had barely known Dimitri before he struck out into the world, and most of what the boy knew came from fantastic-sounding stories. Sitting on a blanket nearby was Paul's baby sister, and another, much tinier baby lay sleeping in a bassinet. Sonya's baby, I realized. She'd been pregnant when I'd visited earlier that summer.

I was used to always being near Dimitri's side, but this was a moment when I knew I had to yield him. He sat on the sofa, and Karolina and Sonya immediately flanked him, wearing expressions that said they were afraid to let him out of their sight. Viktoria, irked at having lost a prime seat, settled down on the floor and leaned her head against his knee. She was seventeen, only a year younger than me, but as she gazed up at him adoringly, she looked much younger. All of the siblings had brown hair and eyes, making a pretty portrait as they sat together.

Olena scurried about, certain we must be famished, and finally settled down when we assured her we were fine. She sat in a chair opposite Dimitri, her hands clasped in her lap as she leaned forward eagerly.

"This is a miracle," she said in accented English. "I didn't believe it. When I received the message, I thought it was a mistake. Or a lie." She sighed happily. "But here you are. Alive. The same."

"The same," Dimitri confirmed.

"Was the first story . . ." Karolina paused, a small frown crossing her pretty features as she carefully chose her words. "Was the first story a mistake, then? You weren't truly . . . truly a Strigoi?"

The word hung in the air for a moment, casting a chill over the warm summer evening. For the space of a heartbeat, I couldn't breathe. I was suddenly far away from here, trapped in a different house with a very different Dimitri. He'd been one of the undead, with chalk-white skin and red-ringed pupils. His strength and speed had far surpassed what he had now, and he'd used those skills to hunt for victims and drink their blood. He'd been terrifying—and had nearly killed me.

A few seconds later, I began to breathe again. That Dimitri was gone. This one—warm, loving, and alive—was here now. Yet, before he answered, Dimitri's dark eyes met mine, and I knew he was thinking of the same things I was. That past was a horrible, difficult thing to shake.

"No," he said. "I was Strigoi. I was one of them. I did . . . terrible things." The words were mild, but the tone of his voice spoke legions. The radiant faces of his family turned sober. "I was lost. Beyond hope. Except . . . Rose believed in me. Rose never gave up."

"As I predicted."

A new voice rang through the living room, and we all looked up at the woman who had suddenly appeared in the doorway. She was considerably shorter than me but carried the kind of personality that could fill up a room. She was Yeva, Dimitri's grandmother. Small and frail with wispy white hair, she was believed by many around here to be a kind of wisewoman or witch. A different word usually came to my mind when I thought of Yeva, though it did sound a lot like "witch."

"You did not," I said, unable to stop myself. "All you did was tell me to get out of here so that I could 'do something else.'"

"Exactly," she said, a smug smile on her wrinkled face. "You needed to go restore my Dimka." She made her way across the living room, but Dimitri met her in the middle. He carefully wrapped her in his arms and murmured what I think was Russian for "grandmother." The insane difference in their heights made it kind of a comical scene.

"But you never said that's what I was going to do," I argued, once she was seated in a rocking chair. I knew I should just drop this subject, but something about Yeva always rubbed me the wrong away. "You can't take credit for that."

"I knew," she said adamantly. Her dark eyes seemed to bore right through me.

"Then why didn't you *tell* me that's what I had to do?" I demanded.

Yeva considered her answer for a moment. "Too easy. You needed to work for it."

I felt my jaw start to drop. Across the room, Dimitri caught my eye. *Don't do it, Rose,* his look seemed to say. *Let it go.* There was a glint of amusement on his face, as well as something that reminded me of our old teacher-student days. He knew me too well. He knew if given half a chance, I would totally battle this out with his ancient grandmother. Likely I would lose. With a quick nod, I clamped my mouth shut. *Okay, witch,* I thought. *You win this one.* Yeva shot me a gap-toothed grin.

"But *how* did it happen?" asked Sonya, tactfully shifting us into less dangerous waters. "The change back to a dhampir, I mean."

Dimitri and I glanced at each other again, but his earlier mirth was gone. "Spirit," he said quietly. This caused a quick intake of breath from his sisters. The Moroi wielded elemental magic, but most of them used only the four physical elements: earth, air, water, and fire. Recently, however, a very rare element had been discovered: spirit. It was tied to psychic abilities and healing and was still something many Moroi and dhampirs had a hard time accepting.

"My friend Lissa used spirit while, um, stabbing him with a silver stake," I explained. While I would gladly go through it all again to save Dimitri, the image of him being staked through the heart was still a little troubling for me. Up until the last moment, none of us had really known if it would just kill him or not.

Paul's eyes widened. "*Lissa?* Do you mean Queen Vasilisa?"

"Oh, yeah," I said. "Her." It was still hard sometimes to remember that my best friend since kindergarten was now queen of the entire Moroi world. Thinking of her now caused a slight knot in my stomach. Her election to the throne a couple weeks ago had been controversial in the eyes of many. Some of her enemies weren't above violence, and leaving her for a week to come here had made me extremely nervous. It was only the guarantee that she'd be surrounded by guardians—along with the need for Dimitri's family to see he was no longer one of the undead—that had made me consent to this trip.

The Belikovs and I stayed up late, answering their many questions. Even before he'd been forcibly turned into a Strigoi, Dimitri had been away from home for a while. He kept trying to find out what his family had been up to these last few years, but they brushed him off. They didn't consider their own experiences important. *He* was their miracle. And they couldn't get enough of him.

I knew the feeling.

When Paul and his sister were both fast asleep on the floor, we finally realized it was time for the rest of us to go to bed too. Tomorrow was a big day. I'd teased Dimitri that his family would have to outdo the memorial party they'd thrown him before, and it turned out I was right.

"Everyone wants to see you," Olena explained as she showed us to our bedroom. I knew "everyone" meant Baia's dhampir community. "As incredible as it is for us, it's even more unbelievable for them. So . . . we just told them to stop by tomorrow. All of them."

I cast a glance at Dimitri, curious as to how he'd respond. He wasn't the type who really reveled in being the center of attention—I could only guess how he felt when it involved the most terrible, traumatizing events of his life. For a second, his face wore that calm, emotionless look he excelled at. Then it relaxed into a smile.

"Of course," he told his mother. "I look forward to it."

Olena returned his smile with a relieved one and then bid us good night. Once she was gone, Dimitri sat down on the edge of the bed and rested his elbows on his knees. He set his head in his hands and muttered something in Russian. I didn't know exactly what he said, but I was guessing it was along the lines of "What have I gotten myself into?"

I walked over to him and sat on his lap, wrapping my arms around his neck so that I could face him. "Why so blue, comrade?"

"You know why," he said, playing with a lock of my hair. "I'm going to have to keep talking about . . . *that* time."

Sympathy burned in me. I knew he felt guilty for what he'd done as a Strigoi and had only recently accepted that it wasn't his fault. He'd been turned against his will by another Strigoi and hadn't been fully in control of himself. Still, it was a hard thing to come to terms with.

"It's true," I said. "But they're only going to talk about that in order to find out the rest of the story. No one's going to focus on what you did as Strigoi. They're going to want to know about how you came back. The miracle. I saw these people earlier this year. They mourned you as dead. Now they're going to want to celebrate you being alive. That's what the focus will be." I brushed my lips against his. "That's certainly *my* favorite part of the story."

He pulled me closer. "*My* favorite part was when you slapped some sense into me and got me to stop feeling sorry for myself."

"Slapped? That's not exactly how I remember it." To be

fair, Dimitri and I had hit and kicked each other plenty of times in the past. It was inevitable with the kind of strict training regimen guardians had. But getting him to overcome his Strigoi days . . . well, that had required less in the way of hitting and more of me trying not to be *too* argumentative while he healed on his own. And yeah, there'd also been one incident involving a hotel room and clothing removal, but I don't really think it had been all that essential in the healing process.

Still, when Dimitri fell backward and took me down on the bed with him, I had a feeling it was that particular memory that was fresh in his mind too. "Maybe you just need to help remind me," he said diplomatically.

"'Remind,' huh?" Wrapped in his arms, I cast an anxious glance at the door. "I feel bad enough having our own room in your mom's house! It's like we're getting away with something."

He cupped my face between his hands. "They're very open-minded," he said. "Besides, after everything we've been through? I think we might as well be married, as far as most of them are concerned."

"I got that impression too," I admitted. When I'd been here for his memorial service, a lot of the other dhampirs had practically treated me like his widow. Dhampir relationships didn't stand much on ceremony.

"Not a bad idea," he teased.

I tried to elbow him, which was kind of difficult, considering how entwined we were. "Nope. Don't go there, comrade." I loved Dimitri more than anything, but despite his occasional suggestions, I'd made it clear I had no intention of getting married until there was a "2" at the beginning of my age. He was seven years older than me, so marriage was more of a reasonable idea for him. For me, even though there was no one else I wanted, eighteen was too young to be a wife just yet.

"You say that now," he said, trying to keep from laughing, "but one of these days you'll crack."

"No way," I said. His fingertips traced patterns against my neck, filling my skin with heat. "You've given some pretty convincing arguments, but you're still a long way from winning me over."

"I haven't even really tried," he said, in a rare moment of arrogance. "When I want to, I can be *very* persuasive."

"Yeah? Prove it."

His lips moved toward mine. "I was hoping you'd say that."

The guests began arriving early. Of course, the Belikov women had been up and awake even earlier—far earlier than Dimitri and me, who were still coping with the time change. The kitchen was a flurry of activity, filling the house with all sorts of mouth-watering scents. Admittedly, Russian food wasn't my favorite cuisine, but there were a few dishes—especially ones Olena made—that I'd grown attached to. She and her daughters baked and cooked enormous quantities of everything, which seemed excessive since almost every person who stopped by also brought a dish to share. The experience was a mirror of Dimitri's memorial service, save that the mood was understandably more upbeat.

At first, there was a little awkwardness on everyone's part. Despite his resolve to focus on the positive, Dimitri still had a little trouble getting over the fact that his Strigoi time was the central focus. Some of the guests were equally nervous, as though maybe the rest of us had made a terrible mistake and he really *was* still a bloodthirsty undead creature. Of course, you only had to spend about five minutes with him to know that wasn't true, and soon the tension melted away. Dimitri knew almost everyone from his childhood and grew more and more delighted to see familiar faces. They in turn were more than happy to rejoice in his being saved.

I watched a lot of this from the sidelines. I'd met many of the visitors before, and while several greeted me, it was clear Dimitri took center stage. Most of the conversation was in Russian too, but it was enough for me to simply watch his face. Once he settled into being among his old friends and family, a quiet joy spread over him. The tension that always seemed to crackle through his body eased a little, and my heart melted to see him at such a moment.

"Rose?"

I'd been watching with amusement while some children interrogated him very seriously. Turning at the sound of my name, I was surprised to find two familiar and welcome faces.

"Mark, Oksana!" I exclaimed, embracing the couple. "I didn't know you'd be here."

"How could we not?" asked Oksana. She was Moroi, nearly thirty years older than me but still very beautiful. She was also one of the few spirit users I knew about. Beside her, her husband Mark smiled down at me. He was a dhampir, which made their relationship scandalous and was why they tended to keep to themselves. Oksana had used her spirit powers to bring Mark back after he was killed in a fight, a feat of healing that rivaled Dimitri's return from the Strigoi. It was called being shadow-kissed.

"We wanted to see you again," Mark told me. He inclined his head toward Dimitri. "And of course, we wanted to see the miracle for ourselves."

"You did it," said Oksana, her gentle face filled with wonder. "You saved him after all."

"And not how I originally intended either," I remarked. When I'd last come to Russia, my goal had been to hunt and kill Dimitri, in order to save his soul from that dark state. I hadn't known then that there was an alternative.

Oksana was understandably curious about the role of spirit in Dimitri's salvation, and I gave her as much information as I was able to. Time flew by. The day gave way to early evening, and people began breaking out the lethal vodka that had been my downfall last time. Mark and Oksana were teasing me about giving it another try, when a new voice suddenly got my attention. The voice's owner wasn't speaking to me, but I was immediately able to pick him out over the hum of the now-crowded house—because he was speaking English.

"Olena? Olena? Where are you? We need to talk about the Blood King."

Following the voice, I soon spotted a guy about five years older than me trying to squeeze his way through the crowd to where Olena stood near her son. Most paid little attention to him, but a few paused and regarded him with a surprise that I shared. He was human—the only human here, from what I could tell. Humans and dhampirs looked virtually indistinguishable from each other, but it was an ability of my race to be able to tell each other apart.

"Olena." Breathless, the human guy reached Olena and gave me my first clear view of him. He had neatly trimmed black hair and wore a very prim gray suit that somehow enhanced his gangly build. When he turned his head a certain way, the light caught one of his cheeks, revealing a golden lily tattoo. And that's what explained his presence. He was an Alchemist.

Olena had been chatting with a neighbor woman and finally turned when the Alchemist said her name three more times. Dimitri's mother remained smiling and pleasant, but I caught the faintest glimpse of exasperation in her eyes.

"Henry," she said. "How nice to see you again."

He adjusted his wire-rimmed glasses. "We need to talk about the Blood King." The more he spoke, the more I could pick out a faint accent. He was British, not American like me.

"This is hardly the time," said Olena. She gestured to Dimitri, who was gazing at Henry with intense scrutiny. "My son is visiting. He hasn't been here in years."

Henry gave Dimitri a polite but curt nod of greeting and then turned back to Olena. "It's *never* the time. The longer we put this off, the more people are going to be hurt. Another human was killed last night, you know."

This brought silence to several people standing nearby. It also brought me striding over to stand beside Dimitri and Olena. "Who was killed?" I demanded. "And who's doing the killing?"

Henry gave me a once-over. It wasn't like a checking-to-see-if-I-was-hot once-over, though. It was more like he was trying to decide if I was worth responding to. Apparently not. His attention went back to Olena.

"You have to do something," he said.

Olena threw up her hands. "Why do you think *I* can do it?"

"Because you're . . . well, you're kind of what passes for a leader around here. Who else is going to organize dhampirs to take care of this menace?"

"I don't lead anyone," said Olena, shaking her head. "And the people here . . . they certainly can't be ordered into battle on a moment's notice."

"But they know how to fight," countered Henry. "You're all trained, even if you didn't become guardians."

"We're trained to defend," she corrected him. "Certainly

everyone here would turn out if Strigoi invaded our town. We don't go out seeking trouble, though. Well, except for the Unmarked. But they're all away right now. Once they return in the autumn, I'm sure they'll happily do this for you."

Henry sighed in frustration. "We can't wait until autumn! Humans are dying now."

"Humans who are too stupid to stay out of trouble," said a grizzled dhampir woman.

"This so-called Blood King is just an ordinary Strigoi," added another man who'd been listening. "Nothing special. Humans need to simply stay away, and he'll leave."

I didn't exactly know what was happening here, but pieces were coming together. Alchemists were among the few humans who knew about the existence of vampires and dhampirs. Although we often lived and interacted with humans, my kind generally did an excellent job of hiding our true natures. Alchemists believed all vampires and dhampirs were dark and unnatural and that humanity was better off without contact. Likewise, the Alchemists feared that if our existence was public knowledge, certain weak-willed humans would jump at the chance to become immortal Strigoi and corrupt their souls. As a result, Alchemists helped us stay hidden and also assisted in covering up Strigoi kills and other ugly business those monsters caused. At the end of the day, though, Alchemists made it clear they were helping humans first and us second. So, if there was something out there threatening his kind, it was no wonder Henry was so worked up.

"Start from the beginning," said Dimitri, stepping forward. He'd listened patiently so far, but even he had limits when someone was trying to order his mother around. "Someone explain who this Blood King is and why he's killing humans."

Henry gave Dimitri an assessment similar to the one he'd

given me. Only, Dimitri apparently passed. "The Blood King is a Strigoi who lives northwest of here. There are some foothills with several caves and twisting paths, and he's taken up residence in there. We don't know exactly which cave, but evidence suggests he's very old and very powerful."

"And so . . . he's what, preying on human hikers that happen to wander nearby?" I asked.

Henry seemed surprised that I'd spoken, but at least answered this time. "No wandering involved. They seek him out. All the people in these villages are superstitious and deluded. They've built up this legendary reputation for him—gave him that Blood King name. They don't fully understand what he is, of course. Anyway, all he has to do is wait around, because every so often, someone gets it into his head that *he's* going to be the one to defeat the Blood King. They rush headlong into those mountain paths—and never come back."

"Stupid," said the woman who'd spoken earlier. I was inclined to agree.

"You have to do something," repeated Henry. This time, he was looking at everyone as he spoke, desperate for help wherever he could get it. "My people can't kill this Strigoi. You need to. I've talked to guardians in the larger cities, but they won't leave their Moroi. That means it's up to you locals."

"Maybe word will eventually get around and humans will stay away," said Olena reasonably.

"We keep hoping that'll happen, but it doesn't," said Henry. Something in the way he spoke made me think he'd explained this many times. If he didn't have such an arrogant demeanor, I'd almost feel sorry for him. "And before anyone suggests it: no, I don't think any human's going to get lucky and kill the Blood King either."

"Of course not."

The room had pretty much gone silent by this point, but Yeva's entrance ensured it stayed that way. How did she always make it seem like she'd appeared out of thin air? She came forward, using a gnarled cane that I suspected she kept on hand just to poke people with. She focused on Henry but seemed pleased to have gotten everyone else's attention.

"Only someone who has walked the road of death can kill the Blood King." She paused dramatically. "I have foreseen it."

From the awed expressions this elicited, it was obvious that no one else was going to question her. As usual, it was up to me. "Oh for God's sake," I said. "That could mean a hundred different things."

Henry was frowning. "I'd have to agree. Walking the road of death could be anything . . . someone who has nearly died, someone who has killed, any warrior or fighter who's—"

"Dimka," said Viktoria. I hadn't even noticed her standing near us. A few people had been in front of her but now moved aside as she spoke. "Grandmother means Dimka. He's walked the road of death and returned."

Murmurs filled the room as all eyes shifted to Dimitri. Many were nodding at Viktoria's declaration. I heard one man say, "Dimitri's the one. He's destined to kill the Blood King." I was pretty sure it was the same guy who'd earlier scoffed and said the Blood King wasn't anything special. Others were in agreement. "Yeva Belikova has declared it to be so," someone else said. "She's never wrong."

"That's not what she said at all!" I cried.

"I'll do it," said Dimitri resolutely. "I'll put an end to this Strigoi."

Cheers broke out, so no one heard me say, "But you don't have to! She never said you did."

Correction—one person heard me. Dimitri. "Roza," he said, his voice carrying through the growing noise. It was only one word, but as often happened, he managed to convey a thousand messages in it, most of which could be summed up as "We'll talk later."

"I'd like to come with you," said Mark. He straightened up to his full height. "If you'll have me." Despite his graying hair, Mark was still lean and muscled, with a look about him that said he was more than capable of kicking Strigoi ass.

"Of course. I'd be honored," said Dimitri gravely. "But that's it." This last part was added because suddenly half the room wanted to go with him. They'd rolled their eyes at Henry's initial request, but with Dimitri on board now, this had just hit heroic odyssey status.

"What about me?" I asked dryly.

A smile twitched at Dimitri's lips. "I figured that was a given."

I wasn't able to speak privately with him until much later. After all, people were still celebrating his return to the living, and now there was this quest to cheer on. The only one more impatient than me, I think, was Henry. He was pleased to have finally gotten help, but it was clear he wanted to start going over logistics and plans with Dimitri *right now.* That obviously wasn't going to happen, and at last, Henry left and said he'd be back tomorrow.

It was nearly the middle of the night when the remaining guests departed and Dimitri and I returned to our room. I was exhausted but still had enough energy left to chastise him.

"You know Yeva didn't specifically say you had to be the one to kill this Blood King guy," I said, crossing my arms to look imposing. "Viktoria—and everyone else—jumped to that conclusion."

"I know," said Dimitri, stifling a yawn. "But *someone* has to kill him. Even if these humans are bringing it on themselves, the threat needs to be removed. My mother's right that dhampirs around here are mostly focused on defense. You and I are the only ones who've gone through an entire guardian's training. And Mark."

I nodded slowly. "That's why you said he could come. I figured it was just because he was the first to ask and not one of those other wannabes trying to get in on your awesomeness."

Dimitri smiled and sat down on the bed. "These people can fight. They'd fight to the death if their homes were attacked. But to go into battle? Mark's the only one of them I'd take. And he's still no match for you."

"Well," I said, coming to sit beside him. "That's the smartest thing I've heard all night." Another realization hit me. "Mark can sense Strigoi too." It was a side effect of being brought back from the dead. "Huh. I guess this might be crazy enough to work."

Dimitri kissed the top of my head. "Admit it. You don't mind going after this Strigoi. It's the right thing to do. Even if they're walking into it, innocents are still dying because of him."

"Yeah, yeah, it's the right thing. I would've volunteered myself eventually." I sighed. "I just hate giving Yeva one more reason to think she controls the fate of the universe."

He chuckled. "If you plan on being a part of this family, then you'd better get used to it."

Dimitri and I had no hangover effects to deal with, fortunately, but neither of us was too thrilled when Henry showed up at the crack of dawn so that we could "get down to business." Like the other Alchemists I'd met, Henry wasn't the type to get his hands dirty. He had no intention of going with us to take on this Blood King. Also like other Alchemists, Henry was swimming in paperwork and plans.

He brought us tons of maps and diagrams of the cavernous area the Blood King inhabited, as well as every report the Alchemists had about sightings and attacks. Alchemists loved reports. Olena made us all some extremely strong coffee that tasted only slightly less toxic than the regional vodka, but the coffee's caffeine buzz went a long way to help us wake up and strategize.

"It's not that big a region," remarked Henry, tapping one of the maps. "I don't understand why no one can ever find him in daylight. This area's small enough that someone could search out every single cave within a day. Yet, they all still end up trapped there at night and get killed."

My mind spun back to another set of caves, halfway around the world. "The caves are connected," I said slowly, tracing the dots that one map used to mark the entrances. "You can search all day and never find him because he moves around underground."

"Brilliant, Roza," murmured Dimitri in approval.

Henry looked startled. "How do you know?"

I shrugged. "It's the only thing that makes sense." I flipped through the pieces of paper. "Do you have an underground map? Did anyone ever do a . . . I don't know . . . a geological survey or something?" It seemed like every other representation of the area was there: satellite images, topographical drawings, analyses of the minerals . . . everything but a glimpse of what was happening below the surface. Henry confirmed as much.

"No," he admitted sheepishly. "I don't have anything like that." Then, as though to save face for Alchemists and their usually meticulous style, he added, "Probably because no one ever actually made one. If it existed, we'd have it."

"That's going to be a disadvantage," I mused.

"Not so much," said Dimitri, finishing off the last of his

coffee. "I have an idea. I don't think we need to go underground at all. Especially with Mark."

I met his eyes and felt a jolt of electricity jump between us. Part of what drew us together was a mutual love of excitement and danger. It wasn't that we sought it out, exactly, but when there was a need to respond, we were both always ready to take on whatever was necessary. I felt that spark kindling between us now as this task loomed closer, and suddenly had a good idea of what his plan was.

"Bold move, comrade," I teased.

"Not by your standards," he returned.

Henry glanced back and forth between us, totally lost. "What are you two talking about?"

Dimitri and I just grinned.

Of course, there weren't many smiles when we set out before dawn the next day. Dimitri's family displayed a conflicting mix of confidence and nervousness. Ostensibly, Yeva's proclamation that Dimitri would triumph guaranteed victory. Yet neither his sisters nor his mother were totally carefree about sending him off to face an old and powerful Strigoi with a long history of kills. The women showered him with hugs and well wishes, and all the while, Yeva looked on in her smug, knowing manner.

Mark was with us, looking tough and battle ready. Henry had said the Baia dhampirs were "local" to the Blood King, but that was kind of a relative term, as the caverns were still about a six-hour drive away. We were simply the closest, since the caves lay in a remote area with little surrounding civilization. In fact, part of the drive's length was a result of the roads in that region being so poorly maintained.

We reached the caverns around midday, which was all according to plan. It was a desolate place and really only a small blip as far as elevation went, hardly able to compete with much grander ranges like the Ural Mountains far to the east. Still, it was higher and steeper than most of the surrounding lowlands, with rock-faced cliffsides that were going to require some sure footing. None of the caves were visible from where we parked the car, but a small, worn footpath meandered off between some of the cliffs. From what we'd seen of Henry's map, this led into the heart of the complex.

"Nothing like a little rock climbing," I said cheerfully, hoisting my backpack over my shoulder. "This could almost be a vacation, if not for the, you know, potentially dying part."

Mark held up a hand to shield his eyes from the sun as he regarded Dimitri and me. "Something tells me you're the kind of people whose vacations always end up that way."

"True," said Dimitri, heading out toward the path. "Besides, we're safe today. We have my grandmother's guarantee, remember?"

I rolled my eyes at the teasing in his voice. Dimitri might love and revere Yeva, but I knew he wouldn't count on any vague prophecy to get this task done. His faith was in the silver stake he carried at his belt.

The path started out easy but soon became a challenge as the elevation rose and more obstacles appeared in our way. We had to climb around boulders and manage some tricky parts where the path all but disappeared, forcing us to cling to the rocky sides. When we reached what was apparently the center of the complex, I was surprised to see how level it was. Cliff faces rose up all around us, like we were in some kind of fortress, but this area provided a small measure of tranquility. I wasn't tired—dhampirs are hardy, after all—but was glad we had reached our destination.

And that was where . . . we stopped.

We settled down on the ground, sorting out the contents of

our backpacks, and proceeded to pretty much lounge around for the rest of the day. Despite the wind blowing up here, the temperature was still summer-warm, and this would've almost made a perfect picnic scene. True, the weathered rock and scattered vegetation were hardly idyllic, but we spread out a blanket and ate a lunch consisting of Olena's fabulous cooking. When we were finished, I lay down next to Dimitri while Mark began whittling a piece of wood.

We kept up a steady stream of small talk. This was all part of the plan too. After Henry had said adventuring humans had gone hunting and been killed, we'd realized that was the downfall: going off and getting trapped inside caves that this Blood King guy obviously knew better than us. We weren't going to do it. We would stay out in the open, making no effort to hide our presence. While Strigoi loved human blood, they loved Moroi and dhampir blood even more. There was no way this Strigoi would be able to ignore us hanging out on his turf. If the violation didn't draw him out, the lure of our blood would. He'd eventually come after us when darkness fell, and we'd fight him on our terms.

"Mark, you and Oksana should come to the U.S.," I said. "Lissa would love to meet you and talk spirit. Lots of people would."

Mark didn't look up from his carving. "That's the problem," he said good-naturedly. "We're worried too many people would, now that everyone's interested in spirit. We don't want to become science experiments."

"Lissa wouldn't let that happen," I said adamantly. "And think of all the amazing things we might learn. Spirit seems to be able to do something new every day." Before I even knew it, my hand found Dimitri's. In saving him, spirit had already done the greatest thing it ever could in my eyes.

"We'll see," said Mark. "Oksana likes her privacy, but I know she's curious about—"

Dimitri shot up from his lounging position, instantly rigid and focused in that way he had. Mark had fallen silent as soon as Dimitri twitched, and now I sat up too. My hand went to my stake, and I saw the guys' hands do the same. Even as I did, the logical part of me knew there was no need—not when we were out in broad daylight. Whatever had spooked Dimitri wasn't Strigoi, but the instinct was hard to shake. His gaze fell on a large pile of rocks and boulders sitting near a cliff face. Wordlessly, he pointed to it and then tapped his ear. Mark and I nodded in understanding.

Glancing down at one of Henry's maps that we'd left open, I immediately spotted the rock formation Dimitri had indicated. It was large and sprawling, with what looked like a small gap between it and the cliff. If there was something lurking and spying on us, it would be possible to sneak behind the formation and catch the spy unawares. I tapped my chest and pointed to the formation on the map. Dimitri shook his head and tapped his chest instead. I glared and started to protest, but then he gestured between Mark and me. In that uncanny way we had of thinking alike sometimes, I immediately knew what Dimitri was saying. Mark and I had been talking when Dimitri had heard whatever startled him. We needed to continue that in order to keep the cover and surprise this potential threat. Reluctantly, I nodded defeat to Dimitri.

He crept away, silent as a cat, and I turned to Mark and tried to remember what we'd been talking about. The U.S.—I'd been trying to convince him he should visit for some reason. Talk. I needed to talk and create a distraction. So I frantically blurted the first thing that came to mind.

"So, yeah, Mark . . . if you, um, come visit . . . we can go out to eat and you can try some American food. No more cabbage." I gave an uneasy laugh and tried not to stare at Dimitri as he disappeared around a rocky corner. "We could, you know, go out for hot dogs. Don't worry—they're not actually dogs. It's just a name. They're these meat things that you put on buns—that's a kind of bread—and then you top them with other things and—"

"I know what a hot dog is," interrupted Mark. His tone was light for the sake of our observer, but his stake had replaced the whittling knife.

"You do?" I asked, legitimately surprised. "How?"

"We're not *that* remote. We have TV and movies. Besides, I've left Siberia, you know. I've been to the U.S."

"Really?" I hadn't known that. I knew very little about his history, really. "Did you try a hot dog?"

"No," he said. His eyes were on the spot where Dimitri had vanished, but they briefly flicked to me. "I was offered one . . . but it didn't look that appetizing."

"What!" I exclaimed. "Blasphemy. They're delicious."

"Aren't they compressed animal parts?" he pushed.

"Well, yeah . . . I think so. But so is sausage."

Mark shook his head. "I don't know. Something's just not right about a hot dog."

"Not right? I think you mean *so right.* They're like the—"

My righteous indignation was interrupted by a yelp, reminding me that there'd been another purpose here besides my defense of one of the greatest foods in the universe. Mark and I moved as one, both sprinting over to the rock pile and source of the noise. There, we found Dimitri pinning down a wriggling guy in a leather jacket and worn blue jeans. I couldn't tell much else about him because Dimitri had the guy's faced pressed into the dirt. Seeing us, Dimitri eased his hold so that the guy could look up. When he did, I saw that he was my age—and human.

He glanced between me and Mark—or, more accurately, he glanced between the silver stakes we both held. Gray-blue eyes went wide, and the captive began babbling in Russian. Mark frowned and asked a question, but didn't lower his stake. The human answered, sounding near-panicked. Dimitri scoffed and released his grip altogether. The human scrambled away, only to trip and land hard on his butt. Mark made some comment in Russian, which Dimitri responded to with a laugh.

"Will someone please tell me what's going on?" I demanded. "In English?"

To my surprise, it wasn't either of my colleagues that answered. "You . . . you're American!" exclaimed the boy, regarding me wonderingly. He spoke with a heavy accent. "I knew the Blood King's reputation had spread, but I didn't know it had gone that far!"

"Well, it hasn't. Not exactly," I said. I noticed then that both Dimitri and Mark had put their stakes away. "I just happened to be in the neighborhood."

"I told you," said Dimitri, speaking to the human. "This is no place for you. Leave now."

The boy shook his head, making his unruly blond hair seem that much messier. "No! We can work together. We're all here for the same reason. We're here to kill the Blood King."

I met Dimitri's eyes questioningly but received no help. "What's your name?" I asked.

"Ivan. Ivan Grigorovitch."

"Well, Ivan, I'm Rose, and while we appreciate the offer of help, we've got this under control. There's no need for you to stick around."

Ivan looked skeptical. "You didn't look like you had it under control. You looked like you were having a picnic."

I repressed a grimace. "We were, uh, just getting ready to go into action."

He brightened. "Then I'm in time."

Mark sighed, clearly out of patience with this. "Boy, this isn't a game. Do you have anything like this?" He pulled out his silver stake again, making sure the point caught the light. Ivan gaped. "I didn't think so. Let me guess. You have a wooden stake, right?"

Ivan flushed. "Well, yes, but I'm very good at—"

"Very good at getting yourself killed," declared Mark. "You don't have the skills or weapons for this."

"Teach me," Ivan said eagerly. "I told you, I'm willing to help! It's what I've dreamed of—being a famous vampire hunter!"

"This isn't a field trip," said Dimitri. Like Mark, he no longer found Ivan so comical. "If you don't leave this area now, we'll carry you out ourselves."

Ivan jumped to his feet. "I can go . . . I can go . . . but are you sure you don't want my help? I know all there is to know about vampires. Nobody in my village has read as much as I have—"

"Go," said Mark and Dimitri in unison.

Ivan went. The three of us watched as he hurried down the path, toward where it had to make its way through rocky obstacles in order to get back out to the main road.

"Idiot," muttered Mark. He put the stake away again and trudged back over to where we'd been sitting before. After a few moments, Dimitri and I followed.

"I feel kind of bad for him," I remarked. "He seemed so . . . I don't know, enthusiastic. But I also start to get why

Henry was freaking out so much. If all the other human 'vampire experts' that come here are like him, I can see why they're getting killed off."

"Exactly," said Dimitri. His gaze was on Ivan's retreating figure, almost impossible to see now as he walked around a stony outcropping. "Hopefully he'll go back to his village and make up some fantastic story about how he killed the Blood King himself."

"True," I said. "The fact that we'll have done it will just back him up when people come here and see no more vampire."

Still, as I settled back down in our makeshift camp, I couldn't forget the zealous look in Ivan's eyes as he'd talked about killing the Blood King. How many others had come in with that same naïve attitude? It was disheartening. I'd grown up with the idea that fighting Strigoi was a duty and a responsibility. It wasn't something you treated as a game.

Mark and I eventually picked up our hot dog debate, much to Dimitri's amusement. Dimitri tended to agree with Mark, which I found shocking. I could only blame the cuisine they'd been raised with for such misguided views. Despite the easy nature of the conversation, though, I could feel the tension building within all of us as the sun began moving down toward the horizon. The silver stakes had returned, and even before darkness fell, our eyes were constantly scanning our surroundings. Shadows darkened the stone walls around us, turning them into something mysterious and ominous.

We'd brought along a couple of electric lanterns and turned them on once it grew too dark to see comfortably. As dhampirs, we didn't need as much light as humans, but we needed some. The lanterns cast just enough to help our eyes without blinding us to our periphery, like a campfire would have. Soon, the skies were completely dark, and we knew we'd entered the time when Strigoi could walk freely. None of us doubted he'd come for us. The question was whether he would wait and try to wear us down or strike suddenly. As more time passed, it appeared as though it would be the former.

"Do you sense anything?" I whispered to Mark. Those who were shadow-kissed felt nauseous when Strigoi were close.

"Not yet," he murmured back.

"We should've brought marshmallows," I joked. "Of course, then we'd have to build a fire for sure—"

An earsplitting scream ripped through the night.

I jumped to my feet, wincing. The problem with superior hearing is that loud noises are *really* loud. My companions were up too, stakes ready. Mark frowned.

"Some Strigoi trick?"

"No," I said, moving toward where the scream had originated. "That was Ivan."

Mark swore in Russian, something I'd gotten used to from Dimitri. "He never left," said Mark.

Dimitri grabbed my arm to slow me down. "Rose, he's in one of the caves."

"I know," I said. I'd already figured that out and turned to face Dimitri. "But what choice do we have? We can't leave him in there."

"This is exactly what we wanted to avoid," said Dimitri grimly.

"And likely a trap set by the Blood King," added Mark, just as another scream sounded. "He wants us but is too smart to come out and get us."

I grimaced, knowing Mark was right. "But that also

means he's probably not going to kill Ivan right away. He's just going to mess with him to lure us in. There's a chance we can save Ivan." I threw my hands up when nobody responded. "Come on! Can you really leave that inept kid in there to die?"

No, of course they couldn't. Dimitri sighed. "This is where we could've used a map of the caves. Better to set up an ambush."

"No such luxury, comrade," I said, walking toward the cave again. "We've got to go in the front door. At least Mark can give us warning."

A debate then broke out between the three of us over who would lead and who would go last to carry a lantern. Dimitri and Mark came up with lame arguments about why they should go ahead of me. Mark's was that, as the oldest, his life was more expendable, which was ridiculous. Dimitri's reasoning was that he was safe, thanks to Yeva's prophecy. That was even more ridiculous, and I knew he was only saying so to protect me. Yet in the end, I was overruled and ended up behind them.

Darkness far deeper than the night engulfed us as we stepped inside. The lantern helped a little but only illuminated a short distance in front of us as we walked further and further into the unknown. None of us spoke, but I had a feeling we were all thinking the same thing. The screams had stopped. It could mean Ivan was dead. It almost certainly meant the Blood King wanted to lead us as far into the caves as possible.

Trouble came when we reached a fork in the tunnel. It not only meant we had to choose a path; it also meant the Blood King had the potential to double back on us. "Which way?" murmured Dimitri.

I glanced between the two options. One was narrower, but that meant nothing. Lines of thought filled Mark's face, and then he indicated the larger tunnel. "There. It's faint, but I can feel him there."

The three of us hurried forward, and the tunnel soon grew wider and wider, finally opening into a large "room" with three other tunnels feeding into it. Before any of us had a chance to question where to go next, something heavy slammed into me and knocked me to the ground. The lantern flew from my grasp and miraculously rolled away, unbroken.

Instinct made me follow suit. I had no clue where my attacker was, but I rolled away as soon as I hit the cave's floor. It was a good decision, because half a second later, I got my first glimpse of the Blood King. The stories were true. He *was* old. Admittedly, Strigoi didn't age once they turned, and at a glance, this guy had the appearance of someone in his midforties. Like all Strigoi, he had ghastly white skin and the look of death about him. If the light had been a little better, I knew I'd see red in his eyes too. His long mustache and shoulder-length hair were black with gray streaks, looking like something you'd see from the imperial days of Russia. But it was more than the antiquated haircut that marked his age. There was something about a Strigoi you could feel, an ancient evilness that went straight to the bone. Also, as age increased, so did their speed and strength.

And man, this guy was *fast*. He'd lunged at the place I'd fallen, striking out with more than enough force to break my neck. Seeing he'd missed me, he didn't waste a moment in coming after me in my new spot, and I hurried to get away. I was fast, but not as fast as him, and he caught hold of my sleeve. Before he could pull me to him, Dimitri and Mark were on his back, forcing the Blood King to release me. My companions were good—among the best—but it took every ounce of their skill to keep pace with him. He dodged every swipe of their stakes with the effortless ease of a dancer.

I sprang to my feet, ready to join in and assist, when I heard a moan coming from one of the tunnels. Ivan. I wanted to join the fray, but Dimitri and Mark had just parried some of the Blood King's attacks, forcing the whole group to move to the far side and put my friends between me and the Strigoi. With no obvious opening for me, I made the decision to rescue the innocent and trust Dimitri's and Mark's skills. Yet, as I moved toward the branching tunnel, I cast an uneasy glance back at Dimitri. Again, I was reminded of that time long ago, in other tunnels. It was there that Dimitri had been bitten and forcibly turned into a Strigoi. Panic seized me, along with an intense, irrational need to go throw myself in front of Dimitri.

No, I told myself. *Dimitri and Mark can handle this. There's two of them and only one Strigoi. It's not like it was last time.* Another moan from Ivan spurred me to action. For all I knew, he could be bleeding to death somewhere. The sooner I got to him and helped, the more likely he'd survive. Going after him meant abandoning the lantern, since Dimitri and Mark needed it more than me. Besides, this tunnel was narrow enough that I could reach out and touch both sides with my hands, giving me some measure of guidance as I entered the darkness.

"Ivan?" I called, half afraid I'd trip over him.

"Here," came an answering voice. It was astonishingly close, and I slowed my pace, reaching out in front of me in the hopes I'd feel him. Moments later, I touched hair and a forehead. I stopped and knelt.

"Ivan, are you okay? Can you stand?" I asked.

"I . . . I think so . . ."

I hoped so. Unable to see him, I had no idea if his blood

was gushing out right in front of me. I found his hand and helped him up. He leaned heavily against me but seemed to have control of his legs, which I took as a good sign. Slowly, we made our way back toward the fight, our maneuvers awkward in the tight tunnel. When we emerged into the light, I was dismayed to see the Blood King still alive.

"Rest here," I told Ivan, moving him toward a wall. He wasn't in as critical a condition as I'd feared. He looked as though the Blood King had—literally—thrown him around a few times, but none of the cuts and bruises looked dire. I expected him to sit so that I could lend my strength to the fight, but instead, Ivan's eyes went wide as he took in the battle. With an energy I hadn't believed possible, he sprang forward with his ridiculous wooden stake and aimed it for the Blood King's back.

"No!" I yelled, hurrying after him.

His stake didn't pierce flesh, of course. It didn't even hurt the Blood King. What it did do, however, was cause the Strigoi to pause for a split second and swat away Ivan. He flew across the cave, landing hard against a wall. In the space of that heartbeat, Dimitri and Mark acted with flawless, wordless efficiency. Dimitri's foot snaked out and knocked the Blood King's legs from under him. Mark surged forward, plunging his stake into the ancient Strigoi's heart. The Blood King froze, and we all held a collective breath as a look of total shock crossed his features. Then death seized him, and his body slumped forward.

I exhaled in relief and immediately looked at Dimitri first, needing to make sure he was okay. But of course he was. He was my badass battle god. It'd take more than some super tough Strigoi—even one with a dramatic name—to take him down. Mark seemed equally fine. Across the cave,

Ivan looked stunned but otherwise uninjured. He was watching us with wonder, and his eyes lit up when he met my gaze. He held his wooden stake in the air in kind of a mock salute and grinned.

"You're welcome," he said.

It turned out part of the reason Ivan hadn't left when we told him—aside from his idiotic sense of heroism—was that he had no means to leave. Some friends from his village had dropped him off, with the intent of coming back in two days to see if he was dead or alive. We could hardly leave him there in such a beaten-up state, so we made the two-hour drive to take him home. The entire time, Ivan kept going on and on about how he'd saved Dimitri and Mark in the nick of time and how they would've met certain death if not for him.

Pointing out that it was only sheer luck that he hadn't gotten them killed seemed useless at this point. We let him talk and were all relieved when we reached his village, a place that made Baia look like New York City.

"Sometimes I hear reports of other vampires," he told us as he got out of the car. "If you want to team up again, I'll let you come along with me next time too."

"Noted," I said.

The only person more infuriating than Ivan was Yeva. After five minutes with her, I was suddenly wishing I was back in the car with him.

"So," she said, sitting in her rocking chair in the Belikov house like it was a throne. "It seems I was right."

I collapsed onto the couch beside Dimitri, bone weary and wishing I could sleep for about twelve hours. Mark had already gone home to Oksana. Still, I had enough spunk in me to argue back.

"No, actually," I retorted, trying to keep a smug smile off my face, "you said Dimitri would kill the Blood King. He didn't. Mark did."

"I said one who had walked the road of death would succeed," she said. "Mark has faced death and survived."

I opened my mouth to deny it, but she had a point. "Okay. But when Viktoria said Dimitri would do it, you didn't deny it."

"I didn't confirm it either."

I groaned. "This is ridiculous! That 'prediction' meant nothing! Hell, it could've applied to Ivan, since he nearly died because of the Blood King."

"My prophecies see many things," responded Yeva—which was really no response at all. "My next one is particularly interesting."

"Uh-huh," I said. "Let me guess. 'A journey.' That could mean me and Dimitri going home. Or Olena going to the grocery store."

"Actually," said Yeva, "I see a wedding in the future."

Viktoria had been listening to the exchange with amusement and clapped her hands together. "Oh! Rose and Dimka!" Her sisters nodded excitedly.

I stared incredulously. "How can you even say that? That can mean anything too! Someone in town is probably getting married right now. Or maybe it'll be Karolina—didn't you say you're getting serious with your boyfriend? If it is me and Dimitri, it'll be years from now—which, of course, you'll claim you foresaw since it was 'the future.'"

No one was listening to me anymore, though. The Belikov women were already chattering excitedly about plans, speculating if the wedding would be here or in the U.S. and how nice it would be to see Dimitri "finally settle down."

I groaned again and leaned against him. "Unbelievable."

Dimitri smiled and put his arm around me. "Don't you believe in fate, Roza?"

"Sure," I said. "Just not in your grandmother's crazy vague predictions."

"Doesn't sound that crazy to me," he teased.

"You're as crazy as her."

He kissed the top of my head. "I had a feeling you'd say that."

ABOUT THE AUTHORS

HEATHER BREWER was not your typical teen, and she's certainly not your typical adult. Her love of the macabre inspired her *New York Times* bestselling series The Chronicles of Vladimir Tod and its spin-off, the Slayer Chronicles. She dresses in black, decorates her office with antique medical instruments, and loves the music of Green Day—in fact, "Misery" was inspired by one of their songs by the same name. Heather lives in St. Louis with her husband, two children, and three very spoiled cats. Visit her online at HeatherBrewer.com.

MEG CABOT was born during the Chinese astrological year of the Fire Horse, a notoriously unlucky sign, but learned at an early age that a good storyteller can always give herself a happy ending. Her books for adults, teens, and tweens have sold more than sixteen million copies worldwide and included multiple number-one *New York Times* bestsellers. Her Princess Diaries series has been published in more than thirty-eight countries and was made into two hit films by Disney. Meg's award-winning books include the Mediator series, *Insatiable, Abandon,* and the Heather Wells mystery series. Meg Cabot (her last name rhymes with *habit,* as in "her books can be habit-forming") lives in Key West with two cats and her husband, who doesn't know he married a fire horse. Please don't tell him.

MATT DE LA PEÑA is the author of four critically acclaimed young adult novels: *Ball Don't Lie, Mexican WhiteBoy, We Were Here,* and *I Will Save You.* He received his MFA in creative writing from San Diego State University and his BA from the University of the Pacific, where he attended school on a full athletic scholarship for basketball. He teaches creative writing at NYU and speaks at high schools and colleges throughout the country. Matt de la Peña lives in Brooklyn, New York.

SIMONE ELKELES is the *New York Times* and *USA Today* bestselling author of the award-winning series Perfect Chemistry, Leaving Paradise, and How to Ruin. Simone was named Author of the Year by the Illinois Association of Teachers of English and loves writing teen novels that appeal to both boys and girls. Find her at SimoneElkeles.net.

KAMI GARCIA is the *New York Times, USA Today, Publishers Weekly,* and internationally bestselling coauthor of the Beautiful Creatures novels. *Beautiful Creatures* has been published in over forty countries and translated into over thirty languages and is in production as a major motion picture. Kami is also the author of *Unbreakable,* the first book in her solo series, the Legion, which is being developed as a major motion picture by Mark Morgan, producer of the Twilight Saga and *Percy Jackson and the Lightning Thief.* When she is not writing, Kami can usually be found watching disaster movies, listening to Soundgarden, or drinking Diet Coke. She lives in Los Angeles with her husband, son, and daughter and their dogs, Spike and Oz (named after characters from *Buffy the Vampire Slayer*). Keep up with her at KamiGarcia.com.

MICHAEL GRANT is the author or coauthor of more than 150 books, including the Animorphs series (with his wife, Katherine Applegate), the Gone series, and the BZRK series. He and Katherine are teaming up again for *Eve and Adam.* He lives in the San Francisco Bay Area.

MALINDA LO, a former entertainment reporter, is the author of several YA fantasy and science fiction novels, including most recently *Adaptation.* Her first novel, *Ash,* a lesbian retelling of the Cinderella story, was a finalist for the William C. Morris Award, the Andre Norton Award, and the Lambda Literary Award. She lives in Northern California with her partner and their dog. Visit her website at MalindaLo.com.

LISA McMANN is the *New York Times* bestselling author of the Wake trilogy, *Dead to You, Cryer's Cross,* and the dystopian fantasy series The Unwanteds. She lives with her husband and their teenage son and daughter in Arizona. Visit her at LisaMcMann.com.

RICHELLE MEAD is an internationally bestselling author of fantasy novels for adults and teens. Her Vampire Academy series has received honors from the American Library Association and was recently followed by Bloodlines, a spin-off series about a secret society keeping the vampire world hidden from humans. Richelle's books have been translated into more than two dozen languages around the world and transformed into graphic novels. A lifelong reader, Richelle loves mythology and wacky humor. When she's not writing, she can be found spending time with her family in Seattle, buying dresses, and watching bad reality TV. For more information about Richelle, visit RichelleMead.com.

SAUNDRA MITCHELL has been a phone psychic, a car salesperson, a denture deliverer, and a layout waxer. She has dodged trains, endured basic training, and hitchhiked from Montana to California. She teaches herself languages, raises children, and makes paper for fun. She is the author of *Shadowed Summer, The Vespertine, The Springsweet,* and the forthcoming novels *The Elementals* and *Mistwalker*. She is also the editor of the upcoming YA anthology *Defy the Dark*. She always picks truth; dares are too easy. Visit her online at SaundraMitchell.com.

DIANA PETERFREUND is the author of eight novels, including the Secret Society Girl series, the killer unicorn novels *Rampant* and *Ascendant,* and the postapocalyptic *For Darkness Shows the Stars.* Her work has been translated into twelve languages, and her short stories have appeared on *Locus*'s Best of the Year list and been included in *The Best Science Fiction and Fantasy of the Year,* volume 5. Learn more about Diana at DianaPeterfreund.com.

CARRIE RYAN is the *New York Times* bestselling author of *The Forest of Hands and Teeth, The Dead-Tossed Waves, The Dark and Hollow Places,* and the original ebook *Hare Moon.* She has contributed to multiple story collections, including most recently *Zombies vs. Unicorns, Kiss Me Deadly,* and *Enthralled*. Her work has been translated into over eighteen languages and her first novel is in production as a major motion picture. Born and raised in Greenville, South Carolina, Carrie is a graduate of Williams College and Duke University School of Law. A former litigator, she now writes full-time and lives in Charlotte, North Carolina. Visit her at CarrieRyan.com.

MARGARET STOHL is the author of the forthcoming sci-fi fantasy novel *Icons* and coauthor of the acclaimed Beautiful Creatures novels, which have sold over a million copies in over forty countries and are being adapted into a feature film. Margaret studied literature at Amherst College, Stanford, and Yale and creative writing at the University of East Anglia in Norwich, England. She lives with her husband, three daughters, and two bad beagles in Santa Monica, California. Visit her at Margaret-Stohl.com.

LAINI TAYLOR is the author of five books, including *Lips Touch: Three Times,* which was a National Book Award finalist, and *Daughter of Smoke and Bone,* named one of Amazon's Top Ten Books of 2011. She resides between raindrops in Portland, Oregon, with her husband, illustrator Jim Di Bartolo, and their greatest collaboration, their daughter, Clementine. Visit Laini at LainiTaylor.com.